Country Locator for Volume 6
ARGENTINA, PARAGUAY, AND URUGUAY

The following countries and political regions are covered in the eleven-volume encyclopedia *World and Its Peoples: The Americas*. Detailed discussion of the following can be found in the volumes indicated in parentheses.

Anguilla (3)
Antigua and Barbuda (3)
Argentina (6)
Aruba (3)
Bahamas (2)
Barbados (3)
Belize (1)
Bermuda (2)
Bolivia (7)
Bonaire (3)
Brazil (5)
British Virgin Islands (2)
Canada (8)
Cayman Islands (2)
Chile (7)
Colombia (4)
Costa Rica (1)
Cuba (2)
Curaçao (3)
Dominica (3)
Dominican Republic (2)
Ecuador (4)
El Salvador (1)
Falkland Islands (6)
French Guiana (5)
Greenland (8)
Grenada (3)
Guadeloupe (3)
Guatemala (1)
Guyana (5)
Haiti (2)
Honduras (1)
Jamaica (2)
Martinique (3)
Mexico (1)
Montserrat (3)
Nicaragua (1)
Panama (4)
Paraguay (6)
Peru (7)
Puerto Rico (2)
Saba (3)
Saint Barthélemy (3)
Saint Eustatius (3)
Saint Kitts-Nevis (3)
Saint Lucia (3)
Saint-Martin (3)
Saint Martin (Sint Maarten) (3)
Saint-Pierre and Miquelon (8)
Saint Vincent and the Grenadines (3)
Suriname (5)
Trinidad and Tobago (3)
Turks and Caicos Islands (2)
United States (9, 10)
Uruguay (6)
Venezuela (4)
Virgin Islands of the United States (2)

WORLD AND ITS PEOPLES

THE AMERICAS

6

ARGENTINA, PARAGUAY, AND URUGUAY

Marshall Cavendish
Reference
New York

SET CONSULTANTS
Joshua Ginsberg, Conservation Operations, Wildlife Conservation Society, New York

Constantine Passaris, Department of Economics, University of New Brunswick, Fredericton, Canada

David Robinson, Department of Geography, University of Syracuse, New York

VOLUME CONSULTANTS
Robert B. Kent, Department of Geography and Planning, University of Akron, Ohio

Joseph L. Scarpaci, Department of Geography, Virginia Polytechnic Institute and State University, Blacksburg

Kathleen Schroeder, Department of Geography and Planning, Appalachian State University, Boone, North Carolina

WRITERS
Jens Andermann, School of Languages, Linguistics and Culture, Birkbeck College, University of London, England

Daniel Balderston, Department of Cinema and Comparative Literature, University of Iowa, Iowa City

Peter Bartok, Latin American Program, University of Houston, Texas

Rachel Bean, Church Stretton, England

Kelvin Bias, Brooklyn, New York

Scott Brown, Coordinator of International Studies, Francis Marion University, Florence, South Carolina

Mark Camburn, Santa Cruz de la Sierra, Bolivia

Kevin Evanovitch, London, England

Michelle Felton, School of Geographical Sciences, University of Bristol, England

Adolfo Garcé, Department of Political Science, University of the Republic, Montevideo, Uruguay

Núria Homedes, School of Public Health, University of Texas, Houston

Simon Lund-Lack, London, England

James Martin, London, England

Jay Moncada, London, England

Dag Retsö, Institute of Latin American Studies, Stockholm University, Sweden

Rachel Simon-Kumar, Faculty of Arts and Social Sciences, University of Waikato, Hamilton, New Zealand

Emerald M. Stone, Edinburgh, Scotland

Della Torra, London, England

Antonio Ugalde, Department of Sociology, University of Texas, Austin

Marshall Cavendish
99 White Plains Road
Tarrytown, New York 10591-9001

www.marshallcavendish.us

© 2009 Marshall Cavendish Corporation

Created by **The Brown Reference Group plc**

All rights reserved. No part of this book may be reproduced or utilized in any form or by any means electronic or mechanical, including photocopying, recording, or by any information storage and retrieval system, without prior written permission from the publisher and the copyright holder.

Library of Congress Cataloging-in-Publication Data

World and its peoples : the Americas.
   v. cm.
   Includes bibliographical references.
   Contents: 1. Mexico and Central America -- 2. Northern Caribbean -- 3. Southern Caribbean -- 4. Colombia, Ecuador, Panama, and Venezuela -- 5. Brazil and the Guiana Coast -- 6. Argentina, Paraguay, and Uruguay -- 7. Bolivia, Chile, and Peru -- 8. Canada and Greenland -- 9. United States. Part I -- 10. United States. Part II -- 11. Indexes.
   ISBN 978-0-7614-7802-7 (set) -- ISBN 978-0-7614-7803-4 (v. 1) -- ISBN 978-0-7614-7804-1 (v. 2) -- ISBN 978-0-7614-7805-8 (v. 3) -- ISBN 978-0-7614-7807-2 (v. 4) -- ISBN 978-0-7614-7808-9 (v. 5) -- ISBN 978-0-7614-7809-6 (v. 6) -- ISBN 978-0-7614-7810-2 (v. 7) -- ISBN 978-0-7614-7811-9 (v. 8) -- ISBN 978-0-7614-7812-6 (v. 9) -- ISBN 978-0-7614-7814-0 (v. 10) -- ISBN 978-0-7614-7815-7 (v. 11)
   1. Geography--America--Encyclopedias.
   G133.W86 2009
   917--dc22
                                                 2008062303

Printed in Malaysia

12 11 10 09 08 1 2 3 4 5

PHOTOGRAPHIC CREDITS
Front cover: Alamy: Pablo Corral Vega; **Shutterstock:** Vera Bogaerts bl, Jose Alberto Tejo br.
Alamy: Arco Images 738, Richard Wareham Fotografie 858, Terry Whittaker 758; **Bridgeman Art Library:** Theodore De Bry/Service Historique de la Marine, Vincennes, France 745; **Corbis:** Yann Arthus-Bertrand 796, Sophie Bassouls/Sygma 813, Pablo Corral Vega 829, Andres Cristaldo/epa 821, John Farmar/Ecoscene 803, Pablo La Rosa/Reuters 842, Enrique Marcarian/Reuters 780, Diego Lezama Orezzoli 749, Pierre Perrin/Zoko Productions 788, Jose Fuste Raga 859, Enzo & Paolo Ragazzini 775, Reuters 764, 808, 839, Andres Stapff/Reuters 844, Horacio Villalobos 774; **Getty Images:** AFP 770; **Mary Evans Picture Library:** 747; **Robert Hunt Library:** 781; **Shutterstock:** Peter Chafer 733, Rafael Martin-Gaitero 734, Lee Torrens 742; **South American Pictures:** 756, 810, 835, 837, 838, Danny Aeberhard 735, Kathy Jarvis 731, Kimball Morrison 792, Tony Morrison 727, 729, 737, 752, 753, 755, 757, 776, 777, 793, 799, 800, 812, 816, 820, 822, 823, 824, 826, 828, 832, 845, 847, 848, 850, 851, 852, 853, 857, Frank Nowikowski 721, 772, 784, 786, Chris Sharp 782, 789; **Topham:** 748, 766, 769, 778, 794, 806, Sonda Dawes/The Image Works 834, 841, 843, Chet Gordon/The Image Works 818, Roger Hart 798, ProSport 817, Adam Tanner/The Image Works 815.

For **MARSHALL CAVENDISH**
Publisher: Paul Bernabeo
Project Editor: Stephanie Driver
Production Manager: Alan Tsai

For **THE BROWN REFERENCE GROUP**
Project Editor: Clive Carpenter
Deputy Editors: Felicity Crowe, Paul Thompson, Aruna Vasudevan
Design: Focus Publishing
Cartography: Encompass Graphics Ltd
Picture Research: Kate Pink
Design Manager: Sarah Williams
Managing Editor: Tim Harris
Indexer: Ann Barrett

CONTENTS

GEOGRAPHY AND CLIMATE	724
HISTORY AND MOVEMENT OF PEOPLES	744

Argentina
Introduction	760
Government	764
Modern History	765
Cultural Expression	773
Daily Life	783
Economy	795

The Falkland Islands — 802

Paraguay
Introduction	804
Government	808
Modern History	809
Cultural Expression	813
Daily Life	819
Economy	825

Uruguay
Introduction	830
Government	834
Modern History	835
Cultural Expression	840
Daily Life	846
Economy	854

Further Research — 860
Index — 862

Geography and Climate

Argentina, and its neighbors Paraguay and Uruguay, occupy the southern part of South America, the so-called Southern Cone. Together, the three nations comprise an area more than twice that of the state of Alaska. The region stretches from subtropical semideserts, grasslands, and forests through vast, open, temperate plains to high mountain ranges and subarctic regions.

PARAGUAY RIVER

The Paraguay River, which is 1,584 miles (some 2,550 km) long, rises in southern Brazil and joins the Paraná River near the Argentine border in the far south of Paraguay. The river is subject to seasonal flooding. The northern basin of the Paraguay in Brazil and northern Paraguay is a seasonal swamp known as the Pantanal. The waterway then forms the border between Paraguay and Brazil before entering Paraguay, where it divides the nation in two: the sparsely populated Occidental region, which contains the dry Gran Chaco, to the west of the waterway; and the Oriental region, which is home to the overwhelming majority of Paraguayans to the east. South of Asunción, the Paraguayan national capital, the waterway forms the border between Paraguay and Argentina until it joins the Paraná.

Unlike many of the major waterways in the region, the Paraguay has not been dammed to provide hydropower. As a result, the river is still navigable, providing passage for small oceangoing ships inland as far as Asunción and for smaller craft upstream. There are plans to improve the navigation, but development, including dam construction, would threaten the Paranal, which is one of the world's largest tropical wetlands.

URUGUAY RIVER

The Uruguay River, which forms the western border of the nation of Uruguay, flows for 990 miles (1,593 km), from southern Brazil to join the delta of the Paraná River in Argentina, where the combined waterway becomes the Río de la Plata. The Uruguay is known as the Pelotas River in its headwaters above the confluence with the Canoas River. South of the confluence, rapids restrict navigation, and the river is only navigable for 190 miles (306 km) upstream from its confluence with the Paraná. A road bridge crosses the Uruguay River to link Argentina with Brazil, and three other bridges connect Uruguay and Argentina.

RÍO DE LA PLATA

Upstream from the Argentine national capital, Buenos Aires, the Paraná and Uruguay rivers join to form a wide combined estuary, the Río de la Plata, whose northern shore forms the south coast of Uruguay; its southern shore forms the north coast of Argentina. The Río de la Plata has a maximum width of about 136 miles (219 km) at its eastern end. Some 180 miles (290 km) long, the funnel-shaped estuary drains around one-fourth of the South American continent.

The muddy waters of the Río de la Plata carry large amounts of silt from the rivers that flow into it. As a result, the estuary has to be dredged constantly to maintain access for ships to ports, such as Buenos Aires. The shallow waters are home to many species of fish, and fishing ports line its shores. The estuary is also home to the rare La Plata dolphin, the only river dolphin that lives in saltwater rather than freshwater.

LAKE ITAIPU

When the Itaipu Dam, along the Paraná River, was completed in October 1982, a reservoir formed behind it. The dam, which houses the largest operational hydroelectric power plant in the world, connects Paraguay and Brazil across the waterway. Itaipu Lake is now more than 564 square miles (about 1,460 sq. km) in area and contains 66 islands. The reservoir is 106 miles (170 km) long and averages 4.4 miles (7 km) wide.

As the reservoir filled, it submerged two of the world's largest waterfalls: Guaíra (or Salto dos Sete Quedras) and Urubupunga, which were, respectively, the second- and sixth-largest waterfalls by volume in the world. The lake has also modified the local climate. Differential heating of land and water generates strong breezes over Lake Itaipu, with breezes flowing from the lake during the day and toward the lake at night. There is, however, no evidence that the presence of the lake has affected local precipitation patterns.

Today, the lake is surrounded by forest, which is protected along both banks in two nature preserves, one national park, and four environmental refuges. The company that constructed the Itaipu Dam reforested large areas adjoining the project, planting around 20 million tree seedlings. An artificial channel connects the lake with the Paraná River to provide passage for fish whose migration to spawning grounds was interrupted by the construction of the dam. The strongly flowing channel is now not only used by migrating fish but also by rafters and for competitive slalom canoeing. Some artificial beaches and facilities, such as marinas, along the lake shore attract tourists.

The Land of Argentina, Paraguay, and Uruguay

Argentina, Paraguay, and Uruguay occupy the greater portion of the Southern Cone, a region that is defined by common physical, historical, and economic characteristics. Physically, the Southern Cone is distinguishable as the triangular-shaped southern half of the South American landmass.

Argentina, Paraguay, and Uruguay form a distinct region that was united in history—as the Spanish viceroyalty (administrative region) of Río de la Plata—until the early nineteenth century. The region is united geographically, forming the greater part of the drainage basin of the Paraná, Paraguay, and Uruguay rivers, which flow to the wide estuary of the Río de la Plata.

In modern times, the three nations are members of the Southern Cone Common Market (or MERCOSUR), along with Brazil and Venezuela. MERCOSUR is an economic trade organization, designed to facilitate trade within the region. Argentina, Paraguay, and Uruguay are also united by Latin American culture, language (Spanish), religion (the overwhelming majority of people in the region are Roman Catholics), and by a regional character.

In terms of population, the Southern Cone is the most urbanized portion of South America. While less than one-half of Paraguay's population live in urban areas, at least 88 percent of the population of Argentina and 87 percent of Uruguayans are considered urban. Much of the region's population is concentrated in the national capitals. Metropolitan Buenos Aires, with a population of more than 12 million (2001 census), contains about one-third of the population of Argentina. More than one-half of Uruguay's population lives in metropolitan Montevideo, which had some 1,750,000 inhabitants (2004 census), and around one-third of Paraguay's population lives in metropolitan Asunción, which had 1,660,000 inhabitants at the 2002 census.

PHYSICAL REGIONS

Despite the characteristics that Argentina, Paraguay, and Uruguay have in common, the three countries include a wide variety of environments. However, ten broad physical regions can be identified. The Andes Mountains divide Chile from Argentina, providing a natural boundary between these two nations. In the north, the wide Andean Altiplano extends well into the northwestern corner of Argentina, where it is known as the Puna. Two major lowland regions, the Gran Chaco and the Pampas, lie between the Andes and the Atlantic Ocean. To the north, the Gran Chaco, which is a semiarid scrubland, covers most of Paraguay and northern Argentina, extending into Brazil and Bolivia. In Argentina, the Andes drop abruptly toward the Gran Chaco. Where the Andes become narrower, south of the Puna, a region of lower mountain ranges, known as the Pampean Sierras or, locally, the Cuyo, gradually descends eastward to the vast Pampa. Lying directly to the south of the Gran Chaco, the Pampas region forms a temperate grassland, or prairie, that covers central Argentina and most of Uruguay.

Northeast of the Pampas and east of the Gran Chaco are a series of smaller regions, all of which form southern extensions of the Brazilian Highlands. These include the Oriental region of eastern Paraguay, the hill ranges of Uruguay, and, lying sandwiched between these two regions, Mesopotamia, which occupies the northeastern spur of Argentina between Paraguay and Uruguay. To the south of the Pampas is the much narrower Patagonian Plateau, which gradually slopes from the peaks of the Andes to the Atlantic coast. This dry, rugged, windy region of valleys and tablelands stretches south to Tierra del Fuego, which is shared by both Chile and Argentina and is separated from the South American mainland by the narrow Strait of Magellan. The Falkland Islands (also known as Islas Malvinas) lie in the South Atlantic Ocean.

THE ANDES, THE PUNA, AND THE CUYO

The Andes is the main physical feature of the Southern Cone; more than one-half of their length lies within the region. The Argentine Andes include the Western Hemisphere's highest peak, Aconcagua, which rises to 22,834 feet (6,960 m) above sea level. On the Argentine side of the border, the Atlantic slope of the Andes includes three physical subregions, the Puna, Cuyo, and the much narrower southern Andes.

In the north, the Andean Altiplano—the high, wide interior flatland lying between the western and eastern ranges of the Andes—extends southward from Bolivia and into the northwestern corner of Argentina, where it is known as the Puna. The term *puna* refers to an altitudinal climate and vegetation zone, where the elevation ranges from around 11,810 feet to 15,090 feet (about 3,600–4,600 m) above sea level and where conditions are dry and cold. In the Puna, as elsewhere in the central Andes, elevations often rise significantly higher, above the snowline. West of the city of San Miguel de Tucumán, the

GEOGRAPHY AND CLIMATE

The sparsely populated Gran Chaco in the Occidental region of Paraguay includes marshy areas where fan palms flourish.

Sierra de Aconquija rises to 17,005 feet (5,183 m). Farther west along the Chilean-Argentine border (but just within Chile), the highest peak in the region is Ojos del Salado, at 22,664 feet (6,908 m), the world's tallest active volcano.

In the Puna in Argentina, the Altiplano begins to narrow and to descend gradually to lower elevations southward and eastward. The word *puna* is used interchangeably with the term *altiplano*, but, unlike the wide, flat Altiplano in Bolivia, the Argentine Puna consists of a series of roughly north-south tending mountain ridges crossed by narrower intermontane plateaus. Consequently, the Puna is more rugged and mountainous than the Bolivian Altiplano. Snow and ice meltwater from the adjacent high mountain peaks collect and evaporate in basins in the Puna to form salt flats, known in Spanish as *salares*. Waterways drain eastward from the high peaks of the Andes down through the foothills and out onto the vast Gran Chaco, where they eventually join the Paraguay-Paraná river system. *Puna* also refers to the cold, dry wind of the Andes.

Puna rural life and land has patterns that are similar to those found in the Altiplano of Bolivia and Peru. Raising animals, such as llamas, vicuñas, and sheep, is common, as is the cultivation of beans, potatoes, and quinoa (used to make flour). Important minerals in the region include lead, zinc, and sulfur. Because of the numerous *salares*, salt is also an important local product.

The lower foothills and valleys of the eastern flank of the Andes contain significant reserves of oil. The foothills are also an important agricultural region whose products include wheat, corn, sugarcane, and tobacco. The major population centers of the Argentine Puna include, from north to south, Jujuy, Salta, San Miguel de Tucumán, and Catamarca, all of which lie in fertile intermontane valleys of the lower Andean piedmont (the region at the foot of a mountain range), adjacent to the lowlands of the Gran Chaco. The climate of these cities in basins is warmer and more subtropical than that of the Puna. Founded during the sixteenth century, these cities were early settlements of the initial wave of Spanish colonial activity in Argentina.

Farther south, the high Andean Puna becomes a much narrower range of high peaks, from which the transition eastward onto the Pampa lowlands is more gradual. High in the Andes, along the Chilean-Argentine border, is the Uspallata Pass, at 12,500 feet (3,810 m), which has long been the only effective transportation link between Santiago, Chile, and Buenos Aires. Nearby, east of the border, is South America's highest peak, Aconcagua. To the east, the Andes descend in a series of lower ranges interspersed by relatively wide intermontane basins. This semiarid region, the Cuyo, is Argentina's principal wine-producing region. Other crops in the Cuyo include olives, potatoes, tomatoes, and fruits. The largest city in the region, Mendoza, which is situated at the foot of the Andes, is a center for the wine trade. Other major population centers in the Cuyo include San Juan, San Luis, and La Rioja.

At the eastern edge of the Cuyo are the Sierra de Córdoba uplands, immediately east of which begins the vast, flat Pampas. Along the eastern foot of this range lies Argentina's second-largest city, Córdoba, with 1,368,000 inhabitants (2002 census) in the metropolitan area. Apart from Buenos Aires, Córdoba is Argentina's most important industrial center.

South of Aconcagua and the Uspallata Pass, the southern Andes narrow to a single mountain range, east of which lies Patagonia. Elevations generally decrease toward the south. The highest peak, Fitz Roy, reaches an elevation of 11,073 feet (3,375 m). Numerous lakes cut by glaciers during the ice age lie within the Andes, south of latitude 40°S. As a result, this region is commonly known as the Lake District. This alpine region is characterized by lofty snow-capped mountains, pine forests, and pristine lakes and has become a major center for tourism. Along the shore of Lake Nahuel Huapi is the town of Bariloche (or San Carlos de Bariloche), which was founded by Austrian and German settlers and has become a popular ski resort.

THE GRAN CHACO

East of the Puna, in Argentina and Paraguay, the Gran Chaco gradually descends eastward toward the Paraguay-Paraná river system and the Brazilian Highlands farther east. The Gran Chaco is a large, flat region that includes the north-central portion of Argentina and all of Paraguay west of the Paraguay River (the so-called Occidental region) and also extends north into Bolivia and Brazil. Three subregions can be identified: the forested Chaco Boreal in the north and the drier Chaco Central and Chaco Austral to the south. This subtropical, semiarid region is characterized by thorn and scrub forests, cacti, grass savanna (a grassland with scattered trees), seasonally flooded marshlands, and hardwood forests and consequently is described as having a tropical to subtropical savanna environment. The most valuable and heavily exploited of the hardwoods is the quebracho tree, which yields tannin, lumber, and fuel.

The Gran Chaco is a hot region and has the highest temperatures in South America. Because of inhospitable conditions, it is sparsely settled. There are no major centers of population within the region; while two-thirds of Paraguay's area lies in the Occidental region in the Gran Chaco, barely 2 percent of that country's population lives there. Only a few cities are located in the southern fringes of the Gran Chaco in Argentina, including Santiago del Estero, near the foot of the Andes, and Resistencia and Formosa, located along the banks of the Paraguay and Paraná rivers. The region is drained by transitory streams that flow from the Andean highlands to the Paraguay River, including the Bermejo and Pilcomayo. In Argentina, the southern fringe of the Gran Chaco is marked by the Salado River and the Río Dulce, both of which flow from the Andes into the Paraná River. The plains of the Pampas stretch south of these waterways.

THE PAMPAS

South of where the Salado River bends southward toward Santa Fé and the Río Dulce discharges onto a marshy plain north of Córdoba, the impoverished soils of the Gran Chaco give way to South America's most productive, prosperous agricultural region, the Pampas. The word *pampa* is a term in the Amerindian Quechua language for "grassland." The Pampas form an undulating to flat prairie that stretches from the Sierra de Córdoba in the west to the Atlantic Ocean in the east and runs from Uruguay in the north to the Río Negro in the south. Three subregions can be distinguished: the Pampa Seca (dry Pampa), the Pampa Húmeda (humid Pampa), and the Uruguayan Pampas. The Pampa Húmeda covers the central portion of Argentina and extends eastward and southward of Buenos Aires, which is located at the head of the Río de la Plata estuary. As the Pampas become drier farther south, west, and north, they are referred to as the Pampa Seca. The Uruguayan Pampa is similar to the Pampa Húmeda, but is more rolling and hilly as it transitions into the Cuchilla ranges along the southern fringes of the Brazilian highlands.

The soils of this rich agricultural region, some of the most fertile in the world, were formed by the deposition of loess, a fine-grained soil that was blown from the Andes. These soils have been enriched over time by the addition of volcanic ash, also from the Andes. The climate is characterized as humid subtropical, with warm, humid summers and winters that are mild to cool, although sometimes quite chilly, especially when cold fronts, locally known as *pamperos*, blow from the south. While freezing temperatures and frosts sometimes occur, snowfall is rare near the coast and light farther inland. The productivity of the soils has been enhanced by high annual precipitation, which is common throughout the year but is a little heavier during late spring and summer, when violent thunderstorms are common. Annual rainfall is heaviest near the coast and decreases gradually inland. This has allowed the growth of native grasses and consequently increased the amount of organic matter in the soil, making this a region of great agricultural potential.

After Europeans pushed nomadic Amerindians off the Pampas in the nineteenth century, they transformed the region into the agricultural heartland of the Southern Cone. Since then, the Pampas have come largely to resemble the vast grasslands of the North American Midwest. The cultivation of wheat and corn and, more recently, soybeans, as well as cattle raising, have been the mainstays of the Pampas for more than a century. As a result, beef and grain form the center of Argentina's diet as well as its economy. Sheep raising is also common, mainly in the drier Pampa Seca, and wool is an important regional commodity. European settlers in the Argentine Pampas built a network of railroads in order to introduce farming and livestock

GEOGRAPHY AND CLIMATE

Pampas grass dotted by small stands of trees covers much of western Uruguay.

grazing on a vast scale throughout the region, and small family farms and large cattle ranches, known as *estancia*s, came to dominate the landscape. The Pampas are traditionally known as the home of the highly romanticized gaucho, the independent cattle herder, comparable to the cowboy of the North American West.

Since the construction of the railroads, the settlement of the Pampas by Spanish and Italian immigrants during the late nineteenth and early twentieth centuries—and the success of farming and ranching—the port of Buenos Aires emerged as the dominant city not only of the Pampas but of Argentina. The city is a major industrial, administrative, commercial, and educational center. Other major cities in the Pampas include Rosario (which had 1,161,000 inhabitants in the metropolitan area at the 2002 census) and Santa Fé (with 454,000 inhabitants in the metropolitan area), both of which emerged as important industrial centers (producing petrochemicals and steel) and river ports along the Paraná River.

Along the Atlantic coast, Mar del Plata, with 542,000 inhabitants, is Argentina's main fishing port, seaside resort, and woolen textile manufacturing center. Farther south, along the coast near the Río Colorado, Bahia Blanca serves as an important seaport for the southern Pampas, exporting wheat and, more recently, petrochemicals.

The Uruguayan Pampas are a continuation of the Argentine Pampa Húmeda, but they are also an extension of the Brazilian highlands. Uruguay's landscape transitions gradually from flat grasslands in the south toward rolling hills in the north. Much of the country is characterized as a gentle rolling plain. Like the Argentine Pampas, cattle raising, sheep grazing, and grain cultivation dominate land use patterns. Most of the country's major cities are located along the Atlantic coast in the south and the Uruguay River in the west, the boundary between Uruguay and Argentina. Along the southern coast, where the Río de la Plata enters the Atlantic Ocean, is the national capital of Uruguay, Montevideo. Economically, it is overshadowed by Buenos Aires across the broad estuary. Farther east, Punta del Este is Uruguay's main seaside resort.

THE HILLS OF URUGUAY

The rolling plains of the Uruguayan Pampas gradually merge into the hilly uplands of the Paraná Plateau, which forms part of the much larger Brazilian highlands. Parts of the Uruguayan Pampas

729

lie on top of an underlying granite rock base, the southernmost extension of the Paraná Plateau. The northern three-fourths of Uruguay are characterized by rolling hills, which are known locally as *cuchillas*, or ridges, the largest of which are the Cuchilla de Haedo (reaching 1,378 feet or 420 m) in the northwest and the Cuchilla Grande farther south. Between these ridges, the Negro flows westward across Uruguay, draining into the Uruguay River.

MESOPOTAMIA

The Argentine region of Mesopotamia is a southward extension of the Paraná Plateau. This narrow northeastern spur of Argentina lies between the Uruguay and Paraná rivers, which respectively form the borders of Uruguay (to the east) and Paraguay (to the west). The region includes not only the Argentine province of Mesopotamia but also the province of Misiones, wedged between Paraguay and Uruguay, as well as the provinces of Corrientes and Entre Ríos, farther south.

Most of Mespotamia is characterized as having a humid subtropical environment. Rainfall is abundant throughout the region and, in the northern province of Misiones, semitropical woodlands with hardwoods and palms are dominant. At the northernmost corner of Misiones, the Paraná River drops from the Paraná Plateau, cascading over a series of large cataracts known as Iguazú Falls, which have become a major tourist attraction.

Corrientes, to the south, is marshy and wooded and also includes low hills. Most of Entre Ríos is covered with fertile pastureland and forms part of the Pampas, sharing characteristics with both the Pampa Húmeda of Argentina, across the Paraná River, and the Uruguayan Pampas, across the Uruguay River. The southernmost part of Entre Ríos province is characterized by swampy lowlands in the Paraná Delta, where the Paraná and Uruguay rivers converge and empty into the Río de la Plata. Mesopotamia is well known for the cultivation of yerba. Yerba leaves are dried and ground and steeped in hot water to make a popular tealike beverage known as yerba maté, which is consumed throughout the Southern Cone.

ORIENTAL REGION OF PARAGUAY

The Paraná Plateau extends westward from Brazil into eastern Paraguay. The plateau region in Paraguay lying between the Paraná River in the east and the Paraguay River in the west is called the Oriental region. The rich soils and dense forests east of the Paraguay River sharply distinguish this area from the much drier and economically marginal Occidental region of Paraguay, to the west of the waterway. Like the northern part of Mesopotamia in Argentina, the Oriental region is characterized as an uneven, hilly plateau covered with semitropical forests rich with hardwoods, palms, and medicinal plants. The region is a major producer and exporter of yerba. A number of food crops

RIVERS OF ARGENTINA, PARAGUAY AND URUGUAY

River	Length in miles	Length in km
Paraná*–Río de la Plata	3,032	4,880
Paraguay*	1,585	2,550
Pilcomayo*	1,554	2,500
Uruguay*	990	1,593
Negro-Nequén	699	1,125
Bermejo	650	1,046
Colorado	528	850
Chubut	503	810
Negro (Uruguay)	497	800
Salado	398	640

* Not all the course of these waterways flows through the region.

such as corn, cassava, wheat, rice, vegetables, and fruits, along with commercial crops such as cotton, vegetable oils, coffee, and tobacco, are also as produced, and cattle ranching is widespread.

The productive Oriental region is home to some 98 percent of Paraguay's population. The national capital, Asunción, which serves as an important river port along the east bank of the Paraguay River, is the economic heart of this region. In the eastern part of the Oriental region is Ciudad del Este, Paraguay's second-largest metropolitan area, with a population of 332,000 at the 2002 census. Ciudad del Este, which is located along the Paraná River on the border with Brazil, is rapidly developing and has a major tax-free trading zone, relying upon customers from neighboring Brazil.

PATAGONIA

South of the Pampas in Argentina, Patagonia occupies the tapering southeastern lowland of the South American continent. This region extends from the Río Negro in the north, on the southern fringe of the Pampa Seca, to Tierra del Fuego in the south. Patagonia is a region of cool, dry, windswept steppes. Unlike the Pampas, which become drier farther inland, Patagonia becomes moister and its grasslands more productive, inland and southward. Patagonia is a rare example of an east coast desert. Gradually sloping from the Andean foothills in the west to the Atlantic coast, Patagonia is characterized by relatively low-lying plateaus and intermittent valleys, incised by eastward-flowing waterways that are fed by Andean snowmelt and glacial lakes. The plateau uplands, known as *mesetas centrales*, form a wall along the Atlantic coast, from where they rise like stair steps toward the Andes. Deep valleys, or *bajos*, are well watered and afford refuge from the relentless winds of the uplands. The *bajos* contain nearly all of Patagonia's productive agricultural lands.

GEOGRAPHY AND CLIMATE

Ushuaia, which had a population of about 64,000 in 2001, is Argentina's most southerly city. In modern times, Ushuaia has developed an important tourist industry.

Most of the region's population centers, including Trelew, Comodoro Rivadavia, and Río Gallegos, are port towns located where rivers meet the coast. This region was settled by Argentines as well as English, Scots, and especially (in the late nineteenth century) Welsh, who settled mainly along the Chubut Valley. The region still has a small Welsh-speaking population. In Patagonia, sheep raising is the dominant and most widespread land use, but irrigated lands in the river valleys permit some vineyards, fruit orchards, and wheat cultivation.

volume of shipping around the southern tip of South America. Ushuaia now serves as an important center for manufacturing and tourism; people flock to see the penguins and seals that gather nearby.

S. BROWN

TIERRA DEL FUEGO

South of the city of Río Gallegos, the South American mainland ends at the Strait of Magellan, beyond which lies the archipelago of Tierra del Fuego, literally, "land of fire." By far the largest island in Tierra del Fuego is Isla Grande, which is roughly the size of Ireland; it is shared by Chile on the west and Argentina on the east. Tierra del Fuego has a subantarctic climate and is cool, with temperature extremes moderated by marine influences. Prevailing winds are from the southwest. The western and southern portions of the island are forested, while the northeast of the island is a treeless plain of sheep farms. The region, which contains oil fields, has numerous ice fields and glaciers. Ushuaia, the southernmost city in Argentina, once served as a major center of ship repair, until construction of the Panama Canal at the beginning of the twentieth century greatly reduced the

The Falkland Islands

Around 300 miles (483 km) east of mainland South America, the Falkland Islands comprise two main islands, East Falkland and West Falkland (separated by Falkland Sound) and some 700 smaller islands. The coast along either side of Falkland Sound is relatively straight, but the islands' other coasts are deeply indented. Both main islands contain mountains and boggy plains, and most of the land is devoted to sheep raising. The islands have a cold, humid, windy climate. The Falkland Islands, a British territory, are claimed by Argentina, which invaded in 1982. At the end of the two-month-long Falklands War, British forces removed the Argentines. At the 2001 census, the islands were home to 2,500 people (excluding British military personnel). The islands' population is of British ancestry, and about 80 percent live in Stanley, the only town.

Geology of Argentina, Paraguay, and Uruguay

The Brazilian Shield, the nucleus of South America, provided a building platform for sediments that form much of Argentina, Paraguay, and Uruguay. The movement of tectonic plates—plates that form Earth's outer layer and move with the molten material beneath—has also shaped the region, particularly through rifting in the east and the formation of the high Andes mountain range in the west.

The Brazilian Shield, the center of South America, provided a platform for the deposition of sediments as the shield eroded through time. Marginal seas periodically transgressed onto the shield, and marine sediments were deposited. As a result, much of the region formed by Argentina, Paraguay, and Uruguay is formed from sedimentary rocks (rocks laid down in layers).

Most of the South American continent is part of the South American Plate, which has migrated over time, floating on the oceanic crust. The plate has changed position from tropical equatorial to polar conditions over hundreds of millions of years. During migration, it has collided with isolated microcontinents and oceanic volcanic island arc systems, which have been added (accreted) to the continent. Because of stresses resulting either from collisions with plates or from changes in thermal conditions in the mantle (the layer extending from the base of Earth's crust to the core), the land masses have undergone brittle failure and have created either significant rift valleys—valleys formed by the sinking of land between two parallel faults—or have formed major fissures in the crust, allowing for the expulsion of extensive lava flows, when magma extrudes from the mantle below. Both rifts and lava flows are evident in the region.

THE EARLIEST SHIELDS AND SEDIMENTS

The geological history of northern Argentina, Paraguay, and Uruguay begins with the Precambrian Shield (dating from before 545 million years ago), an area of old hard rocks exposed in northeastern Paraguay and eastern Uruguay and extending southward into northern Argentina below the surface. An appendage of the shield, the Asunción Arch, extends from northern Paraguay into Argentina and is exposed at the surface near Asunción, the capital of Paraguay. The arch forms a major divide between the south Brazilian Paraná Basin, which includes eastern Paraguay, Uruguay, and part of northeastern Argentina, from the Chaco Basin of Paraguay and northern Argentina.

The earliest sediments in the region are in northeastern Paraguay where Cambrian (545 through 495 million years ago) limestones edge the Brazilian Shield. Progressively, sediments, including sandstones and shales (a sedimentary rock made of clay particles), were added as the shield area built out during the Paleozoic era (545 through 248 million years ago), extending from Paraguay and across northern Argentina. In Uruguay, the exposure of these sediments is limited because all Paleozoic rocks in western Uruguay are buried under deep lava flows. Where the Paleozoic sediments are exposed, they are of marine origin and contain rich fossil assemblages, particularly graptolites (colonial animals related to coelenterates) and brachiopods (marine invertebrates). The presence of these fossils allows for accurate dating of the sediments and correlation of the sediments across the region. The climatic conditions of the region during most of the Paleozoic were cold polar, and Silurian (443 to 417 million years ago) to Permian (290 to 248 million years ago) glacial deposits are documented across southern South America.

MICROCONTINENTS

Along west-central Argentina, two microcontinents—the Precordillera and the Patagonia Massif—collided with the southern Brazilian Shield from the Pacific. The Precordillera, near the city of Mendoza, collided during the late Paleozoic. In the south, during the Permian period, the Patagonia Massif, which covers around one-third of Argentina, also collided with the shield. The attachment of Patagonia is related to a global mountain-building process known as the Hercynian orogeny. Hercynian remnants extend from Patagonia, along the Andes, through North America, and into Europe. The Hercynian event resulted from the collision of the ancestor of North America (Laurentia) with South America and Africa (Gondwana or Gondwanaland), creating the supercontinent of Pangea. As a result, Eurasia, Africa, and the Americas formed one continent, allowing diverse animal species to migrate across the vast landmass. Dinosaur species, in particular, became widespread, and the dinosaur fossil record allows for detailed correlations of similar aged rocks.

RIFTING

By the Jurassic (206 through 144 million years ago) and Cretaceous (144 through 65 million years ago) periods, the Gondwana supercontinent, which linked what are now Argentina

GEOGRAPHY AND CLIMATE

The Iguazú Falls mark the boundary of a band of hard volcanic rock, formed from lava that flowed across much of the region during Mesozoic times.

and Uruguay directly to southwest Africa, began to strain as it migrated northward to lower latitudes. The most obvious effect of the strain was the separation of South America and Africa. The rift event is well documented by geological evidence from thousands of deep oil wells drilled offshore in the South Atlantic.

When the initial breakup occurred, the edges were rough and irregular, and shoulders of higher land developed near the edges of grabens (elongated troughs formed by subsidence of the crust between faults). Examples of the grabens include the Salado graben at the mouth of the Río de la Plata. The shoulder of the Salado graben and other principal South Atlantic graben systems formed highlands that are exposed in eastern Uruguay. Similar grabens continue along the South Atlantic coast as far south as Tierra del Fuego.

Grabens form many of the sedimentary basins of Argentina, including the Colorado and San Jorge basins, in southern Argentina, and, in part, the Neuquén Basin (in central southern Argentina). Organic material laid down in these basins is now represented by hydrocarbons, and these regions are the main oil and natural gas producers in Argentina. The Neuquén Basin is located between the Precordillera and the Pampean Massif and formed as a consequence of strain between these two terrains (areas within which particular rocks and physical characteristics are prevalent) as South America underwent deformation.

VOLCANIC ACTIVITY

The massive volcanic fields of the Brazilian Paraná Basin, extending into eastern Paraguay, northern Argentina, and covering all of western Uruguay, are an additional result of the major rifting event in the region. The total area covered by the Mesozoic Paraná lava flow is more than 386,000 square miles (some 1 million sq. km), and laval rocks in the region have a total thickness of more than 1 mile (over 1.6 km). Volcanic activity persisted for more than 10 million years, and similar contemporaneous volcanic flows are recorded in South Africa and central India. Air pockets in the Mesozoic Paraná lava flow form geodes (cavities lined with crystals), which contain commercially important amethyst crystals.

ARGENTINA, PARAGUAY, AND URUGUAY

The most spectacular physiographic feature resulting from the flows is the Iguazú Falls, along the Paraná River, where a series of more than 20 cataracts (averaging 200 feet or 60 m high) fall over the hard band of rock formed by the lava flows. The Iguazú Falls are the fifth-largest falls in the world in terms of the volume of water.

MOUNTAIN BUILDING

During the Jurassic and Cretaceous periods, western Argentina was covered by the sea, and extensive marine sedimentation occurred until the plate collision that formed the Andes closed the access to the Pacific Ocean. Through most of the Cenozoic era (from 65 million years ago), the Pacific Nazca Plate moved eastward, being subducted under the South American Plate. In the process, the crust was folded and shortened, and the Andes range was formed. As the Andes pushed toward the east, they resulted in folding of the western Argentine crust, creating several new basins. These form part of a string of similar features known as the Sub-Andean Basins.

The Perito Moreno glacier, in southern Argentina, is a remnant of the glaciation that occurred in the region until about 11,000 years ago.

In subduction, the crust melts along the edges, resulting in volcanism. Active volcanoes line the Andes (the plate boundary) through northern and southern Argentina. The Andean region is also subject to deep-seated earthquakes, up to 500 miles (800 km) deep.

GLACIATION

In recent geological time, a glacial period affected the high Andes, with ice spreading from the far south around 9 million years ago. During the ice age, which did not end in the region until some 11,000 years ago, U-shaped valleys were eroded by glaciers, which also formed cirques (high mountain basins, forming the blunt end of a valley) and hanging valleys (valleys that join other valleys that are much deeper than the tributary). Above the level of the ice sheets, frost-shattered peaks formed.

P. BARTOK

GEOGRAPHY AND CLIMATE

Climate of Argentina, Paraguay, and Uruguay

Argentina, Paraguay, and Uruguay together cover a large area of southern South America. Stretching from latitude 18°S through 55°S, they have a diverse climate, from tropical through subarctic.

The main influences on the climate in Argentina, Paraguay, and Uruguay are the prevailing northwesterly winds over the mid-latitudes (30°S to 60°S), the prevailing southeasterly trade winds over the tropical regions (0° to 30°S), the South American monsoon, cold polar frontal weather systems, and the El Niño phenomenon. The high mountainous terrain is also a strong influence on the local climate. Argentina and Uruguay both have an eastern coastline along the Atlantic Ocean, and maritime influences are also a factor in shaping the climate.

The strong prevailing wind in Tierra del Fuego causes trees and other vegetation to bend as they grow.

Because the region spans a wide range of latitude and terrain, it has strong contrasts in climate. The region may be divided into five broad climatic-geographic regions: the Andes highlands; the Pampas and the plains of Uruguay; the Chaco region of northeastern interior Argentina and Paraguay; western Argentina; and Patagonia. The climate is also often named simply by the altitude of the land: *tierra caliente* (literally, "hot land") is from sea level to about 2,950 feet (900 m), *tierra templada* ("temperate land") from 2,950 feet to 5,900 feet (900–1,800 m), *tierra fría* ("cold land") from 5,900 feet to about 9,840 feet (1,800–3,000 m), and *páramos* ("high land') or altiplano ("high plain") above around 9,840 feet (3,000 m).

735

ARGENTINA, PARAGUAY, AND URUGUAY

EL NIÑO

The El Niño phenomenon is a shift of the region of warmest Pacific Ocean surface temperature (more than 82°F or 27.5°C) from the western Pacific to the central and eastern Pacific. This shift tends to weaken the easterly trade winds and changes the Pacific Ocean currents along the western coast of South America and the global circulation in the atmosphere. El Niño events occur every three to seven years, usually lasting for between six and nine months, and are strongest in December. These events have major impacts on the climate worldwide, as well as in South America. Warm El Niño events, in which coastal waters along Peru become warmer, bring increased rainfall and flooding in Paraguay, Uruguay, and central Argentina as the midlatitude weather systems become more active. Conversely, cold events bring lower rainfall, often leading to drought.

ANDES HIGHLANDS

The Andes highlands and plateaus run northward through western Argentina and contain the highest peak in the Andes, Aconcagua, at 22,834 feet (6,960 m). In northern Argentina, the Andes mountains are mostly more than 9,840 feet (3,000 m) above sea level, and the range has a relatively low annual precipitation, with a high snowline up to 19,685 feet (about 6,000 m). The Andes in southern Argentina have a higher annual precipitation, a lower snowline, and many glaciers and permanent snowfields. Summers are less warm than in the neighboring lowlands, and the winters are colder (and much colder in the southern Andes). Differences between daytime and nighttime temperatures are also greater in the highlands than in the lowlands.

Salta, in northern Argentina, at an elevation of 4,003 feet (1,220 m), has a typical highland climate. Maximum monthly temperatures are 80°F (27°C) in January, while in June, maximum temperatures are significantly cooler at 65°F (18°C). At night, the monthly average minimum temperature drops to 40°F (4°C). Annual rainfall is 27.3 inches (69 cm).

In central western Argentina, a local dry wind, named the *zonda*, blows along the eastern slopes of the Andes. It is formed when humid maritime air is lifted over the mountains from the west, loses its moisture as snowfall over the mountains, and then descends down the eastern mountain as much drier air. The *zonda*, which tends to blow for a few hours in the afternoon from May through November, is particularly frequent in the San Juan, Mendoza, and La Rioja provinces of Argentina.

PREVAILING WINDS

Prevailing westerly winds blow in the midlatitudes, and prevailing easterly trade winds blow over the tropics. These winds blow because there is a global-scale circulation of air from the high pressure areas to lower pressure areas, which, together with the effects of Earth's rotation, produces the global pattern of prevailing winds. Winds blowing from over the Atlantic Ocean are moist, bringing adequate precipitation for agriculture to eastern and coastal regions.

THE PAMPAS AND THE URUGUAY PLAINS

The Pampas is a region of relatively flat plains covering northeastern Argentina and extending into western Uruguay. Eastern Uruguay is more hilly, but the hills are fairly low and climatic differences between west and east are slight. This region

GEOGRAPHY AND CLIMATE

Distinct wet and dry seasons (although with occasional drought) support grasslands in much of Uruguay.

has a temperate climate, generally mild winters, and warm summers, with fairly distinct wet and dry seasons, and an average annual rainfall of about 20–40 inches (around 50–100 cm). Because the region is generally flat, high winds and weather systems can quickly sweep over the plains.

Frost and snow are rare, only occurring briefly if cold polar fronts from Antarctica reach into the region. High temperatures are also rare. There is significant rainfall every month, but most rain tends to fall in a few heavy showers. Droughts occasionally occur, and, during dry weather, grassland fires can be common. The weather is moderately sunny, with eight to ten hours of clear sunshine per day in summer, and four to five hours of sunshine a day in winter. The western Pampas in Argentina are drier and warmer in summer than the southern or coastal Pampas.

Buenos Aires is typical of the southern Pampas. In summer, the city has average monthly maximum temperatures in January of 84°F (29°C), and average minimum temperatures of 63°F (17°C). The monthly precipitation is fairly constant at 2–5 inches (about 5–12 cm) throughout the year, with an annual average of more than 47 inches (more than 120 cm).

Victoria is typical of the western Pampas, but the city is at a slightly higher elevation than Buenos Aires. It has an annual precipitation of 22.2 inches (56.4 cm), which falls mostly from October through March. Average summer maximum temperatures are 93°F (34°C) in January, with an average minimum temperature of 59°F (15°C). By contrast, in June the average minimum temperature is 32°F (0°C), and the average maximum is 59°F (15°C). Paysandú has a climate typical of western Uruguay. The city has an annual precipitation of 47.1 inches (some 120 cm), falling throughout the year, peaking in October and April. It has an average monthly maximum temperature of 86°F (30°C), with night minimum temperatures of 71°F (22°C) in summer (in January). In winter, the July maximum temperature in the region is 60°F (16°C), and the minimum temperature is 48°F (9°C).

The Pampas and Uruguay experience local winds called the *sondo* and the *pampero*. The *sondo* is a hot, humid north wind, which blows in summer, arriving ahead of a depression system

737

ARGENTINA, PARAGUAY, AND URUGUAY

High temperatures and reliable rainfall in eastern Paraguay allow a rich cover of forest to grow.

(area of low pressure) moving eastward. The *pampero* wind is a particularly cold winter wind that can occur abruptly, bringing cold air northward across the Pampas.

THE CHACO REGION

The Chaco climatic region covers northeastern interior Argentina and northwestern Paraguay as well as part of Bolivia. It has a mostly tropical climate and is warmer than the Pampas, with generally high temperatures and often high humidity. Precipitation falls throughout the year, peaking between March and May, and also around October. Southern Paraguay has a similar climate, but because it is at a higher elevation, with rolling hills, it is subtropical with slightly cooler temperatures and slightly higher rainfall. Otherwise, the terrain of the Chaco is generally flat. Occasionally, temperatures dramatically drop to below freezing, but normally winters are mild. The rainfall is lower toward the west.

Resistencia, a city in northeastern Argentina, has a climate typical of this region. It has monthly maximum temperatures of 90°F (32°C) and monthly minimum temperatures of 71°F (22°C) in January. In winter, the monthly average maximum temperature is 69°F (21°C), and the minimum temperature is 51°F (11°C) in July. The annual precipitation of 52.5 inches (around 130 cm) falls mostly during October to May. Farther west, Santiago del Estero has an annual rainfall of 21.5 inches (some 55 cm), falling mostly from December through March. Summer temperatures in January are an average maximum of 90°F (32°C), falling to a minimum average of 70°F (21°C) at night. In winter, July maximum monthly temperatures average 67°F (19°C) and the minimum temperatures average 43°F (6°C).

WESTERN ARGENTINA

Western Argentina, including the northernmost Andes, is a dry semiarid region, similar to the deserts of northern Chile on the western side of the Andes. Even on the high mountains, snowfall is light. This semiarid desert region reaches across the eastern foothills of the Andes south to 35°S. The region is a rainshadow, a dry region on the leeward side of mountains, over which rain-bearing air deposits its moisture before reaching the rainshadow. The annual rainfall in most parts is less than 10 inches (some 25 cm) and is variable from year to year. There are frequent droughts, especially in winter months. Summers are generally hot and sunny, with about ten hours of sunshine per day. Mendoza has a climate typical of the region. In summer, January average maximum temperatures are 90°F (32°C), falling to minimum temperatures of 61°F (16°C) at night. July maximum temperatures are 59°F (15°C), with minimum temperatures averaging 36°F (2°C). Monthly rainfall is low, at 1.1 inches (about 3 cm) maximum in February and March, and as low as 0.2 inch (0.5 cm) in July, and an annual total rainfall of 3.6 inches (9.3 cm).

PATAGONIA

Patagonia covers the southern one-third of Argentina and generally has a cool temperate and fairly dry climate. The region is sheltered from the prevailing midlatitude westerly winds by the southern Andes Mountains. Sarmiento, at an elevation of 879 feet (some 270 m), has a climate typical of the region. In summer, January average monthly maximum temperatures are 79°F (26°C), and minimum temperatures are 52°F (11°C), and there are nine hours of sunshine per day. In winter, July monthly maximum temperatures average 45°F (7°C) with minimum temperatures of 28°F (−2°C), and there is an average of three hours of sunshine per day. Farther south, summers are cooler, with extensive snow and frost during the winter months, although the cold is moderated by the warmer coastal temperatures. Rio Grande is in the extreme south, with average winter minimum temperatures of 28°F (-2°C) and average maximum temperatures of 36°F (2°C). The average temperature is below 32°F (0°C) for about four months of the year.

CLIMATIC HAZARDS

Strong El Niño warm events can bring torrential rain and flooding to the region, which can damage sanitation facilities, drinking water, and the general infrastructure. Cold El Niño events can bring droughts, which can cause crop failure and water shortages. Cold fronts can sometimes suddenly bring extremely cold air, as in July 2003, when temperatures in the Andean highlands rapidly dropped to 4°F (-20°C) in some regions, resulting in human deaths and widespread loss of livestock. Climatic conditions are only suitable for a malarial mosquito cycle in a small region of northwest Argentina and southeastern Paraguay, while Uruguay is free of malaria.

CLIMATE CHANGE

Global climate change is predicted to have strong impacts in this region of South America. Mean annual temperatures over much of Argentina, Paraguay, and Uruguay are predicted to increase, with the greatest rise over northern Argentina and Paraguay. The warming is already having dramatic effects on the glaciers in most of South America's high mountains, including the Upsala Glacier of Argentina, which has melted significantly since the 1950s. The disappearance of glaciers threatens drinking water supplies, as well as the generation of hydroelectricity from glacial meltwater. Increased rainfall is expected in Uruguay and northeastern Argentina, while lower rainfall is predicted in western Argentina.

M. FELTON

CLIMATE

ASUNCIÓN, PARAGUAY
25°15'S 57°40'W Height above sea level 291 feet (81 m)

	J	F	M	A	M	J	J	A	S	O	N	D
Mean maximum												
(°F)	93	91	90	82	77	73	73	77	79	84	88	90
(°C)	34	33	32	28	25	23	23	25	26	29	31	32
Mean minimum												
(°F)	73	72	70	66	61	57	55	57	61	66	68	72
(°C)	23	22	21	19	16	14	13	14	16	19	20	22
Precipitation												
(in.)	5.8	5.1	4.6	6.5	4.4	3.2	1.5	2.9	3.5	5.2	6.5	5.9
(cm)	14.7	12.9	11.8	16.6	11.3	8.2	3.9	7.3	8.8	13.1	16.4	15.0

BUENOS AIRES, ARGENTINA
34°40'S 58°30'W Height above sea level: 16 feet (5 m)

	J	F	M	A	M	J	J	A	S	O	N	D
Mean maximum												
(°F)	84	84	79	73	66	61	59	63	66	73	77	82
(°C)	29	29	26	23	19	16	15	17	19	23	25	28
Mean minimum												
(°F)	63	63	63	57	50	46	45	48	50	55	61	61
(°C)	17	17	17	14	10	8	7	9	10	13	16	18
Precipitation												
(in.)	4.8	4.8	6.1	4.2	3.6	2.0	2.1	2.5	3.1	5.5	5.2	4.1
(cm)	12.2	12.3	15.4	10.7	9.2	5.0	5.3	6.3	7.8	13.9	13.1	10.3

USHUAIA, ARGENTINA
54°48'S 68°19'W Height above sea level: 16 feet (5 m)

	J	F	M	A	M	J	J	A	S	O	N	D
Mean maximum												
(°F)	59	57	54	50	43	41	41	43	48	52	55	54
(°C)	15	14	12	10	6	5	5	6	9	11	13	13
Mean minimum												
(°F)	43	41	39	36	32	30	30	30	34	36	39	41
(°C)	6	5	4	2	0	-1	-1	-1	1	2	4	5
Precipitation												
(in.)	1.2	1.3	1.9	2.0	2.2	2.2	1.8	2.4	1.6	1.4	1.4	1.6
(cm)	3.1	3.3	4.9	5.0	5.5	5.5	4.6	6.1	4.0	3.5	3.5	4.1

Flora and Fauna of Argentina, Paraguay, and Uruguay

The region that comprises Argentina, Paraguay, and Uruguay includes a wide range of habitats from tropical and subtropical forests, through dry grasslands and deserts, to temperate and subarctic regions.

Although the region covered by Argentina, Paraguay, and Uruguay contains may different habitats, some five broad climatic-vegetation regions can be identified: the Gran Chaco and savanna, the Pampas grasslands, the steppes, Patagonia, and Tierra del Fuego. Within these regions, many smaller ecosystems occur, and while human activity has greatly modified the environment in some areas, other districts are unpopulated enough, and remote enough, to be relatively unchanged.

THE GRAN CHACO AND THE SAVANNA

A dry, wooded grassland dominates a region, stretching from eastern Brazil through northern Paraguay and into northern Argentina. The northern and western sections form the Gran Chaco (or Chaco), a savanna region of tropical and subtropical grasses containing scattered trees and drought-resistant undergrowth. This thorny forest forms the northernmost region of Argentina and Paraguay.

The Chaco is bounded by the Andes foothills to the west and the Paraguay and Paraná rivers to the east. Western parts of the Chaco are very dry because the region lies within the rain shadow of the Andes (a rain shadow is a dry area on the leeward side of hills or mountains, on the other side of which moist air gives rain). Characteristic plants of this arid zone include algarrobos, a group of thorny, drought-resistant shrubs that are at their most diverse in this part of South America. They have deep root systems that help them trap water. A rich herbaceous understory below the algarrobos includes other thorn-bearing plants such as bayonet bromeliads and star cactus.

Lack of water makes life in the arid Chaco difficult, but the region contains a rich diversity of animals, mainly because large tracts remain only sparsely populated and there was relatively little pressure from hunting by Amerindians in the past—although the name *chaco* is a Quechua Amerindian word meaning "hunting ground." Mammals in the region include the Chacoan tuco-tuco and other rodents such as maras and agoutis. Azara night monkeys clamber among the thorns, and there are thought to still be small populations of guanaco and pampas deer living in the Chaco. The region is home to the burrowing, ant-eating pink fairy armadillo, and the Chaco also has a number of other armadillo species. Exploration and research in parts of this thorny, arid wilderness were long delayed by its remoteness and difficult conditions, and new animal species were discovered as late as the last quarter of the twentieth century, including the pig-sized Chaco peccary, or tagua. The birds of the region are similarly diverse, with resident species including black-legged seriemas, many-colored Chaco finches, Chaco earthcreepers, Chaco pipits, and Chaco chachalacas.

Toward the east, the Chaco becomes increasingly less arid, with the algarrobo woodland giving way to patches of forest dominated by three species of quebracho. These wooded patches are interspersed with cactus-rich grassland and thorny shrub, rich with algarrobos but also containing acacias and parkinsonias, as well as stands of caranday palms. The grasslands hold small populations of animals such as greater rheas, maned wolves, and giant anteaters, while the more densely wooded areas are home to species such as jaguars, collared peccaries, and black howler monkeys.

There are some important wetland areas within the eastern humid Chaco, including pools dug by ranchers for their cattle, as well as natural bogs in lowland areas that are susceptible to flooding. Chaco wetlands are an important habitat for birds. Shallow, salty lagoons in the heart of the Chaco hold populations of Chilean flamingos, coscoroba swans, plumbeous ibises, collared plovers, and ringed teals, and they are an important stopover for long-distance migrants such as pectoral sandpipers. The wetlands are home to mammals such as marsh deer, Chacoan maras, and capybaras (large semiaquatic rodents), and these large herbivores support a range of reptilian predators, including yellow anacondas and spectacled caimans.

The Chaco grades to the east into an expanse of tall grasses, dotted with wetlands and forests of willows. The savanna extends through Uruguay into southern Brazil. Like all the grasslands of central and eastern South America, the Chaco is under serious threat from ranching and conversion to agriculture. Most larger mammals of the Uruguayan savanna are confined to zones of forest along the waterways. They include gray brockets and Pampas deer, capybaras, and giant otters, while seasonally flooded grasslands are important for globally threatened birds such as marsh and Entre Rios seedeaters and saffron-cowled blackbirds. Grassland species such as Pampas meadowlarks, yellow cardinal, and ochre-breasted pipits live in drier areas, while scattered copses are home to range-restricted species such as chestnut-backed tanagers, glaucous-blue grosbeaks, and red-rumped warbling finches.

GEOGRAPHY AND CLIMATE

Surviving Fire

Although the Pampas are largely devoid of trees, there is one treelike species that does grow on this vast grassland, the ombú, a fast-growing herbaceous plant that is a close relative of pokeweed, the plant that is sometimes harvested in the United States for poke salad greens. The ombú is equipped with a variety of adaptations that allow it to grow where other trees cannot.

A large evergreen with a wide canopy, ombús can grow up to 60 feet (18m) tall. As is the case for all plants on the Pampas, water conservation is essential. A plant that has adapted to the environment, ombú has sap that contains mammal-specific toxins that deter browsers, while the leaves are waxy to minimize water loss. Water is stored deep within the massive base of the plant, from which multiple trunks often develop. Despite these water-saving adaptations, ombús rarely grow closely together because of the scarcity of this precious resource.

To survive on the Pampas, plants must share one important adaptation—fire resistance. Pampas grasses burn in the frequent naturally occurring fires, but their seeds can withstand the heat. Ombús survive by having fire-resistant trunks. Regular blazes remove other large plants, allowing the ombú to grow largely without competition for light, space, or water.

THE PAMPAS

South of the Uruguayan savanna lie the Pampas, a grassland that covers much of lowland Argentina. This habitat is seriously threatened by human activities. Because of its temperate climate and rich soil, much of the region has been turned over to agriculture or livestock, especially cattle. The Pampas are typified by a nearly total absence of trees, except along rivers and streams, due to frequent fires in summer, when the dry grasses provide an exceptional kindling. Although the composition of the flora changes with water availability from the arid grasslands of central Argentina to the wetter east, perennial grasses and herbaceous plants dominate throughout. A typical species of the region is the hardy Pampas grass, which can form stands up to 10 feet (3m) tall.

Grassland is a demanding habitat for small mammals, and a lack of cover from aerial predators such as cinereous harriers and Harris's hawks causes many rodents, such as guinea pigs, to confine periods of feeding and other activity to dawn or dusk. Species such as Pampas viscacha (of the chinchilla family) and hairy armadillos spend much of the day in burrows in the soil, and abandoned mammal burrows often become home to burrowing owls. Small mammals are prey to a range of carnivores, which include maned wolves, Pampas foxes, lesser grisons, and Geoffroy's cats. Larger mammals of the Pampas include Pampas deer, guanacos, and, in low-lying wetland areas, coypus, which provide food for predators, such as pumas. American black and turkey vultures are among the region's scavengers. Seed-eating birds such as finches and buntings are diverse on the Pampas and include saffron finches, long-tailed reed finches, and double-collared seedeaters. Other grassland bird species include the greater rhea, South America's largest bird.

The Pampas are girdled to the south and west by a dry, thorny deciduous shrub-forest, the espinal. Dominated by algarrobo and acacia, the region is similar to the more northerly Chaco, although it has fewer species. The espinal grades into a dry evergreen scrub, the monte, which extends to the foothills of the Andes. Typical large plants of the monte include creosote bushes, verawoods, and acacias, with an understory of bougainvilleas, cacti, and bromeliads. Rodents are diverse and include Patagonian maras, tuco-tucos, and viscachas, which are

741

ARGENTINA, PARAGUAY, AND URUGUAY

A female capybara, the world's largest rodent, feeding her young.

prey to gray zorros, Patagonian weasels, and rufous-thighed hawks. The endangered crowned solitary eagle tends to feed on larger prey such as hog-nosed skunks and armadillos. Characteristic smaller birds of the monte include golden-billed saltators, austral blackbirds, and white-crested elaenias.

ISOLATED MOUNTAINS

In central Argentina, the expanse of the pampas is interrupted by a series of isolated mountain chains, the Sierras Centrales. Separated from the Andes to the east by dry, lowland plains of grass, these highlands are rich in endemic plant and animal life (species found nowhere else). Quebracho woodland dominates on the sunnier, drier slopes, while cloudier, wetter areas support forests of citruses. At around 6,000 feet (some 1,800 m) these forests are replaced by a species-rich montane grassland. The isolation of the region has allowed endemic animal species to evolve, including short-tailed opossums and a number of endemic birds, such as Olrog's and Córdoba cinclodes, which feed on invertebrates around fast-flowing mountain streams. These mountainous highlands also provide a refuge for several Andean species, including Andean tinamous, and they are home to the easternmost population of the huge Andean condor.

STEPPE IN THE FOOTHILLS

The Pampas extend throughout the eastern half of Argentina, while to the west, beyond the monte, where the Andes begin to rise, is another grassland habitat, the Andean steppe. Plants in this region must be able to survive cold, windy, and exceptionally dry conditions. The makeup of plant communities varies with altitude, humidity, and degree of slope (which affects rain run-off), although there are three broad levels. The so-called yellow belt, named for the predominant color of the foliage, occurs in the foothills up to around 9,000 feet (some 2,700 m). It consists mainly of grasses with stands of shrubs, many of which are endemic. Most of the flora in the yellow belt bears thorns and tough internal fibers to deter herbivores. The llareta belt, named for the dense cushions of plants that grow there, occurs at higher elevations up to 11,000 feet (around 3,300 m). Plants of the llareta belt are short and often flattened, which minimizes the effect of water loss to the fierce wind. Temperatures are also a little higher closer to the ground and can be significantly increased by the plant's cushionlike form, which allows an insulating blanket of dead leaves to collect. The dead leaves give the added benefit of slowly releasing nutrients back into the soil as they decay and are reabsorbed by the plant. A third group of plants occurs up to around 15,000 feet (some 4,500 m). These species survive extreme cold, very little water, howling winds, a nutrient-poor soil, and frequently shifting scree slopes.

While the Andean steppe has many endemic plants, it has far fewer endemic vertebrates. Those present include birds such as creamy-rumped miners, rufous-tailed plantcutters, and greater yellow finches, but there are also a number of species that visit the steppe only to breed. The black-fronted ground-tyrant, for example, migrates north to the puna (a high-elevation montane grassland in Bolivia and southern Peru) in winter.

The Andean steppe hosts a rich variety of small mammals, including mountain viscachas, Andean cats, and the critically endangered long-tailed chinchilla, which is on the brink of extinction because of hunting for the fur trade; its close relative, the short-tailed chinchilla, is probably already extinct. Larger mammals include vicuñas and guanacos and carnivores such as pumas and culpeo foxes.

PATAGONIA AND TIERRA DEL FUEGO

A second South American steppe biome lies to the south of the monte: the Patagonian steppe, a cold, perpetually windy semidesert scrub, with high levels of endemism. As on the Andean steppe, many plants form cushions and almost all are dwarfed, but the region is dominated by coirón grass, with extensive patches of tussocky *Poa* and *Stipa* grasses among the scrub. There are some wet meadows in valleys and lowland areas, where sedges and rushes occur. Birds of the Patagonian steppe include lesser (Darwin's) rhea, least seedsnipes, Patagonian tinamous, black-throated finches, ashy-headed geese, and chocolate-vented tyrants, while raptors such as gray eagle-buzzards and striated caracaras soar overhead. Small mammal species include viscachas, Patagonian maras, Patagonian hog-nosed skunks, and two species of opossums, the tiny dwarf mouse opossum and the endangered Patagonian opossum.

Separated from mainland South America by the Strait of Magellan, Tierra del Fuego is a unique wilderness, home to large stands of old-growth deciduous forests, alpine meadows in the highlands, bogs, wide rivers, and deep coastal fjords. The steppe gives way to dense, wet forests of southern beech, while lenga and coigue trees dominate nearer the coast. These forests are rich in bird life, with a range of spectacular species such as Magellanic woodpeckers, white-throated treerunners, and the world's most southerly parrot, the austral parakeet.

As well as forests and grasslands, the island of Tierra del Fuego boasts a number of wetlands, which are home to internationally important populations of birds such as austral rails, rosy-billed pochards, and hooded grebes. The wetlands also provide wintering grounds for a number of shorebirds, including Hudsonian godwits, which make a long journey to southern South America from breeding sites in Alaska and northern Canada each year. The region is similarly rich in marine life. Coastal waters abound with cormorants, grebes, gulls, geese, steamer ducks, skuas, and terns, while seabirds such as albatrosses and petrels skim low across the waves offshore. Beaches provide breeding grounds for southern elephant seals, South American fur seals, and South American sea lions. The young of these species are prey for orcas, which also feed on penguins that breed along the coasts of Tierra del Fuego. Penguin species in the region include large colonies of rockhoppers and macaroni, and Magellanic penguins, plus a smaller population of gentoos.

REMOTE ISLANDS

A habitat similar to the Patagonian steppe covers the Falkland Islands, 300 miles (around 480 km) to the east in the Atlantic Ocean. These islands provide a vital breeding ground for a range of animals that spend most of their lives at sea. The islands are home to six species of penguins, including king and royal penguins. Black-browed albatrosses breed in the Falklands, as do a range of other seabirds including slender-billed and fairy prions, white-chinned petrels (also known as shoemaker petrels), sooty and great shearwaters, and gray-backed storm petrels, while the beaches serve as breeding grounds for sea lions, southern elephant seals, and fur seals. Breeding colonies attract predators and opportunist scavengers, including turkey vultures, striated and crested caracaras, brown skuas, and sheathbills.

Trees are largely absent on the Falklands, but the tussocky grass shelters a surprisingly wide range of herbaceous plants, which support a range of insects, including the beautiful queen of the Falklands fritillary butterfly. With the exception of the pinnipeds (seals and sea lions), the Falklands now lack native mammal species. The only mammal known from the islands, the Falkland fox or warrah, was exterminated by sheep farmers in the mid-nineteenth century; how the ancestors of this species crossed miles of open ocean to reach these remote islands is an enduring zoogeographical mystery. There remains, however, a diverse land-bird fauna, including two endemic species, the flightless steamer duck and Cobb's wren, as well as distinct subspecies of a number of Patagonian species, including blackish cincloides, sedge wrens, and austral thrushes.

J. MARTIN

History and Movement of Peoples

Pre-Columbian Amerindian Societies

Before the Spanish arrived in what are now Argentina, Paraguay, and Uruguay, small numbers of indigenous people inhabited the region. The Amerindians comprised several different peoples, with the majority in the north.

Modern Paraguay, and the adjoining areas of Argentina, Uruguay, and Brazil, were historically populated by the Guaraní Amerindians, who today are still the most populous indigenous group in the region. Other Amerindian groups included the Charrúa, who lived in most of what is now Uruguay, while small numbers of Araucanians lived in southern Argentina. The Querandí inhabited the region of Buenos Aires. To the south, Tierra del Fuego was home to several different Amerindian communities, who were collectively known as the Fuegians.

THE GUARANÍ

During the fourteenth and fifteenth centuries, several Tupian-speaking people migrated into the region along the Paraná and Paraguay rivers from tropical areas to the north. Eventually known as the Guaraní (also known as Tupí-Guaraní), they became the principal Amerindian people of the region, and from the fourteenth century onward they moved into what is now Paraguay.

Guaraní society was semiagricultural, and their main food staples were cassava, corn, cotton, and yams. The women primarily tended the fields, while the men hunted and fished. Organized into tribes, Guaraní families tended to live together in large, rectangular, wooden houses that were thatched. Although large groups often resided together under one roof, each family had its own partitioned area. Every five to six years, the tribes were forced to move when the soil had become exhausted because of the slash-and-burn style of farming that the Guaraní practiced.

In the early 1500s, the first Europeans to make contact with the Guaraní were Spanish and Portuguese explorers, who were searching for an overland route to the silver mines of Peru. At that time, some experts believe that there may have been as many as 150,000 Guaraní living in the region. The Spanish captured Guaraní women, keeping them captive along the coast. From the early seventeenth century onward, Spanish Jesuits founded missions, known as *reducciones* (or reductions), with the aim of converting the Guaraní to Catholicism. The Jesuit missionaries taught the Guaraní weaving, carpentry, and other skills. In exchange for tending cattle or the fields, the Guaraní received food, clothing, and housing. In time, the *reducciones* came to resemble small townships. Unlike some other Amerindian languages in the region, Guaraní was preserved because the Jesuits adopted it as the language used in the conversion of local people to Christianity.

By 1730, there were approximately 30 missions with a resident Guaraní population of about 140,000. Spanish authorities came to view the settlements along Río de la Plata in particular with favor, seeing them as a bulwark against a Portuguese invasion from the north. However, many Spanish colonists resented the *reducciones*, which they believed took away their supply of forced labor, and they began to object to the Jesuits' power. After 1767, when the Jesuits were expelled from South America, some Guaraní returned to their former way of life, but many others were forced into slavery. Many Guaraní and Spaniards had children together and gradually the cultures became enmeshed, particularly in Paraguay, where Guaraní remains the predominant language and culture.

THE CHARRÚA

The Charrúa Amerindians inhabited what is now Uruguay and parts of neighboring southern Brazil. A nomadic people, the Charrúa lived by fishing, hunting, and gathering fruits and plants. The Charrúa did not build houses, but constructed simple temporary shelters. The hostility of the warlike Charrúa people delayed the colonization of Uruguay by the Spanish in the sixteenth century, and subsequently Spanish settlers killed many Charrúa, greatly reducing the population. Most of the remaining Charrúa were massacred in 1831 at Salsipuedes Creek in Uruguay, when they were ambushed by a group of Spanish soldiers. As a result, the Charrúa were effectively wiped out, and scholars claim that no Charrúa of unmixed Amerindian ancestry survive.

THE QUERANDÍ

The Querandí inhabited the area between Cabo Blanco along the Atlantic coast of Argentina and the Córdoba Mountains along the western shores of the Río de la Plata. A nomadic tribe, the Querandí warred against the Spanish and against other

HISTORY AND MOVEMENT OF PEOPLES

A Guaraní village, as painted by a Spanish settler.

indigenous tribes. They began to die out in the second half of the seventeenth century, and it is believed that no remnants of their language survive.

FUEGIANS

Tierra del Fuego, the rocky, rainy, cold island group at the southernmost tip of South America, was home to several Amerindian tribes, including the Alacaluf, Chono, Haush, Ona, and Yahgan (also known as the Yámana). The name Tierra del Fuego, literally "land of fire," is said to have been given to the islands by Portuguese explorer Ferdinand Magellan (c. 1480–1521), who is said to have named the territory for the many large fires that his expedition saw along its shores. Some historians have speculated that the local Amerindians lit the fires as signals warning of the intruders.

The indigenous peoples of Tierra del Fuego are known collectively as Fuegians. Their different tribes are divided into two distinct cultural and linguistic groups. The Ona (also called Selk'nam) and Haush peoples made up the first group, while the Alacaluf, Chono, and Yahgan made up the other linguistic group. The Ona and Haush were nomadic, and their members lived mainly in the inland forest areas of the largest island. These tribes, also referred to as "foot Indians," subsisted by hunting guanacos (small camelid relatives of the llama), rheas, and rodents. To capture their prey, the Fuegians used a device called a bola. Consisting of stone or clay balls tied to the end of a rope, the bola was thrown at running animals, and the rope wrapped around the animal's legs, causing it to fall to the ground.

The Alacaluf, Chono, and Yahgan lived along the coast, subsisting mainly on seafood. They were adept at making and utilizing canoes to travel through the dangerous waters in and around the Strait of Magellan. The Yahgan are considered by many historians to be the original inhabitants of Tierra del Fuego. They seldom camped in the same place for more than a few days and heavily relied on gathering shellfish. Yahgan canoes were characterized by pointed ends and a fireplace in the middle. The Alacaluf culture was similar to those of the Chono and Yahgan. Despite the cold weather, most Fuegians wore little or no clothing; they decorated their bodies with paint and used grease on their skin to protect them from the rain and the ocean spray.

As more European settlers came to the region and their culture and lifestyle began to dominate that of the native peoples, some Fuegians tribes began to assimilate, intermarrying with Europeans or forming relationships with them that resulted in children of mixed ancestry. Others contracted virulent diseases, that the Europeans brought with them, such as measles and smallpox, to which Amerindians had no immunity. In the nineteenth century, there were approximately 3,000 Yahgan left. In 1884, a measles outbreak in Argentina wiped out about 50 percent of the remaining Yahgans. There were virtually no Fuegians of unmixed ancestry by the late twentieth century.

K. EVANOVITCH

Spanish Discovery and Settlement

In the early sixteenth century, European expeditions in the Americas concentrated their efforts in the Caribbean area. Mineral wealth and the riches of the Inca Empire (centered in modern-day Peru) later attracted the Spanish to western South America. Until the eighteenth century, the region that is now occupied by Argentina, Paraguay, and Uruguay received less attention from Spanish colonists.

Before European geographers and cartographers had any exact idea of the configuration of the New World, sporadic Spanish and Portuguese expeditions reached the east coast of South America during the sixteenth century. Among the first expeditions was one led by Portuguese navigator Pedro Álvares Cabral (c. 1467–c. 1520) in 1500. Cabral never reached farther south than what is now the city of Bahia, in Brazil, but, in the following year, Italian explorer Amerigo Vespucci (1454–1512), for whom America was named, sailed along the entire east coast as far south as the Río de la Plata, the combined estuary of the Paraná and Uruguay rivers.

Fifteen years after Vespucci's voyage, the Spaniard Juan Díaz de Solís (1470–1516), the founder of the first permanent European colony on the mainland of the American continent—in Panama in 1506—also visited the Río de la Plata estuary. However, he was killed shortly afterward by Querandí Indians, a tribe of hunter-gatherers who lived a nomadic life on the vast grasslands of the interior, the Pampas.

Early in 1520, Ferdinand Magellan (1480–1521), the Portuguese navigator who discovered the sea route to the Pacific Ocean from the Atlantic and whose expedition was the first to circumnavigate the earth, also made a short stop in the Río de la Plata estuary. However, he did not claim the area for Portugal, and the region was later to become a Spanish rather than a Portuguese possession.

RÍO DE LA PLATA

The first permanent colony in the Río de la Plata area was not founded until 1526, when Sebastian Cabot (Sebastiano Caboto; c. 1476–c. 1557), who was of Italian origin but was in the service of Spain, established a small fort. Cabot's colony, which was called Sancti Spíritu, was located along the lower Paraná River between the modern Argentine cities of Santa Fé and Rosario. In the following years, Cabot explored the surrounding area in the search for the passage that was believed to exist from the Atlantic Ocean to the Pacific Ocean. In the expectation that silver would be found in the region, Cabot gave the estuary the name Río de la Plata (meaning "river of silver").

In 1529, a Spanish aristocrat, Pedro de Mendoza (1487–1537), made an offer to the Spanish monarch to explore the hinterland of the Río de la Plata. In return, the king made him military governor and granted him huge tracts of land in the area. Hopeful that he would find the silver that the region's name seemed to promise, Mendoza arrived in the Río de la Plata estuary in 1536 with 2,500 troops on 14 ships and founded Ciudad de Nuestra Señora Santa María del Buen Ayre (literally, "the city of Our Lady of Good Air"), on the site of what is now the Argentine national capital, Buenos Aires. However, the hostility of the Querandí Amerindians toward the colonists was vigorous and, at one time, thousands of Amerindians besieged Mendoza's forces, killing about two-thirds of them.

As a result, the colony was abandoned in 1541, leaving behind only some horses and cattle. In time, the horses and cattle ran wild in the interior, establishing breeding herds on the Argentine Pampas.

PARAGUAY

Three other Spanish colonists, Juan de Ayolas (died 1538), Domingo Martínez (1509–1556), and Juan de Salazar (died 1560), turned their attention inland and sailed northward up the Paraná River to explore the region inland along both the Paraná and its major tributary, the Paraguay River. In 1537, Salazar eventually established a fort in the territory of the Guaraní Indians, at a place he called Nuestra Señora de la Asunción (meaning "Our Lady of the Assumption"). The settlement became the first capital of the province of Río de la Plata and, later, became the national capital of Paraguay.

In the early colonial period, Asunción rather than Buenos Aires was the hub of Spanish colonialism in southern South America, and Paraguay became the center of the missionary activities of the Catholic Jesuit order, which established large missionary settlements, known as *reducciónes*, or reductions, in the region. Consequently, Asunción was the principal center of population in southeastern South America during the second half of the sixteenth century.

In 1542, a new governor arrived in the province of Río de la Plata, Álvar Núñez Cabeza de Vaca (c. 1490–c. 1556), who had earlier explored the areas along the Gulf of Mexico coast between Florida and Texas. Cabeza de Vaca helped develop the Asunción region and was conciliatory toward the indigenous Guaraní population, but he became involved in a political conflict within the Spanish community in Asunción. He was strongly resented

HISTORY AND MOVEMENT OF PEOPLES

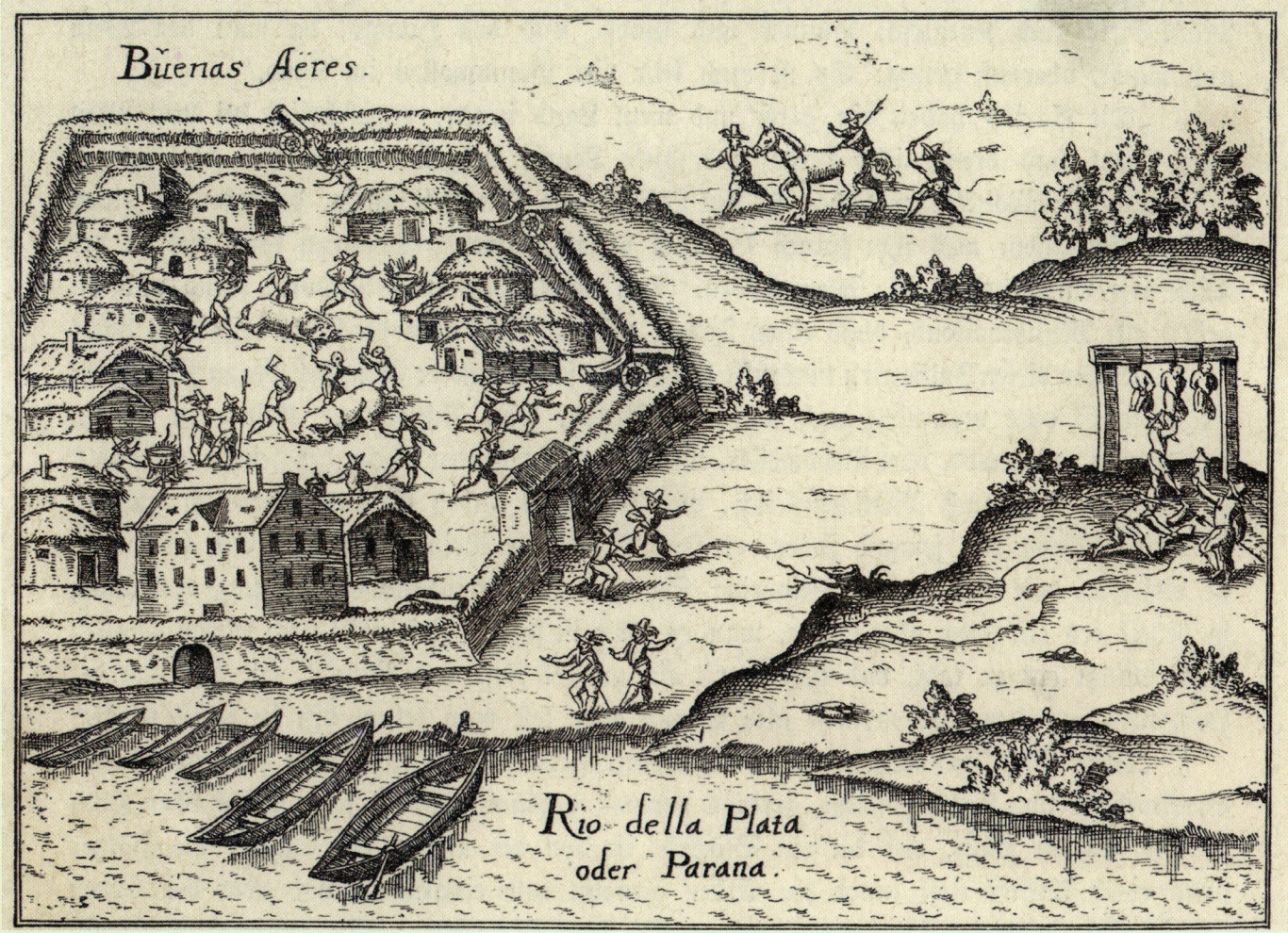

This sixteenth-century illustration shows the small Spanish colony of Ciudad de Nuestra Señora Santa María del Buen Ayre, on the site of the modern Argentine national capital Buenos Aires, being overrun by Amerindians in 1541. The Europeans subsequently abandoned the settlement for nearly two generations.

by the veterans of the Mendoza expedition and was deposed and imprisoned by Domingo Martínez, who subsequently governed the colony until his death in 1556.

COLONIZATION IN THE ARGENTINE INTERIOR

After the Spanish had conquered the Inca Empire in the Andes, they moved southward during the 1540s into what would become northwestern Argentina. There, the Spanish founded a number of cities, including Santiago del Estero (in 1553), Jujuy (1561), and Salta (1582). Farther south, Spaniards crossing the Andes from Chile founded the cities of Mendoza (in 1561) and San Miguel de Tucumán (1565), as well as Córdoba and Santa Fé (1573). San Miguel de Tucumán became the principal center of the entire region and the point of departure for the mule trains heading for the rich silver mine in Potosí, in Upper Peru or Charcas (modern Bolivia).

Many of these cities retain sixteenth- and seventeenth-century buildings, including cathedrals, other churches, Jesuit missions, public buildings, and universities. Córdoba, for example, is home to a university, which was founded in 1613 (the oldest in what is now Argentina), and a group of buildings known as the Manzana Jesuitica (usually referred to in English as the Jesuit Block). In 2000, the Jesuit Block, one of the most important groups of Spanish colonial buildings in South America, was listed as a UNESCO World Heritage site.

In 1580, Mendoza's colony along the Río de la Plata estuary was refounded by a Spanish expedition from Asunción under the leadership of Juan de Garay (1528–1583). The revived settlement became known as Buenos Aires, and it soon was the hub of a growing cattle trade with the Pampas inland. By then, the size of the herds of horses and cattle, which were descended from animals left behind by Mendoza's expedition in the early 1540s, had increased to such an extent that they had become a source of livelihood for a new group on the Pampas, seminomadic hunting, herding, Hispanic people, known as gauchos. Skilled in riding, the gauchos soon became the archetype of the South American cowboy and, in the nineteenth and twentieth centuries, a potent symbol of Argentine national identity.

747

ARGENTINA, PARAGUAY, AND URUGUAY

San Francisco church, in Santa Fé, was established in 1680, a century after the city was founded by Spanish from Peru. Santa Fé grew at the mouth of the Salado River along the Paraná River and was an important river port in colonial times.

TRADE RESTRICTIONS

Sebastian Cabot's ambition to discover silver in the La Plata region turned out to be hopeless. However, after large deposits of silver were discovered at Potosí, Upper Peru, in 1545, the Spanish authorities in the region subsequently concentrated their colonial development in South America in Upper Peru and along the coastal districts of neighboring Peru, where the city of Lima was located. Lima, the capital of the huge viceroyalty (administrative region) of Peru, was the center of administration for virtually all of Spanish South America until the last quarter of the eighteenth century. Consequently, the Río de la Plata area became peripheral to the heart of the Spanish possessions in South America and remained relatively undeveloped for more than 150 years.

According to the Spanish colonial system in South America, all trade between the Río de la Plata region and Spain had to pass through Peru and the viceregal capital, Lima. As a result, exports had to be carried along the difficult route over the Andes to the Pacific Ocean, and then across the Panama isthmus to the Caribbean Sea and the Atlantic Ocean beyond. Because of this trade route, the northwestern parts of what is now Argentina had stronger ties with coastal Peru than with Buenos Aires, which was little more than a satellite colony of the more important inland settlement at Asunción.

This awkward system, which ignored the relative ease with which trade could be directly developed between Buenos Aires and Spain, was part of the centralizing policies of the Spanish administration under which trade was recorded and taxes were imposed at the capital, Lima. As part of the same system, goods imported into the region followed a similarly circuitous route. As a result, prices for merchandise were high in the Río de la Plata area, impeding the region's economic development.

The Spanish colonial system also prohibited trade between Spanish colonies and the colonies of other nations. In the case of the neighboring Portuguese colony of Brazil, this restriction was particularly difficult to enforce. As a result of the extremely high prices of merchandise in Buenos Aires and the proximity of Brazil (from which items could be obtained more cheaply than importing them through Lima), a large-scale, profitable smuggling trade grew between the Río de la Plata region and Brazil. The British South Sea Company, which after 1713 held the exclusive rights to furnish Spain's American colonies with African slaves (a right known as the *asiento*), maintained a trading post in Buenos Aires. The company soon became involved in the illegal introduction of British merchandise into Spanish America.

THE CHURCH

The Roman Catholic Church played a key role in establishing colonial rule in parts of the region. The church aimed to convert the indigenous people to Christianity, and the spread of the religion was one of the reasons given to justify Spanish colonialism. In much of the region, conditions were different from those in Spanish possessions west of the Andes, where Amerindians lived in much greater numbers. Only in what is now Paraguay and neighboring parts of Argentina and northwestern Uruguay were indigenous people more numerous. There, Jesuit missions were established, with small townships clustered around a large church, surrounded by buildings for the missionaries and homes for the Amerindians, who were gathered from the surrounding countryside to establish settlements and farm the land. In other parts of the region, the church was nevertheless economically important. Religious orders other than Jesuits were also active, particularly the Franciscans, and the church hierarchy loaned money to settlers and promoted development.

EARLY COLONIAL TRADE

The fertile Pampas grasslands around the Río de la Plata were ideal for raising cattle, and the region developed the production of jerked beef (*tasajo*), hides, grease, and tallow. This trade mainly

HISTORY AND MOVEMENT OF PEOPLES

took place within the framework of the Spanish colonial system. The exports of animal products from the Río de la Plata area went to other parts of the Spanish Empire, particularly Cuba, which in the early days of Spanish colonization had produced *tasajo* but which, from the eighteenth century, specialized in the production of sugar for the European market.

COLONIAL RIVALRY

In the seventeenth century, the extraction of silver in Peru began to decline, leading to economic problems for the Spanish authorities and, in turn, a weakening of Spain's military capacity. Because Spain was unable to mobilize the resources necessary to maintain military defenses throughout its possessions in the New World, competing European powers, including the English and the French as well as the Dutch, took the opportunity to seize a number of islands in the Caribbean. The loss of Spanish possessions in the Caribbean began with the English occupation of the island of Saint Christopher (modern Saint Kitts) in 1623. In 1625, the English also seized Barbados from the Spanish. Soon, Spain faced other, more serious, incursions into its colonial territories in South America. The greatest threat was Portuguese penetration southward and westward from their colony of Brazil into the northern part of the Río de la Plata region.

The Portuguese, from their colony of Brazil, founded the fort at Colónia (or Colónia do Sacramento) as part of a campaign to annex Banda Oriental (modern Uruguay). Portuguese merchants operated a flourishing smuggling trade from Colónia into the Buenos Aires area, in contravention of the restrictions on trade imposed by the Spanish colonial authorities.

COMPETITION FOR THE BANDA ORIENTAL REGION

By 1532, the Portuguese explorer Martim Afonso de Sousa (died 1564) had visited the northern shores of Río de la Plata and, during the seventeenth century, further overland explorations were carried out by slave-hunters from Brazil, who captured Guaraní and Charrúa Amerindians. Spanish expeditions simultaneously explored the region east of the Uruguay River, the so-called Banda Oriental (literally, "east bank"; modern Uruguay). Consequently, Banda Oriental became a region of increased rivalry between the Spanish and the Portuguese. (In modern times, a relic of the name Banda Oriental survives in the official name of Uruguay, the Oriental Republic of Uruguay.)

At an early stage in the colonization of the New World, Spain and Portugal had signed the 1494 Tordesillas Treaty, under which the two nations delineated two distinct spheres of interest, defined by longitude. Under the terms of the treaty, Spain had the

749

legitimate right to Banda Oriental, but after the Spanish and Portuguese crowns merged in 1580, the treaty temporarily became irrelevant. After Portugal regained national sovereignty in 1640, competition for territory between the two countries intensified, and, in 1680, the Portuguese founded Colónia (or Colónia do Sacramento), in contravention of the 1494 treaty, at a site across the Río de la Plata estuary from Buenos Aires.

THE CITY OF COLÓNIA

The Spanish did not immediately respond to the Portuguese challenge in Banda Oriental, and it was not until 1726 that the Spanish authorities established a secure presence in the region with the foundation of Montevideo, now the national capital of Uruguay. The potential conflict between Spain and Portugal over Banda Oriental was temporarily solved through the Madrid Treaty of 1750, which declared the Tordesillas Treaty to be null and void but ceded Portuguese Colónia—along with all of Banda Oriental—to Spain.

However, the treaty also stipulated the transfer to the Portuguese of seven Spanish missions established by the Jesuits to the east of the Uruguay River, a provision that the Guaraní Amerindians in the area refused to accept. The indigenous people trusted the Jesuits and looked to them for protection from predation by slave traders who were based in Brazil. In response to the dispute concerning the missions, the Portuguese postponed the evacuation of Colónia, and the Madrid Treaty ceased to be effective by 1761.

During the Seven Years' War (1756–1763)—a war between major European powers that was also fought in their colonial territories in both the New World and in Asia (particularly in India)—Spanish forces took Colónia by force. At the same time, Spanish troops also seized parts of southern Brazil, basing their claim on the rights accorded to them in the Tordesillas Treaty. However, in the aftermath of the war, both Spain and Portugal relinquished their overlapping claims.

In a new treaty signed in 1777, Spain withdrew from southern Brazil, abandoning any territorial claims in the region, and the Portuguese, in turn, finally removed their forces from the city of Colónia, recognizing Spanish sovereignty in the area. Temporarily, the territorial claims in Banda Oriental were settled, but these border disputes would be inherited by the independent countries of Brazil and Argentina early in the nineteenth century, leading to wars and a delay in the emergence of the independent nation of Uruguay.

THE COLONIAL SYSTEM

The centralization of administration and the collection of taxes in Lima, the capital of the huge viceroyalty of Peru, focused colonial and urban development away from the Río de la Plata region. Spanish administrators in Lima were concerned not only with the productive mining region of Upper Peru but also with the northwestern regions of South America, the region now occupied by the nations of Colombia, Ecuador, and Venezuela. Consequently, the colonial administration was not only unwieldy but also inefficient. The districts around the Río de la Plata estuary were also relatively ignored by the Spanish because they were sparsely populated, lacking a large enough Amerindian population to supply an enforced labor force. Peru and some other parts of Spanish America had a much larger indigenous population, which was economically exploited.

The peoples of the region—except in Paraguay, where Guaraní Amerindians were overwhelmingly in the majority—were largely descended from settlers from Spain, although there was also a minority of mestizos (people of mixed European and Amerindian ancestry). The region was also home to African slaves, who were mainly from the coastal regions of western central Africa. Although people of unmixed Spanish ancestry, called *criollos* (creoles), formed a social and cultural elite, they were largely excluded from the colonial administration, which was reserved for officials from Spain. The *criollos* were able to exert political influence only in the councils of towns and cities in the region, and this exclusion from power was another element in the settlers' growing resentment of the Spanish colonial authorities. At the same time, merchants in Buenos Aires and the ports along the Paraná River and its tributaries sought reform of the restrictive trade regime that prohibited direct trade with foreign destinations. However, smuggling brought some prosperity to the region.

THE CALL FOR REFORM

A new dynasty in Spain, when the Bourbons came to power under Philip V (1683–1746; reigned 1700–1746), provided an impetus for change. Under the so-called Bourbon Reforms, the Spanish authorities introduced some elements of modern, national government advocated by thinkers of the Enlightenment, an eighteenth-century philosophical movement that emphasized reason. The Bourbon Reforms included economic, military, and administrative changes, which were designed to create a more efficient system.

As part of the reform program, the Spanish authorities abolished the existing corrupt system of local administration and established a network of intendants, local administrators who had direct access to the Spanish authorities. However, the new system eventually proved to be as prone to corruption as the old.

The reforms had an important impact on the Río de la Plata region. The old trade restrictions, centering commercial activity in Lima, were abolished, and the viceroyalty of Peru was divided into three. While modern Colombia, Ecuador, and Venezuela in the north became the viceroyalty of New Granada, what are now Argentina, Paraguay, and Uruguay, plus some adjoining areas, became the viceroyalty of the Río de la Plata. As a result, Buenos Aires started a long period of development that saw it grow to become the largest city of Spanish-speaking South America.

D. RETSÖ

The Missions

The colonization of parts of the New World by the Spaniards, and also by the Portuguese, was partly motivated by religion. The papacy gave its blessing to the project as a means of converting the Amerindians to Roman Catholicism, and Catholic religious orders were particularly active in the colonization of what is now Paraguay and northeastern Argentina.

In the Americas, missionary activities were carried out by various Roman Catholic religious orders, but the Jesuits—the Society of Jesus, founded in 1534 by Spanish student of religion Ignatius of Loyola (originally Iñigo de Oñaz y Loyola; 1491–1556)—were particularly prominent. The order was approved by the papacy in 1537, the same year that Loyola became a priest.

THE JESUITS

Jesuits first arrived in northeastern Brazil in 1549 but did not reach Paraguay until 1588. Their most important areas of influence in South America would later be around the Paraná and Uruguay rivers in the center of the continent. They preached zealously to the seminomadic hunter-gatherers of the forests and displayed great courage in their penetration of the wilderness, most often walking unarmed and barefoot, in search of new converts. Their missionary activities were conscious imitations of the preaching practices of the first Christian congregations, and the conversion of the New World was considered by some, at the time, as a peaceful extension of the medieval reconquest (known as the Reconquista) of the Iberian Peninsula by Christian monarchs.

In 1610, the Jesuits established seven colonies or missions (in Spanish America called *reducciones*, in Portuguese-speaking Brazil known as *aldeias*) east of the Uruguay River. In English, *reducciones* is usually translated as "reductions." The Jesuits soon extended their activities into the Mato Grosso region of Brazil as well as into modern Argentina and Paraguay, where some 30 missions were eventually established.

LIFE IN THE MISSIONS

The greatest concentration of Jesuit reductions was in Paraguay and what are now the Argentine provinces of Misiones and Corrientes, a region that was home to Guaraní Amerindians. Within the missions, converted Guaraní were settled and were taught Christian doctrine as well as agriculture, cattle-rearing, art, music, and other skills by the Jesuits. Each Amerindian family was also allowed to hold a plot of land for its own subsistence. In return, the indigenous people were expected to contribute their labor two days a week on the common agricultural land belonging to the reduction. In this way, the missions became highly efficient and virtually self-sufficient economic units producing sugar, tobacco, cotton, cacao, and maté tea with little integration with the rest of the empire, economically or politically. The largest reductions were the size of towns. The Jesuit mission system has variably been described by historians as "Christian socialism" and "theocratic capitalism." Within the reductions, the Jesuits created an authoritarian and paternalistic society, in which the indigenous people were regarded as children in need of continuous spiritual guidance by the Jesuits, and the conduct of the Amerindians living in the missions was strictly regimented.

THE COLONIAL AUTHORITIES

The attitude of the Spanish authorities, both in Spain and in the colonies, toward the Jesuit endeavors was ambiguous but was initially sympathetic. The colonial authorities considered that the missionary work of the Jesuits among the indigenous people along the borders of colonial society, where the civil authorities had little influence, contributed to the pacification and settlement of potentially hostile nomadic tribes. Christianized and Hispanicized, the Amerindians would constitute no threat to the white settlers. In that way, the Jesuits were a highly useful agent for the Spanish authorities and were regarded as paving the way for a successful outcome of the entire colonial project. An additional advantage to the Spanish was that the costs for this type of colonization fell upon the Jesuits rather than the crown, while the benefits were shared by both.

On the other hand, the conquest and colonization of America was not only a religious project. Spanish colonization was economic and commercial as well, and the Spanish authorities encountered difficulties in the development of the region. Because of a low population density, there was a scarcity of labor. Most of the colonization was effectively carried out by private entrepreneurs rather than by the crown itself, and the colonial authorities had to address the needs of the secular colonists, particularly their desire for enforced labor of the Amerindians. Under the *encomienda* system, Amerindians retained the right to farm their land but were taxed by *encomenderos* (Spanish landlords, who were granted rights over the indigenous people). The *encomenderos* could summon the

ARGENTINA, PARAGUAY, AND URUGUAY

The ruins of the seventeenth-century Jesuit church at San Ignácio Miní, in Argentina, are the most impressive remains of what was once a large settlement.

local people to work for them for nothing, and the system rapidly came to resemble slavery. Because of the scarcity of labor, the colonists were jealous of the Jesuits' access to labor in the reductions, and they claimed that the missions deprived them of a workforce. The Amerindians were economically important to the missions and to the secular colonies. The *encomienda* system gradually lost importance in other parts of South America, where the population eventually increased enough to encourage development, but in Paraguay the colonists continued to rely on tribute from and the labor of the indigenous people. As a result, the system endured to the benefit of Spanish colonists in Paraguay almost until the end of the colonial era in the early years of the nineteenth century.

THE COMUNEROS

Repeatedly during the colonial period, secular colonists in Paraguay took direct action in an attempt to secure an adequate labor force. In 1721, the governor in Asunción, who sympathized with the Jesuits, was deposed by a group of landowners, known as the *comuneros* (citizens organized to defend their rights against the authorities). A lawyer from Upper Peru (modern Bolivia), José de Antequera y Castro (1690–1731) was sent to Asunción by the colonial authorities to investigate complaints by the colonists that the governor had not addressed their interests in securing a labor force. Antequera sided with the colonists and effectively made himself governor of a province in rebellion against the Spanish authorities. For four years, the *comuneros* governed the colony in virtual independence from the viceroyalty of Peru, the huge administrative region that, at the time, covered most of Spanish South America. The leaders of the *comuneros* asserted the rights of the people against those of the Spanish crown and the authorities. Antequera was captured by the colonial authorities and subsequently beheaded in 1731, but the rebellion of the junta against the Spanish authorities continued until it was put down in 1733.

THE BANDEIRANTES

Adventurers from Brazil, the *bandeirantes* (also known as *paulistas*, because many of their number came from the city of São Paulo) also sought to supply the hunger for Amerindian labor in the colonial economy. The *bandeirantes* roamed in bands across the vast South American interior in search of precious metals and indigenous people, who could be sold as slave labor to the sugarcane planters of northeastern Brazil.

According to the 1494 Tordesillas Treaty (which divided the New World into Spanish and Portuguese sectors), the Jesuit missions along the upper Uruguay and the Paraná rivers were located in Spanish territory. However, the treaty—which in practice had been annulled by the union in 1580 between the Spanish and the Portuguese crowns (resulting in Portugal's loss of independence until 1640)—meant little to the Brazilian slave traders. The boundary between Spanish and Portuguese territory was also poorly delineated, and it was not easy for the *bandeirantes* to determine exactly where, in the unmapped wilderness of the interior, the border ran.

Unintentionally, the Jesuits facilitated the task of the *bandeirantes*. The Jesuits concentrated indigenous people in the missions, which the *bandeirantes* attacked, capturing as many Amerindians as possible and taking them into slavery. The Jesuits formed local armed groups to defend the missions from these attacks, but their military capacity was limited, and the reductions were virtually defenseless. According to Jesuit sources, *bandeirantes* captured some 300,000 Amerindians between 1614 and 1639. Although this is probably an exaggerated figure, it gives an indication of the seriousness of the problem; by 1702, the indigenous population of the Jesuit missions in Paraguay totaled only around 114,000 people. This number suggests that the scale of abduction by the *bandeirantes* was considerable.

EXPULSION OF THE JESUITS

The Spanish colonial authorities increasingly received complaints from the colonists concerning the reductions, which they held responsible for their lack of enforced laborers. However, when the Spanish finally took action against the Jesuits in the eighteenth century, it was mainly to serve their own economic interests; in addition, there was a growing climate of opposition to the Jesuits in Europe, where for various political and economic reasons a number of European governments agitated against the order.

By the eighteenth century, the string of Jesuit missions across central South America seemed to have developed into a theocratic state within the state, beyond the control of the civil authorities. The Jesuits had accumulated enormous wealth and huge tracts of land in their estates, which were exempt from taxes. The secular authorities increasingly resented the fact that these resources were outside their control. In the eighteenth century, the colonial governments in Spanish and Portuguese territories in South America embarked upon programs of reforms, and the semi-independent Jesuit missions were seen as obstacles to increased colonial control. The clash between the Jesuits and the interests of the crown was made more complicated by the fact that the Jesuits claimed supremacy over the secular authorities on behalf of the papacy in Rome. A conflict between church and state developed, and, in 1759, the Jesuits were expelled from Brazil by the Portuguese and their property was confiscated. In 1767, the Spanish authorities also expelled the Jesuits and took their property. The result was an exodus from America of some

The Jesuits taught the Guaraní Amerindians who lived at the missions many skills, including stone carving. This carved head at La Santisima Trinidad de Paraná, in Paraguay, is typical of Guaraní art.

2,200 Jesuits, who went into exile in Italy. In 1767, the Jesuits were suppressed in Spanish and Portuguese territories (in Europe and the colonies), in France, and in some Italian states. By 1773, the Jesuits were suppressed everywhere, except Russia (which then included parts of Poland, where the order survived). The Society of Jesus was eventually restored in 1814.

In Paraguay, the expulsion of the Jesuits was met with some resistance on the part of the Amerindians, who had been protected by them and who feared increased attacks by slave traders. With the expulsion of the Jesuits, from 1759 through 1767, an important agent for cultural transformation disappeared from the scene. Although historians differ in their opinions about the legacy of the Jesuits in the region, the contribution of the order toward the development of Paraguay was major. In comparison with most of the Catholic clergy and other religious orders active in the region at the time, the Jesuits were known for morality and exemplary conduct. For many Amerindians, the Jesuits were the only Europeans they had met who did not wish to exploit them. However, while the Jesuits defended the indigenous people against the aggressive slave traders from Brazil and protected them from the inhumane working conditions on the plantations, they also contributed to the extinction of much of Native American culture.

With the disappearance of the Jesuits, the reductions were soon abandoned, and the Guaraní returned to many aspects of their previous lives, although Hispanic culture and the practice of Roman Catholicism remained. The huge, impressive buildings of the reductions soon fell into ruins. In modern times, the ruins are preserved as historic monuments, including the extensive remains at La Santisima Trinidad de Paraná in Paraguay and San Ignácio Miní in northeastern Argentina.

D. RETSÖ

The Viceroyalty of the Río de la Plata

In 1776, the Spanish reformed the restrictive colonial system in South America, and through the last quarter of the eighteenth century, the region rapidly developed. However, by the end of the first quarter of the nineteenth century, the colonial era in the region had ended and Argentina and Paraguay were independent nations, although Uruguay was still struggling toward sovereignty.

In the eighteenth century, the merchant community of Buenos Aires complained about what it felt was excessive control by the Spanish authorities in Lima, where the administration of the huge viceroyalty (administrative region) of Peru was based. The merchants also protested against the centralization of taxation in Lima and the enforced direction of colonial trade through that city, although unoffficial trade links and smuggling, particularly with the Portuguese colony of Brazil, flourished. During the eighteenth century, the Spanish colonial authorities slowly recognized the need for administrative and economic reforms in the colonies, and a change of dynasty in Spain—under Philip V (1683–1746; reigned 1700–1746)—introduced a program of reform, the so-called Bourbon Reforms.

The reforms, in 1776, loosened the confines of the previously strict colonial system, and all of southeastern Spanish America was separated from the vast viceroyalty of Peru to constitute a new division, the viceroyalty of the Río de la Plata with Buenos Aires as its capital. The viceroyalty consisted of present-day Argentina, Paraguay, and Uruguay and some adjoining areas.

The creation of the new viceroyalty was not only an attempt to establish a more efficient form of government but also a recognition of a continuing threat to the Río de la Plata region from the Portuguese in Brazil. The Spanish authorities believed that an administration based in Buenos Aires would be better able to maintain defenses against the Portuguese and would also be able to address the problem of smuggling across the Río de la Plata estuary.

ECONOMIC GROWTH

The first holder of the viceregal office, Pedro de Cevallos (1715–1778; in office 1776–1778), was a temporary appointment, but, although his tenure was brief, he was able to push back Portuguese intrusion into the region. Cevallos then laid the foundations for the administraton of the viceroyalty in Buenos Aires. Juan José de Vértiz y Salcedo (1719–1799; in office 1778–1784), the first permanent viceroy, assumed office in 1778, the same year that the merchants of Buenos Aires were allowed direct trade with Spain as well as with other Spanish colonies. The result of this economic reform was a remarkable period of economic growth and increased trade in the Río de la Plata region's traditional exports of hides, tallow, horn, and wool.

The reform also led to a long-desired decline in local prices. Imports had previously had to follow the same circuitous route through Lima to Buenos Aires and other cities in the Río de la Plata region, although smuggling had supplied some items at cheaper prices. Economic conditions were also improved by the fact that some of the silver mines of Upper Peru (modern Bolivia) were included within the viceroyalty of the Río de la Plata. As a result, much of the flow of silver to Spain from Upper Peru passed through Buenos Aires rather than through Lima.

PENINSULARES AND CRIOLLOS

Political decision making remained firmly in Spanish control, and all important political offices were still reserved for Spanish-born residents, so-called *peninsulares*. People of unmixed Spanish ancestry born in South America, the creoles (*criollos*), were largely excluded from high office. The monopoly of power of the *peninsulares* was emphasized by the establishment in 1783 of a royal court, an *audiencia*, in Buenos Aires, whose members were officials from Spain. The only arena for political influence for the locally born *criollos* was the town councils (*cabildos*). The contradiction of increased economic prosperity and continued political exclusion created tension between Spanish officials and the Latin American *criollos* in general and, in the Río de la Plata region, the merchants of Buenos Aires were particularly discontented with a regime in which they had no say.

BRITISH INTERVENTION

The British became active in the region in the eighteenth century. During the first half of the century, they acquired the sole right to import African slaves into Spanish South America, and, later, the British sought to acquire territory in the region. The British landed in the Falkland Islands (Islas Malvinas) in 1765, one year after the French. In 1770, France sold its claim to the islands to Spain, which expelled the British. However, involvement in the Falklands had given Great Britain a toehold in the region.

From 1792, various European powers attempted to contain revolutionary France through a series of coalitions. Spain made peace with France in 1795, during the First Coalition (1792–1797), and, in 1796, Spain became an ally of France under the terms of

The city of Córdoba, with the surrounding region, resisted the centralizing junta in Buenos Aires at the beginning of the nineteenth century.

the Treaty of San Ildefonso. The Franco-Spanish alliance provided Britain with an excuse to acquire territories at the expense of Spain in the New World. At the same time, British merchants, who had long been impatient with the restrictive Spanish monopoly of trade with South America, became more active in the area.

The viceroyalty's trade had flourished after Buenos Aires had been opened to direct commerce with Spain. The cattle-raising grasslands of the Pampas in the interior began to prosper when ranchers met a great demand for salted meat from other Spanish possessions in the Americas and also frrom Brazil. Soon Buenos Aires was exporting hides as well as meat, and the British were increasingly impatient for a share of the trade. In June 1806, a British naval squadron arrived in the Río de la Plata estuary and landed 1,600 soldiers led by Brigadier-General William Carr Beresford (1768–1854). Two days later, they seized Buenos Aires, and the Spanish viceroy, Rafael de Sobremonte (1746–1827; in office 1804–1807), fled. However, the resistance of the *criollo* inhabitants of Buenos Aires was strong and, on August 12, a large popular revolt against the British managed to expel Beresford's troops. Beresford was captured and put on trial, and he was sent, along with 1,200 of his troops, as prisoners to the interior. (Beresford, later released, successfully held command in the Peninsular War of 1808 through 1814 in Spain and Portugal.)

Sobremonte returned, but the episode had a profound impact upon the people of Buenos Aires, who had defeated the British through their own efforts. The *criollos* grew in confidence and ability to defend and administer themselves, while the increasing weakness of the Spanish colonial power had been made evident.

The British did not give up their attempt to acquire the Río de la Plata. In February of the following year, another contingent of British troops landed in Montevideo in the region known as Banda Oriental (modern Uruguay) across the Río de la Plata, capturing the city after a siege. British reinforcements followed during the next six months; in early July 1807, the British tried

José de San Martín (1778–1850) led the forces of the junta in Buenos Aires against opposition from Spanish loyalists. He eventually decided to invade Peru and Chile to remove the Spanish threat.

once more to seize Buenos Aires. Again Sobremonte fled. However, misjudging the scale of local opposition to their intervention, the British were again defeated and expelled, and, shortly afterward, they were forced to abandon Montevideo.

The incidents in Buenos Aires and Montevideo in 1806 and 1807 had several important consequences. The inability of Spain to defend its own colonies was now clear to the peoples of the region. Spain's weakness, along with growing impatience among the *criollos* of Buenos Aires with their lack of political power over local affairs, encouraged some *criollos* in the belief that a successful revolution against rule by Spain was possible, and some local people adopted the goal of independence.

THE BUENOS AIRES JUNTA

In May 1808, the Spanish king, Ferdinand VII (1784–1833; reigned 1808 and 1813–1833), was deposed by the French ruler Napoléon I (1769–1821; reigned as emperor 1804–1814 and 1815) and was replaced by the latter's brother, Joseph Bonaparte (1768–1844; reigned 1808–1813). A junta in the southern Spanish city, Cádiz, resisted the new regime and claimed to represent the legitimate Spanish king. Subsequently, on May 13, 1810, the city council of Buenos Aires declared in favor of Ferdinand and deposed the unpopular viceroy, Baltasar Hidalgo de Cisneros (1775–1829; in office 1809–1810), stating that his continuation in office could trigger a general popular upheaval. As a result, power in the viceroyalty was handed over to a provisional junta, marking the first step toward independence.

Royal power in the viceroyalty, represented by the *audiencia*, remained in place, however, and soon the junta and the *audiencia* were issuing contradictory orders. The result was an increasingly confused situation, in which no one knew who was exercising power. The provinces of Córdoba and Banda Oriental refused to recognize the rights of the Buenos Aires junta to represent Spanish royal power, and the authorities in both ignored its orders. In Banda Oriental, armed resistance to the junta was led by Santiago (or Jacques) de Liniers (1753–1810; in office 1807–1809), who was a former acting viceroy of French origin.

THE PATH TOWARD INDEPENDENCE

In 1813, the French were expelled from Madrid, the Spanish national capital, but Ferdinand VII was not able to return to the city to regain power until the following year. Once reinstalled, however, he immediately tried to reestablish control in Spanish America, where local *cabildos* had exercised power in his name. The *criollos* were unwilling to give up the authority they had exercised and made new demands for increased autonomy and political influence as a precondition for recognizing direct Spanish rule again. The Spanish monarch refused to accept the demands, but the Spanish authorities in the region were not powerful enough to reimpose control, and the administration of the viceroyalty of the Río de la Plata gradually passed out of Spain's hands.

INSTABILITY AND SECESSION

The junta was threatened by internal strife and dissolution. The core of the problem facing the new authority was that the junta in Buenos Aires wanted to maintain the territorial unity of the

Delegates from across the Río de la Plata met in July 1816 in this building in San Miguel de Tucumán to proclaim independence.

vast viceroyalty through a strongly centralized government, while the inland provinces favored a loose federation or independence of their own. The people of the interior, the *estancieros* (the large cattle-raising landowners) and the seminomadic gauchos, had enjoyed virtual autonomy from all centers of power, including Buenos Aires, a commercial city whose interests were regarded as different from those of the Pampas.

The *criollos* in Buenos Aires did not immediately opt for independence. For a time, they sought autonomy within the Spanish Empire. Some members of the junta suggested the creation of a constitutional monarchy, with the Spanish monarch as king. Ferdinand, however, abruptly rejected the proposal.

In Paraguay, the citizens of Asunción, the provincial capital, refused to accept the authority of Buenos Aires, in part because of long-standing rivalry between the two cities. In 1811, a force under Miguel Belgrano (1770–1820), sent by the junta to subdue Asunción, was repulsed, and Paraguay declared independence.

The junta still felt threatened by loyalist Spanish forces in Lima on the other side of the Andes, and, in 1812, the leaders of the junta appointed José de San Martín (1778–1850), a *criollo* officer who had had a distinguished military career in Spain, to organize a corps to defend Buenos Aires. In 1813, San Martín defeated the loyalists at San Lorenzo, along the Paraná River, and then reinforced San Miguel de Tucumán, which had been held by Belgrano for the junta against loyalist forces. San Martín then decided to cross the Andes to confront the loyalists.

With Spain unwilling to negotiate, the *criollo* leaders in Buenos Aires had no choice but to opt for independence. In 1816, an assembly of the Río de la Plata provinces was summoned to San Miguel de Tucumán. There, on July 9, the independence of the United Provinces of the Río de la Plata was declared, but the new nation was confined to modern Argentina and Uruguay. No further serious attempt was made to bring Paraguay back under the rule of Buenos Aires. Banda Oriental was annexed by Brazil in 1825 and became independent in 1828.

For subsequent history, see pages 765–772, 809–812, and 835–839.

D. RETSÖ

Peoples of Argentina, Paraguay, and Uruguay

The three nations of the southeastern region of South America have different population profiles. Whereas Uruguay is largely Spanish in heritage, Argentina also has a significant population of Italian ancestry. Paraguay, by contrast, is home to many people of mixed Amerindian ancestry.

Argentina, Paraguay, and Uruguay are overwhelmingly home to people of Spanish ancestry and, compared with other parts of South America, most of the region has relatively small populations of Amerindian and African ancestry. In Argentina, 97 percent of the population is of unmixed European ancestry, while the remaining 3 percent comprises mestizos (people of mixed Amerindian and European ancestry), Amerindians, and others. Some 88 percent of Uruguayans are of unmixed European ancestry, while 8 percent are mestizos, and 4 percent are of African ancestry. Paraguay offers a contrast. About 95 percent of Paraguay's people are mestizos and almost all of the remaining 5 percent are Amerindians.

HISPANICS

From the sixteenth century through the beginning of the nineteenth century, the region was part of the Spanish Empire. A steady flow of Spanish settlers came to the region, which soon had a large population of creoles (*criollos*, people of unmixed Spanish ancestry born in the Western Hemisphere). Their descendants are the dominant community in both Argentina and Uruguay. They are overwhelmingly Roman Catholic and are Spanish-speaking. Spanish is the official language in Argentina and in Uruguay, and one of two official languages in Paraguay. A dialect of Castilian Spanish (the standard form of the language in Spain) is used throughout the region, but some different pronunciations and local elements of vocabulary occur. The three nations share this common version of Spanish, although the sound of the Spanish spoken in Argentina is different from that spoken in other South American countries; spoken Argentine Spanish resembles Italian in its inflections.

While most people of Guaraní ancestry in Paraguay are mestizos and are fully assimilated into the modern life of the nation, a few members of a Guaraní community of unmixed ancestry, such as these, live a more traditional way of life.

ITALIANS

Large-scale immigration from Italy to Argentina in the nineteenth and early twentieth centuries changed the population profile of the nation. In modern times, almost one-half of Argentines have an Italian ancestor. Many people in Argentina have Italian names, and some 2 percent of the population still speak Italian as a first language. Argentina's Italian community has had considerable economic and political influence, and Italian culture shapes many facets of Argentine society. Italian immigrants also settled in Uruguay, but they did not arrive in such numbers or have such an impact on society as did Argentina's Italians.

OTHER EUROPEAN MINORITIES

In the nineteenth century, settlers from Great Britain became major players in the commercial activities of Argentina. Today, Argentina has a larger community of people of British ancestry than any other South American country. Uruguay also has a small community of people of British ancestry, and almost all of the inhabitants of the Falkland Islands (known to Argentines as Islas Malvinas), a British dependent territory in the South Atlantic, are of British or Irish ancestry. Patagonia in south Argentina was the destination of emigration from Wales in the late nineteenth century, and the region still has a small community of Welsh speakers. Other Europeans—Germans (especially in Uruguay), Poles, Hungarians, Russians, and Ukrainians—also settled in Argentina, Paraguay, and Uruguay. People of mixed Brazilian Portuguese and Hispanic ancestry, who live in northeast Uruguay, speak Portuñol, a combination of Spanish and Portuguese.

HISTORY AND MOVEMENT OF PEOPLES

ASIAN AND AFRICAN MINORITIES

Emigrants from western Asia settled in parts of northern Argentina and the Buenos Aires region in the late nineteenth and early twentieth centuries. Some were Lebanese, but the majority were of Syrian ancestry. Most of the Syrians were Jews or Christians, with only a small minority of Muslims. The larger cities of southeastern South America are also home to a small Chinese community.

The Spanish colonial authorities imported slaves from West Africa to work plantations and other large holdings, such as cattle ranches, in South America. In much of southeastern South America, however, Amerindians were enslaved to work for the Spanish and there was less demand for African slaves. In what is now Uruguay, where the number of Amerindians was small and the indigenous population was soon reduced by colonial warfare, slaves were imported. As a result, 4 percent of Uruguayans are of African ancestry, while in Argentina and Paraguay, the population is much smaller.

AMERINDIANS

Compared to rest of the South American continent, the region has a small Amerindian population. The largest indigenous group is the Guaraní, who live in northern Argentina and parts of Uruguay—where they form small minorities—but also in Paraguay, where Guaraní culture is dominant. In Paraguay under the dictatorship of José Gaspar Rodríguez de Francia (1766–1840; chief of state 1813–1814, 1814, and 1814–1840), there was an official attempt to erase the cultural imprint of three centuries of Spanish colonial rule. Francia prohibited marriage between creoles and, as a result, Paraguayan creoles married Guaranís. Subsequently, the Guaraní language became the most commonly used in Paraguay. In modern times, 91 percent of Paraguayans speak Guaraní as a first language, and it is one the nation's two official languages.

Northern Argentina is also home to Quechua Amerindians in the region near the Bolivian border. What is now Uruguay contained a population of Charrúa peoples, who were never numerous. Strongly independent, they resisted Spanish colonial rule. Consequently, many Charrúa were killed and a massacre in the 1830s wiped out most of the remaining Charrúa. Most ethnographers believe that there are now no Charrúa of unmixed heritage. Mapuche (or Araucanian) people, who migrated to Patagonia from Chile under the Spanish, form a small minority in southern Argentina.

Various peoples, collectively known as Fuegians, lived in the islands of Tierra del Fuego, to the south of the Argentine mainland. The Fuegians are usually categorized in two linguistic and cultural groups: the Ona and Haush peoples, who were hunters, living inland, and the Alacaluf, Chono, and Yahgan peoples, who were coastal fishers and gatherers of shellfish. Adapted to life in harsh climatic conditions, some Fuegians were assimilated by the Spanish colonists. However, the majority died after exposure to diseases to which they had no immunity. As a result, the Fuegian community was decimated in the nineteenth century, and very few Fuegians of unmixed ancestry remain.

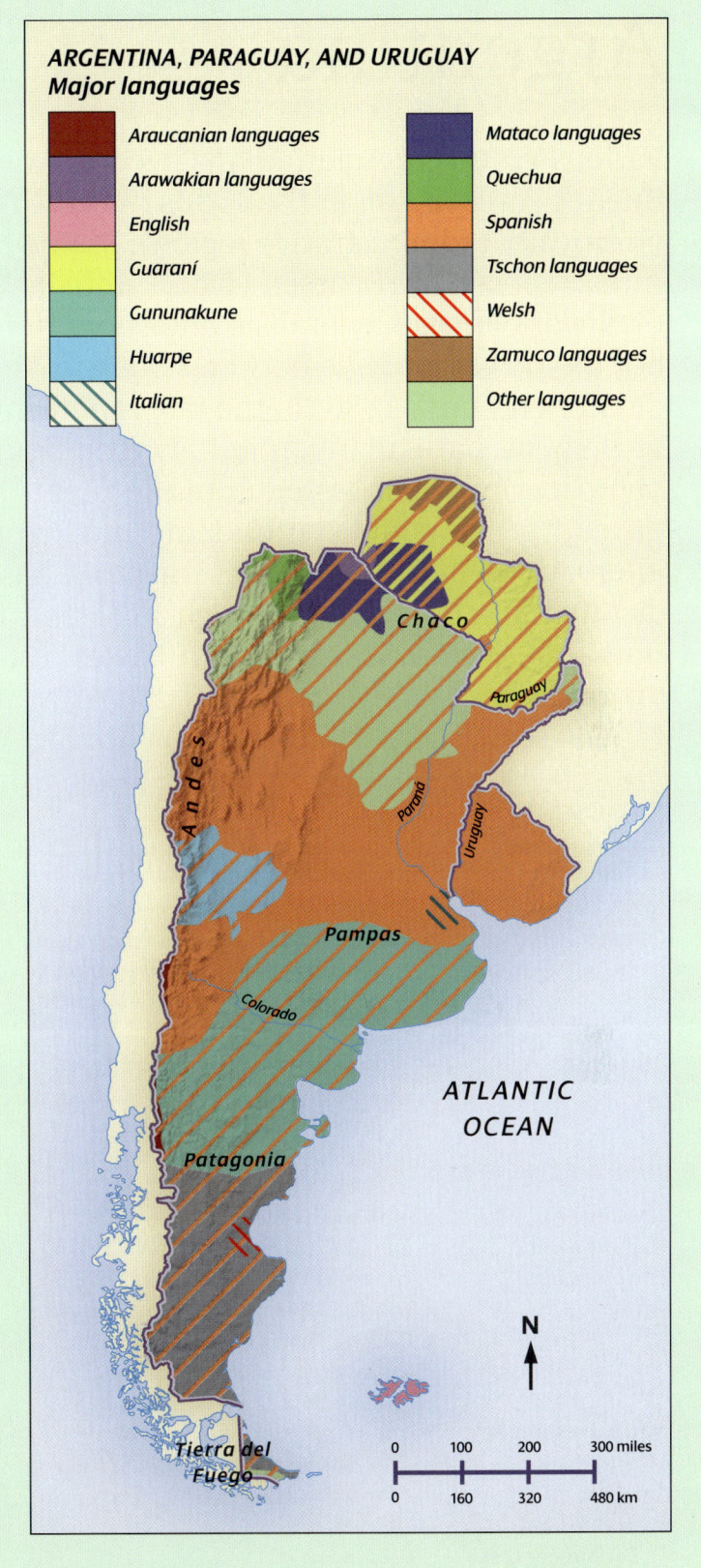

C. CARPENTER

Argentina

Various groups of Amerindians lived in Argentina before the Spanish colonized the Buenos Aires region in the 1530s. In 1776, the area became the center of a Spanish viceroyalty (administrative region), Río de la Plata. In 1810, a local junta in Buenos Aires deposed the Spanish viceroy and, in 1816, Argentina declared independence. Civil war between federalists and supporters of a centralized system ended in 1853, but the power struggle between Buenos Aires, the national capital, and the provinces did not end until 1880. In the late nineteenth century, large-scale European settlement, particularly from Italy (combined with British investment), led to a period of prosperity, which lasted until the Great Depression (1929–mid-1930s). From 1946 through 1955, populist president Juan Perón (1895–1974) greatly increased state intervention in the economy. Argentina has since experienced two periods of military dictatorship, from 1966 through 1973 and 1976 to 1983, when there were many human rights abuses. Civilian rule was restored in 1983, but the nation suffered a major economic crisis in 2001.

GEOGRAPHY

Location	Eastern South America, along the South Atlantic Ocean
Climate	Temperate through most of the country; subtropical in the north; arid in the southeast; subarctic in the southwest
Area	1,068,302 sq. miles (2,766,890 sq. km), excluding territories claimed by Argentina (the Falkland Islands, or Islas Malvinas, and the Argentine claim in the Antarctic)
Coastline	3,101 miles (4,989 km)
Highest point	Cerro Aconcagua 22,834 feet (6,960 m)
Lowest point	Laguna del Carbón -344 feet (-105 m)
Terrain	Low fertile plains (the Pampas) in the north; a plateau (Patagonia) in the south; the rugged Andes mountains in the west
Natural resources	Natural gas, tin, lead, petroleum, hydroelectric power potential, copper
Land use	
Arable land	10.0 percent
Permanent crops	0.4 percent
Other	89.6 percent
Major rivers	Río de la Plata, Uruguay, Paraná, Salado, Colorado, Negro, Chubut
Major lake	Nahuel Huapí
Natural hazards	Earthquakes (regionally), floods

METROPOLITAN AREAS, 2001 POPULATION

Urban population	88 percent
Buenos Aires	12,047,000
Buenos Aires City	2,769,000
San Justo–La Matanza	1,254,000
Lomas de Zamora	591,000
Quilmes	519,000
Almirante Brown	514,000
Merlo	469,000
Lanus	453,000
General San Martín	405,000
Moreno	380,000
Florencio Varela	343,000
Caseros	336,000;
Avellaneda	330,000;
Córdoba	1,368,000
Córdoba City	1,268,000
Rosario	1,161,000
Rosario City	906,000
Mendoza	849,000
Mendoza City	111,000
San Miguel de Tucumán	738,000
San Miguel de Tucumán City	526,000
La Plata	694,000
La Plata City	553,000
Mar del Plata	542,000
Salta	469,000
Salta City	463,000

ARGENTINA

Santa Fé	454,000
Santa Fé City	368,000
San Juan	422,000
San Juan City	116,000
Resistencia	360,000
Resistencia City	274,000
Santiago del Estero	328,000
Santiago del Estero City	230,000
Neuquén	291,000
Neuquén City	202,000
Posadas	280,000
Posadas City	253,000
San Salvador de Jujuy	278,000
San Salvador de Jujuy City	231,000
Bahía Blanca	275,000

Source: Argentine national census, 2001

NEIGHBORS AND LENGTH OF BORDERS

Bolivia	517 miles (832 km)
Brazil	784 miles (1,261 km)
Chile	3,299 miles (5,308 km)
Paraguay	1,168 miles (1,880 km)
Uruguay	360 miles (580 km)

POPULATION

Population	39,356,000 (2007 government estimate)
Population density	36.8 per sq. mile (14.2 per sq. km)
Population growth	0.9 percent a year
Birthrate	16.5 births per 1,000 of the population
Death rate	7.6 deaths per 1,000 of the population

ARGENTINA

Population under age 15	24.9 percent
Population over age 65	10.7 percent
Sex ratio	105 males for 100 females
Fertility rate	2.1 children per woman
Infant mortality rate	14.3 deaths per 1,000 live births
Life expectancy at birth	
Total population	76.3 years
Female	80.2 years
Male	72.6 years

ECONOMY

Currency	Argentine peso (ARS)
Exchange rate (2007)	$1 = ARS 3.1
Gross domestic product (2006)	$608.8 billion
GDP per capita (2006)	$15,200
Unemployment rate (2006)	8.7 percent
Population under poverty line (2006)	27 percent
Exports	$46.5 billion (2006)
Imports	$32.6 billion (2006)

GOVERNMENT

Official country name	Argentine Republic
Conventional short form	Argentina
Nationality	
noun	Argentine
adjective	Argentine
Official language	Spanish
Capital city	Buenos Aires

FLAG

The flag of Argentina comprises three horizontal bands, pale blue, white, and pale blue. The white band has a yellow sun, the so-called Sun of May, at the center. The original flag is said to have been designed by General Manuel Belgrano (1770–1820) and was first flown before a battle along the banks of the Paraná River in the Argentine War of Independence in 1812. The sun was added in 1818.

Type of government	Republic; democracy
Voting rights	18 years and over; universal and compulsory
National anthem	"Marcha de la Patria" (March of the fatherland)
National day	Revolution Day, May 25 (the anniversary of the beginning of the struggle for independence from Spain in 1810)

TRANSPORTATION

Railroads	19,827 miles (31,902 km)
Highways	142,414 miles (229,144 km)
Expressways	456 miles (734 km)
Other paved roads	42,309 miles (68,075 km)
Unpaved roads	99,649 miles (160,335 km)
Navigable waterways	6,837 miles (11,000 km)
Airports	
International airports	15
Paved runways	154

POPULATION PROFILE, 2006 ESTIMATES

Ethnic groups	
European ancestry	97 percent
Mestizo (Amerindian and European), Amerindians, and others	3 percent
Religions	
Roman Catholic	91 percent (less than 20 percent practicing)
Various Protestant churches	3 percent
Jewish	2 percent
Others and nonreligious	4 percent
Languages	
Spanish	97 percent
Italian	2 percent
Others	1 percent
Adult literacy	97 percent

CHRONOLOGY

1st century CE	Amerindians who grow corn live in the foothills of the Andes in what is now Argentina.
late 15th century	The Inca Empire extends into northern Argentina. Guaraní Amerindians live in the northeastern region of Argentina.
1516	Spanish navigator Juan Díaz de Solís (1470–1516) visits the coast of Argentina.
from 1530s	The Spanish colonize the Buenos Aires region, establishing a permanent settlement at Buenos Aires in 1580. Argentina later becomes part of the Spanish viceroyalty (administrative region) of Peru, based in Lima.
1776	A separate viceroyalty of Río de la Plata, comprising Argentina, Paraguay, and Uruguay, is established.
1806–1807	British forces unsuccessfully invade the Río de la Plata region.
1810–1811	While Spain is occupied by French forces, the Spanish in Argentina declare their own autonomous junta in Buenos Aires.
1811–1816	From 1811 through 1813, forces of the Buenos Aires junta resist attempts by Spain to retake the region. Argentine independence from Spanish rule is achieved in 1816.
1825–1826	Argentina and Brazil fight a war, largely over control of Uruguay.
late 1820s–1853	Civil war between federalists and supporters of a centralized system destablizes Argentina. In 1853, unity is achieved and a constitution introduced.
1865–1870	In the War of the Triple Alliance, Argentina, Brazil, and Uruguay fight Paraguay.
late 19th century	Large-scale European settlement, particularly from Italy and Spain, and British investment lead to economic development and a period of prosperity.
1929–mid-1930s	The Argentine economy collapses in the Great Depression.
1946–1955	Populist leader Juan Perón (1895–1974) greatly increases state spending in favor of unionized workers, whose social and political rights are greatly expanded.
1955	A military coup forces Péron from office.
1966–1973	A military junta rules Argentina.
1973–1974	Perón is again elected to the presidency; he dies in office in 1974.
1976–1983	A military junta rules Argentina. Opponents of the regime disappear, and there are many human rights abuses. Left-wing guerrilla movements commit acts of terror.
1982	Argentine forces invade the Falkland Islands (Islas Malvinas), which Argentina has always claimed as part of its national territory. After two months, British forces recapture the islands.
since 1983	Democratic civilian rule is restored.
2001	Because of massive foreign debt, Argentina suffers a major economic crisis, leading to widescale unrest and riots. The economy recovers after 2003.

GOVERNMENT

Argentina is a federal republic headed by an executive presidency. The powers of the central government and of the provinces were defined by the 1853 Argentine constitution.

The early history of Argentina was characterized by nearly constant civil war between the government of Buenos Aires, which advocated a strong central authority, and the provinces, which fought for a considerable degree of autonomy within a loose confederation. For much of the 1830s and 1840s, a central Argentine authority hardly existed, and the first effective national constitution did not come into force until 1853. The constitution established a republic that is, in theory, federal, but in which the powers of the constituent provinces are limited. The constitution has been suspended at different periods, when military governments have ruled Argentina.

THE CHIEF OF STATE AND THE LEGISLATURE

The chief of state of Argentina is a president, who is elected by universal adult suffrage. The voting age is 18, and voting is compulsory. Presidents originally served a nonrenewable six-year term but, since 1994, the president has been elected for a maximum of two consecutive four-year terms. The chief of state

Carlos Menem (born 1930), a member of the Justicialist Party, was president of Argentina from 1989 through 1999, during which time the presidential term was shortened from six to four years.

appoints a cabinet of ministers and the principal officers of state, is commander-in-chief of the armed forces, directs the nation's foreign policy, and, in certain circumstances, can rule by decree.

The legislature, or National Congress, comprises two houses, the Senate (upper house) and the Chamber of Deputies (lower house). The Senate has 72 members, three members elected from each province to serve for six years plus three representatives of the city of Buenos Aires. Not all the provinces hold elections to the Senate at the same time—one-third of the provinces hold senatorial elections every two years. The vice president, who is elected on the same ticket as the president, chairs the Senate.

The Chamber of Deputies has 257 members, who are elected from the provinces and Buenos Aires under a system of proportional representation. Each province forms a single constituency. One-half of the deputies are elected every two years to serve a four-year term. The provinces return members roughly in proportion to their population, with a minimum of five deputies representing each province. Ten of the 23 provinces each elect five members, while only the provinces of Santa Fé (with 19 deputies), Córdoba (18), and Buenos Aires (70), including the city of Buenos Aires (25), return more than ten deputies.

POLITICAL PARTIES

Three political movements have evolved from the populist center-right Justicialist Party (PJ) founded by Juan Perón (1895–1974; in office 1946–1955 and 1973–1974): the (majority) Front for Victory (FPV), the PJ, and the Judicialist Front. These are formally factions of the PJ but operate independently. Other parties include the (center-right) Radical Civic Union (UCR), the (center-left) Alternative for an Egalitarian Republic (ARI), and the (center-right) Republican Proposal (PRO).

LOCAL GOVERNMENT

Argentina is divided into 23 provinces and the city of Buenos Aires, which covers the downtown area and the inner suburbs of the city. Each province is administered by a directly elected governor and an elected provincial legislature. Buenos Aires has an elected mayor and legislature. The provinces are divided into municipalities, each of which has an elected council and mayor.

C. CARPENTER

MODERN HISTORY

Civil War and the Formation of the State

After the struggle for independence from Spanish rule at the start of the nineteenth century, Argentina experienced a long period of civil war when the provinces resisted the centralization of power in Buenos Aires.

In the late eighteenth century, Buenos Aires increased in importance to become the major Atlantic trade outlet of Spanish South America. At the same time, radically conflicting interests emerged in the Río de la Plata region. In the port city of Buenos Aires, merchants exercising monopoly trade rights with Spain (*monopolistas*) clashed with free-trade supporters (*librecambistas*), who sometimes aligned themselves with foreign traders.

THE STRUGGLE FOR INDEPENDENCE

Between 1806 and 1807, the British attempted to invade the Río de la Plata region. Local militias resisted the British forces and effectively seized power from the regular Spanish army. In 1808, the French invaded Spain, deposing the Spanish monarch. As a result, the Spanish in the Río de la Plata viceroyalty (administrative region)—which included modern-day Argentina, Uruguay, and Paraguay—eventually established a local council, or junta, to replace the Spanish-appointed authorities until legitimate rule was restored in Spain.

On May 25, 1810, militia commander Cornelio Saavedra (1761–1829) deposed the Spanish viceroy. Saavedra became president of a junta, with the leaders of the *librecambista* faction, Manuel Belgrano (1770–1820), Juan José Castelli (1764–1812), and Mariano Moreno (1778–1811), among its members. Consequently, the Río de la Plata region had an autonomous government, which ruled in the name of the deposed Spanish king, Ferdinand VII (1784–1833; reigned 1808 and 1813–1833). Although the junta received the support of many other cities and regions, some districts—Asunción (now in Paraguay) and Montevideo (Uruguay) among them—remained loyal to Spain. In response, the junta in Buenos Aires dispatched military forces led by Castelli and Belgrano to prevent a Spanish counterattack.

Despite initial victories at Córdoba and Suipacha in the northwest of the viceroyalty, the insurgent armies suffered humiliating defeats in 1811 and 1813. The junta subsequently lost part of the viceroyalty, which eventually became the independent republic of Paraguay in 1811. The junta in Buenos Aires also faced the possibility of a Spanish invasion from Banda Oriental (the opposite bank of the Río de la Plata, present-day Uruguay), but the threat was warded off in 1811 by a rural uprising under José Gervasio Artigas (1764–1850), a local militia leader, whose forces surrounded and besieged the Spanish at Montevideo (later the capital of Uruguay).

When Ferdinand VII was restored in Spain in 1813, he proved unpopular. Many supporters of the junta were unwilling to abandon autonomy and return to direct Spanish rule. Consequently, on July 9, 1816, a nationalist assembly met in the city of San Miguel de Tucumán and declared independence as the United Provinces of the Río de la Plata. Spanish royalists resisted the nationalists for several years, but, with the fall of Montevideo to Artigas in 1814, Spain was deprived of its last remaining regional port along the Atlantic and the possibility of easily introducing military reinforcements. In 1817, forces from Buenos Aires and several other cities under José de San Martín (1778–1850) crossed the Andes into Chile and defeated the Spanish at the battles of Chacabuco (1817) and Maipú (1818).

INTERNAL CONFLICT

With the break from Spain, patterns in trade changed, and the export of meat replaced the export of precious metals (from what is now Bolivia) as the mainstay of Buenos Aires. As a result, merchant groups in Buenos Aires faced the growing power of a new, cattle-raising landowner class. The interior provinces, in turn, resisted the centralization of power and wealth in Buenos Aires, resulting in a series of regional uprisings while the war against the Spanish was still under way.

When politicians in Buenos Aires sought to concentrate power in the port city and abolish existing trade monopolies, to the benefit of the local merchants, rural militia leaders in the

In this contemporary engraving of the Battle of Caseros (1852), troops loyal to Argentine dictator Juan Manuel de Rosas (1793–1877) are attacked by a combined Brazilian and Uruguayan force led by his former deputy, Justo José de Urquiza (1801–1870). Rosas was subsequently defeated and exiled.

interior favored regional autonomy and the maintenance of trade barriers to protect local producers. In Banda Oriental, Artigas turned against his former allies in Buenos Aires, gaining the support of the city of Córdoba and the provinces of present-day northern Argentina along the Paraná River. In response, Buenos Aires and its supporters, the so-called unitarians, called a constituent assembly, which attempted to impose a unitary constitution over all of the former viceroyalty of Río de la Plata. Artigas was exiled from Banda Oriental by a Portuguese invasion of Montevideo in 1817, but his former federalist allies repudiated the unitarian constitution, invaded Buenos Aires, and forced the authorities in the city to accept the principle of regional autonomy. However, the federalists' loose alliance of local warlords (caudillos) soon fell apart, and Buenos Aires reassumed control over the provinces along the Paraná. Consequently, Buenos Aires regained direction over regional trade and customs duties, and the city resumed its dominant role.

BUENOS AIRES AND THE FEDERALISTS

Bernardino Rivadavia (1780–1845), government secretary in Buenos Aires, became the dominant political figure between 1821 and 1827. Through a series of reforms, including the creation of a national bank, a university, new electoral laws, and the leasing of landed property, Rivadavia attempted to stabilize the fledgling state of the United Provinces. A new constitution was adopted in 1826, and Rivadavia was elected president of the United Provinces (in office 1826–1827). Only a year later, he was forced to step down because of continued resistance from the caudillos in the interior and also because of a financially disastrous war with Brazil, which had annexed Banda Oriental in 1822. In 1825, local forces supported by Buenos Aires cornered the Brazilians in Montevideo. The Brazilians responded with a naval blockade of Buenos Aires. The impasse continued until 1828, when Manuel Dorrego (1787–1828; in office as governor of Buenos Aires 1820 and 1827–1828) agreed to the creation of an independent republic in the area that is now Uruguay.

Unitarian commanders José María Paz (1791–1854) and Juan Lavalle (1797–1841) attempted to reverse their faction's decline. Paz occupied Córdoba and quickly established power over much of the interior of the United Provinces. Lavalle attacked Buenos Aires, only to be driven out the following year by a rural uprising led by a major landowner, Juan Manuel de Rosas (1793–1877; governor of Buenos Aires 1829–1832 and 1835–1852; supreme chief of the Argentine confederation 1851–1852). Rosas was elected governor with "extraordinary powers" in 1829.

JUAN MANUEL DE ROSAS

Rosas quickly formed an alliance with the remaining provincial warlords, Estanislao López (1786–1838) and Juan Facundo Quiroga (1788–1835), defeating Paz's unitarian forces in 1831.

Rosas delayed subsequent attempts to recall the constituent assembly and draw up a federalist constitution. He used the status quo to his own advantage. As a result, Buenos Aires was left in control of foreign trade and customs for the United Provinces, but there was no effective Argentine central government. Stepping down in 1832 to command a military campaign on the southern frontier, Rosas was recalled by the Buenos Aires congress in 1835 and was invested once more with dictatorial powers. Alternating military threats and economic subsidies, Rosas soon brought most of the interior provinces into submission. He remained in power for almost 20 years despite various attempted coups by unitarian opponents and French and British naval blockades of Buenos Aires—trying to force open the navigation of the Paraná River—in 1838 and 1845. Eventually, in 1852, an army of unitarian, Uruguayan, and Brazilian forces under Rosas's former deputy Justo José de Urquiza (1801–1870; in office as provisional director 1852–1854 and as president of Argentina 1854–1860) defeated the dictator and drove Rosas into exile in Great Britain.

One of the most controversial figures in Argentine history, Rosas is portrayed by his detractors as a tyrant, while others have described him as an early anti-imperialist and economic nationalist who had popular mass support. Rosas made it mandatory to wear the federal colors in public and ordered that even personal correspondence should begin with the phrase "Long live the federation, and death to the savage unitarians!" Rosas's police killed dozens of opponents when his rule was threatened in the late 1830s, but he also enjoyed the support of landless peasants (gauchos) and the urban black proletariat. Although he never formally abolished slavery, many black people acquired their freedom through military service. Foreign imports were heavily taxed, while national produce, especially meat and grains, were exempted from taxation. Rosas's policies chiefly benefited major landowners and cattle ranchers like himself, but his downfall was principally the result of discontent among rural landowners with the increasing militarization of the regime, which caused severe labor shortages in the countryside. His dictatorship brought about a truce of sorts between the forces of Buenos Aires and the provinces, but it was only after his overthrow that a centralized, modern state started to emerge.

THE CONSOLIDATION OF THE STATE

Urquiza—like Rosas, a major landowner—became the new political power with the title of provisional director. The interior provinces once again attempted to enforce a federalist constitution on Buenos Aires and, in 1853, liberals in Buenos Aires overthrew the governor imposed by Urquiza and rejected a constitutional agreement that the provinces had signed the previous year. Urquiza subsequently proclaimed himself president of the Argentine Confederation in 1854, moving the capital to his own province of Entre Ríos. Tensions between the confederation and Buenos Aires rose until, in 1859, Urquiza defeated the forces of Buenos Aires in battle. However, two years later, Urquiza was forced to retreat by Bartolomé Mitre (1821–1906; in office as president of Argentina 1862–1868), Buenos Aires's new governor, who had rallied the support of disaffected factions in the interior. Urquiza was defeated not for military reasons but because of the failure of the provinces to channel foreign trade through their ports along the Paraná River rather than through Buenos Aires. As a result, the provinces suffered a financial crisis.

THE ARGENTINE REPUBLIC

Buenos Aires finally approved a constitution that returned the federal government to the city. In 1862, Mitre was elected first president of the Argentine Republic. He subsequently implemented a nationwide judicial system, a postal service, and a federal army, and he developed the transportation system. Construction of the Central Railroad from Rosario to Córdoba began in 1862 and was completed in 1870, by which time Buenos Aires was also connected by railroad to the cities of Chivilcoy and Chascomús to the south. In 1890, the railroad reached Bahía Blanca, Mendoza, and San Miguel de Tucumán. The economic benefits of infrastructural integration were far greater for Buenos Aires than for the interior provinces, but the creation of a state bureaucracy allowed Mitre to coopt provincial support through the distribution of public offices. This support broke the influence of the local caudillos, and remaining islands of federalist resistance were violently crushed.

External conflict accelerated Mitre's creation of a national army as an instrument to repress internal dissent. In 1865, Argentina joined forces with Brazil and their Uruguayan allies (the local unitarians, or Blancos) against the Paraguayan dictator Francisco Solano López (1827–1870; in office 1862–1869), who had intervened in the Uruguayan civil war between the Blancos and their opponents, the Colorados. During the ensuing war, the War of the Triple Alliance (1865–1870), power transferred from Buenos Aires to provincial elites that were emerging as a result of state consolidation. Domingo F. Sarmiento (1811–1888; in office 1868–1874), a veteran liberal from San Juan, became president with support of the military and of factions in Buenos Aires that were opposed to Mitre. In 1874, Mitre was again defeated in presidential elections, this time in favor of Nicolás Avellaneda (1837–1885; in office 1874–1880), another provincial candidate. An uprising of Mitre's supporters was crushed by federal troops.

In 1880, another revolt occurred when the presidential candidate from Buenos Aires, Carlos Tejedor (1817–1903), rebelled against the president-elect, Julio Argentino Roca (1843–1914; in office 1880–1886 and 1898–1904). As minister of war, Roca had led the army in the so-called Desert Campaign in 1879, advancing the southern frontier of Argentina into lands previously occupied by indigenous groups. On taking office, Roca decreed the separation of the federal capital from the surrounding province of Buenos Aires, which, as a result, no longer had such a dominant role in Argentine affairs.

J. ANDERMANN

The Era of Prosperity

From 1880, Argentina experienced a period of increased exports, economic development, and mass immigration. The era of prosperity ended with an economic crisis, a military coup in 1930, and a seizure of power by the army in 1943.

A program of large-scale economic development began under the presidency of Julio Argentino Roca (1843–1914; in office 1880–1886 and 1898–1904). In 1879, as minister of war, Roca had conducted the so-called Desert Campaign, which led to the rapid military conquest of Patagonia in the south and the Gran Chaco region in the far north. In both regions, the indigenous inhabitants were killed or deported, and their vast lands were sold to landowners in Buenos Aires and abroad. The acquisition of so much new land for agriculture led to a sharp rise in meat, wool, and grain exports, as well as to feverish financial speculation because of the influx of foreign capital. Immigration from overseas, particularly from Italy and Spain, also dramatically rose. However, because landed property was concentrated in relatively few hands, most immigrants settled in coastal cities, particularly Buenos Aires, and in cities along the Paraná River.

ECONOMIC DEVELOPMENT

The Argentine government effectively subsidized the speculative gains of the landholding elite, and foreign debt rose. This provoked a stock-exchange crash in 1890. Salaries and real estate prices fell by around 50 percent, generating widespread discontent with the government of Miguel Juárez Celman (1844–1909; in office 1886–1890). With little success, Juárez Celman tried to combat inflation by selling state assets, such as railroads, to foreign corporations.

In 1890, Juárez Celman was toppled by a coalition including supporters of the veteran politician Bartolomé Mitre (1821–1906; in office 1862–1868), who had remained a powerful figure long after his presidency. The coalition included Catholics alienated by the government's secularization of education and of marriage law, and the Civic Union, a movement of urban professionals and skilled workers, which campaigned against electoral fraud. Mitre made a secret deal with Roca, allowing the acting vice president Carlos Pellegrini (1846–1906; in office 1890–1892) to take over from Juárez Celman, while Roca promised to support Mitre in forthcoming elections. However, in 1892 and 1895, Roca was instrumental in the election of compliant allies before becoming president again himself from 1898 through 1904.

Meanwhile, sectors of the Civic Union—disillusioned after the failed revolution of 1890—founded the Radical Civic Union (the UCR, or Radicals), which staged several armed uprisings in the interior between 1891 and 1893. Immigrant workers from Europe also started to organize themselves, introducing traditions of class struggle from their countries of origin. Anarchist ideas spread among unskilled immigrants from the Mediterranean region of southern Europe, while socialism attracted trained workers and professionals, many of whom came from industrialized regions of northern Europe.

Although export and immigration figures soon regained their pace of growth after 1890, rising popular discontent with the closed system of government began to alarm the ruling elite. In response, a nationalist faction campaigned for restrictions on immigration, a ban on foreign-language education, and the deportation of working-class activists, which Congress authorized in 1902. Modernizing factions, meanwhile, advocated more inclusive citizenship laws and the extension of political participation to prevent social unrest. Their agenda appeared to gain urgency in 1905 after another Radical rebellion gained support from the lower ranks of the army. Led by Roque Saenz (1851–1914; in office 1910–1914), the modernizers eventually prevailed over Roca and the conservatives and attempted to secure their hold on power by introducing limited electoral reforms in 1912. However, the legislature of one province after another was captured by the Radicals, who had ended their policy of electoral abstention. In 1916, Hipólito Yrigoyen (1852–1933; in office 1916–1922 and 1928–1930), the UCR's leader, narrowly won the presidential election, ending decades of rule by the conservative landowning elite.

DEMOCRATIC POPULISM

Yrigoyen introduced measures of social welfare and some modest reforms, such as government loans to agricultural producers, in an attempt to widen his rural support. His strategy of reducing the conservatives' power, using federal powers to replace provincial governors and senators in the national legislature, had partly succeeded by 1918. In the same year, the government supported a student movement for university reform.

The main beneficiaries of Yrigoyen's policies were the emergent middle classes, which gained access to education and social mobility. His attempts to wrest working-class support away from the socialists were less successful, even though the government intervened on the side of labor in the dockworkers' strike of 1916 and in other labor disputes. However, in the so-called Semana Trágica, or Tragic Week, of January 1919, a steelworkers' strike was violently crushed by a paramilitary group, the Argentine Patriotic League, which also killed dozens

In the early twentieth century, Buenos Aires rapidly developed as a major port, exporting agricultural produce from the interior, and as a growing industrial and service center, attracting many settlers from Europe, particularly Italians and Spaniards.

of Jewish immigrants, accusing them of being Communist agents. Under pressure from the right wing, Yrigoyen sent the army to suppress a rural strike in Patagonia in 1921–1922, which resulted in the deaths of hundreds of workers.

Attempts by the Radicals to consolidate popular support by increasing government spending inflated public debt. Meat exports to Europe, which had enjoyed a boom during World War I (1914–1918), sharply declined after 1921. Marcelo T. de Alvear (1868–1942; in office 1922–1928), Yrigoyen's successor, unsuccessfully tried to keep inflation in check by reducing public expenditure and raising taxes on imports. However, while protectionism did nothing to change the conservative elite's hostility toward the government, budget austerity alienated middle-class support. In 1924, the UCR split between a conservative wing under Alvear and a populist movement campaigning for a second Yrigoyen presidency. In 1928, Yrigoyen was reelected, promising a return to the social welfare agenda of his first presidency, financed by the nationalization of Patagonian oil. Yrigoyen was initially successful in crushing conservative opposition in the Senate, but the Great Depression of 1929–mid-1930s (a world-wide economic downturn) forced his government again to cut public spending, while inflation greatly increased. Yrigoyen's support crumbled in the midterm elections in March 1930, and in September of the same year, a military coup under General José Félix Uriburu (1868–1932; in office 1930–1932) brought the conservative elite back to power.

MILITARY REGIMES

Uriburu's faction, which had emerged from the Argentine Patriotic League, sympathized with Spanish and Italian fascism and sought to create a corporative police state. Yrigoyen and other leading Radicals were imprisoned, and strikes and protests were violently repressed. However, the liberal wing of the regime, in a pact with anti-Yrigoyen Radicals and some other politicians, formed an alliance known as the *concordancia*, whose presidential candidate, Agustín P. Justo (1876–1943; in office 1932–1938), was elected in 1932. The *concordancia* stayed in power during the 1930s through systematic electoral fraud.

The *concordancia* governments confronted the economic crisis with fiscal reforms. Prices for domestic products were protected by tariffs. In a series of bilateral agreements with other governments, such as the Roca-Runciman Treaty with Great Britain in 1933, Argentina agreed to drastic reductions in import taxes to maintain its previous levels of agricultural exports. The treaties were heavily criticized by nationalists, who promoted their candidate, the ultra-right-wing Ramón S. Castillo (1873–1944; in office 1942–1943), as running mate to the liberals' Roberto M. Ortíz (1886–1942; in office 1938–1942) in 1938.

Suffering from illness, Ortíz had to leave the government in Castillo's hands in 1940, and, when Ortíz died, Castillo succeeded him. At the outset of World War II (1939–1945), despite its trade links with the Allies, Argentina had a government with fascist sympathies, but it remained neutral. Opposition groups, however, rejected neutrality, and Castillo was overthrown in a coup of lower-ranked officers. Among these officers was Juan Perón (1895–1974; in office 1946–1955 and 1973–1974), who was to dominate Argentine politics for decades to come.

J. ANDERMANN

Juan Perón

Juan Perón (1895–1974; in office 1946–1955, and 1973–1974) was one of a group of army officers who seized power in Argentina in 1943. Eclipsing his colleagues, he founded a populist political movement that held power for a decade.

Following the military coup of 1943, the president, Pedro Ramírez (1884–1962; in office 1943–1944), was Argentina's leader in name only. The military leaders, also known as the "Colonels," formed a junta, *Gobierno, Orden, Unidad* (GOU; Government, Order, Unity), which effectively ruled the country. Over the next two years, Perón emerged as the most powerful member of the GOU. He first rose to prominence as the secretary of labor and social welfare and, by 1945, he had added the offices of vice president and minister of war to his portfolio, solidifying his power base. A popular figure in the military, Perón was also successful in gaining the support of the laboring poor. Perón's beautiful and charismatic mistress, former radio actor Eva Duarte (popularly known as Eva Perón or Evita; 1919–1952), helped Perón win support among underprivileged workers, whom she referred to as the "shirtless ones."

THE PEOPLE'S LEADER

In early October 1945, Perón was arrested and removed from office by politicians and army officers who favored constitutional government. With the help of her associates in the labor unions, Duarte organized mass protests among workers in the Buenos Aires area. As a result of Duarte's efforts, Perón was released from prison on October 17. Later that evening, he made a memorable speech to a crowd of more than 300,000 people from the balcony of the presidential palace. In his speech, which was broadcast via radio across the country, Perón promised to make Argentina a powerful nation. A few days later, he married Duarte in secret.

THE PERÓN PRESIDENCY

Perón was elected president in February 1946, winning 56 percent of the vote. He founded the Justicialist Party (Partido Justicialista), popularly known as the Perónistas. He aimed to make Argentina the military, political, and financial leader of Latin America. Adopting a strong anti-American and anti-British stance, Perón followed the "Third Position," a doctrine that lay between capitalism and communism. He nationalized the railroad system and other utilities and embarked on a program of industrialization and state intervention. He awarded wage increases to industrial workers and implemented social programs for their benefit.

In 1951, Perón was reelected by a slightly larger margin; however, his administration became more dictatorial. He censored the press and ruthlessly suppressed opponents to his regime. Nonetheless, his popularity among the masses remained strong and, when Evita died of cancer in 1952, the majority of Argentines mourned. Evita's body was laid in state, and four people died and 2,500 were injured in the frenzy to view her.

Following his wife's death, Perón modified some of his polices, but opposition to his rule increased. By 1955, the Roman Catholic Church, which had initially supported Perón, had also turned against him after he legalized divorce and prostitution and took measures to reduce the church's power.

THE FALL OF PERÓN

Public discontent and opposition to Perón's regime increased as inflation grew. On September 19, 1955, Perón was overthrown by army and military leaders. Forced to resign, Perón first fled to Paraguay, eventually settling in Madrid, Spain. The Perónistas remained active, however, and Perón served as president again from 1973 through 1974, and died in office. Perónism remains an influential political movement in Argentina.

K. BIAS

Juan Perón (1895–1974) used radio broadcasts to spread his ideas for reshaping Argentine society.

Modern Argentina

During the second half of the twentieth century, Argentina experienced several coups and two periods of military rule (from 1966 through 1973, and 1976 through 1983), fought a short war with Great Britain for ownership of the Falkland Islands (Islas Malvinas), and ended the century on the brink of a major economic crisis.

After the fall from power of Argentine dictator Juan Perón 1895–1974; in office 1946–1955 and 1973–1974) in 1955, support for the ideas of the political movement he had founded, the populist Justicialist Party (Partido Justicialista), remained strong. The political legacy of Perón, who was exiled in Spain, was important, and the former president and his party eventually returned to power in the 1970s.

CIVILIAN AND MILITARY GOVERNMENTS

Having deposed Perón and banned his party, a military junta took control of Argentina in 1955. The military leaders reinstated the constitution of 1853, which was largely based on the U.S. constitution. In 1958, presidential and legislative elections were held, and the leader of the Radical Civic Union party, Arturo Frondizi (1908–1995), became president. Frondizi, whose party had been suppressed by Perón's government, initiated a program that cut government spending, limited wage increases, and took other measures aimed at stopping the country's rising inflation. However, these measures were in direct opposition to the ideas of Perón's supporters, known as the Perónistas, who advocated state intervention and high public spending.

The Perónistas, whose party was banned, nevertheless still had the support of the labor unions, and some military leaders became increasingly concerned that, with enough pressure, Frondizi would lift the ban on the Justicialist Party. At the same time, the middle classes, who supported Frondizi's economic policies, shared with the Perónistas a concern about the growing leftist nature of Frondizi's foreign policy, particularly when it became known that Frondizi had held a secret meeting with Argentine-born revolutionary Che Guevara (Ernesto Guevara de la Serna; 1928–1967), who was acting as the envoy of Cuban leader Fidel Castro (born 1926). In 1962, Frondizi lost the support of the military and subsequently resigned. The military established an interim government, and two army factions—one sympathetic toward and the other opposing the Perónistas—struggled for power. Eventually, in 1963, new elections were held, and the Radicals were returned to power. However, support for the Perónistas grew and, in 1966, the Perónistas supported a successful military coup.

Military rule from 1966 through 1973 was marked by increasing civil unrest, labor strikes, violence, and many protests against military corruption and inefficient government. Student riots in 1969 protested unpopular economic policies, and terrorist groups, such as the People's Revolutionary Army and the Montoneros, became active, staging bank robberies, and kidnapping and assassinating opponents. Juan Carlos Onganía (1914–1995; in office 1966–1970), a civilian politician who ruled with military backing, was unable to restore order, and the murder of former president Pedro Eugenio Aramburu (1903–1970; in office 1955–1958) by the Montoneros prompted the army to take direct control. In March 1971, a military regime, led by General Alejandro Agustín Lanusse (1918–1996; in office 1971–1973), seized power, pledging a return to constitutional democracy by the end of 1973.

PERÓN'S RETURN

In 1973, Perónistas won the presidency under Héctor J. Cámpora (1909–1980; in office 1973). Perón, who had briefly returned from exile in Spain in November 1972, made a permanent return to Argentina in June 1973. At a celebration for his return, deep animosity between conflicting groups of Perónistas led to violence, and 34 people were killed and 342 wounded in fighting. Unrest and political instability increased in Argentina, and, less than a month later, Cámpora resigned. Later that same year, Perón was elected president by a large margin. However, he died of influenza within nine months in 1974, and his third wife, Isabel (born 1931; in office 1974–1976), who was vice president, became president. Isabel was the first female president in the Western Hemisphere, but she was unpopular, partly due to the influence that the controversial social welfare minister, José López Rega (1916–1989), was believed to have over her, and partly because the country suffered high inflation, debt, and unrest during her administration. The Perónista movement effectively split, and terrorist activities by right-wing extremists and human rights abuses by the military increased. In March 1976, a military junta arrested Isabel Perón, took control, and dissolved Congress.

THE MILITARY REGIME

The military junta that held power from 1976 through 1983—the period that came to be known as the Dirty War—began a campaign to stop terrorism, but their actions led to numerous abuses of civil rights and killings. The military cracked down on opposition members, branding them radical and subversive leftists. Government-sponsored death squads were active, and torturous interrogations, rape, and abduction were used by the military for political purposes. At least 10,000 Argentines were killed or disappeared as a result of the military's activities between 1976 and 1981. Those dissenters and opponents of the military who were never found are referred to as *los desaparecidos* ("the disappeared ones"). Mothers of the *desaparecidos* formed a group to protest the fate of their relatives. Gathering for the first time in 1977 in downtown Buenos Aires, they became known as the Mothers of the Plaza de Mayo, after the square in which they gathered every Thursday afternoon through the period of the dictatorship. Some of these women were subsequently detained and tortured.

On April 2, 1982, Argentine forces invaded the British-held Falkland Islands. The Falklands, which were known as Islas Malvinas to Argentines, are a rocky group of two main islands and many smaller ones, east of the southern tip of South America in the South Atlantic. The islands had been disputed by Argentina and Great Britain since the 1830s, but most of the few thousand people living in the islands were of Scottish, Irish, or Welsh descent. A force of about 5,000 Argentine troops quickly overran the small British force in the islands, but Great Britain immediately sent a fleet of nearly 30 ships to the region, recapturing the Falklands in June.

The campaign to capture the Falklands briefly gained support for the military regime in Argentina. However, the Falkland Islands War added to the nation's economic problems, and chief of state Leopoldo Galtieri (1926–2003; in office 1981–1982) was forced to step down. Defeat in the Falklands precipitated the end of military rule, and free elections were held in late 1983.

CIVILIAN RULE RESTORED

In December 1983, Radical Civic Union leader Raúl Alfonsín (born 1927; in office 1983–1989) took office as head of a civilian government. Under Alfonsín, tribunals were held to investigate human rights abuses committed by previous governments. As a result, in 1985, three former presidents and many high-ranking military officers were sentenced to prison.

However, Argentina's economic difficulties continued as inflation rapidly increased. Prices doubled and then tripled for basic goods such as bread and milk. Carlos Menem (born 1930; in office 1989–1999), a Perónista, was elected president in 1989, pledging to address the country's economic problems. During his first term, Menem greatly reduced inflation and opened Argentine markets to foreign investment. Menem was reelected in 1995 and was succeeded by Fernando de la Rúa (born 1937; in office 1999–2001) in 1999.

Argentina's political and economic difficulties continued in the twenty-first century. After Menem's two terms, inflation, foreign debt, and budget deficits again mounted, and the economy contracted. Consumer and investor confidence diminished and, in December 2001, Argentina defaulted on its

The Mothers of the Plaza de Mayo wear white shawls or head scarfs, representing the diapers of lost children, to protest the disappearance of relatives during the 1976–1983 military dictatorship.

massive foreign debt. Angered by the country's economic collapse, some Argentines looted stores and supermarkets in cities across the country. In Buenos Aires, protesters surrounded the presidential palace, and 27 people were killed in violent clashes with the police. Four days after the riots started, de la Rúa resigned and, from late 2001 through early 2003, five different presidents held office. The economic crisis reduced many Argentines to poverty. The downturn lasted until 2003, when Perónista candidate Néstor Kirchner (born 1950; in office 2003–2007) became president. In office, he repealed the amnesty that had protected many army officers from prosecution for human rights abuses during the 1976–1983 military dictatorship. Personality clashes split the Perónista movement in three (all formally part of the Justicialist Party). Kirchner's Front for Victory emerged as the largest group, and its candidate, Kirchner's wife, Cristina Fernández de Kirchner (born 1953), became president in 2007.

K. BIAS

CULTURAL EXPRESSION

Literature

Argentine literature is an important part of the Spanish-language literary heritage, and the country has produced a number of internationally famous writers, including Jorge Luis Borges (1899–1986). Although Spanish literature and culture influenced Argentine writers, other European cultures, particularly French, also had a major part in shaping Argentine literature.

What became Argentina was a relatively sparsely populated part of the Spanish Empire in the New World, and few notable local writers emerged during the colonial era (early sixteenth century through early nineteenth century). Works about Argentina before the 1800s were most often travelers' accounts; among the best known are those of the German mercenary Ulrich Schmidel (1510–1579) and the Spanish traveler Alonso Carrió de la Vandera (1715–1778), known by the pen name Concolocorvo. Schmidel's 1567 account includes lively discussions of indigenous customs. Concolocorvo, traveling with muleteers in the northern part of the country, wrote an important early (1775) account of the life of the gaucho, the Argentine cowboy.

NINETEENTH-CENTURY LITERATURE

Argentine literature at the time of independence consisted of patriotic poetry (the Argentine national anthem dates from this period) and of the first examples of what is known as *poesía gauchesca* ("gauchesque poetry"), written in the voice of gauchos and using popular language and familiar verse forms. One of the defining early Argentine intellectuals was Esteban Echeverría (1805–1851), best known for his 1837 poem "La cautiva"—about a white woman taken captive by the Indians of the Pampas—and *El matadero*, a prose sketch of life in a Buenos Aires slaughterhouse during the dictatorship of Juan Manuel de Rosas (1793–1877; governor of Buenos Aires 1829–1832 and 1835–1852). *El matadero* is usually considered the first short story in Spanish-speaking America, although it was published posthumously in 1871.

Facundo: Civilización i barbarie (1845; *Facundo: Civilization and Barbarism*, 2004) by Domingo F. Sarmiento (1811–1888; in office as president of Argentina 1868–1874) and the epic *El gaucho Martín Fierro* (1872, second part 1879; The gaucho Martín Fierro) by José Hernández (1834–1886) are generally considered masterpieces of nineteenth-century Argentine literature. Sarmiento wrote *Facundo*, an account of life in the Pampas and the interior, while he was in exile in Chile. Hernández's epic is the culmination of the tradition of what have been called "gaucho-political" poems, in this case the response by Hernández to the treatment of the gauchos by the government of Sarmiento. Other important writers of the late nineteenth century include Lucio V. Mansilla (1831–1913), who is known for his lively account of an 1870 visit to the Ranquel Amerindians, and Eduardo Gutiérrez (1851–1889), famous for his popular serial novels about bandits of the pampas.

LUGONES AND LATIN AMERICAN *MODERNISMO*

In the last decade of the nineteenth century and the first several decades of the twentieth century, the dominant figure in Argentine literature, and one of the central figures in Latin American *modernismo* (a movement that swept across the Spanish-speaking world with a reinvention of poetic language), was the poet, essayist, and short story writer Leopoldo Lugones (1874–1938). Initially a socialist, Lugones became a nationalist with close ties to fascism, as became evident in his 1924 speech known as the "Hour of the Sword." His bold use of metaphor was an inspiration to the younger poets of the avant-garde, including Borges, although his ideas about poetry and about the national tradition were widely criticized.

Other important writers of the period were Alfonsina Storni (1892–1938), poet and feminist journalist; Victoria Ocampo (1890–1978), founder of the literary magazine *Sur* in 1931 and writer of essays and a five-volume autobiography; the experimental novelist Macedonio Fernández (1874–1952); Ricardo Güiraldes (1886–1927), author of a nostalgic novel of gaucho life, *Don Segundo Sombra* (1926; English version, 1995); and the Uruguayan-born short story writer Horacio Quiroga (1878–1937), celebrated for his tales set in the subtropical region of Misiones in northern Argentina (near the frontier with Paraguay and Brazil).

Jorge Luis Borges (1899–1986) was a poet, translator, and critic as well as the writer of the short stories for which he is best known in the English-speaking world.

BORGES

The most influential Argentine writer was the poet, essayist, and short story writer Jorge Luis Borges (1899–1986). A central figure in the avant-garde movement, Borges turned in the 1930s to the short story, first in the collected short stories, essays, and embellished translations of little-known works in *Historia universal de la infamia* (1935; Universal history of iniquity; published in English as part of *Collected Fictions*, 1999), and then in the vivid stories collected in *Ficciones* (1944) and *El Aleph* (1949), including the stories "El sur" (The south) and "El jardín de senderos que se bifurcan" (The garden of forking paths). Borges's works are generally considered to be among the most important contributions to the short-story genre in world literature in the twentieth century. Borges explores the tensions between fiction and other kinds of writing, and between high and low culture, in stories that play with intellectual puzzles (crime fiction, labyrinths in space and time, and intrusions from imaginary into real worlds). His essays are equally meditations on intellectual problems: creativity and tradition, the nature of time, the role of the reader, and the relation of imagination to experience.

Argentine literature after Borges was centrally concerned with these questions, and (unlike earlier periods, which focused on rural life) would highlight the uneven modernity most strikingly represented in the Argentine metropolis of Buenos Aires. Borges's contemporaries included the novelist and journalist Roberto Arlt (1900–1942), who explored the world of popular inventors, anarchists and other revolutionaries, and of marginalized groups such as prostitutes and criminals.

MODERN WRITERS

Noted writers who came to prominence in the middle of the century were the fiction writer Julio Cortázar (1914–1984), author of the important experimental novel *Rayuela* (1963; *Hopscotch*, 1966), whose chapters can be read in different orders, and of several collections of short stories; Adolfo Bioy Casares (1914–1999), author of the novel *La invención de Morel* (1940; *The Invention of Morel*, 1964) and coauthor with Borges of crime fiction and screenplays; and Silvina Ocampo (1904–1994), author of the disturbing short stories "La furia" (1959) and "Las invitadas" (1961) and of a significant body of poetry. Manuel Puig (1932–1990), the novelist whose works include the celebrated *El beso de la mujer araña* (1976; *The Kiss of the Spider Woman*, 1979), about a prison-cell dialogue between a flamboyant homosexual raconteur and a revolutionary, focused his work on the impact of popular culture on gender and sexual identity.

Ricardo Piglia (born 1940), especially in his novella *Homenaje a Roberto Arlt* (1976; published in English as *Assumed Name*, 1995) and the 1980 novel *Respiración artificial* (1980; Artificial respiration), explores the tensions in modern Argentine culture between tradition and innovation, the local and the global, the vernacular and the cosmopolitan. Other central figures of modern Argentine letters are the fiction writer Juan José Saer (1937–2005), author of a novel about the first Spanish expedition to the Río de la Plata, *El entenado* (1983; *The Witness*, 1991); the writer and critic Sylvia Molloy (born 1938), author of important studies of Borges and of autobiography in Latin America; and the poets Alejandra Pizarnik (1936–1972), Néstor Perlongher (1949–1992), and Diana Bellessi (born 1946).

D. BALDERSTON

The Argentine Press

Argentina has many newspapers and magazines, but the sector declined around the turn of the twenty-first century when circulations decreased because of the recession. At the same time, a growing number of papers have free circulation and are paid for by advertising. The media are largely privately owned, and many daily newspapers are regional, published in a provincial capital and catering to a provincial readership, rather than national. The largest-circulation newspaper in Argentina and Latin America is *Clarín*, which is published in Buenos Aires. *Clarín*'s owners, Grupo Clarín, owns television and radio stations, cable TV operations, and is an Internet provider. While *Clarín* is generally centrist, the other mass-circulation newspaper in Buenos Aires, *La Nación*, is right-wing. International agencies report that Argentine journalists are sometimes threatened with libel action by provincial officials.

Art and Architecture

Argentine art ranges from pre-Columbian ruins and artifacts to notable examples of Spanish colonial architecture. However, Argentina's artistic heritage is perhaps best known for the French-influenced nineteenth-century architecture of its national capital, Buenos Aires, which is sometimes known as the "Paris of South America."

Although Argentina lacks the impressive pre-Columbian monuments of some Latin American countries, it was home to widely varying cultures before the arrival of the Spanish in the first half of the sixteenth century. Early hunter-gatherer societies made rock paintings, such as those at the Cueva de las Manos in Santa Cruz province, the earliest of which date from the eighth century BCE. The most extensive pre-Columbian remains survive in the Andean region in the northwest of the country, where many settled cultures flourished and made pottery vessels, metal objects (particularly in bronze), and woven textiles. The Quebrada de Humahuaca, the valley of the Río Grande, long a trade route and place of settlement, contains architectural remains, including terraced fields and *pucará* (defensive, stone-built, fortified settlements), which date from around 1000 CE onward. *Pucarás* at Tilcara and Quilmes have been restored as examples.

SPANISH COLONIZATION

The arrival of Spanish conquistadors and missionaries in the sixteenth century initiated far-reaching cultural changes in the region. The first significant colonial cities were established in the region by expeditions sent by the authorities of the viceroyalty (administrative region) of Peru, which, at the time, included most of the Spanish possessions in South America. The first cities included Santiago del Estero (in 1551), San Miguel de Tucumán (1565), Córdoba (1573), Salta (1582), La Rioja (1591), and Jujuy (1592). The towns were laid out on a grid plan around a large square (*plaza major*), which was surrounded by a government house, city hall, and church. The materials used in their construction varied according to locality. In Salta, for example, the first houses had stone walls and wooden roofs, while in Córdoba—which was initially the center of the region—the buildings were of adobe (mud brick) and thatch. As elsewhere in Latin America, a local variant of the highly decorative baroque style became widespread in the seventeenth and eighteenth centuries.

The Jesuit order played an important role in the colonization of northern Argentina and in the creation of religious art and architecture. The Jesuits constructed fine buildings for their city headquarters in Córdoba—the Manzana Jesuítica (the so-called Jesuit Block and a UNESCO World Heritage Site since 2000), which included the church of La Compañia (1645–1674) and the university (1613)—and established *reducciones* (reductions), large, self-sufficient communities where the local Amerindians were housed and converted to Christianity. One of the best preserved of these colonies in Argentina is San Ignacio Miní, in Misiones province. Founded in 1611, it follows a standard design, with a church, school, house for the Jesuits, and dwellings for the Amerindians, arranged around a large square. The Jesuits also set up workshops to train indigenous artisans, using religious paintings and sculptures from Bolivia and Peru, as well as from Europe, as models. Local artists became skilled at oil painting and the creation of carved and gilded decorations, retables, and pulpits in the baroque style. Fine examples of their work include the stone carving at San Ignacio Miní and the carved and gilded pulpit in Jujuy Cathedral. In the mid-eighteenth century the Spanish attacked the *reducciones*, expelled the surviving Jesuits and Amerindians, and left the communities to fall into ruin.

DECORATIVE ARTS

The missions and growing cities also created a demand for ecclesiastical and domestic gold and silverwork. Like other art forms, this work reflected the baroque styles of Bolivia and Peru, although often with more restrained forms, and was also influenced by artists from Europe. Silver accessories for horses and riders became increasingly popular in the nineteenth century, including mounts for stirrups, bridles, and saddles, as

This decorated saddle is typical of the intricate leatherwork that is traditionally produced for gauchos in Argentina.

Palacio Barolo on Avenida de Mayo in Buenos Aires is a grand townhouse built in the French style in the 1920s.

well as spurs, daggers, whips, drinking horns, and flint strikers for gauchos. The region developed a leatherwork tradition, including high-quality saddlery and horse tack.

ART AND ARCHITECTURE IN NINETEENTH-CENTURY ARGENTINA

After Argentina achieved independence in 1816, art and architecture flourished when the authorities in the major provinces recruited architects from Europe to work in Argentine cities. Spanish and Italian, as well as French and British, architects designed many official buildings in fashionable European styles, notably the neoclassical and Renaissance styles. A number of European artists, such as the British painter Emeric Essex Vidal (1791–1861), also came to Argentina, depicting the landscapes and people of the Río de la Plata region around the rapidly expanding city of Buenos Aires.

The burgeoning of Argentine art and architecture came in the closing decades of the nineteenth century, however, as a result of the huge economic growth of Buenos Aires and the city's final undisputed assumption of the role of national capital in the 1850s. From the 1880s, Buenos Aires was transformed following the example of Baron Georges-Eugène Haussman (1809–1891), who remodeled Paris, in the 1850s and 1860s. Wide avenues, long vistas, squares, and parks were laid out, and the French Beaux-Arts style, with its classical features and mansard roofs, was widely adopted. The Argentine architect Antonio Buschiazzo (1846–1917) created the gracious Avenida de Mayo (1888–1894), and key buildings such as the Congreso Nacional (Congress building; 1898–1906), Casa de Gobierno (government palace; 1885–1898), and Teatro Colón (1908) all date from this time.

The period also saw a flowering of Argentine painting and sculpture, promoted by the foundation of the Escuela Nacional de Bellas Artes (1878) and the Museo Nacional de Bellas Artes (1895–1896). The realist style, as taught in the art academies of Europe, was favored by the government for the monuments and sculptures celebrating Argentine national heroes that it commissioned to adorn public spaces. Leading painters such as Ernesto de la Cárcova (1866–1927), Eduardo Sívori (1847–1918), and Angel Della Valle (1855–1903) had academic training but often turned to local, everyday subjects.

MODERN ART AND ARCHITECTURE

Although Argentina suffered economic downturn and periods of military government during the twentieth century, Argentine architects and artists continued to engage with current trends in the arts. The art nouveau, art deco, and modernist styles all took root in Buenos Aires. The city got its first skyscraper in 1923 with the 22-story Palacio Barolo. Clorindo Testa (born 1923) emerged as one of the most innovative urbanists and architects of the 1960s and 1970s. At the turn of the twenty-first century, glass-and-steel high-rise buildings such as the sleek Edificio Telefónica (completed 1997) designed by Argentine-born architect César Pelli (born 1926), transformed the skyline of the capital. Among Pelli's international commissions are the Manhattan World Financial Center, in New York City, and the Petronas Towers, in Kuala Lumpur, Malaysia, at one time the tallest building in the world.

Many Argentine artists in the twentieth century used their work to explore social themes and injustice, notably the Artistas de Pueblo group, the painter Antonio Berni (1905–1981), and the sculptor Rogelio Yrurtia (1879–1950). Artists also brought their own interpretation to experimental tendencies emerging in Western art: they included the painter Xul Solar (1888–1963) and other artists of the Grupo de Florida; the sculptor Antonio Sibellino (1891–1962), who experimented with abstraction; Emilio Pettoruti (1892–1971), who pursued cubism; and Juan Batlle Planas (1911–1966), who worked in a surrealist vein. From 1959, the Art Informel movement explored abstract expressionism, while artists such as Eduardo Macentyre (1873–1932) practiced geometric abstraction. Others, such as the sculptors Alberto Heredia (1924–2000) and Juan Carlos Distéfano (born 1933), dealt with political themes. Early in the twenty-first century, Argentine artists were working in a wide variety of approaches and media, from figurative painting to digital technology. Leading artists include Gumier Maier (born 1953), Marcelo Pombo (born 1959), Pablo Siquier (born 1961), Rosana Fuentes (born 1962), and experimental theater director Guillermo Kuitca (born 1961).

R. BEAN

Music and Performing Arts

Argentine music and performing arts are among the most diverse in Latin America, absorbing elements of European and African as well as Amerindian cultures. Argentina has a longer tradition of classical music than most Latin American states, but the country is most famous for the music of the tango, also the national dance.

European, largely Spanish and Italian, sacred and courtly music was introduced to the region from the sixteenth century onward, in the Spanish colonial era. The main centers of musical education were in the city of Córdoba and the missions along the Paraná and Paraguay rivers, where Jesuits were active in teaching and often used music to help convert local peoples. In Buenos Aires, the first opera house opened in 1757, mostly performing an Italian repertoire but also playing compositions by local residents such as the Italian-born Bartolomé Massa (1721–1796), who set to music several comedies by Spanish dramatist Pedro Calderón de la Barca (1600–1681).

Spanish musical genres and instruments were introduced to the region, and, by the time Argentina gained independence in the early nineteenth century, those musical traditions were firmly established in the country's culture. Many musicians and composers were of indigenous or African origin, among them the cembalist and instrument maker José Antonio Ortiz (1764–1794), who was a Guaraní Amerindian, and the violinist Teodoro H. Guzmán (1750–1794).

CANDOMBE

Afro-Argentines were influential in the development of music in Argentina. African dances, known under the generic name of *candombe*, were based on drumming and were accompanied by cane flutes, with a call-and-response style of singing providing the melody line. In Argentina, *candombes* became public parades during carnival as well as on religious and civic holidays. Often prohibited because of public disorder in the eighteenth and nineteenth centuries, *candombe* reached the height of popularity in the 1830s and 1840s, when up to 6,000 members of African societies in Buenos Aires (the Banguela, Angola, Conga, and Mondongo) escorted their ceremonial "kings" and "queens" to the central Plaza de la Victoria. The *candombe* tradition survives in *murga* (carnival) societies, which combine dance and percussion with satirical songs and dialogues during carnival parades. *Candombe* is also one of the roots of tango, a musical form that began to develop in the mid-nineteenth century when black musicians started to adapt their African repertoire to European social dances. Leading Afro-Argentine musicians included Fernando Espinosa (1820–1872), who was a pianist and composer of waltzes, mazurkas, and polkas, and Zenón Rolón (1856–1902), who wrote several operas and operettas.

CLASSICAL MUSIC

Opera became popular in Argentine cities in the last decades of the nineteenth century. In 1854 alone, 30 new productions of operas were staged in Buenos Aires. The country's leading opera house, Buenos Aires's Teatro Colón, opened in 1856 with a production of *La Traviata*—by Italian composer Giuseppe Verdi (1813–1901)—featuring gaslight illumination and modern stage technology. Internationally acclaimed singers and conductors have performed at Teatro Colón, and the nation's prosperity, as well as strong Italian and Spanish cultural influences, encouraged a flourishing classical music sector. Argentine composers include Alberto Ginastera (1916–1983), who wrote piano and chamber music as well as operas.

The tango combines elements of African and Amerindian dances with European social dance. Its popularity in Argentina revived in the late twentieth century.

Revolutionary singer-songwriter Mercedes Sosa (born 1935) was banned from returning to her native Argentina until the fall of the military dictatorship in 1983.

MODERN MUSIC

In the second half of the twentieth century, Argentine singers faced censorship under two military regimes, from 1966 through 1973, and from 1976 through 1983. Some musicians were forced into exile abroad in order to continue performing. The singer Mercedes Sosa (born 1935), known as the "Voice of Latin America," suffered harassment from the authorities after she released several politically and socially critical songs. Sosa lived in France and Italy during her time in exile.

In modern times, Buenos Aires is a major center of Spanish-language rock music. This style of music dates back to the mid-1960s, when a Uruguayan band called Los Shakers became popular. Young Argentine musicians, including the band Los Gatos, initially copied the styles of British bands but soon developed their own particular style of rock, which drew on traditional Argentine music. Argentine rock became popular throughout Spanish-speaking South America, and rock bands such as La Renga, Los Redontitos (whose songs are known for their powerful existential lyrics and controversial subjects), and Divididos had a large following throughout the continent into the twenty-first century. Local musicians, such as keyboard player Charly García (born 1951) and guitarist Luis Alberto Spinetta (born 1950), have also been very influential in the emergence and development of rock music in Latin America.

Tango

Tango, Argentina's most famous and universal cultural export, was initially scorned because of its low social origins. The dance emerged around 1870 in the brothels and bars of the working-class suburbs and docks of Buenos Aires. A word of African origin, *tango* became the name of a new dance combining the native traditions of the *milonga* and the Afro-Argentine *candombe* with European social dances. Its novelty lay in the erotically charged way in which it introduced *candombe* movements into the *pareja abrazada* (literally, "embraced couple") of European-style ballroom dancing, the *quebrada* ("break," a rapid contortion with one leg enveloping that of the partner), and the *corte* ("cut," a suggestive, sudden pause in the movement).

Early tango lyrics were often sexually explicit, praised suburban rogues (*compadrito*s), and denounced social misery. The new dance became popular in the brothels of the wealthier districts, where most musicians, such as the pianist Rosendo Mendizábal (1868–1913), performed. Tango sheet music, usually for piano, was published from the 1890s, and the most successful pieces sold up to 100,000 copies. A purged form of the dance, the *tango liso* ("smooth tango"), was incorporated into middle-class leisure by 1900, and professional tango dancers, such as "El Cachafaz" (Ovidio José Bianquet; 1885–1942), started to appear. Guitar ensembles and trios composed of violin, *bandoneón* (similar to a concertina), and piano first recorded tangos around 1900 and, by 1910, the predominant formation was the more opulent *orquesta típica*, also featuring a double bass.

A more lyrical tango repertoire had started to appear with the 1912 song "Mi noche triste" (My sad night), by poet and guitarist Pascual Contursi (1888–1932), which nostalgically invoked lost loves and Buenos Aires neighborhoods (barrios). The song's first performer, Carlos Gardel (1891–1935), became tango's most famous star, touring the United States and Europe and appearing in several Hollywood films. *Tango de salón* (literally, "tango for the ballroom") conquered Paris around 1910, making it socially acceptable for upper-class Argentines to dance at home. In the 1920s and 1930s, the tango was popular in the elite ballrooms of downtown Buenos Aires. Large orchestras, such as those of *bandoneonist* Aníbal Troilo (1914–1975) and pianist Osvaldo Pugliese (1905–1995), performed a more complex and melodic tango repertoire. From the 1950s, lack of innovation in music led to a decline until *bandoneonist* and composer Astor Piazzolla (1921–1992) introduced the revolutionary *tango nuevo*, incorporating contemporary classical and jazz influences. At the end of the twentieth century, the tango became a popular dance again, and, in modern times, the tango remains the musical signature of Argentina.

DANCE

Outside Buenos Aires, regional folk music often combines European dances such as the polka or the contre dance with Amerindian and mestizo traditions, mostly performed by couples or groups of dancers facing one another with little or no physical contact. Variations of the Andean *huayno* (a rhythmic, accelerated dance) and *yaraví* (a melancholic, melodic dance) are

Argentine Film

The Argentine film industry is one of the most respected in Latin America. Despite experiencing censorship and political repression as recently as during the military dictatorship from 1976 through 1983, Argentina's new filmmakers have produced several influential and award-winning films in the last decades of the twentieth century and into the twenty-first century.

In 1897, Eugene Py (1859–1924), a French photographer living in Argentina, shot *La bandera Argentina* (The Argentine flag), heralding the beginning of the country's film industry. Over the next 30 years, Argentine filmmakers produced more than two hundred silent movies, including comedies, thrillers, and dramas. The arrival of sound, in 1933, and the establishment of film companies, such as Argentina Sono Film, brought a new impetus to movie production. By the 1950s, Argentina released more than 40 films a year, many of which were exported all over Latin America. Notable filmmakers of this period include Luis Moglia Barth (1903–1984), who directed the hugely successful movie *Tango!* (1933), and Francisco Múgica (born 1907), who directed the 1939 comedy *Así es la vida* (Such is life).

During the administration of Juan Perón (1895–1974; in office 1946–1955 and 1973–1974), government intervention in the film industry increased; there was extreme censorship, blacklisting, and interference in the distribution of certain films. One of the artists who suffered from blacklisting was the actor and singer Libertad Lamarque (1908–2000), who allegedly slapped a young actor named Eva Duarte (1919–1952); she later became more famous as Perón's wife and was known more popularly as Evita.

Competition from films imported from North America and Europe gradually resulted in a decline in the popularity of domestically produced movies, although in the period after Perón's fall from power, the government set about promoting the domestic industry. In 1957, the Cinema Act was passed and the Instituto Nacional de Cinematografía (INC, National Cinema Institute) was created. Prominent filmmakers of this period included Leopoldo Torre Nilsson (1924–1978), who helped bring Argentine film to an international audience with his 1957 movie *La casa del angel* (released in the United States as *The Age of Innocence*). Also in the 1950s, Fernando Birri (born 1925) founded the first documentary film school in Argentina. Birri was one of many filmmakers later forced into exile because of his opposition to the 1946–1973 military government. Among the important filmmakers to come to prominence in the 1960s as part of the so-called Third Wave of Cinema (a genre of films with a leftist stance) was Fernando E. Solanas (born 1936), who along with the Cine Liberacion collective made the influential *La hora de los hornos* (The hours of the furnaces) in 1966.

In the 1970s and 1980s, the Argentine film industry suffered from both the repressive censorship of military dictatorships and an economic downturn. Domestic production fell, and Argentine distributors began exhibiting greater numbers of foreign-made films. In 1983, Argentine film production was at an all-time low—just 12 films—and more than 40 percent of foreign films shown in the country originated in the United States. During this period, cinema attendance also fell by 50 percent, as did the actual number of cinema houses, which declined from more than 2,000 to fewer than 1,000. The government tried to promote domestic film and ended censorship. By the end of 1984, domestic production had more than doubled.

In the 1980s, Argentine cinema again began to attract international attention through such films as the 1985 movie *La historia oficial* (The official version), which won its director, Luis Puenzo (born 1949), an Oscar for best foreign-language film, and the 1989 movie *La boda secreta* (The secret wedding) by Alejandro Gresti (born 1961). In 1994, the government passed a law applying new taxes to videos and films broadcast on television, a percentage of which was meant to subsidize Argentine film. The screening of *Historias Breves*, a collection of short films, in 1995 marked the beginning of *el nuevo cine argentino* (new wave of Argentine film). At the end of the twentieth century and into the twenty-first century, Argentine film saw a resurgence through the movies of such filmmakers as Fabián Bielinsky (born 1959), Lucretia Martel (born 1966), Esteban Sapir (born 1967), and Pablo Trapero (born 1974).

---

danced in northern Argentina. Other dances include the playful *carnavalito*, as well as slower dances such as the *vidalita*, mostly accompanied by the *vigüela*, a small guitar. The *chamamé*, popular in Corrientes and the northeast, is a derivative of the European polka. The *milonga*, accompanied by a guitar, is a rural precursor of the tango. *Payadores*, the performers of the *milonga*, often challenged each other to poetic duels (*payadas*), during which each contender improvised poetry to the accompaniment of a guitar.

THEATER

Argentine theater has its origins in the circus, where performers such as actor and clown José Podestá (1858–1937) performed short pantomimes based on popular serial novels. The gaucho adventure *Juan Moreira* by Eduardo Gutiérrez (1851–1889) was adapted for the stage by Podestá in 1884. Other traditions include the *sainete*, a broad comedy of Spanish origin, transformed into so-called Creole Grotesque by writers such as Armando Discépolo (1887–1971). Such works combined absurd humor with acid social critique. Argentine theater features a combination of dramatic acting, pantomime, acrobatics, and dance, and this has influenced the creations of the avant-garde Teatro Abierto (founded 1981), whose plays protested the military dictatorship of 1976 to 1983. Other theater and dance companies that have been influenced by these features include the De la Guarda theater and dance company (founded in Buenos Aires in 1993), whose performances, which tour internationally, often are interactive spectacles.

J. ANDERMANN, E. M. STONE

Festivals and Ceremonies

Argentines celebrate around 15 days of public holidays every year. Some are religious holidays, and others mark events in the history of the nation. Argentina also hosts a wide variety of festivals, some of which attract international attention.

The overwhelming majority of Argentines are Roman Catholics, and major Christian religious feasts and celebrations are public holidays in Argentina. Maundy Thursday, Good Friday, the Immaculate Conception (December 8), Christmas Eve (a half-day holiday), and Christmas Day are all holidays. All Saints' Day (Día de Todos Santos), November 1, is also widely celebrated, although it is not a formal public holiday. Before Lent, Buenos Aires holds a spectacular carnival, which culminates on Shrove Tuesday (Mardi Gras).

FESTIVALS

Most cities and towns in Argentina have local festivals, usually the feast day of a patron saint. Other festivals are cultural, such as the National Folklore Festival, which has been held every year in Cosquin, in late January since 1961. The festival attracts musicians and dancers from across Argentina. The city of Mendoza, situated at the foot of the Andes, is the center of Argentina's wine-producing region. In late February, Mendoza holds the Fiesta Nacional de la Vendimia, a wine festival to celebrate the grape harvest of the region's grape, the Malbec. Each district of the city selects a "princess" to compete in the Reina de la Vendimia ("harvest queen") competition and holds a parade of floats during two days of the fiesta.

Buenos Aires, the Argentine national capital, stages an annual tango festival, honoring the national dance. Both Buenos Aires and Mar del Plata hold film festivals, while Bue international music festival, featuring rock and world music, is also held in Buenos Aires. At Villa General Belgrano, in Córdoba province, a German-style Oktoberfest is held, introduced by German settlers in the region. Oberá, in Misiones province, stages the Immigrants' Festival, which features performers from the many different nationalities that have settled in Argentina.

SECULAR HOLIDAYS

May 25 is Revolucion de Mayo (May Revolution or Revolution Day), which marks the installation in Buenos Aires in 1810 of the first junta (government) that was effectively independent of the Spanish authorities. In modern times, not only is May 25, the National Day, an annual public holiday, but a variety of other events in the week leading up to the holiday are also celebrated during the so-called Semana de Mayo (May Week).

Día de la Bandera, or Flag Dag, is held on June 20, the anniversary of the death of General Manuel Belgrano (1770–1820), one of the leaders of the revolution that brought Argentina independence. Belgrano is said to have designed the flag in 1812 before a battle along the banks of the Paraná River at Rosario. The light blue and white stripes are believed to represent the way the clouds parted in the sky before the battle. August 17, the anniversary of the death of General José de San Martín (1778–1850), who was instrumental in the Argentine independence struggle and also helped liberate Chile, Bolivia, and Peru, is also a public holiday. July 9, Independence Day, celebrates the anniversary of the declaration of independence by an Argentine assembly at San Miguel de Tucumán in 1816. The anniversary of the landing of Christopher Columbus in the New World in 1492, Día de la Raza ("race day," commemorating the first contact between Europeans and Amerindians), is marked on October 12.

Argentina has always disputed British possession of the Falkland Islands (Islas Malvinas), and June 10, Dia de las Malvinas (Malvinas Day), commemorates the Argentine claim. The Day of the War Veterans and the Fallen in the Malvinas Islands, on April 2, marks the landing of Argentine forces on the islands in 1982.

D. TORRA, J. ANDERMANN

Members of the Kamarr carnival group perform during the popular annual Carnaval del Pais in Gualeguaychú.

Sports in Argentina

Sports play an important role in Argentine culture and, in international competition, success in team sports, as well as the exploits of individual sportswomen and sportsmen, contribute to the national identity. Argentina first gained success in equestrian sports. The equestrian skills demanded by a rural cattle economy in nineteenth-century Argentina led to the development of activities in which riders could show their strengths and compete against other people. The *doma* was a public taming of horses, similar to the North American rodeo, while the *pato* (literally, "duck"), which was first recorded in 1611, is a team sport in which two groups of riders have to drive a rubber ball (originally a duck in a bag, hence the name) through a hoop at the opposite end of the field. The similarity of skills required helps explain the success of polo, which was introduced to Argentina by British residents in 1875. The River Plate Polo Association was founded in 1892, and the wealthy Argentine Heguy family promoted the sport. In the Paris Olympics of 1924, the Argentine team won the first of many gold medals in polo. In modern times, Argentina, which breeds some of the world's finest polo ponies, is one of the few nations in which polo is a professional sport.

British residents in Argentina introduced other sports that were initially upper-class pastimes, including rowing (with the first regattas organized in 1871) and rugby and field hockey (which established Argentine federations in 1899 and 1908, respectively). Argentina is now the leading rugby-playing nation in the Americas.

Spanish immigrants introduced ball games such as the *frontón* or *pelota vasca* (Basque ball) around 1800. A century later, Italian settlers founded Argentina's first cycling club. Tennis became fashionable in the first decades of the twentieth century, but it was only from the 1970s that Argentine players such as Guillermo Vilas (born 1952), José Luis Clerc (born 1958), and Gabriela Sabatini (born 1970) would win major tournaments. Basketball became a major team sport, particularly in the main cities of the interior, from the 1930s. In 1950, Argentina beat the United States to win the first FIBA (International Basketball Federation) world championship in a contest held in Buenos Aires.

Boxing became popular when, in 1923, the Argentine Luis Angel Firpo (1894–1960), known as the "Bull of the Pampas," narrowly lost his challenge for the world heavyweight title against U.S. boxer Jack Dempsey (1895–1983). Motor sports are also popular in Argentina, and Juan Manuel Fangio (1911–1995), Argentina's most famous Formula-1 competitor, was five-time world champion in the 1950s.

Undoubtedly the most popular sport in Argentina is soccer. The first local club, the Buenos Aires Football Club, was founded in 1867 by British residents, almost exclusively comprising British members. Belgrano Athletic and English High School soon followed, also with British players and followers. Toward the end of the century, local players started to be admitted, but the game's ethos continued to be based on an elite value system of amateurism. With the appearance of clubs dominated by Argentines and Italian immigrants, such as the archrivals River Plate (founded 1901) and Boca Juniors (1905), in the working-class neighborhoods of southern Buenos Aires, players started becoming professional, and a new style of play emerged, based on individual dribbling skills. In 1925, Boca Juniors toured Europe, beating major European teams as well as the French national selection.

Celebrated Argentine sportsman Juan Fangio (1911–1995) won four Formula 1 motor-racing world titles with four different teams: Alfa Romeo, Ferrari, Maserati, and Mercedes-Benz.

In the first soccer World Cup, held in neighboring Uruguay in 1930, Argentina only lost to the hosts in the final. The *albiceleste* (or "white-and-blues," as the national team is known for its shirt colors) won its first soccer World Cup at home in 1978. A second world title followed in 1986, when the Argentine selection was captained by arguably its most famous player, Diego Maradona (born 1960).

Food and Drink

Argentine cuisine is characterized by its superb beef and by the influence of recipes introduced from Europe. Argentine cooking is considered to be more Mediterranean in style than the cuisines of other Latin American countries.

Argentines normally eat three meals a day: a light breakfast, a more substantial lunch around midday, and a late dinner, which is eaten around nine o'clock in the evening. Meat, particularly beef, forms a large part of the Argentine diet, and barbecues (*asador*) and grills (*parallada*) are particularly popular. In addition, light snacks such as empanadas (pastries filled with meat or cheese and vegetables) and *sandwiches de miga* (thin-crusted sandwiches filled with ham and cheese) are popular. Donutlike sweets called *churros*, served plain or filled with the popular *dulce de leche* (made from boiled milk and sugar) or chocolate, are also favorites. *Dulce de leche* is also used in other desserts and cookies such as *alfajores* (shortbread sandwiched with *dulce de leche* or jam). Cheese is served with quince jam (*dulce de membrillo*).

Argentines often hold barbecues on Sundays, gathering family and friends to dine together. Traditionally, the whole animal is cooked on an iron cross and everything from the offal to the best cuts is consumed. At these events, salads, baked potatoes, and pasta may also be served. *Paralladas* are also extremely popular and typically feature chicken, ribs, beef, and sausages, although sweet breads (*mollejas*), offal, and intestines may also be served. *Parillas* (restaurants serving mixed grills) are popular throughout the country. Meat from the cattle regions of central Argentina, the Pampas, is readily available and affordable throughout Argentina, and *carne asado* (barbecued beef) and breaded meats are often eaten. Spanish dishes such as tortillas and paella are also common.

ITALIAN AND GERMAN DISHES

From the late nineteenth century, large number of Italians settled in Argentina. As a result, Italian foods such as pizza and pasta are common and, in central Argentina, where the majority of Italian Argentines live, these dishes have been adapted to become regional dishes. Pasta, such as *sorrentinos* (stuffed with mozzarella and basil, and served with tomato sauce), is often served with bread, a style not typical in Italy. The influence of German settlers in Argentina can be seen in sweets and desserts such as *facturas* (pastries).

REGIONAL CUISINE

Indigenous influences are found in the cuisine of northwest Argentina, which includes the areas of Salta and San Miguel de Tucumán. Grains such as quinoa and staples such as avocados and corn form an important part of the local diet and are made into tamales and *el locro*, a corn-based stew. Most of Argentina's best wines also come from this region. Northeastern Argentina is famous for mandioca, rice, freshwater fish (such as dorado, surubí, and boga), and maté (herbal tea). The region produces most of the yerba maté consumed in Argentina and also grows oranges, pineapples, and bananas.

A mixture of many different ethnic groups and habitats give Patagonia and Tierra del Fuego in the south a rich cuisine. Freshwater fish from rivers and barbecued sheep meat from flocks in the open plains are common ingredients. The region's small Welsh community in the Chubut district still makes scones.

DRINK

Argentines drink a lot of coffee. *Cafe chico* (a thick coffee served in a small cup), *cortado* (a small coffee served in a glass with a little milk), and *café con leche* (coffee with a larger serving of milk) are commonly drunk. In northern Argentina in particular, people drink maté, often served as a welcome drink to visitors. Argentina has a thriving wine industry; it also produces whiskey and gin, including *ginebra bols* (a ginlike spirit), as well as *caña* (made from sugarcane), which is a national drink.

J. MONCADA

An Argentine gaucho drinks maté, a traditional herbal tea.

DAILY LIFE

Religion

Argentina is a predominantly Roman Catholic country, with some 91 percent of the population recorded as Catholic. However, fewer than one Argentine in five regularly attends mass and can be regarded as a practicing Catholic. Around 3 percent of Argentines belong to various Protestant churches and 1 percent are Jewish. The remaining 4 percent is made up of members of other faiths, including Muslims (1 percent) and nonreligious people. The constitution protects the right to practice any religious faith.

Catholicism was first introduced into the region by Spanish colonists in the sixteenth century, and missions—particularly of the Jesuits, who began their activities in Salta in 1586—played an important part in colonization. The Catholic Church had a leading role during the Spanish colonial era (from the early sixteenth century through the beginning of the nineteenth century). In the late nineteenth century, Italian Catholic immigrants also settled in Argentina, solidifying the influence of Catholicism.

CHRISTIANITY IN MODERN ARGENTINA

In modern times, there are 70 Catholic dioceses and archdioceses in Argentina, and—although the fourteenth article of the Argentine constitution allows freedom of religion—religious practices in Argentina, and in many cases the nation's politics, are dominated by the Roman Catholic Church. Most Argentine Catholics attend church solely on religious holidays, such as Christmas and Easter, as well as for weddings and funerals, but, despite the gradual implementation of restrictions on the power of the Catholic Church by the state since the establishment of an effective Argentine national government in the 1850s, the church still exercises considerable authority, and its presence is evident through the large cathedrals and other churches in the cities and the ubiquitous small local churches in rural communities. The basilica of Luján and the cathedral at La Plata (one of the largest in the world) are prominent among major Argentine church buildings.

Protestants, who make up about 2 percent of the population, include Anglicans (the descendants of settlers from Great Britain) and Methodists, as well as Lutherans and members of Reformed churches whose ancestors were immigrants from Germany and northern Europe. Various Orthodox churches, including Russian, Greek, and Syrian churches, are also active in Argentina.

Argentina's Secretariat of Worship, part of the Ministry of Foreign Affairs, International Trade, and Worship, handles the government's relations with the Catholic Church and other churches and religious organizations. The Secretariat of Worship maintains a national registry of about 2,800 organizations comprising around 30 religious groups and denominations. The principal Catholic festivals (Good Friday, the Immaculate Conception, and Christmas) are observed as national holidays, and Argentine law allows for paid leave for citizens observing the major Jewish and Islamic holy days.

ISLAM AND JUDAISM

Argentina has the largest Muslim minority population in Latin America, but the number is disputed. Most Argentine Muslims are descended from migrants from Syria and Lebanon in the twentieth century, but the majority of Syrian and Lebanese settlers were either Christian or Jewish. Argentina is also home to the second-largest Jewish population in the Americas, but there are no reliable statistics regarding the size of the Jewish minority. Although the followers of most religious groups and denominations in Argentina coexist peacefully, anti-Semitism is a problem. Jewish community leaders have made claims of anti-Semitism in the Argentine military, and a Jewish cemetery was desecrated in the Buenos Aires suburb of Berazategui in 2002. In July 1994, a bomb leveled the seven-story Israeli-Argentine Mutual Association (AMIA) Jewish community center in downtown Buenos Aires, causing some 100 fatalities, and, in March 1992, a truck filled with explosive materials blew up outside the Israeli embassy in Buenos Aires. There is no proof that Argentine citizens were involved in these attacks and, in August 2003, several Iranian officials were indicted in connection with the AMIA attack. Investigations into

The King Fahd Islamic Cultural Center in Buenos Aires caters to one of the largest communities of Muslims in Latin America. Most Argentine Muslims are Syrian or Lebanese immigrants.

these episodes were incomplete and were still ongoing several years later. Early in the twenty-first century, there were also reports of increasing anti-Muslim agitation in the country.

CATHOLICISM AND ARGENTINE SOCIETY

The Argentine constitution states that the government "sustains the apostolic Roman Catholic faith," and the Catholic Church is given a leading role by the government, receiving approximately $4 million dollars a year in subsidies. These subsidies are primarily used for schools and, despite the freedom of religion defined in the constitution, similar provisions are not offered to other faiths or denominations. Until a constitutional revision of 1994, Argentina's president and vice president had to be Roman Catholics. Despite the change, Argentine political observers still regard it as highly improbable that a non-Catholic could be elected to the presidency.

Catholic feast days are widely celebrated in Argentina. The most notable feast day is held on May 8 for the patron saint of Argentina, the Virgin of Luján. More than 1 million Argentines make the annual pilgrimage—many thousands on foot from Buenos Aires—to Luján, a city about 40 miles (some 64 km) west of the capital. The origins of the festival date to the early 1600s (the precise year varies in different accounts), when a statue of the Virgin Mary was carted from place to place. According to popular legend, the cart became stuck in Luján, and, realizing it could not be moved, the villagers constructed a chapel at the site to protect the statue. The basilica and city of Luján grew up around where the chapel once stood. Another prominent pilgrimage occurs in the far northern city of Salta, where the feast of Our Lord of Miracles is celebrated on September 15.

Although the Catholic Church has tried to remain neutral in political and social crises, it has also increasingly acted as a critic of alleged abuses or wrongs. In the second half of the twentieth century, Catholic leaders initially supported the populist leader Juan Perón (1895–1974; in office 1946–1955 and 1973–1974), because many of his policies were aimed at addressing poverty. However, in 1955, church leaders withdrew their support, after Perón legalized divorce and prostitution.

In the following decades, the Catholic Church often had to work under oppressive conditions. During the military dictatorship of 1976 through 1983, many human rights abuses occurred and opponents of the regime disappeared. In 1979, the military junta's repression of the church helped to virtually eliminate so-called *comunidades* ("base communities") of Catholic movements that were becoming popular in other regions of Latin America and that worked with the poor and disenfranchised.

In modern times, most Argentines do not adhere to the Catholic Church's ruling against the use of contraceptives. There is increasing support in Argentina for the right to have an abortion, which the Catholic Church opposes. In the early twenty-first century, gay civil unions were legalized in Buenos Aires, bringing the civil authorities and the Catholic Church again into conflict.

K. BIAS

Family and Society

Argentine society is strongly influenced by European culture, most Argentines (some 97 percent) are of unmixed European ancestry. Mestizos (people of mixed Amerindian and European ancestry) and Amerindians form a much smaller group than in most South American countries (most of the remaining 3 percent). There are also small Afro-Argentine, Arab, and Asian communities.

As a result of the country's colonial history as a Spanish possession from the mid-sixteenth century through the early nineteenth century, Argentina is overwhelmingly Hispanic. From the mid-nineteenth century onward, large numbers of immigrants came to Argentina from Europe, particularly Italians, British, Germans, and Irish. Argentine culture is closely linked to cultures in Europe. Toward the end of the nineteenth century, Argentina was the leading economic power in Spanish-speaking America. Argentines, particularly those in Buenos Aires (the national capital), followed European fashions and ideas, and it is often claimed that Argentines are more European than Latin American. Argentine Spanish even sounds a little like Italian because of the introduction of Italian inflections and words into the language, and it is, therefore, different from the Spanish spoken in other Latin American countries.

ARGENTINE ITALIANS

Italians form a core element of Argentine society and their influence is important. Many Argentines have Italian names, and it is estimated that nearly one-half of the Argentine population has at least one Italian ancestor. Since the mid-1950s, seven of Argentina's chiefs of state have had Italian family names. Italian Argentines, many of whom maintain ties with family in Italy, are generally prosperous and have professional, middle-class occupations. Italian culture pervades many aspects of Argentine life, and many Argentine musicians, writers, painters, and other artists descend from Italian stock. In modern times, Italian is still the first language of 2 percent of Argentines.

MINORITIES

British settlers in Argentina in the nineteenth century concentrated in the Buenos Aires region but were involved in commercial activities throughout Argentina, for example, in constructing the country's railroads. Modern Argentina has a larger community of people of British ancestry than any other Latin American country, and the Argentine British have an influence out of proportion to their numbers—for example, the majority of private schools in Buenos Aires are British.

Patagonia is home to a small community of Welsh speakers, descended from immigrants from Wales in the late nineteenth century, while northern Argentina and Buenos Aires are home to a small Arab community, largely of Syrian ancestry. Only a minority of the Syrian community, which includes Jews and Christians of different denominations, are Muslims.

Argentina has a much smaller percentage of Amerindians than most South American countries. Guaraní and Quechua Amerindians live in the far north, the former in regions adjoining Paraguay and the latter near the Bolivian border. Tehuelche peoples form a small minority in Patagonia, where Mapuche (or Araucanian) people, who migrated to Patagonia from the western side of the Andes during the Spanish colonial period, also live. A number of different peoples, collectively known as Fuegians, lived in Tierra del Fuego. However, exposure to diseases, such as smallpox and measles, to which the Fuegians had no immunity, decimated their numbers in the nineteenth century, and few Fuegians of unmixed ancestry remain.

FAMILY STRUCTURE

The structure of the Argentine family was shaped by Spanish law and the dominant Roman Catholic faith, which is followed by 91 percent of the population (although around one-fifth are practicing). Argentine families were traditionally patriarchal. The father was seen as the head of the household, while women were responsible for domestic affairs. It was also common for newly married couples and young families to stay in the family home. Family and personal honor were socially important, and the cohesion of the family unit was valued.

In contemporary Argentina, this family structure is no longer widespread. There is a rising trend of nuclear families, smaller units comprising parents and one or two children. Although most domestic work is still done by women, they are becoming more independent by working outside the home and exerting rights of equality within the family. Children tend to stay with the families well into their twenties and usually move out when they begin their own family units. The number of households in which women are the head of the family is also rising. A 2001 official estimate suggests that the principal income earners in at least 27 percent of households in Buenos Aires were women.

The Hurlingham Club, in Buenos Aires, was founded by wealthy British settlers in 1888. The club hosts polo, cricket, golf, tennis, and field hockey and is an important social center for Buenos Aires's influential community of British ancestry.

The social makeup of families has undergone considerable change since the 1950s. Despite the powerful influence of the Roman Catholic Church, divorce was legalized in Argentina in 1986 (divorce had also briefly been allowed from 1955 through 1956), allowing couples to remarry. In modern Argentina, the number of marriages is declining, rates of divorce are increasing, and there is a tendency for couples to cohabit without the formality of marriage. Children born outside marriage are now not uncommon, and there are more single-parent families, which were rare before modern times.

THE ROLE OF WOMEN

Despite traditional legal and social structures that favored men, the influx of European immigrants helped bring a shift in attitudes about gender during the late nineteenth century. Women, mostly from wealthy backgrounds, were enrolled in secondary school by the turn of the twentieth century. Eva Perón (1919–1952), the influential wife of Juan Perón (1895–1974; in office as president of Argentina 1946–1955 and 1973–1974), helped promote improvements in the conditions of working-class women. From the 1950s, large numbers of women were able to participate in the public spheres of work, politics, and education.

The military regime that was in power from 1976 through 1983 placed restrictions on women's rights, attempting to crush the feminist movement and enforcing traditional roles for women. However, in 1977, a group of 14 women began a weekly public protest against the military, demanding information about their (adult) children who had disappeared because of their opposition to the regime. The women became internationally famous as the Mothers of the Plaza de Mayo, named for the Buenos Aires square in which they met. Since the restoration of democratic civilian government in the 1980s, Argentine governments have enacted laws guaranteeing women's rights. In 1994, a constitutional reform introduced a quota system under which 30 percent of candidates for legislative elections must be women. In 2007, Cristina Fernández de Kirchner (born 1953) was elected president.

URBAN AND RURAL POPULATIONS

Around 88 percent of Argentina's people live in urban areas, with one-third in the Buenos Aires metropolitan area. In the second half of the twentieth century, many families migrated to the cities in search of employment, especially during periods of economic difficulty. Cities are divided along social lines, in the case of Buenos Aires with prosperous and middle-class suburbs in the west and poorer districts, including shantytowns with few amenities, in the urban fringe. The iconic view of life in rural Argentina involves a traditional Argentine culture of large ranches (*estancia*s) and cattle-raising gauchos, but, at the turn of the twenty-first century, social divisions in the countryside widened during a severe economic crisis. More than one-third of the rural population are now estimated to live in poverty, and migration from rural areas is extremely high.

Following a severe recession, which affected every sector of society, a class of the so-called "new poor" emerged, many of whom were professionals. The crisis brought social upheaval and violence, and levels of alcoholism, crime, and domestic violence rose. Although the economy has greatly recovered since the 2001 crisis, only a minority have benefited from the upturn, and emigration from Argentina has increased.

R. SIMON-KUMAR

Health and Welfare

By many socioeconomic indicators, Argentina is a modern society. The nation is, in some respects, more European than Latin American—particularly in its citizens' perceptions—and, as a result, Argentines have high expectations concerning the provision of health care and welfare.

At the end of the nineteenth century, Argentina was prosperous and a high standard of living had been achieved, based on great agricultural and mineral resources. However, from the mid-twentieth century and into the twenty-first century, Argentina experienced repeated economic crises, in part because of international recessions and reductions in the prices of the nation's agricultural products on the world market but also because of political instability and huge foreign debt. As a result, trade, unemployment rates, and state revenue fluctuated greatly, and, with different levels of funding available, social security and health care provision also varied. In times of economic crisis, major regional differences in the distribution of wealth as well as class differences and poverty rates increased. In modern times, a new category of "new poor," many of whom are former professionals, emerged because of a severe economic downturn in 2001.

HEALTH

Toward the end of the nineteenth century, Argentine prosperity encouraged large-scale migration from Europe. The consequent rapid growth of Argentine cities brought demands for improvements in sanitation, which the government implemented, but medical care provision was left to the private sector. Labor unions organized insurance programs for their members, known as Obras Sociales, and migrants organized health cooperatives (*mutuales*) based on national backgrounds, neighborhood associations, or church parishes. These institutions also provided a variety of welfare programs from recreational facilities to financial assistance and pension plans. Welfare and health provision remained largely unchanged through the nation's period of great prosperity, which ended with a major world economic downturn from 1929 through the mid-1930s.

In the late 1940s and early 1950s, populist president Juan Perón (1895–1974; in office 1946–1955 and 1973–1974) began greater state intervention in the economy and introduced social benefits for the working class. However, much of the basis of the present health care funding system dates from the 1960s, when membership in the union-based Obras Sociales became obligatory for all workers in the formal labor force. At the same time, medical coverage was extended to the family members of workers. Funding came from a payroll deduction and contributions from employers. A health insurance program (the Integrated Medical Care Program, known as PAMI) was also organized for retired workers and was financed by a deduction from pensions as well as by contributions by workers in the labor force. By 1984, about 75 percent of the population were covered by these programs.

HEALTH CARE REFORMS

The system of Obras Sociales imposed constraints. Workers could, for example, only affiliate to the Obra Social of their own labor union, and, consequently, those workers whose unions had fewer resources or were smaller—and, sometimes, not efficient—received fewer benefits or benefits of lower quality. Increasingly, the Obras Sociales and PAMI contracted out of the system and made agreements with private providers, adding to the costs of the programs. Several unsuccessful attempts were made to reform the system. President Raúl Alfonsin (born 1927; in office 1983–1989) tried to establish a state-run national health insurance program but, for various reasons, the labor unions resisted the attempt. The severe economic crisis of the 1980s added to unemployment and poverty levels, and, by 1991, the number of people covered by the Obras Sociales and PAMI had declined to some 58 percent of the population.

The World Bank, which was involved in helping Argentina toward economic recovery, promoted a model of health care to President Carlos Menem (born 1930; in office 1989–1999), whose government embarked on a neoliberal program of privatization, reducing the functions of the state, making working conditions more flexible, and reducing employers' contribution to workers' health insurance. The health reform program, which was financed by World Bank loans, was based on three basic ideas: decentralizing public health services to the provincial governments, promoting self-management and cost recovery in public hospitals (intended to reduce government hospital funding), and a basic mother-child primary health care package. However, the program did not succeed. Decentralization failed to improve the quality of care or to increase coverage, and autonomy did not improve public hospital efficiency or quality. According to some public health experts, the implementation of the policies led to a decline in health care provision, and private health insurance companies did not opt to invest in Argentina, in part because of worries concerning the nation's economy.

In 2001, Argentina faced the worst economic depression of its history. Income fell, unemployment rapidly increased, and the Obras Sociales, PAMI, and public services declined in quality

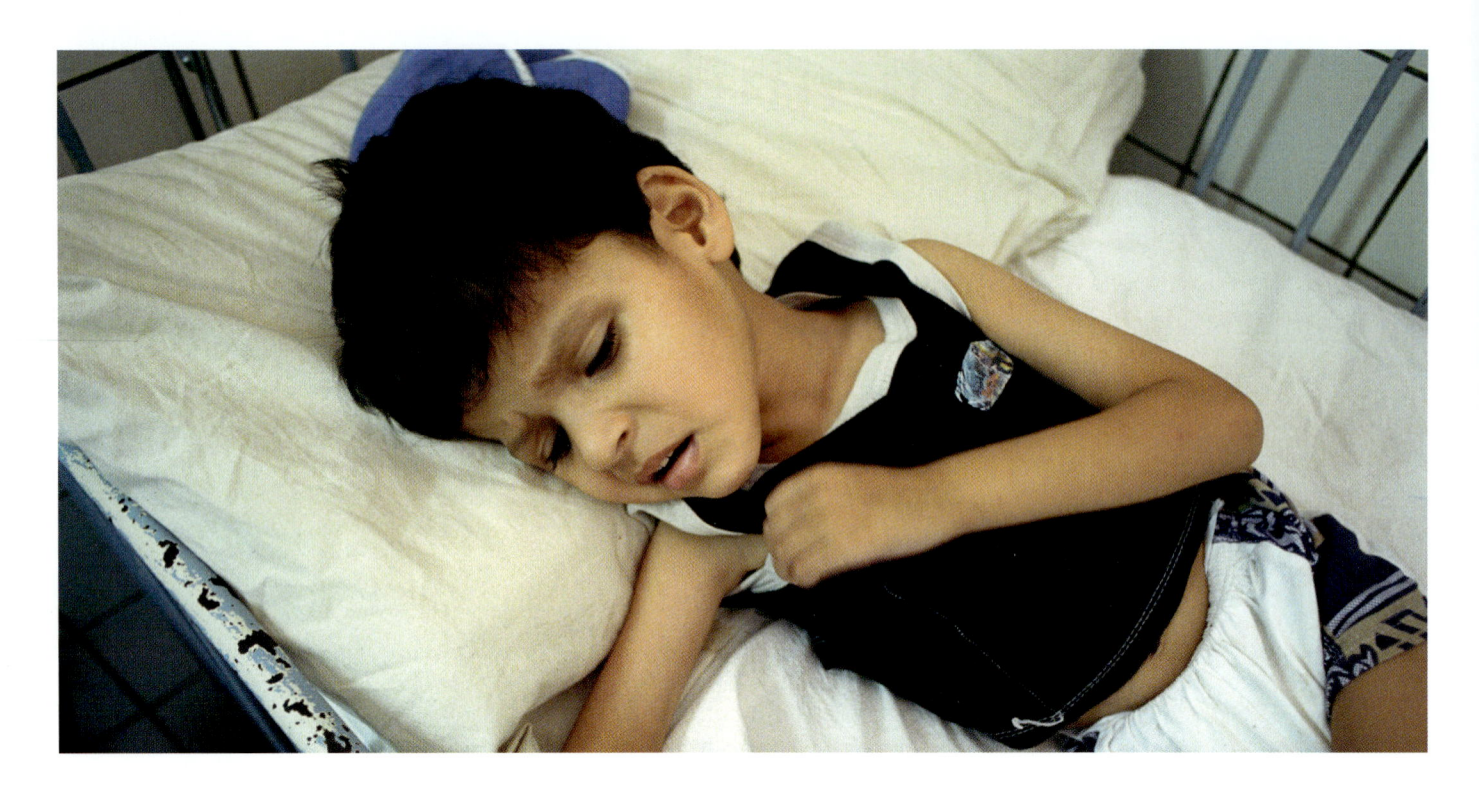

A young patient attends a community clinic in a poor neighborhood of Buenos Aires.

and coverage. A relatively large number of Argentines did not have access to any health services or medications, and the provision of health care became critical.

As the country recovers economically, its health system remains highly fragmented and inefficient. Political conflicts among and within parties, particularly in the regions, delay the organization of a national health system or social insurance program that most modern societies have. However, some health indicators reflect Argentina's modernity and developed-nation status. Life expectancy is high for women, 80.2 years in 2006, although lower for men, 72.6 years in the same year. The principal causes of death are cardiovascular diseases, which account for around one-third of mortality; cancers are the second-largest cause of death. At the same time, the typical communicable diseases of developing societies—such as dengue, chagas, cholera, malaria, yellow fever, and rabies—have either been brought under control or have been eradicated.

The Argentine health care sector employs large numbers of personnel. The nation has, for example, 3.2 physicians per 1,000 people, compared with 2.1 doctors for 1,000 people in Canada. Argentina also has a relatively high provision of hospital beds—4.1 per 1,000, the same figure as Canada. The larger modern hospitals are in the cities and, in some remote rural areas, people must travel a distance to health centers or hospitals. Hospitals and health clinics that cater to the wealthy tend to offer better facilities.

SOCIAL SECURITY

Argentina lacks a comprehensive state-run health care system, but the state social security system covers old-age pensions, unemployment benefits, and disability payments. Two pension programs operate: the Reparto (or RPP) is managed by the state, while the Régimen de Capitalización (known as the Sistema Mixto; literally, "mixed system") is run by private pension funds but is supervised by the state. The Reparto provides a relatively modest basic pension for women from age 60 and men from age 65 and a higher pension for advanced old age, defined as more than 70. The system, which also includes payments for widows, widowers, and dependent children, is funded by employee contributions. The Sistema Mixto provides greater flexibility, with people being able to choose contribution rates through programs run by private companies, although this arrangement may not result in a higher pension than the Reparto.

HOUSING

Wealthy Argentines live in villas, on estancias in the countryside, and in elegant townhouses and apartments in cities such as Buenos Aires; the middle-classes tend to live in suburban communities that resemble the residential districts of U.S. cities. Around 20 percent of the population, however, live in neighborhoods in which housing needs have not been met and public health and sanitation standards are low; for example, they lack drinking water and indoor toilets and have dirt or temporary floors. Argentina's rural communities make up around 12 percent of the population, and housing in rural areas tends to be in traditional single-story, single-family adobe (mud brick) houses.

A. UGALDE, N. HOMEDES

Education

Education is highly valued in Argentina—around 97 percent of the population are literate—and, despite the economic and political upheavals experienced in the country in the second half of the twentieth century, Argentine governments, including military regimes, have invested heavily in education.

The government of Domingo Sarmiento (1811–1888; in office 1868–1874) was the first to develop a set of initiatives for public education in Argentina. A noted educator, writer, and believer in free thinking, he saw universal education as necessary for Argentine citizens to develop and prosper economically. Sarmiento founded public schools and public libraries, and the implementation of his policies doubled enrollment in schools. Public support for education continued, and, in 1884, under the presidency of Julio A. Roca (1843–1914; in office 1880–1886 and 1898–1904), Law 1420, General Common Education, was passed, making public, free, secular education compulsory in Argentina.

The overwhelming majority of Argentines are Roman Catholic, and, in the nineteenth and early twentieth centuries, the Catholic Church made several attempts to influence the educational system. In 1943, religious education was introduced as a compulsory subject in school, but it was withdrawn again in 1954, when relations between the government and the church authorities deteriorated after divorce was legalized. At different times in the twentieth century, Argentina was ruled by military governments, and, particularly under the junta from 1976 to 1983, the authorities attempted to use the educational system to disseminate and promote their ideology.

Most wealthier Argentine students, particularly in Buenos Aires, attend private schools, such as this one. Most private facilities are run along the lines of British private schools.

THE SCHOOL SYSTEM

More than 88 percent of school-age children enroll and complete primary and secondary (high-school) education. Following legislation in 2006, all Argentine students must complete 13 years of compulsory education. Pupils who fail to pass a grade level must generally repeat it. Students enter primary school at age 6 after kindergarten, which is not compulsory, and must remain within the educational system until age 18. Schooling is divided into primary (Educación General Básica, known as EGB) and secondary (called Polimodal) education. Both primary and high schools follow a common national curriculum set by the Argentine National Council of Education. At high school, the curriculum includes Spanish, a foreign language (normally English), math, social sciences, natural sciences, physical education, information science, and life skills (including sex education, which was introduced in 2006, despite protests by the Catholic Church).

The country has nearly 10 million students (from kindergarten through university level), the majority of whom are in public schools. Argentine private schools generally offer better facilities and obtain higher examination grades. While public schools offer free tuition, parents must pay for books, other materials, and transportation. Although schooling in Argentina is considered to be among the best in Latin America, rural education is not as well resourced as schools in the city, and because of the poverty in some rural families, it is not uncommon for children to drop out of school after age 11.

UNIVERSITIES

The first Argentine university was opened by Jesuit priests in Córdoba in 1622. Today, there are 97 universities, 43 public (at which tuition is free) and 54 private. In the 1990s, a program of university expansion included the foundation of 22 private and 12 public universities. Argentine universities offer academic and vocational courses. To enter university, secondary students must attend five years of high school education and pass the *bachillerato* exam. The main language of instruction is Spanish, but the government encourages English-language study, which it believes is essential for international communication. As well as the universities, there are more than 1,000 colleges in Argentina, offering higher and further education courses.

R. SIMON-KUMAR

Buenos Aires

Buenos Aires, the Argentine national capital, is home to one-third of the population of Argentina. At the 2001 census, the metropolitan area had 12,047,000 inhabitants, and 2,769,000 people lived within the city limits. The metropolitan area includes San Justo–La Matanza (which had 1,254,000 inhabitants in 2001), Lomas de Zamora (591,000), Quilmes (519,000), Almirante Brown (514,000), Merlo (469,000), Lanus (453,000), and General San Martín (405,000).

Buenos Aires adjoins the Pampa Húmeda (the humid pampa), one of the most productive agricultural regions in the world. The region produces beef, dairy products, wheat, corn, tobacco, lamb and wool, and a range of other products, which are processed in the Buenos Aires metropolitan area. When the Pampas region was settled by Spanish, Italian, and other immigrants in the late nineteenth century, ranches were established and a network of railroads and highways was built, converging on Buenos Aires. As a result, the city became a major port, exporting the agricultural produce of the region. However, Rosario, along the Paraná River, remained Argentina's major port for exports until 1942, and Buenos Aires has not always been the unchallenged leading city of Argentina.

BUENOS AIRES IN HISTORY

The first Spanish explorers came to the region in 1516, but opposition from the local Amerindians discouraged them from establishing a settlement. In 1536, the Spanish founded Ciudad de Nuestra Señora Santa María del Buen Ayre (literally, "the city of Our Lady Saint Mary of the Good Air"), but Amerindians attacked the settlement, which was abandoned in 1541. The focus of Spanish settlement moved upstream along the Paraná River, and Asunción, now the national capital of Paraguay, became the leading city in southeastern Spanish South America.

In 1580, an expedition from Asunción refounded Buenos Aires, and the port along the wide estuary of the Río de la Plata began to develop. By the seventeenth century, Buenos Aires was one of the leading cities in the region. However, development was held back by the insistence of the Spanish colonial authorities to route trade through Lima, the capital of the vast viceroyalty of Peru, which initially covered most of the Spanish possessions in South America. In 1776, the huge viceroyalty was divided, and Buenos Aires became the administrative center and focus of trade for the new viceroyalty of the Río de la Plata, which included not only present-day Argentina but also Paraguay and Uruguay. As a result, Buenos Aires grew rapidly.

In 1806 and 1807, the British unsuccessfully attempted to invade the Río de la Plata estuary, which had become a center of growing opposition to Spanish rule. The advantages in trade long enjoyed by Lima had been deeply resented in Buenos Aires, whose citizens were at the forefront of the nationalist movement that developed from 1810, when an autonomous junta—to rule the region while Spain was under French occupation—was declared in Buenos Aires. However, the decisive step toward nationhood was taken not in Buenos Aires but inland in San Miguel de Tucumán, where independence was declared in July 1816 by a nationalist assembly.

Independent Argentina (then called the United Provinces of the Río de la Plata) was destabilized by intermittent civil war until 1853. The interests of the merchants of Buenos Aires were countered by those of the rich, landowning cattle ranchers of the interior; the city of Córdoba, in particular, emerged as a strong rival to Buenos Aires. Federalists opposed centralists, but, for much of the period, there was no effective central government. Nevertheless, the Argentines became involved in regional wars, largely fought in Uruguay. When the French, and later the British, became involved on the side of Uruguayan nationalists, a French fleet blockaded Buenos Aires in the late 1830s, and a combined British and French fleet blockaded the port in the mid-1840s.

In the early 1850s, the central government in Buenos Aires imposed its authority across Argentina, and the city was able to develop as the national capital. In 1855, Buenos Aires had a population of 99,000; by 1880, the city was home to 249,000 people. Also in 1880, the city of Buenos Aires was removed from the province of the same name; consequently, the political influence of the city was reduced. By the turn of the twentieth century, Buenos Aires had 615,000 inhabitants, and the city continued to expand through the early twentieth century, reaching a population of 1,780,000 in 1923.

A CULTURAL CENTER

In the late nineteenth and early twentieth centuries, Buenos Aires emerged as a leading cultural center. The city regarded itself as being the equal of the major European capitals and, when architects from Europe redesigned parts of the city along French lines from the 1880s onward—with wide boulevards, parks, and elegant public spaces—Buenos Aires earned the nickname "Paris of South America."

DAILY LIFE

Plaza de Mayo, the political center of downtown Buenos Aires, is flanked by Casa Rosada, the presidential palace, the massive metropolitan cathedral, and other public buildings.

Theaters, including Teatro Colón (1908), a famous opera house, opened in the city, and the first subway in South America followed. Many buildings were constructed in the French Beaux-Arts style, with classical features. The Argentine architect Antonio Buschiazzo (1846–1917) was responsible for the elegant Avenida de Mayo (1888–1894), and many key public buildings, such as the Congreso Nacional (Congress building) and Casa de Gobierno (government palace), were also constructed at the end of the nineteenth century.

Buenos Aires became the cultural capital of Spanish-speaking Latin America, with an important film industry and a rich musical tradition, including the tango, which developed in the city's poor suburbs. In modern times, Buenos Aires celebrates the dance in an annual Tango Day, in December. Buenos Aires has movie houses, internationally renowned symphony orchestras, sports facilities including large stadiums for soccer and rugby, a zoo, and botanical gardens. The city is home to more than 20 universities, including the large University of Buenos Aires, which is one of the most prestigious in South America.

THE MODERN CITY

Buenos Aires is the administrative, commercial, financial, and industrial capital of Argentina. The city has a large retail sector, including many shopping malls, and its stock exchange is one of the most important in Latin America. Apart from major industries processing meat, cereals, dairy products, and other farming products, the city has a wide and diverse range of industries including engineering and metalworking, oil refining, machinery, textiles, and a wide range of consumer goods.

The port is the largest in Argentina and one of the busiest in South America. The importance of the port to the city is echoed by the name *porteño*s (literally, "port dwellers"), which is used to describe citizens of Buenos Aires. The city is a transportation hub and has a major international airport (Ministro Pistarini International Airport), while a second airport mainly serves domestic flights. The subway system now has 80 stations, and development in the first decade of the twenty-first century will double the length of track by 2011. An extensive railroad network in the suburbs brings commuters into the city to work, while many others use buses (including the city-owned *colectivo* buses).

Although it is still the dominant city in the region, Buenos Aires, along with Argentina itself, suffered a relative decline in importance, beginning in the 1929–mid-1930s Great Depression (a worldwide economic downturn), when its exports were greatly reduced. The city has also suffered much social and political upheaval through periods of military rule in the late twentieth century, as well as a major severe economic crisis in the early twenty-first century. As a result, poverty in Buenos Aires increased and, in modern times, there are considerable differences in standards of living between the rich quarter in the west and the slums in the south.

One of the most powerful images of the modern city is the silent vigil of the Mothers of the Plaza de Mayo, the mothers of people known as the "disappeared," who were kidnapped and believed to have been killed by the military regime that held power from 1976 through 1983. At great personal risk, the women met every week in the downtown Plaza de Mayo to protest the illegal detentions and killings, continuing their weekly vigil even after the end of the military dictatorship. Many of them were, in turn, detained or disappeared.

C. CARPENTER

Córdoba

Córdoba, the second-largest city in Argentina, was home to 1,368,000 people at the 2001 Argentine national census; some 1,268,000 people lived within the city limits.

Córdoba lies along the Primero River, where the northern part of the Pampas, the vast stretch of grasslands that cover much of Argentina, meets the foothills of the Córdoba Mountains. The city's central location within Argentina has helped it develop as a center of trade and a route hub.

CÓRDOBA IN HISTORY

Spanish colonists founded Córdoba in 1573, naming it for the city of Córdoba in southern Spain. From 1599 onward, Jesuit missionaries became active in the region and, in 1613, they founded a university in Córdoba, the first in what is now Argentina. Córdoba became an important regional center within the huge Spanish viceroyalty (administrative region) of Peru, which was governed from Lima. However, when the Spanish established the separate viceroyalty of Río de la Plata in 1776—which included the countries that are now known as Argentina, Paraguay, and Uruguay—Córdoba began to suffer as a hub for trade when economic activities in the new viceroyalty became centered in the viceroyalty's center, Buenos Aires.

As a result of opposition to centralization, as well as a growing rivalry with Buenos Aires, Córdoba supported federalism when Argentina gained independence from Spanish rule in the early nineteenth century. Through the 1830s and 1840s, Córdoba was often the scene of armed conflict between advocates and opponents of the central government in Buenos Aires.

THE MODERN CITY

In modern times, Córdoba is an important industrial city. Córdoba's economic development began in the 1860s, when the city was connected by railroad to the coast and the Primero River was dammed to provide domestic and irrigation water and, later, hydroelectric power. The city's industries process the agricultural products of the surrounding countryside, fruits, grains, meat, and hides. While leather, food processing, and textile industries still dominate Córdoba's industrial sector, the engineering (including railroad engineering), glass, automobile (Fiat, Renault, and Volkswagen), chemical, agribusiness, and consumer goods industries are now also important. After World War II (1939–1945), the Argentine government located the nation's aircraft industry in Córdoba, employing German engineers and designers to work there. The city is the principal center of electronic engineering and high-tech industries in Argentina, and it is home to the Argentine space industry, the Centro Espacial Teófilo Tabanera, where satellites are made.

Large international corporations, including Motorola and Intel, have regional offices in Córdoba. The city is also a major highway and railroad hub and has a busy airport. A regional administrative and media center, Córdoba is an educational center, containing not only the historic university but other higher educational institutions, including the prestigious UTN (Universidad Tecnológica Nacional) engineering university.

The city retains many of its historic buildings, including the eighteenth-century cathedral and the viceroy's palace, as well as a number of churches and convents that date from the Spanish colonial era. Córdoba's most famous religious monument is the Manzana Jesuítica (known as the Jesuit Block), a seventeenth-century complex of buildings, which was declared a UNESCO World Heritage site in 2000. The city has a growing tourist industry, and visitors are also attracted to resorts that are located nearby in the mountains.

C. CARPENTER

Downtown Córdoba contains historic public buildings, such as the eighteenth-century cathedral, around a central square.

Rosario

Rosario is a major river port along the Paraná River, some 180 miles (about 290 km) upstream from Buenos Aires on the Río de la Plata estuary. At the 2001 census, Rosario had a population of 1,161,000, and 906,000 people lived within the city.

Rosario began to grow around a villa called Pago de los Arroyos, which lay at the center of a rural district from 1689. The settlement was named Rosario in 1725.

ROSARIO IN HISTORY

At the start of the nineteenth century, Rosario was one of the centers of opposition to Spanish rule in the region. In 1812, General Manuel Belgrano (1770–1820) raised the Argentine flag for the first time before a battle along the banks of the Paraná River at Rosario. The city grew slowly during the first half of the nineteenth century, when Argentina was in a state of nearly constant civil war between the forces of Buenos Aires and those of the provinces, which resisted the imposition of a central government. In 1819, much of Rosario was burned to the ground during the civil war and, in 1829, the city suffered wide-scale destruction in a naval bombardment.

By 1850, Rosario had a population of only 3,000, and the development of the port was restricted by a decree in 1841 of the Argentine dictator Juan Manuel de Rosas (1793–1877; governor of Buenos Aires 1829–1832 and 1835–1852), who banned foreign ships from Rosario. In 1852, the ban was lifted, and Rosario was declared a city. After this date, the Argentine authorities successfully encouraged the growth of the port, which shipped the agricultural produce of its hinterland to Buenos Aires and abroad. By 1880, Rosario had become one of the world's largest grain-exporting centers.

The city's growth was rapid, and, by the 1920s, Rosario was home to more than 400,000 people. Rosario became a regional highway and railroad hub for the region west of the Paraná River, and the port developed under foreign ownership. It remained Argentina's largest port for exports until 1942, when the Argentine government nationalized the port and encouraged competition from other ports within the country. As a result, Rosario lost its leading role.

THE MODERN CITY

Although the Paraná River is liable to silt, and consequently needs regular dredging, the port can take oceangoing ships with a draft of 34 feet (10.4 m). Rosario exports wheat, corn, soy, and other grains, meat and hides, wool, and timber. The city's industries process the agricultural produce of the region; the food processing industries (particularly flour milling and making vegetable oils) are important employers. Other industries include agricultural machinery, engineering, iron and steel, consumer goods, and automobiles. The city's economy was boosted in 1976 by the establishment in the port of a free-trade (tax-free) zone for landlocked Bolivia.

In the late 1980s and through the 1990s, the economic collapse of Argentina greatly affected the city. Agricultural exports decreased, and the city's industries suffered adversely from foreign competition. Unemployment rose to such a degree that by 1995, one-fifth of the labor force in Rosario was out of work. Inner-city poverty grew in the 2001 economic crisis, exacerbated by the migration of unemployed rural poor to the city. The city experienced a growth in shantytowns during this period. After 2001, a boom in agricultural exports led to a recovery, but the city has not fully returned to former levels of prosperity.

Although a bridge, constructed in 2003, across the Paraná River connects Rosario with the city of Victoria, Rosario's transportation links with the region to the east of the waterway are still restricted. Rosario is an educational center, with several universities, and has a growing tourist industry. The historic downtown area centers around the Plaza 25 de Mayo, which is lined by major buildings, including the Palacio de los Leones, the cathedral, and the museum of decorative arts.

C. CARPENTER

The Monument of the Flag in Rosario commemorates the 1812 raising of the Argentine flag for the first time.

ECONOMY

One of the most prosperous countries in the world at the turn of the twentieth century, Argentina suffered a series of major economic crises during the following century. As a result, the nation, although rich in resources, has declined in economic importance, compared with other South American nations.

Argentina has an export-led economy in which agricultural products, particularly meat and grain, play a major role. The nation also has abundant natural resources, including fertile soil, hydroelectric power potential, rich fisheries, and reserves of minerals, petroleum, and natural gas. Argentina has a diverse industrial base and a large services sector. In 2001, the country suffered one of its worst economic crises, which many economists believed would require many years of recovery. However, the Argentine economy has recovered and has achieved strong growth since then.

ECONOMIC CHALLENGES

One of the greatest challenges faced by the Argentine economy is that of meeting the high expectations of the Argentine people. While forming part of South America, Argentina has long considered itself different from the rest of the continent. Argentina and its people have a far closer affinity with Europe than many of its neighbors, and, for much of the twentieth century, many sectors of society enjoyed living conditions on a par with those found in continental Europe. At the start of the twentieth century, Argentina was one of the ten richest countries in the world, with a per capita income equivalent to that of traditionally powerful economies such as France and Germany. At that time, many believed that the nation would become one of the world's leading economic powers. However, because of a series of economic and political crises through the twentieth century and into the twenty-first century, Argentina has not fulfilled its economic potential or its citizens' expectations.

At the turn of the twentieth century, Argentina exported agricultural products, such as corn, flax, and meat, bringing prosperity to the country. By the end of the century, it had experienced severe economic problems, beginning with the Great Depression (a global economic downturn from 1929 through the mid-1930s). In the period following World War II (1939–1945), during which Argentina benefited from the export of its agricultural products to the Allies, a populist government—under the presidency of Juan Perón (1895–1974; in office 1946– 1955 and 1973–1974)—attempted to provide jobs and to subsidize health care and education. Perón's government nationalized sectors of the economy, including the railroads, and increased state intervention in the economy, embarking on a program of industrialization. The new industries were protected from foreign competition by tariffs. For working and middle-class families, these policies brought some short-term stability. There were, however, fundamental economic problems and insufficient funding to develop industries. Consequently, inflation and unemployment sharply rose, deeply affecting the lives of ordinary people.

In the late 1970s, Argentina pursued a program of economic reforms and reconstruction. At the time, about two-thirds of the population were middle class, but, by the 1980s, Argentina was struggling economically and many Argentines were impoverished. At the end of the 1980s, the nation, which had been restored to democratic government after a period of military government from 1976 through 1983, had a huge foreign debt and suffered hyperinflation (up to 3,000 percent in 1989). The government of Carlos Menem (born 1930; in office 1989–1999) attempted to solve the problem through the neoliberal economic policies that were popular with many foreign governments at the time and closely abided by the advice provided by the International Monetary Fund (IMF). The strategy had three main pillars: trade liberalization, labor deregulation, and privatization. In a program of trade liberalization, taxes on imports and exports were reduced, removing protection for national industries. Labor deregulation made it easier to hire and fire staff, and in a program of privatization of state-owned firms, state corporations, such as energy and telecommunications providers, were sold to private companies.

As a quick-fix strategy to control hyperinflation, Menem decided to peg the local currency (the peso) to the U.S. dollar on a 1-to-1 basis. As a result, Argentines could freely convert their local currency into the equivalent amount of dollars, make transactions in both currencies, and open bank accounts and

Standard of Living

In 2006, GDP (gross domestic product) per capita in Argentina was $15,200, adjusted for purchasing power parity (PPP), a formula that allows comparison between living standards in different countries. Since 2001, there is a wider disparity in the distribution of income in Argentina, and many formerly middle class Argentines have become poorer. In 2006, some 27 percent of the population lived below the official poverty line.

The oil wells near Comodoro Rivadavia in Chubut province are part of the extensive network of hydrocarbon reserves that make Argentina self-sufficient in fuel.

take out loans in dollars. The initial effects of the policy were positive, cutting inflation to lower levels and generating one of Latin America's fastest growing economies.

Late in the 1990s, economic growth slowed, and although Argentina received loans from the IMF, the economy did not revive. By 2001, the country had one of the largest national debts of any developing nation. Much of the debt was accumulated during the period of military dictatorship prior to 1983, when huge loans were taken out for major infrastructure projects, which were often left incomplete or unsuccessful. Because corruption was rampant during the military dictatorship, large amounts of the money borrowed never reached the projects the investment was supposed to benefit. Additionally, under civilian government in the 1990s, public spending based on foreign loans remained high, leading to foreign debt increasing in value rather than decreasing. By the end of 2001, as the crisis hit, Argentina's debt became economically unmanageable.

Another of the factors leading to the crisis was the very policy that led to the economy's success in the early 1990s: the pegged currency. While pegging the peso to the U.S. dollar helped eliminate hyperinflation, it also led to the creation of an economy that became increasingly overvalued toward the end of the decade. At the time, the dollar was strong with respect to other global currencies, and, consequently, Argentina's exports became expensive and uncompetitive. The situation was made worse when Brazil devalued its currency in 1997, making its own exports far more competitive than Argentina's. As a result, Argentine exports decreased, while, at the same time, the level of imports increased, as rising quality of living standards led to more demand for consumer goods that were not produced in Argentina. In this way, capital, and in particular dollars, began to leave the country (for the purchase of foreign goods). Investors began to withdraw their capital from Argentina, partly as a result of the receding economy, but also because of nervousness induced by economic crises in Mexico and Brazil.

As the economy declined, unemployment rapidly increased and wages (especially in the public sector) were cut. Fernando de la Rúa (born 1937; in office 1999–2001) resigned as president in December 2001 amid violent and widespread protests. The economy was in disarray, and, in the following 12 days, two interim presidents came and went, during which time Argentina defaulted on $93 billion of debt, the largest-ever global debt default. President Eduardo Duhalde (born 1941; in office 2002–2003) finally dismantled the fixed exchange rate.

In the early twenty-first century, Argentina's economy has strongly recovered, and living standards and real wages have risen, but the benefits have not extended throughout society, and large numbers of people remain in poverty. In 2006, around 27 percent of Argentines were below the official poverty line, including the so-called "new poor," former professionals. As a result of the decline in living standards, some 300,000 people opted to emigrate, many to Europe.

ECONOMY

ARGENTINA
Industry and Resources

- Principal oil fields
- Principal gas fields
- Agricultural industries
- Auto construction
- Building materials/Cement
- Chemicals
- Clothing/Footwear
- Consumer goods
- Decorative arts
- Electronics
- Engineering
- Fishing
- Food processing
- Glass
- Hydroelectric power
- Iron and steel
- Metalworking
- Services/Commerce
- Textiles
- Timber
- Tourism

Mineral deposits
- (S) Salt

Transportation
- Major roads
- Minor roads
- Major railroads
- Major airports
- Major ports

RESOURCES

Argentina's greatest natural resource is the rich land of the Pampas, the vast grasslands that occupy most of central Argentina around the cities of Buenos Aires, Córdoba, Rosario, and Santa Fé. The region offers ideal growing conditions for a wide array of agricultural crops. Argentina's economy also benefits from reserves of lead, zinc, tin, copper, iron ore, manganese, uranium, petroleum, and natural gas.

Argentina has Latin America's third-largest natural gas fields and has come to depend on this resource to fulfill most of its energy needs. The country had proven reserves of 18.9 trillion cubic feet (0.53 trillion cubic m) in 2006, and its annual production reached 1.4 trillion cubic feet (0.04 trillion cubic m) in 2003. The main reserves are located in the southern Neuquén province, with further reserves in the northern province of Salta and the southern provinces of Santa Cruz and Tierra del Fuego. Domestic consumption accounts for 85 percent of production, allowing Argentina to export its natural gas surpluses to neighboring Chile.

Argentina also has sufficient supplies of petroleum to satisfy national demand. With estimated proven reserves of 2.3 billion barrels and a consumption rate of 440,000 barrels per day (bbl/d), the production rate of 763,000 bbl/d provides a surplus of 323,000 bbl/d, which is exported to Brazil and Chile. The production of petroleum is focused on two main oil fields, the Neuguina field, in western-central Argentina, and the Golfo San Jorge field along the southeast of the country. Between them, these two fields account for more than 85 percent of domestic petroleum production. Because of a reliance on these two fields, and a lack of investment in new machinery and new exploration, petroleum production has been in decline since 1998. Nevertheless, current exploration, both on and offshore in southern Argentina, could potentially reverse this trend.

ARGENTINA

The traditional cattle-raising estancia *(large estate) economy of much of the Pampas grassland region depends upon the labor of* gauchos *(cowboys).*

ARGENTINA'S GDP

Argentina's gross domestic product (GDP) was $608.8 billion in 2006. The figure is adjusted for purchasing power parity (PPP), an exchange rate at which goods in one country cost the same as goods in another. PPP allows a comparison between the living standards in different nations.

MAIN CONTRIBUTORS TO ARGENTINA'S GDP

Agriculture	8.5 percent
Industry	35.9 percent
Services	55.6 percent

Source: CIA, Factbook, 2006

The production of hydropower is partly related to the problem of controlling water supplies to industry in the semiarid north. Dams and reservoirs ensure water flow regulation and flood control and, at the same time, the dams are harnessed to supply hydroelectric power. Early in the twenty-first century, Argentina had 35 hydropower plants, most of which were on large dams. However, only around 25 percent of the nation's hydroelectric power has been harnessed. On major waterways along the national borders, the large Yacyretá and Salto Grande facilities, both binational facilities (with Paraguay and Uruguay, respectively), provide a major share of the nation's hydropower.

AGRICULTURE

Agriculture directly contributes 8.5 percent of Argentina's GDP, although much the nation's industry is based on agricultural products. The farming sector has grown strongly since the economic crisis of 2001, with agro-industry (particularly the production of soybeans) considered as one of the keys to economic recovery.

Argentina's economy has long been based upon growing cereals and cattle raising. In the seventeenth and eighteenth centuries, the plains of the highly fertile Pampas region were exploited by cattle ranchers, who took advantage of open grasslands to rear large herds of cattle. With the influx of labor during the late nineteenth and early twentieth centuries, as a result of large-scale and predominantly European immigration (mainly from Spain and Italy), the Pampas region began to be exploited for other types of farming. The immigrants not only provided Argentina with the labor needed to further develop the region, but they also brought with them new techniques and technologies, which helped turn the region from grassland into highly productive cropland, initially specializing in the production of wheat, oats, corn, and barley. The foreign influx also brought with it European investment, which was geared toward the improvement of infrastructure. Consequently, the region was opened up by new roads and railroads, and the export of agricultural products was facilitated through the construction of seaports along the Atlantic coast and river ports along the Paraná waterway system. Subsequently, Argentina became a major producer and exporter of agricultural goods, both cereal crops and traditional livestock-based exports (meat and leather). Cattle raising remains important both within the Pampas region and increasingly in peripheral regions.

Agricultural production in Argentina has varied according to world demand and the opening up of new productive areas. The Pampas region remains the most agriculturally productive part of the country, although many of the crops it traditionally produced have been overshadowed by the rapid expansion of soybeans, which have been extensively farmed since the 1980s. As a result, Argentina has become the world's third-largest soybean producer, leading to the emergence of huge agro-industries, which use technology to exploit the land to its full potential. However, the spread of large-scale soybean production has led to the failure of many small- and medium-sized family farms, which are unable to compete with larger producers.

In other parts of Argentina, where soils are less fertile but still productive, other cash crops have increased in importance. For example, the western Cuyo region, around the cities of Mendoza, San Juan, and La Rioja, has become a major wine-producing area, specializing in the cultivation of grape vines and the production and export of high-quality red and white wines. The northern region around the city of Tucumán is a major producer of sugarcane, while in the southern Patagonia region, sheep farming remains the predominant agricultural activity.

EMPLOYMENT IN ARGENTINA

The Argentine government has not published figures for the labor force by occupation since 1996. Since then, a major economic crisis has partially changed the structure of the economy. As a result, the figures below give only an indication of the relative size of the workforce in major economic sectors.

Sector	Percentage of labor force
Agriculture and mining	2.2 percent
Manufacturing industry	18.5 percent
Commerce	18.1 percent
Transportation and communications	10.3 percent
Public administration and defense	9.5 percent
Services and other (including unemployed)	41.4 percent

Source: Government of Argentina, 1996

In 2006, 8.7 percent of the labor force was unemployed.

Although some of the coastal waters of Argentina contain relatively rich fishing grounds, the Argentine fishing industry is not highly developed, in large part because fish forms a small proportion of the national diet in comparison to red meat. Since the 1970s, government financial incentives have helped enlarge and modernize the fishing fleet, and, subsequently, the marine catch more than doubled in a generation. Commercially the most important species are pejerrey (which is related to the mackerel), squid, the salmonlike dorado, and hake.

INDUSTRY

Industry contributes nearly 36 percent of the Argentine GDP. The major industries in Argentina are the production of motor vehicles and parts (including automobiles, farm equipment, and transportation vehicles), iron and steel, home appliances, textiles, chemicals and petrochemicals, metallurgy, wood processing, and food processing and packing (particularly meat processing, packing, and freezing, flour milling, and vegetable oils).

Industrial production varies widely, with industries commonly situated close to sources of agricultural raw materials. The main industrial centers are Buenos Aires, Córdoba, and Rosario. Buenos Aires, whose industries include those based on imported raw materials, has a widely varied industrial production, specializing in food processing (based on the raw grains and cereals produced in the Pampas region), consumer goods and home appliances, chemicals and petrochemicals, and motor vehicle production (based on local steel production).

The Argentine grape industry in the Mendoza region produces increasing quantities of wine for export. These wines compare in quality with Chilean and California wines.

Galerias Pacifico is one of the upmarket shopping facilities that makes Buenos Aires the leading retail center of South America.

Córdoba, situated at the heart of both the Pampas region and central to Argentina, has become a key center for food processing, particularly in the production of soybean derivatives (flour, oil, and dairy products). The city is also a major metal-producing area (steel and iron), and, consequently, it has become the center of motor vehicle production in Argentina. This industry has become increasingly important since the 1980s, as Argentina has sought to develop its steel-producing capacity. By the end of the 1950s, only around 30,000 automobiles were produced in Argentina. By the end of the 1990s, the figure had increased to around 450,000 units (although production fell to 235,000 after the economic crisis of 2001). Several foreign automobile companies also have facilities in Argentina.

The third major Argentine industrial center, Rosario, has come to specialize in the production of steel, the processing of agricultural goods (cereals and bovine products), and the production of chemicals and petrochemicals. The city is home to several major oil refineries, which are linked into the national network of oil and gas pipelines, bringing raw materials to the area from oil and gas fields in the north and south of the country.

The northwestern city of Tucumán, in the traditional sugarcane growing area, is home to Argentina's major sugar refineries. The city of Mendoza, in western Argentina, is a center for wine production, based on local grapevines. The northern Chaco region specializes in the production of cotton, and its cities house many cotton mills.

SERVICES

The service sector was one of the hardest hit areas of the Argentine economy in the major downturn of 2001. In 1995, the service sector represented almost 66 percent of GDP, with healthy growth figures of 3.1 percent during the period of 1985 through 1995. The sector continued to grow until 2000, although at a slower rate, and, by 2006, its contribution to GDP had dropped to just 55.6 percent of GDP, in part because of the faster growth of other sectors. Growth figures over the period of 1995 through 2005 were just 0.4 percent. Nevertheless, by 2005, the sector had partially recovered, registering a healthy growth rate of 6.8 percent.

Retail, wholesale, real estate, and other business activities make up the largest parts of the service sector. Retail and wholesale have recovered strongly since the 2001 crisis, growing by 143 percent from 2002 through 2006. Buenos Aires, Argentina's main retail center, is renowned for its fashion goods, and the city's shopping facilities have a good reputation throughout South America. The real estate and business activities sectors have also grown, and the development in these markets has encouraged the recovery of the Argentine economy in general, with consumer confidence returning, allowing citizens to spend more freely, both in the retail sector and for other services.

The growth of tourism has helped boost the service sector, by increasing spending in retail and wholesale, transportation, and hotels and restaurants. The return of stability has led to an increase in domestic travel, with Argentines visiting many of the varied tourist destinations within their own country, including beach resorts such as Mar del Plata. At the same time, Argentina is becoming an increasingly popular international tourist destination, and, in 2005, Argentina received 3.7 million foreign tourists.

TRADE

One of the major factors that led to the economic crisis of 2001 was a long-running trade deficit—the total value of imports was far greater than the total value of exports. In the years leading up to the crisis, when the Argentine peso was pegged to the U.S. dollar, the country's export products proved uncompetitive on the international market because of unfavorable exchange rates. At the same time, this monetary policy, which made exports uncompetitive, helped make imports relatively cheap in comparison.

The success of the stabilization program in curbing inflation and raising GDP, in the same period, led to greater demand for household commodities, which were not widely produced locally, and were, therefore, imported from abroad. These factors led to a sustained period of trade deficit, reaching a low in 1998, when the total value of exports was just $28 billion, while imports were valued at nearly $34 billion.

In modern times, the competitiveness of Argentine products has been restored, leading to a boom in exports and a healthier balance of trade. In 2006, Argentina exported goods and services with an estimated value of $46.5 billion, while importing goods and services worth $32.6 billion. Argentina's exports are dominated by agricultural products, with soybeans and their derivatives accounting for almost one-quarter of all exports. Cereal crops, such as wheat and corn, make up a further 8 percent. Other major farm-based goods, such as bovine products (beef, leather, milk, and cheese) and fruits and vegetables, contribute another 9 percent of exports.

The second-largest export sector is petroleum and its derivatives, accounting for 20 percent of all exports. The automobile industry contributes 7 percent, while mining and the production of steel and iron account for another 3 percent.

The industrial sector provides the biggest demand for imported goods. In 2005, 36 percent of all imports were intermediate goods (raw materials that are transformed into other goods), a further 24 percent were capital goods (goods used in the production of commodities), and imported parts for the maintenance of capital goods represented another 17 percent. Compared with many other nations, Argentina spends little on the importation of fuel. The country is virtually self-sufficient in energy, importing fuels valued at only $1.5 billion—representing just 5 percent of all imports. The remainder of the country's imports consists mainly of consumer goods and motor vehicles.

Argentina is a member of MERCOSUR (the trade organization whose other members are Brazil, Uruguay, Paraguay, and Venezuela). Founded in 1991, MERCOSUR facilitates free trade between member states as well as reducing restrictions on the flow of goods, peoples, and currency within the region. Along with Brazil, Argentina is one of the main players in MERCOSUR, whose creation has led to a huge increase in trade among member countries. Argentina has benefited both from new markets for its products and cheaper import sources, particularly for its industries. In 2005, MERCOSUR countries received more than 20 percent of all exports from Argentina and provided more than 40 percent of imports.

Argentina also enjoys good trade relations with the NAFTA (North American Free Trade Agreement) trading area, which was created in 1994 and includes the United States, Mexico, and Canada. NAFTA provides a further 18 percent of imports, while receiving 15 percent of exports. The principal destinations of exports from Argentina are Brazil (which received 17 percent of Argentine exports in 2006), Chile (9 percent), the United States (8 percent), China including Hong Kong (7 percent), Germany, Italy, France, and Uruguay. Other trade partners in the region include Paraguay, Venezuela, and Bolivia.

The main sources of imports into Argentina are Brazil (which supplied 36 percent of imports in 2006), the United States (15 percent), China including Hong Kong (6 percent), Germany (5 percent), Spain, the Netherlands, Italy, and Uruguay.

TRANSPORTATION AND COMMUNICATION

Because Argentina relies on exports, particularly of agricultural products, the country has developed an advanced transportation infrastructure. At the start of the twentieth century, Argentina received major foreign investment to open up the interior through the construction of highways and railroads. At the same time, investment was directed to the construction of seaports and river ports to allow the export of the country's products. As a result, Argentina developed one the world's larger railroad systems, linking all the major cities and the farming regions to the ports, and providing commuter services in the Buenos Aires metropolitan area. The state-run railroads were privatized during the 1990s and, after privatization, many lines were shut down or reduced to carrying freight rather than passengers. As a result, in 2007, there were 19,827 miles (31,902 km) of track in use. The government is beginning to reopen some of the passenger lines that were shut down in the 1990s and is also constructing a new high-speed rail service between Buenos Aires and Rosario. Buenos Aires has a subway, a light railroad system, and a streetcar system. Rosario has a light railroad.

The nation has an extensive highway network of 142,414 miles (229,144 km), of which 456 miles (734 km) are expressways and another 42,309 miles (68,075 km) are other paved roads. Multilane expressways now link Buenos Aires and Córdoba and some other cities.

Water transportation is important in Argentina, and more than 90 percent of all foreign trade is carried by sea. An extensive navigable waterway system covers 6,837 miles (11,000 km), much of which forms part of the Paraná-Paraguay river network, which links the MERCOSUR nations of Argentina, Uruguay, Paraguay, and Brazil and is a major artery of trade between them. Rosario, along the Paraná River, is a major inland port and, until 1942, was Argentina's largest port for exports. Other major commercial ports include Buenos Aires, Bahía Blanca, and La Plata. However, Argentina's sea trade is, in part, limited by the fact that it does not yet possess a deepwater port, capable of receiving the largest bulk and oil carriers and container ships.

Argentina has more than 1,380 airports and airstrips, including 15 airports that handle international flights. Two national companies, Aerolineas Argentinas and Lineas Aereas Privadas Argentinas, dominate internal air transportation.

In 2006, there were some 9.5 million main telephone lines in operation in Argentina, and more than 31.5 million Argentines had mobile cellular phones. The telecommunications sector opened to international competition in the 1990s, improving the telephone network, but remote areas still have poor telephone service. In 2006, 8.2 million Argentines had Internet access.

M. CAMBURN

The Falkland Islands

Reached by Europeans in 1592, the Falkland Islands (known to Argentines as Islas Malvinas) were settled by the French in 1764 and the British in the following year. In 1770, France sold its claim to the Spanish, who expelled the British. Early in the nineteenth century, Argentina inherited the Spanish claim to the islands. However, the British recolonized the group in 1833, and the islands are the subject of an ongoing territorial dispute. Argentine forces invaded the islands in April 1982, but the British regained them in June of the same year. The Falkland Islands are bleak, rocky, wet, and windy, and are sparsely populated by sheep farmers. Since the late 1980s, the sale of fishing licenses to foreign trawlers has been the principal source of revenue, and although oil has been found in territorial waters, its exploitation is not yet commercially viable. A British military garrison of more than 1,500 is important to the economy of the islands. More than four-fifths of the population lives in Stanley, the only town.

GEOGRAPHY

Location	In the South Atlantic Ocean, east of Argentina
Climate	Cold and wet with strong winds
Area	4,698 sq. miles (12,170 sq. km)
Coastline	800 miles (1,288 km)
Highest point	Mount Usborne 2,312 feet (705 m)
Lowest point	Atlantic Ocean 0 feet (0 m)
Terrain	Rocky and mountainous with some marshy plains
Natural resources	Fish
Land use	
Arable land	0 percent
Permanent crops	0 percent
Other	100 percent (99 percent permanent pastures; 1 percent other)
Major rivers and lakes	n/a
Natural hazards	Gales

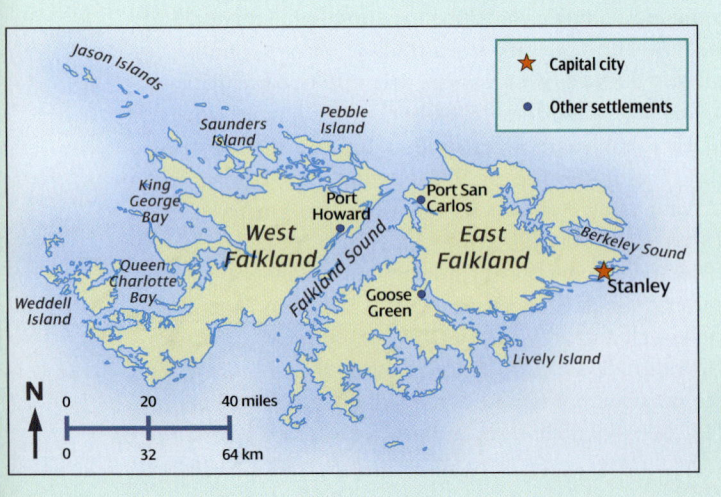

METROPOLITAN AREAS, 2006 POPULATION

Urban population	80 percent
Stanley	2,100

Source: Falkland Islands census, 2006

POPULATION

Population	2,500 (2006 census)
Population density	0.2 per sq. mile (0.5 per sq. km)

ECONOMY

Currency	Falkland pound (FKP), which is on a par with the British pound
Exchange rate (2007)	$1 = FKP 0.5
Gross domestic product (2002)	$75 million
GDP per capita (2002)	$25,000
Unemployment rate (2006)	None; there is a labor shortage
Population under poverty line	n/a
Exports	$125 million (2004 CIA estimate)
Imports	$90 million (2004 CIA estimate)

FALKLAND ISLANDS

Founded in 1843, Stanley, the only town in the Falklands, contains the islands' only shops and school.

GOVERNMENT

Official name	Falkland Islands
Conventional short form	Falkland Islands
Nationality	
noun	Falkland Islander
adjective	Falkland Island
Official language	English
Capital city	Stanley
Type of government	British colony
Voting rights	18 years and over; universal
National anthem	The British national anthem
National day	Liberation Day, June 14 (the anniversary of the end of Argentine occupation in 1982)

TRANSPORTATION

Railroads	n/a
Highways	273 miles (440 km)
Paved roads	31 miles (50 km)
Unpaved roads	242 miles (390 km)
Navigable waterways	n/a
Airports	
International airports	1
Paved runways	2

POPULATION PROFILE, 2006 ESTIMATES

Ethnic groups	
British ancestry	almost 100 percent
Religions	
Anglican	more than 50 percent
Protestant churches, Roman Catholic, and nonreligious	less than 50 percent
Languages	
English	100 percent

FLAG

The flag of the Falkland Islands is dark blue, with the British flag (the red, white, and blue Union flag) in the canton, the upper quarter near the flagpole. In the center of the fly (the part farthest from the flagpole) is the pale blue state badge, which includes a white sheep, white waves, and a sixteenth-century sailing ship.

803

Paraguay

Before the first Spanish settlement in the early sixteenth century, what is now Paraguay was home to Guaraní Amerindians. From the seventeenth century through 1767, Paraguay was effectively controlled by Jesuit missionaries. Part of the Spanish viceroyalty of Río de la Plata, landlocked Paraguay achieved independence in 1811. In the nineteenth century, periods of dictatorship and the disastrous War of the Triple Alliance (1865–1870) against Argentina, Brazil, and Uruguay, in which Paraguay lost more than one-half of its population, held back the nation's development. Paraguay gained most of the Gran Chaco region after a war with Bolivia (1932–1935). For much of the twentieth century, Paraguay was under military rule, including the dictatorship of General Alfredo Stroessner (1912–2006; in office 1954–1989). In modern times, Paraguay has a civilian government, although the nation remains poor, with many subsistence farmers and a large informal (largely unrecorded) economy.

GEOGRAPHY

Location	Central South America, between Brazil and Argentina
Climate	Subtropical and tropical; arid in the west
Area	157,048 sq. miles (406,752 sq. km)
Coastline	None
Highest point	Cerro San Pedro 2,788 feet (850 m)
Lowest point	At the junction of the Paraguay and Paraná rivers 138 feet (42 m)
Terrain	Plains and hills east of the Paraguay River (Oriental Paraguay); marshy plains and dry forest west of the river (Occidental Paraguay)
Natural resources	Hydroelectric power potential, timber, iron ore, limestone, manganese
Land use	
Arable land	7.5 percent
Permanent crops	0.2 percent
Other	92.3 percent
Major rivers	Paraguay, Paraná, Pilcomayo
Major lake	Itaipu Reservoir
Natural hazards	Floods

METROPOLITAN AREAS, 2002 POPULATION

Urban population	46 percent
Asunción	1,660,000
Asunción City	512,000
San Lorenzo	204,000
Luque	171,000
Capiatá	154,000
Lambaré	120,000
Fernando de la Mora	114,000
Limpio	73,000
Némby	72,000
Mariano Roque Alonso	65,000
Villa Elisa	53,000
Itauguá	46,000
Ciudad del Este	332,000
Ciudad del Este City	222,000
Presidente Franco	47,000
Hernandarias	47,000
Encarnación	67,000
San Pedro Caballero	65,000
Caaguazú	49,000
Coronel Oviedo	49,000

Source: Paraguayan national census, 2002

NEIGHBORS AND LENGTH OF BORDERS

Argentina	1,168 miles (1,880 km)
Bolivia	466 miles (750 km)
Brazil	848 miles (1,365 km)

POPULATION

Population	5,163,000 (2002 census)
Population density	33 per sq. mile (13 per sq. km)
Population growth	2.4 percent a year

PARAGUAY

Birthrate	28.8 births per 1,000 of the population
Death rate	4.5 deaths per 1,000 of the population
Population under age 15	37.2 percent
Population over age 65	5.1 percent
Sex ratio	105 males for 100 females
Fertility rate	3.8 children per woman
Infant mortality rate	26.5 deaths per 1,000 live births
Life expectancy at birth	
Total population	75.3 years
Female	78.0 years
Male	72.8 years

ECONOMY

Currency	Guaraní (PYG)
Exchange rate (2007)	$1 = PYG 4,745
Gross domestic product (2006)	$31.3 billion
GDP per capita (2006)	$4,800
Unemployment rate (2005)	9.4 percent
Population under poverty line (2005)	32 percent
Exports	$4.8 billion (2006 CIA estimate)
Imports	$5.8 billion (2006 CIA estimate)

FLAG

The flag of Paraguay is unusual in that the obverse and reverse are different. Both sides have three horizontal bands, red, white, and blue, but the two sides have different symbols at the center. Red represents heroism or justice, white symbolizes peace or unity, and blue represents liberty or knowledge. The symbol at the center of the reverse shows the words "Républica del Paraguay" and a green wreath surrounding a gold star. The obverse coat of arms portrays a lion and a Phrygian cap, with the inscription "Paz y Justicia" (peace and justice).

805

PARAGUAY

The Paraguay River, here at Asunción, divides Paraguay into a sparsely populated western region (Occidental) and an eastern region (Oriental) that includes 98 percent of the nation's people.

GOVERNMENT

Official country name	Republic of Paraguay
Conventional short form	Paraguay
Nationality	
noun	Paraguayan
adjective	Paraguayan
Official languages	Spanish, Guaraní
Capital city	Asunción
Type of government	Republic; democracy
Voting rights	18 years and over; compulsory to age 75
National anthem	"Paraguayos, República o muerte!" (Paraguayans, the republic or death!)
National day	Independence Day, May 14 (the anniversary of independence from Spain in 1811); the holiday is observed on May 15

TRANSPORTATION

Railroads	22 miles (36 km)
Highways	18,334 miles (29,500 km)
Paved roads	9,314 miles (14,986 km)
Unpaved roads	9,020 miles (14,514 km)
Navigable waterways	1,927 miles (3,100 km)

Airports	
International airports	1
Paved runways	12

POPULATION PROFILE, 2006 ESTIMATES

Ethnic groups	
Mestizo (Amerindian and European)	95 percent
Guaraní Amerindian	5 percent
Religions	
Roman Catholic	89 percent
Various Protestant Evangelical churches	5 percent
Mennonites, other Christians, and nonreligious	6 percent
Languages	
Spanish (as a first language)	7 percent but almost universally understood
Guaraní Amerindian	91 percent
Others	2 percent
Adult literacy	94 percent

CHRONOLOGY

1st millennium CE	Guaraní Amerindians live in what is now Paraguay.
1537	Spanish colonists explore the region, founding Asunción, now Paraguay's national capital.
17th century–1767	Paraguay is effectively controlled by the Jesuits, who establish missions across the region.
1776	Paraguay becomes part of the Spanish viceroyalty (administrative region) of Río de la Plata.
1811	Paraguay declares independence from Spanish rule.
1814–1840	José Gaspar Rodríguez de Francia (1766–1840) is virtual dictator of Paraguay, isolating the nation from outside influences. He seizes church property, nationalizes the land, and suppresses dissent.
1865–1870	In the disastrous War of the Triple Alliance against Argentina, Brazil, and Uruguay, Paraguay loses more than one-half of its population. After the war, Paraguay takes decades to recover.
1887–1904	Under governments of the Colorado Party, Paraguay makes a gradual economic recovery.
1904 to late 1930s	The Liberal Party dominates Paraguayan political life.
1920s–1930s	Paraguay and Bolivia establish military posts in the Gran Chaco region, where the border between the two nations is disputed.
1932–1935	In the Chaco War, Paraguay gains most of the Gran Chaco region, despite being initially heavily outnumbered by Bolivian forces. However, the cost of the war ruins Paraguay's economy.
1947	Paraguay fights a civil war, which is eventually won by forces led by General Alfredo Stroessner (1912–2006).
1954–1989	Stroessner rules Paraguay as a dictator. He maintains economic stability, but corruption and abuses of human rights are common. Freedom of speech is restricted and censorship is imposed.
1970	Construction of the Itaipu Dam, which houses the world's largest operational hydroelectric power plant, begins. The first power is generated in 1984.
1989	Stroessner is ousted in a coup.
since 1989	Civilian democratic rule is restored in Paraguay, but the Colorado Party, the party of government under Stroessner, retains power.
1993	The Colorado Party wins a majority of seats in the first free multiparty elections; the first free presidential election is won by Colorado Party candidate, Juan Carlos Wasmosy.
2002–2003	President Luis González Macchi (born 1947; in office 1999–2003) stands trial for impeachment over charges including corruption. He is cleared in February 2003.
2002–2006	Rapid economic growth is achieved, with a flourishing reexport trade. Much of the nation's economy is informal and unrecorded.
2006	González Macchi is sentenced to eight years in jail for illegal financial affairs.

GOVERNMENT

Since the overthrow of a military dictatorship in 1989, Paraguay has had free multiparty elections. The country is a presidential republic in which power rests with the chief of state and the legislature.

Paraguay's chief of state is a directly elected president, who—under the terms of a new constitution, ratified in 1992—may serve for one nonrenewable term of five years. The voting age is 18 years, and voting is compulsory to age 75. However, the legal obligation to vote is not widely enforced, and more than one-third of the electorate generally chooses not to vote.

The president appoints a cabinet of ministers, which she or he chairs. Although the chief of state appoints many of the principal officers of state, the 1992 constitution diluted some of the powers of a highly centralized presidential system. For example, the nine-member supreme court is now appointed by the upper house of the legislature and by the president.

THE LEGISLATURE

The Paraguayan legislature, the National Congress, comprises two houses, the Chamber of Senators (the upper house) and the Chamber of Deputies (the lower house). The Senate has 45 members, who are elected for five years under a system of proportional representation, with political parties returning senators in proportion to the percentage of the vote that they receive in national legislative elections. The 80 members of the Chamber of Deputies are also elected under a system of proportional representation for five years but are elected from individual constituencies, which return two or more members.

Nicanor Duarte Frutos (born 1956), of the Colorado Party, was elected president of Paraguay in 2003.

POLITICAL PARTIES

The 1992 constitution guarantees the rights of all political parties to operate, but Paraguayan political life has been dominated by two parties for more than a century. Paraguay's two major political parties were formed in 1887: the (right-wing) Colorados, in modern times known as the National Republican Association/Colorado Party (ANR/PC), and the liberals, now called Authentic Radical Liberal Party (PLRA). At various times in Paraguayan history, both parties have engaged in unconstitutional activities, supported dictators, and fought civil wars. The Colorados supported the seizure of power by General Alfredo Stroessner (1912–2006; in office 1954–1989) in 1954.

After the Stroessner dictatorship was toppled in 1989, the Colorados retained power as a populist movement and maintained their position as Paraguay's largest political party. The PLRA was the only significant movement of the center-left until the 2008 presidential election campaign. The party then became a major component of the disparate Patriotic Alliance for Change (APC), whose candidate, Fernando Lugo (born 1951), was victorious, becoming the first non-Colorado president of modern times.

LOCAL GOVERNMENT

Paraguay is traditionally divided into two provinces, Oriental (the region east of the Paraguay River) and Occidental (the region west of the waterway). These two broad divisions have no administrative significance. The principal units of local government are 17 departments, each of which has a governor who is elected by popular vote.

Oriental, which is home to the overwhelming majority of Paraguayans, comprises 14 departments plus the city of Asunción, the national capital. Occidental has only three departments—two sparsely populated western departments were abolished in 1992, when boundaries in the western region were redrawn. The departments are divided into municipalities, each of which has an elected council, headed by a mayor.

C. CARPENTER

MODERN HISTORY

The First Century of Independence

Paraguay declared independence from Spanish rule in 1811, but through much of the nineteenth century, the nation was ruled by dictators. In the costly War of the Triple Alliance (1865–1870), Paraguay lost more than one-half of its population.

When the viceroyalty (administrative region) of Río de la Plata was created in 1776, through the division of the vast viceroyalty of Peru, the administration of Paraguay was transferred from Lima to Buenos Aires. The transfer was resented in Asunción, where Buenos Aires was considered a commercial rival. The authorities in Buenos Aires favored the city's own merchants in the traffic along the Paraná and Paraguay rivers, the only outlet to the sea for landlocked Paraguay. As a result, the Paraguayan elite were suspicious of any authority based in Buenos Aires.

INDEPENDENCE

When the city council of Buenos Aires formed a junta to rule the Río de la Plata provinces and deposed the Spanish viceroy in May 1810, the Paraguayans rejected the idea that Buenos Aires could represent their interests. An unsuccessful attempt was made by (limited) armed forces from Buenos Aires to subdue Paraguay. One year later, a leading Asunción citizen, José Gaspar Rodríguez de Francia (1766–1840; chief of state 1813–1814, 1814, and 1814–1840), staged a coup and forced the city's council to declare Paraguay independent. In October 1813, Paraguay adopted a governmental system in which two consuls (chiefs of state) each served four months on rotation. The system of dual executives proved unworkable and, after a period of near-anarchy, was subsequently abolished. Francia, one of the two consuls, was appointed sole chief of state, with the title of supreme dictator. In 1816, he was made ruler for life.

FRANCIA'S DICTATORSHIP

The authorities in Buenos Aires did not accept Paraguay's secession from the Río de la Plata federation, however, and adopted a policy of sanctions, repeatedly blockading the Río de la Plata to Paraguayan trade. To the east, Brazil, which sought to expand its sphere of influence by way of trade along the waterways of central South America, also threatened Paraguay's independence. Francia responded to these threats by attempting to turn Paraguay into a closed, self-sufficient economy, isolating Paraguay from Brazil, Argentina, and the rest of the outside world.

Francia nationalized the land and industry, taking farms and factories into state ownership. He also maintained a state monopoly in vital parts of the agrarian sector. In order to erase the legacy of three centuries of Spanish influence, he banned marriage between creoles (people of unmixed Spanish ancestry). As a result, Paraguay became one of the most mixed nations on the continent as creoles and Guaraní Amerindians married, and the Guaraní language became more commonly used in daily life than Spanish. Under Francia, Paraguay was isolated, peaceful, and stable but subject to a harsh, despotic system. He banned foreign trade and most travel outside Paraguay. He also reduced the privileges of the traditional ruling elite and took measures to control the Roman Catholic Church, such as nationalizing church property. As a result of Francia's policies, Paraguay became impoverished.

THE WAR OF THE TRIPLE ALLIANCE

Francia's successors, who ruled with the title of president from 1844, Carlos Antonio López (1792–1862; in office 1841–1862) and his son, Francisco Solano López (1827–1870; in office 1862–1869), continued to rule Paraguay as a dictatorship. However, they slowly abandoned Francia's isolationist policy. Solano López had imperialistic dreams and embarked on an aggressive foreign policy against Brazil and Argentina. He not only defended Paraguayan independence but also tried to expand its territory. His ambitions clashed with those of an equally expansionist Brazil, to which Paraguay was an obstacle.

Paraguayan troops are transported to the front during the Chaco War (1932–1935).

Greatly overestimating Paraguay's resources, Solano López became involved in a civil war in Uruguay and escalated border disputes with his neighbors, leading to the War of the Triple Alliance (1865–1870) against Argentina, Brazil, and Uruguay. Initially, the prospects for success seemed promising for Paraguay, whose 30,000-strong army was the largest in Latin America. Also, none of the three allied opponents was prepared for war. However, the combined strength of the allies proved too great for Paraguay, and the War of the Triple Alliance became a national catastrophe for the country. When the war ended in 1870, with the final defeat and death in battle of Solano López (who had effectively been replaced as president in 1869), Asunción had been occupied and sacked, and 250,000 people—more than one-half of the country's population—had been killed. Paraguay also lost around 25 percent of its territory. It took more than 30 years for Paraguay to recover from the war, which was among the bloodiest ever fought in Latin America.

RECONSTRUCTION

After the war, the state-controlled economy was dismantled through extensive land sales, mainly to foreigners. However, Paraguay's independence was respected by the three victors, although Brazilian forces remained in Asunción for several years. In the following decades, attempts were made to diminish the role of the state and to empower Paraguayan citizens, but the new liberal constitution, which had been imposed by the Brazilians in 1870, proved unrealistic for a country whose inhabitants had almost no history of democracy. The result was almost constant chaos, widespread electoral fraud, numerous military coups, political assassinations, and brief civil wars.

In 1887, the Liberal Party was founded and, in reaction later the same year, the traditional elite founded a party of its own, the National Republican Association, more commonly known as the Colorados. The two parties came to dominate Paraguayan political life and are still the major political organizations in the country. The Colorados were in power between 1887 and 1904 and the Liberals from 1904 through 1936. At the same time, popular participation in the political process slowly grew. Nevertheless, both parties were based more on personal allegiances to party bosses and populism rather than political ideology, and Paraguay was far from being a democratic society.

THE CHACO WAR

The Gran Chaco area in the northwest was a disputed region between Paraguay and Bolivia. In the 1920s, Bolivia, which had become landlocked when it lost its Pacific coast to Chile in the War of the Pacific (1879–1884), began to search for an outlet to the sea to the east. The navigable Paraguay River seemed to be an obvious route to explore. However, the border in the Gran Chaco was poorly delineated, and both Paraguay and Bolivia established forts there, particularly from the 1920s onward, when there were border clashes.

Both Bolivian and Paraguayan interest in the region further increased when oil corporations prospected in the Gran Chaco. In 1932, after Bolivia attacked a Paraguayan garrison, the Chaco War broke out. However, the Bolivian army was at a disadvantage. Bolivia's troops were predominantly highland Amerindians who were unused to the tropical heat of the lowland regions, where they tired easily and were susceptible to diseases. They were driven back by the Paraguayans, who received supplies and intelligence from neighboring Argentina. The result was a stalemate and, although the war was economically damaging to both nations, when a cease-fire was negotiated in 1935, Paraguay, controlling the greater part of the Gran Chaco, made considerable territorial gains at Bolivia's expense.

D. RETSÖ

Modern Paraguay

Democracy in Paraguay slowly gained ground in the first decades of the twentieth century, but a military coup in February 1936 disrupted that evolution and inaugurated a long period of military rule and political repression. The military regime was ousted in 1989; since then Paraguay has had a civilian government.

From 1887 through 1936, Paraguay's two principal political parties alternated; the (right-wing) Colorados were in power between 1887 and 1904 and the Liberals from 1904 through 1936. However, a military coup in February 1936 ousted the Liberals and began more than 50 years of repressive rule. The coup also marked the beginning of a period of state-led economic development in line with the protectionist economic policies then followed by most Latin American states.

The coup of February 1936 also triggered an almost 20-year-long cycle of infighting within the armed forces among charismatic leaders and their adherents. Several coups and counter-coups resulted, and short-lived presidencies preceded the seizure of power by General José F. Estigarribia (1888–1940; in office 1939–1940). When Estigarribia died in an airplane crash, he was succeeded by General Higinio Morínigo (1897–1983; in office 1940–1948). Morínigo was a supporter of Nazi Germany and facilitated the entry into Paraguay of several Nazi war criminals in 1945 after World War II. He exercised absolute power, suspending the constitution and banning all political parties. However, Morínigo faced growing unrest, including a number of politically motivated strikes.

THE PARAGUAYAN CIVIL WAR

In 1946, Morínigo lifted the ban on political parties but, in the following year, one element of Morínigo's supporters defected because they believed the president was favoring the Colorados (who formed the greater part of Morínigo's government). The defectors then allied with the Liberals and communists. Sectors of the army had also grown impatient with Morínigo's favoritism within the regime and attempted yet another coup. This led to a short civil war in 1947, when some sections of the army as well as the (river-based) navy opposed Morínigo. Forces loyal to Morínigo were victorious, but renewed unrest followed. Morínigo was obliged to resign and went into exile, and, in 1949, there were no fewer than three military coups.

STROESSNER

In 1954, General Alfredo Stroessner (1912–2006; in office 1954–1989) seized power in a coup and finally managed to end the cycle of military unrest. However, social order was only achieved at the cost of Paraguay's still weak democratic institutions. Under Stroessner's long leadership, the so-called *stronato*, Paraguay became one of the most repressive dictatorships on the South American continent.

Domestically, Stroessner based his regime on his control over the military. Such a policy was not new—ever since the dictatorship of José Gaspar Rodríguez de Francia (1766–1840; chief of state 1813–1814, 1814, and 1814–1840) nearly all of Paraguay's leaders had done the same. The difference that Stroessner introduced, which secured power for him for more than three decades, was that he mobilized popular support to counterbalance the power of the military establishment. The instrument for that support was the Colorado Party, which in his control became a mass party with an extensive national organization that penetrated society on all levels. At the same time, a personality cult evolved around Stroessner himself, and potential political opponents were bought off with rewards in the form of public funds and grants of public offices within the administration.

Corruption became an institutional feature of the *stronato*. Although elections were held under Stroessner, Paraguay was ruled by an institutional triumvirate comprising the military, the Colorado Party, and Stroessner's state apparatus, which to an increasing extent became identified with each other. The result was Stroessner's undisputed leadership, and he was reelected president eight times in consecutive flawed elections.

The support he enjoyed from the government of the United States contributed to the longevity of the Stroessner dictatorship. Stroessner had come to power at a stage in the Cold War (the period of rivalry between communist countries led by the Soviet Union and Western nations led by the United States; 1945–1991) when the United States needed allies in Latin America against alleged Soviet activities. Although communism was practically absent in Paraguay, Stroessner opportunistically adopted the U.S. national security doctrine in order to emphasize his support for the United States. In turn, Stroessner acquired U.S. support for his regime. In the 1970s, Stroessner took the initiative to create a secret intelligence cooperation program between the military regimes of the Southern Cone, the countries of the south of the continent. The program, named Operation Condor, aimed at tracking down and eliminating supposed left-wing elements.

The alleged Soviet threat to national security was utilized as an excuse for violent crackdowns on any attempt at organized opposition from students, peasants, or workers. Human rights violations became common during the *stronato*. At the same

Alfredo Stroessner (1912–2006) headed a repressive military regime that held power in Paraguay for 35 years, until his overthrow in 1989.

time, national security motivated lavish spending on the military, which received a large share of the state budget. This policy secured loyalty within the armed forces toward Stroessner.

GROWING DISCONTENT

From 1978, a limited political liberalization was allowed, and an opposition group called Acuerdo Nacional was founded. However, in the 1980s, political repression increased again. The crackdown followed the 1980 assassination in Asunción of Anastasio Somoza (1926–1980; in office as president of Nicaragua 1967–1972 and 1974–1979 but effectively dictator 1967–1979), who had been ousted by the left-wing Sandinista revolution in Nicaragua and subsequently granted political asylum in Paraguay, by Nicaraguan secret agents. Fearful of political violence against him, Stroessner imposed renewed political repression. As a result, leading politicians of the Paraguayan opposition went into exile, and, in 1987, the only opposition newspaper, *El Pueblo*, was outlawed.

However, as repression increased through the 1980s, so did political opposition. The spread of democracy throughout Latin America could not be ignored in Paraguay. Mismanagement of the economy and the virtual monopoly of state employment enjoyed by Colorado Party members finally turned the business community against the regime.

In February 1984, the first demonstration in 30 years was held, and antigovernment political graffiti appeared on walls in Asunción. A visit by Pope John Paul II (1920–2005; reigned 1978–2005) in 1987 also spurred the opposition to demonstrate against the regime. At the same time, a deep division within the hitherto monolithic and unambiguously pro-Stroessner Colorado Party appeared between those who most strongly supported Stroessner and wanted his son to succeed him (the so called *militantes*), an increasingly anti-Stroessner faction (the *éticos*), and a third group whose members wanted to keep the Colorado Party in power but in order to do so wished to remove the Stroessner family from power (the *tradicionalistas*).

PARAGUAY AFTER STROESSNER

On February 3, 1989, a *tradicionalista* army general Andrés Rodríguez (1923–1997; in office 1989–1993) staged a coup. Stroessner went into exile in Brazil, where he died in 2006. Rodríguez immediately initiated a moderate democratization process as well as economic reforms to bring Paraguay more in line with the rest of the continent. However, the practices of corruption and paternalism that had characterized the Stroessner era did not end.

In modern times, the Colorado Party is deeply split between factions led by charismatic leaders at the head of extensive and deeply ingrained networks that still permeate not only the party but society in general. However, even though the competing factions normally function as virtually independent parties, the Colorados still join forces in times of election and managed to retain power and rule the country without interruption from 1948 through 2008.

Bitter infighting within the Colorado Party, as well as the democratic deficit in Paraguay, surfaced in March 1999 when the vice president was assassinated by unidentified assailants, who were widely believed to be members of another Colorado faction. President Raúl Cubas (born 1943; in office 1998–1999) was obliged to resign after riots followed the assassination. Then, another Colorado Party member, army commander General Lino Oviedo (born 1943), who had been jailed for a coup attempt in 1993 but later pardoned by Cubas, was accused of planning a coup. Oviedo fled but returned to Paraguay in 2004 and was imprisoned. In 2007, his conviction was overturned. Luis González Macchi (born 1947; in office 1999–2003) became president in 1999, but, dogged by allegations of corruption, he lost the 2003 presidential election and was convicted of corruption in 2006. In 2003, yet another Colorado Party member, Nicanor Duarte Frutos (born 1956), was elected president. However, in 2008, former Roman Catholic bishop Fernando Lugo (born 1951), the candidate of the Patriotic Alliance for Change (APC), an electoral coalition of widely different parties, won the presidential election and ended more than 60 years of Colorado rule.

D. RETSÖ

CULTURAL EXPRESSION

Literature

European, largely Spanish, settlers came to what is now Paraguay in the sixteenth century and, as a result, the nation's literature is mainly Spanish. However, Guaraní, the language of the indigenous population, is now spoken by the majority of the people of Paraguay and, in modern times, Guaraní literature is increasingly published.

Although indigenous groups in Paraguay had a strong oral literary tradition, much of it was lost after the late sixteenth century when European settlers first arrived in the region. The Jesuits converted thousands of Guaraní people to Christianity, often preaching in Guaraní, which became the *lingua geral* (official language) of the missions. Much of the religious literature from this time was written in Guaraní, but, as increasing numbers of Amerindians became Christian, most of their cultural traditions and oral literature were lost.

Historiography, essays, and poetry formed much of the literature of nineteenth- and early twentieth-century Paraguay. Juan E. O'Leary (1879–1969) was a leading historian and poet of this period. O'Leary, who was also a politician and diplomat, was one a group of poets who, at the turn of the twentieth century, promoted the preservation of the Guaraní language and culture from the pervasive influence of Spanish. During the twentieth century, Paraguayan writing in both Spanish and Guaraní flourished.

Augusto Roa Bastos (1917–2005), Paraguay's most famous novelist, spent much of his career in exile from the military dictatorship, living in Argentina and France.

BASTOS

The best-known Paraguayan writer is the novelist Augusto Roa Bastos (1917–2005), whose works have been translated into many languages. Bastos wrote the celebrated novel *Yo el supremo* (1974; translated into English as *I, the Supreme*, 1986), which focused on the Paraguayan dictator José Gaspar Rodríguez de Francia (1766–1840; chief of state of Paraguay 1813–1814, 1814, and 1814–1840), who secured Paraguay's independence. The novel addressed the issue of dictatorship, and Bastos, who sided with the opponents of Paraguayan dictator Alfredo Stroessner (1912–2006; in office 1954–1989), had to move to Buenos Aires, Argentina, during Stroessner's military dictatorship, living there until 1976, when he moved to France. After Stroessner was ousted from power in 1989, Bastos was able to return to Paraguay.

MODERN LITERATURE

During Stroessner's dictatorship, the country endured extreme censorship. José Ricardo Mazó (1927–1987), an academic and prominent poet, was a member of Promoción del 50, a group of poets, mainly based in the Academia Universitaria and the philosophy faculty in Asunción, who wrote socially and politically focused poetry. Many Paraguayan writers joined Bastos in moving abroad during Stroessner's rule, and much of the important literature of this period was written by writers in exile. Among the exiles were the novelist Gabriel Casaccia (1907–1980) and the poets Hérib Campos Cervera (1905–1953) and Elvio Romero (born 1926), who all lived in Argentina.

Since 1989, many Paraguayan writers have returned to their homeland. In the last decades of the twentieth century and in the early twenty-first century, many writers have focused on the reality of living under a dictatorship and the struggle for democracy. There has also been a resurgence in Guaraní literature, through such publishers as the Arandura Press.

E. M. STONE

Art and Architecture

Paraguay's distinctive art and architecture evolved after the arrival of the Spanish in the sixteenth century. The influence of the missions set up by the Jesuits in the seventeenth and eighteenth centuries was great, but an artistic style blending Amerindian and European cultures gradually emerged in Paraguay.

Paraguay's earliest cultures were developed by Guaycurú peoples, who lived in the Gran Chaco region, and Guaraní-speaking peoples, who inhabited lands to the east of the Paraguay River. Although comparatively few artifacts remain from the pre-Columbian period, a number of pottery vessels survive, notably from the Chaco region. They include simply shaped cooking pots, jars, urns, and bowls, which were built up from coils of clay and decorated with incised decorations. While the Chaco and Guaraní cultures were distinct, both used stylized, often geometric decorative patterns. Examples can still be seen in the traditional basketwork made by both peoples today. Another indigenous art form still being practiced is featherwork, in which ceremonial objects and clothing are decorated with feathers.

SPANISH COLONIZATION

Spanish settlers founded a settlement at Asunción in 1537, and the city soon became the center of Spanish power in the La Plata region—which included Argentina—until Buenos Aires was refounded in 1580. Asunción's first buildings, like those of the local Guaraní peoples, were of timber and straw, although they were soon replaced with more permanent structures made from adobe (mud brick) and palm thatch. These early structures included official buildings, a cathedral, and townhouses laid out around courtyards in the Spanish tradition.

Unlike most other colonial cities of Spanish South America, Asunción was not laid out on a grid, largely because of its hilly site on a headland and along a bay of the Paraguay River. When a checkerboard plan was imposed on the city during the nineteenth century, most of the city's Spanish colonial buildings were lost in the redevelopment.

JESUIT MISSIONS

Because Paraguay lacked the rich reserves of minerals that attracted Spanish colonists to some other parts of South America, the region received less attention from the colonial authorities and settlers. As a result, the civil authorities played a smaller part in commissioning architecture and artworks than their wealthier counterparts in other parts of Latin America. In Paraguay, by contrast, the great patrons of the arts were Roman Catholic religious orders, such as the Franciscans and Jesuits, who came to convert the indigenous population to Catholicism.

The Jesuits, in particular, were instrumental in introducing and imposing Christianity and European cultural practices outside Asunción in the seventeenth and eighteenth centuries. In 1609, the Spanish crown granted the Jesuits the right to administer the lands around the Paraná and Uruguay rivers. During the following century and a half, the Jesuits set up some 30 *reducciones* (reductions, settlements of Amerindians directed by the order). Eight reductions were in present-day Paraguay, where they brought together Guaraní peoples in large, self-contained settlements, which had a standard plan. The reductions comprised a church, college, workshops, living quarters for the Jesuits, and dwellings for the Guaraní, all laid out around a large central square.

Although most reductions were abandoned after the expulsion of the Jesuits in 1767 (when the Jesuit order was temporarily suppressed by the Catholic Church for a variety of political and economic reasons), some form the basis of present-day towns, for example, San Ignacio Guazú, which was founded in 1684. Other reductions have survived as ruins, the best preserved of which are at La Santísima Trinidad (1706).

MESTIZO CULTURE

The Jesuit and Franciscan missions became the settings for a new type of art, as Guaraní and European cultures interacted, although European styles remained dominant. The resultant mestizo style (part Amerindian, part European) is characteristic of Paraguay. Despite the prescriptions of the church authorities, indigenous artisans often left their mark. At the large, stone, classical-style church of La Santísima Trinidad, for example—which was designed by an Italian Jesuit architect—Guaraní artisans combined indigenous motifs, such as the Paraguayan harp and local flora, with Christian imagery in their carved decoration of the building. Mostly, however, the mission workshops directed indigenous artists to copy existing statues and paintings of holy figures (some from Europe, others from Peru and Bolivia) to instruct people in the Christian faith. There are many examples of polychrome (painted) sculptures and carved altarpieces from missionary workshops, although fewer paintings have survived.

The ruins of the Jesuit reduction at La Santísima Trinidad in Paraguay extend over a wide area. The settlement was constructed in the early eighteenth century as a virtually self-sufficient city.

Mestizo styles were also evident in popular art made outside the missions, reflecting the wider melding of the Spanish and Guaraní communities, with European culture in the leading role. Rural artisans carved wooden images of saints, which were unfettered by conventions of naturalism and the baroque style that bound official religious art. Artists also introduced figurative decoration and animal-shaped vessels into their pottery. Traditional textile-making was also affected by European culture. Elaborate cotton embroidery work known as *ñandutí* and a type of lace called *yu* both have their origins in the ecclesiastical robes made for missionaries.

ART IN INDEPENDENT PARAGUAY

After Paraguay declared its independence in 1811, its new leader, José Gaspar Rodríguez de Francia (1766–1840; in office 1814–1840), isolated the nation from the outside world and neglected the arts. His successor, Carlos Antonio López (1792–1862; in office as chief of state 1841–1844 and as president 1844–1862) and his son, Francisco Solano López (1827–1870; in office 1862–1869), however, embraced European culture and commissioned many new buildings, monuments, and official portraits to embellish Asunción, the national capital. They invited European artists to Paraguay and sent Paraguayan artists to train in Europe. The López family favored the neoclassical style, which had its origins in the French academies and had associations with national independence, and they transformed Asunción with new or remodeled buildings. The most famous examples of Asunción's neoclassical buildings include the Palacio de Gobierno (government palace), the Palacio de Congresso (Congress Building; begun in the mid-1850s), the oratory of Nuestra Señora de la Asunción (begun mid-1850s), and the domed National Pantheon of Heroes.

The disastrous War of the Triple Alliance (1865–1870), when Paraguay fought Argentina, Brazil, and Uruguay, brought an abrupt end to artistic patronage in Paraguay and severely curtailed artistic activity. A long period of political instability followed, and the country also went through the costly Chaco War (1932–1935) and later military dictatorships. As a result, state patronage of the arts was not a priority, and Paraguayan artists had few opportunities for commissions or to exhibit their works.

ART IN MODERN PARAGUAY

From the middle of the twentieth century, a number of Paraguayan artists began to produce experimental paintings and sculptures and to question the country's conservative traditions. Inspired by wider developments in Latin American art, particularly in Buenos Aires and Rio de Janeiro, these groups included the Arte Nuevo group (founded 1954), the Los Novísimos group (1964), the Neofiguración movement in the late 1960s, and the Re-Figuración movement in the mid-1970s. While artists have explored abstraction and other international trends, figuration remains a feature of Paraguayan arts; artists often use their work to explore social, political, and historical themes. These trends can be seen in the work of Carlos Colombino (born 1937), who is major figure in Paraguay's modern art scene.

R. BEAN

Music and Performing Arts

The music and performing arts of Paraguay mix European and indigenous traditions. The majority of Paraguayans speak both Spanish and Guaraní, an Amerindian language, but most songs and performances are in Guaraní.

Although there is a vast repertoire of Paraguayan music, most of it was not written down until the twentieth century. Music is important to Paraguayan culture and owes much to both Spanish and Guaraní influence. From the sixteenth century, the Spanish brought European instruments—guitars, harps, and wind instruments—to Paraguay, and Jesuit missionaries used music to help convert the local peoples to Christianity. The harp gradually overtook the organ or harpsichord in popularity in church services and at celebrations, and it has been a major influence on the development of Paraguayan music. The modern Paraguayan harp is a simplified version of the original instrument and has 38 strings tuned to one major diatonic scale (a seven-note scale).

DANCE

The Paraguayan polka (or *galopa*) is one of the country's most celebrated styles of music. It combines ternary (three-form) and binary rhythms, whereas the European polka only uses binary. Many Paraguayan composers wrote polkas, including the guitarist Agustín Barrios (1885–1944) who composed Danza Paraguaya as a testament to this type of dance. U.S. composer and guitarist John Williams (born 1932) has recorded many of Barrios's works.

As well as the polka, Paraguay is also famous for *la galopera*, or the bottle dance, during which the performer balances a full bottle or jug of water on top of her or his head. *La galopera* is meant to show the dancer's skill and grace as the performer must not drop any water during the dance. The Ballet Cambacuá performs the traditional dances of Cambacuá, an Afro-Paraguayan community of about two thousand people. In January each year, crowds flock to Cambacuá, east of Asunción, to watch the ballet group perform at a local festival. Paraguay also has its own national ballet company, the Ballet Nacional de Paraguay, which performs classical dance. Some modern dance groups mix elements of traditional folk dance with ballet.

SONGS AND GROUPS

The *zarzuela* (Spanish opera), another early popular form of entertainment, mixes folklore and musical comedy traditions. Songs in Paraguay are usually performed in Guaraní, Spanish, or Jopara (combination of Guaraní and Spanish). The *guarania*, created by the Paraguayan musician José Asunción Flores (1904–1972) in 1925, is another well-known form of indigenous music and mixes slow rhythms with melancholic melodies. Paraguayan harpists, such as Feliz Perez Cardozo (died 1952), helped popularize this style of music.

DICTATORSHIP AND CULTURE

Paraguayan culture was largely cut off from outside cultural influences by the censorship imposed by military dictator Alfredo Stroessner (1912–2006; in office 1954–1989). Modern music, particularly rock music, was not broadcast; nevertheless, several rock bands were formed in Paraguay. Paraguayan popular music flourished from the 1990s onward with such bands as Flou, Revolber, and the ska-punk band Ripe Banana Skins. Lizza Bogado (born c. 1964; birth date not published), considered by many to be one of the best popular and traditional Paraguayan singers, has established an international reputation in the Spanish-speaking world. Bogado promotes music education and dance through her role as director of the arts foundation Fundación Libre in Paraguay.

E. M. STONE

The Paraguayan harp, the national instrument, gives the nation's music a distinctive sound.

Festivals and Ceremonies

Major religious holidays are widely observed in Paraguay and, along with a number of festivals that commemorate events in the country's political history, are the principal national holidays.

As well as national holidays, Paraguayans celebrate a large number of local festivals, the majority of which are saint's days, many of which are restricted to particular cities or localities. However, the festival of San Juan (Saint John) is widely celebrated with local dishes and *asado*s (barbecues), at which friends and family gather. In a few localities, some people mark the festival by walking on hot embers. Some cities and towns stage cultural festivals, and Nanduti Festival, held in Itauguá in June, is a folk celebration of art. In Carapeguá in November, the Poyvi Festival is marked by music and displays of decorative art.

RELIGIOUS HOLIDAYS

The overwhelming majority of the Paraguayan population are Roman Catholic, and major Catholic festivals are national holidays. On August 15, the national capital, Asunción, celebrates the religious festival of the Assumption (Día de la Virgen de la Asunción), which is also the anniversary of its foundation in 1537. The day is a public holiday throughout Paraguay and is marked in the city with official speeches and parades, including an armed forces parade of vehicles and troops. Citizens of Asunción commemorate the holiday with traditional music and dancing. December 8 is Día de la Virgen (the Immaculate Conception), which, although it is a national holiday, is particularly celebrated in the city of Caacupé, whose imposing Basilica de Nuestra Señora de los Milagros draws many thousands of people each year on pilgrimage on the feast day.

February 3 is Día de San Blas, the saint's day of Saint Blaise, one of the national patrons of Paraguay. Although the festival is a public holiday throughout the country, celebrations are especially important in Ciudad del Este, a city along the Brazilian border. On the saint's day, masses are held. Other religious holidays include Epiphany (January 6; known as Three Kings' Day), Maundy Thursday and Good Friday, and Christmas Day. The day before Lent is also a public holiday. Celebrations are liveliest in Asunción and have been heavily influenced by the enthusiastic carnivals held in Brazil.

SECULAR HOLIDAYS

March 1 is Día de los Héroes (Heroes' Day, also known as National Defense Day). The public holiday commemorates the founding fathers of Paraguay as well as those Paraguayans who lost their lives in two wars, the disastrous War of the Triple Alliance (1865–1870), and the Chaco War (1932–1935). Parades, dances, and parties are held on Independence Day on May 15, which commemorates the ousting of the Spanish governor in Asunción in May 1811. September 29 is Boquerón Battle Day, (Victory Day), celebrating Paraguay's success in a border conflict with Bolivia in 1930, before the Chaco War. New Year's Day, Labor Day (May 1), Flag Day (May 14), and Children's Day (August 16) are also public holidays.

National holidays are often an occasion for sports. Although equestrian sports and activities along the main waterways, such as canoeing and fishing, are popular, the national sport is soccer, and holidays are used as a time to watch both live games and matches on television. Professional teams in Asunción, such as Olimpia and Cerro Porteño, have large and loyal followings, but the greatest enthusiasm is reserved for the achievements of the national team, for example in the 2006 World Cup games.

D. TORRA

Paraguay's national soccer team (pictured here in blue, playing against England) qualified for the 2006 soccer World Cup. Paraguayans love to watch soccer and often go to see matches on public holidays.

Food and Drink

Paraguayan cuisine reflects both Guaraní (local Amerindian) and Spanish cultures. Paraguay grows a diverse range of vegetables and fruits, which form a large part of the national diet, along with beef, pork, lamb, goat, other meats, and also freshwater fish. Grains, such as corn, and mandioca (cassava, or manioc) are usually eaten with each meal.

Mandioca (manioc), corn, and beans were among the leading crops traditionally grown by the Guaraní native peoples, and these staple foods still form an essential part of the Paraguayan diet. Mandioca has been grown in the region for several centuries; along with corn, it is a main ingredient in Paraguayan cuisine. The country's subtropical and tropical climate allows Paraguayans to grow a wide range of vegetables and fruit, including gourds, squashes, tomatoes, onions, carrots, pineapples, peaches, bananas, avocados, mangoes, and apples.

Paraguayans tend to eat a light breakfast of bread, jam, and tea (or the herbal tea maté, made from yerba maté) or coffee. They may also eat more traditional dishes such as *rora con leche* (a corn dish with milk) and *mbeju* (unleavened bread made with mandioca starch), or drink *maté cocido* (a yerba maté drink). Lunch is a more substantial meal, as in other Latin American countries, but dinner is the most important meal of the day and is often eaten late at night and may last several hours. A variety of dishes, usually meat, may be eaten.

Paraguayan small farmers commonly sell fruit from their land at the roadside.

NATIONAL DISHES

The Paraguayan diet typically contains large quantities of meat, particularly beef. Like their Argentine neighbors, Paraguayans often eat *parillados* (mixed selections of grilled meat from offal to fine cuts). Families and friends often gather at weekends and celebrations for an *asado* (barbecue) at which meat, usually beef but sometimes a whole pig, is roasted on a spit and served with boiled mandioca and *sopa paraguaya* (a corn flour and cheese bread). Famous for their soups, Paraguayans mix meat with corn or mandioca in dishes such as *sooyo-sopy* (a soup of cornmeal, rice, or noodles mixed with ground beef) and *bori-bori* (chicken soup with cornmeal dumplings). *Locro* (a corn stew) and *chipas* (corn bread mixed with egg and cheese) are national favorites. *Chipa soo* is a popular dish made from corn bread filled with meat, while *chipa guazú* is a cross between *sopa paraguaya* and a soufflé. Surubí, a local freshwater fish, is often grilled or served in a fish pie. Desserts include *suspiros de yemas* (made from egg yolks and sugar), and *mbaipy-he-é* (made from corn, milk, and molasses).

In addition, various ethnic foods are available in Paraguay, particularly Italian, Japanese, Korean, Chinese, and Arab cuisines. Japanese settlers came to Paraguay in the late 1950s, settling in the area between Encarnación and Caazapá. Koreans began emigrating to Paraguay from the mid-1960s, followed by Arabs, Iranians, and Taiwanese who have also settled in and around Ciudad del Este. Each nationality has introduced its own distinctive dishes and ingredients to Paraguayan cuisine.

DRINKS

Paraguayans consume large quantities of maté, an herbal tea that is the national drink, made from the leaves and stems of the yerba maté plant. Related to the holly, yerba maté is grown for both domestic and export purposes. Maté is served either hot or cold as a drink called *tereré*. Sugarcane drinks such as the nonalcoholic *mosto* and the alcoholic *caña* are also drunk by local people. Domestically produced beers are popular, and wines, particularly from Argentina and Chile, are imported for home consumption.

J. MONCADA

DAILY LIFE

Religion

Some 89 percent of Paraguayans are Roman Catholics. Around 5 percent of Paraguay's people are members of various Protestant evangelical churches, while the remaining 6 percent include Mennonites and other Christians, members of various Asian religions, and nonreligious people.

Christianity first reached the area that is now Paraguay in 1526, when Franciscan priests accompanied the first Spanish expedition that sailed up the Paraná River. From the beginning of Spanish settlement in Paraguay, Catholic missionary priests set about converting the indigenous Guaraní peoples. During the administration of Álvar Nuñez Cabeza de Vaca (c. 1490–c. 1557; in office 1542–1544), governor of the Río de la Plata province, increasing numbers of indigenous people were converted to Christianity and, in 1547, the bishopric of Asunción was created.

ROMAN CATHOLICISM AND THE STATE

In the late 1580s, the first Jesuits arrived in the region to establish settlements or *reducciones* where indigenous converts, primarily the Guaraní, lived and worked. The Jesuits were finally expelled from Paraguay in 1767, when the Catholic Church temporarily suppressed the Jesuits for a variety of political and economic reasons. The *reducciones* were abandoned, and their populations were integrated into local society.

José Gaspar Rodríguez de Francia (1766–1840; in office 1813–1814, 1814, and 1814–1840) secured Paraguay's independence in 1813 and ruled the nation as dictator. Francia favored a secular state and sought to control the clergy. He cut off communication with the Vatican in Rome, suppressed the clergy, and relieved the church of its possessions. The clergy in Paraguay also suffered under the presidency of Francisco Solano López (1827–1870; in office 1862–1869). Solano López ordered the execution of Asunción's bishop and other members of the clergy after he discovered their involvement in a plot to overthrow him. By 1870, there were fewer than 50 priests left in the country. The 1870 constitution revised relations between church and state and established Roman Catholicism as the state religion, although it also protected the rights of other faiths.

Through the twentieth century, the relationship between church and state was initially close, but the Catholic Church emerged as a leading voice of dissent against abuses of human and civil rights by the authorities. In the late 1960s, members of the clergy, including several bishops, criticized the dictatorship of Alfredo Stroessner (1912–2006; in office 1954–1989) for its repressive policies. Some priests moved into poor neighborhoods and organized community groups, establishing a newspaper and radio station to promote their views. These community groups sponsored welfare and educational programs, improving literacy among the poor and providing support to families in need. The government subsequently harassed, arrested, and ill-treated priests and nuns, and expelled foreign-born clergy from Paraguay. Through the 1970s and 1980s, church and state came increasingly into conflict as clerics emerged as important critics of the Stroessner regime and defenders of the poor.

Following the overthrow of Alfredo Stroessner in 1989, a new democratic constitution in 1992 separated church and state and gave wider protection to the civil rights of citizens, including religious freedom. Although the Catholic Church remains an influential force in Paraguay, the new constitution offers no political or legal advantages to membership in any religion.

OTHER RELIGIONS

The arrival of immigrants from Russia in 1917, after the Russian Revolution, brought communities of Mennonites (an Anabaptist Christian denomination) to the New World, including the Gran Chaco region of western Paraguay. Other Mennonite communities arrived from Germany and Canada, and Mennonites are now the largest Protestant group in Paraguay. The country's Occidental Region contains a number of Mennonite settlements, the most important of which is Filadelfia.

In modern times, the size of religious minorities in Paraguay has increased, in part through the activities of various Protestant evangelical churches but also through settlement by Arab, Taiwanese, and Iranian traders, particularly in Ciudad del Este, and there are now Buddhist and Muslim congregations in Paraguay.

E. M. STONE

Family and Society

Family and kinship are the center of social life in Paraguay, a nation in which an Amerindian language and culture, Guaraní, plays a leading role. In Paraguay, the Guaraní language is spoken by people of all social classes, not only by those of Guaraní ancestry, and is considered a measure of national identity.

Paraguay's population of nearly 5.2 million (at the 2002 national census) is divided between mestizos (people of mixed Amerindian, mainly Guaraní, and European ancestry), who account for about 95 percent of Paraguayans, and people of unmixed Guaraní ancestry, accounting for almost all of the remaining 5 percent. There is also a small Asian community.

FAMILY

Paraguayans are loyal to their extended family and use their political, business, and other connections to help each other prosper. It is not uncommon for well-off families to sponsor their poorer relatives during times of need. The system of *compadrazgo* (literally, "co-parenthood"), or selecting godparents, is an important social practice. Godparents share responsibility, along with the birth parents, for bringing up a child, and the relationship between godparents, the godchild, and his or her family is very important.

The most common form of family structure is the nuclear family, comprising a father, mother, and dependent children. Traditionally, Paraguay is a patriarchal society in which the father is the head of the house, and the mother manages the domestic sphere. Until modern times, it was accepted that men had an active social life outside the home, which often included extramarital relations.

The Roman Catholic religion, which is followed by 89 percent of the Paraguayan population, is a strong influence on society. Paraguayan women were encouraged to develop an attitude of *marianismo*, or being pure and tolerant like the Virgin Mary. However, in modern Paraguay, there have been considerable changes to these attitudes. Divorce was legalized in Paraguay in 1991. Although marriage is still important, and Paraguay is still generally a conservative society, both unions and children outside of formal marriage are gaining acceptance. Women as heads of households—either as main income earners or single women living apart from their husbands—are becoming more common and, by the early twenty-first century, women were the head of around 25 percent of Paraguayan households. Households headed by women are also a result of the migration of male members of families to cities, such as Asunción (the national capital) and Cuidad del Este (a growing commercial center), in search of work. Paraguay is becoming urbanized, although only 46 percent of Paraguayans live in cities.

Mestizos, such as these children of mixed Hispanic and Guaraní ancestry, form the majority of Paraguay's population.

Social differences are pronounced. A minority of households (under 2 percent) own nearly 80 percent of the land, while the majority of rural families eke out a hard living. Some authorities estimate that nearly 60 percent of rural families live in poverty, while official figures in 2005 showed that 32 percent of Paraguayans were poor.

THE ROLE OF WOMEN

After 1989, the democratic government supported measures to improve women's rights in Paraguay. The 1992 Civil Code established equality for men and women in public affairs. Women were also given equality in land ownership. The authorities have enacted laws against domestic violence and sexual harassment and established a Women's Secretariat to address gender issues. Few Paraguayan women participate in politics: in the 2003 legislative election, only 8 percent of seats in the legislature were held by women. Since 2003, women have also been allowed into military schools. However, abortion is illegal in the country, Paraguayan women still face discrimination in the labor market, and women's wages are often up to 40 percent lower than those of their male counterparts.

R. SIMON-KUMAR

Health and Welfare

Paraguay has social welfare and health care systems that provide basic care for the nation's citizens but, in a highly stratified society, facilities are unevenly distributed and the provision of medical care in poorer areas is sometimes inadequate.

In Paraguay, government officials, military leaders, wealthy landowners, and members of the business sector, who comprise the country's small upper class, obtain health care through private funding. A growing middle class, living mainly in Asunción (the national capital) and Ciudad del Este, also has better access to medical care and social welfare programs than the rural poor.

Lack of safe, clean drinking water is a major health problem in the country, particularly in rural areas. As many as one-fifth of the urban population do not have a potable water supply, while less than one-fifth of the rural population have access to clean water. As a result, people living in rural areas in Paraguay are more susceptible to waterborne diseases. The majority of rural Paraguayans also do not have indoor plumbing, and bathroom and kitchen facilities are housed in sheds adjoining their homes.

HEALTH CARE

Communicable diseases are more common in Paraguay than its southern neighbors, Argentina and Uruguay, in part because immunization programs are less developed than in most other Latin America countries. Despite large-scale immunization programs through the 1980s and 1990s, 10 percent of the population have not been immunized against diphtheria, and around one-quarter have not received the BCG (Bacilli Chalmette Guerin) vaccine, which is effective in preventing tuberculosis. Malnutrition, particularly in rural areas, lowers resistance to disease. Cases of dysentery, hepatitis, measles, tuberculosis, typhoid fever, and acute respiratory infections have been reported, and cases of both malaria and leprosy still occur in Paraguay, although less frequently than in the past.

Paraguayan health services, which are overseen by the Ministry of Public Health and Social Welfare, provide medical and basic dental care, prescription drugs, and hospital treatments for workers, their spouses, and children under age 16 through the Instituto de Previsión Social (Social Security Institute). The system is funded by contributions from employers and employees. Pensioners also contribute from their state pensions to benefit from the program. A separate health agency provides care for members in the military, while wealthier Paraguayans opt for private health care.

According to 2002 World Health Organization (WHO) figures, Paraguay has around 6,350 doctors, more than 9,700 nurses, 535 midwives, about 3,180 dentists, and nearly 1,870 pharmacists. There is approximately only 1 doctor per 1,000

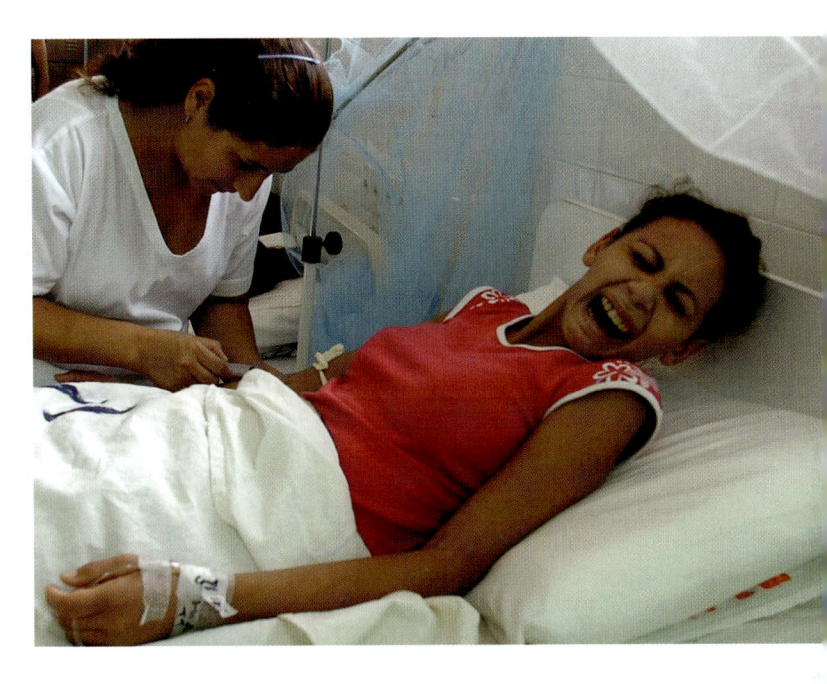

A health worker assists a young patient suffering from dengue fever in a health center in Asunción.

people and 1 dentist for every 2,000 people. Most health care professionals and the majority of hospitals are located in the Asunción region, and, as a result, people living in rural areas sometimes travel great distances to receive basic medical care.

SOCIAL SECURITY

The Instituto de Previsión Social provides cash payments to help cover the expenses of temporary illnesses, maternity, and death. The program is funded by contributions from the government, employers, and employees (who usually contribute about 10 percent of their salaries). However, the system is generally considered inefficient and is not comprehensive. Paraguay currently spends about 8 percent of its GDP (gross domestic product, the total value of all the goods and services produced in a country in a fixed period, usually one year) on health and welfare, but some 60 percent of this total is private funding. Relatively modest old-age pensions are provided—funded by employee contributions to the Social Security Institute—from age 60, or from age 55 for those who have contributed to the program for 30 years.

K. BIAS

Education

The Paraguayan educational system has received substantial investment since 1989, when the dictatorship of Alfredo Stroessner (1912–2006; in office 1954–1989) was ended. Consequently, educational standards are now little different from those of many other South American nations.

Paraguay has a high level of literacy. In 2006, 94 percent of adults could read and write, and there was very little difference in literacy levels between men and women. Public education is free and compulsory from age of six to 14. Enrollments in primary school represent about 96 percent of those eligible to attend.

THE SCHOOL SYSTEM

The educational system in Paraguay is divided into primary, secondary (high school), and university sectors. Primary schooling, which is compulsory, is a six-year course. Secondary schooling is divided into two phases, each of which lasts for three years. The first phase is, in theory, compulsory, while in the second (optional) phase, students follow either vocational training or study for a *bachillerato* degree, which is a qualification to enter the university sector. Many children, especially in rural areas, are either bilingual or more fluent in Guaraní, an Amerindian language, which is one of the nation's two official languages. Schooling, however, is in Spanish.

High-school students wait for a bus to take them to school. Although tuition is free, parents pay for transportation, books, and other materials.

Government spending on education increased steadily from 1989, but international observers of the educational system in Paraguay consider that there is much to be done to raise standards. Enrollments in secondary schools are still low (at about 25 percent of those eligible), and only around 8 percent of Paraguayans go to university. Levels of rural illiteracy are high in comparison to the cities. The minimum legal age at which children can start employment is 12, and many children, especially from poor families, have to work despite the legal requirement to remain in school until age 14.

The shortcomings of the educational system in modern Paraguay derive from the country's political and economic history. In the nineteenth century, education was considered elitist and was largely restricted to the wealthy. The first secondary school in Paraguay was opened as late as 1877, and the first university in 1896. Despite the country's involvement in a number of economically damaging wars through the late nineteenth and early twentieth centuries, the educational system expanded, although slowly because of lack of funding. In the second half of the twentieth century, the development of the educational system suffered under the dictatorship of Alfredo Stroessner. However, the new democratic constitution of 1992 recognized the right to education, and subsequent governments have addressed these obligations, for example, by modernizing the school curriculum and raising the salaries of teachers.

THE UNIVERSITY SECTOR

The two principal universities in Paraguay are located in Asunción, the national capital. One is a public institution, the National University of Asunción, which offers free tuition, and the other, a Catholic university, charges fees. Since 2000, the government has encouraged access to higher education through the expansion of the university sector. There are now also two other private universities (which obtained their university status in 1991) and a second public university (founded in 1994), which has campuses in Asunción and Ciudad del Este. A range of arts and science programs are offered at the universities, where the medium of instruction is Spanish. Enrollments in universities doubled from 1995 through 2003, when it was estimated that there were more than 200,000 students in the sector. Currently, about one-half of university graduates are women.

R. SIMON-KUMAR

Asunción

Asunción, the national capital of Paraguay, is the center of an extensive metropolitan area that is home to one-third of Paraguay's population. At the 2002 Paraguayan census, the metropolitan area had 1,660,000 inhabitants, while some 512,000 people lived within the city limits.

Some of Paraguay's largest cities and towns adjoin Asunción. The urban agglomeration is situated along and back from the east bank of the Paraguay River. On the western bank of the waterway, Argentina faces the southern part of the Asunción metropolitan area across the river. The satellite cities include San Lorenzo, which had a population of 204,000 in 2002, Luque (with 171,000 people), Capiatá (154,000), Lambaré (120,000), and Fernando de la Mora (114,000).

SETTLEMENT AND DEVELOPMENT

Originally called Nuestra Señora de la Asunción (Our Lady of the Assumption), the city is one of the oldest founded by the Spanish in South America. Established as a fort on Assumption Day in 1537, Asunción became a base from which the Spanish explored a large region. Asunción developed as an important provincial center and, for much of the sixteenth century, it was the seat of the Spanish colonial administration for most of southeastern South America. The city also flourished as a major center for the conversion to Christianity of the Guaraní Amerindians of the region. From 1588 through 1767, Paraguay was greatly influenced by the Jesuits, who dominated missionary activities in Paraguay. However, with the administrative separation of the Buenos Aires–La Plata estuary region from Paraguay in 1617 and the subsequent development of the city of Buenos Aires, Asunción declined in importance. From 1776, Paraguay was part of the Spanish viceroyalty (administrative region) of Río de la Plata, and the development of Asunción slowed as Buenos Aires came to dominate the region.

In 1811, Paraguay declared independence from Spain and secession from the emerging loose confederation that was to become Argentina. As a result, Asunción became the capital of an independent nation. However, from 1814 through 1840, the development of the city stalled during the dictatorship of José Gaspar Rodríguez de Francia (1766–1840), who isolated the nation from outside influences.

Paraguay's presidential palace is one of a group of nineteenth-century buildings in the downtown area of Asunción.

The city of Asunción spreads along a bay of the Paraguay River.

President Carlos Antonio López (1792–1862; chief of state 1841–1844; in office as president 1844–1862) improved the infrastructure of Asunción, building schools, a railroad, and factories. The strategic position of Asunción, a river port and the head of navigation along the Paraguay River (at the point at which it is joined by the Pilcomayo River), was of regional importance, and the city was fought over by Paraguay's neighbors in the War of the Triple Alliance (1865–1870). In the war, Paraguay suffered an overwhelming defeat at the hands of Argentine, Brazilian, and Uruguayan forces, and Paraguay lost more than one-half of its population. Asunción was damaged in the fighting, greatly reduced in population, and occupied by the Brazilians in 1868. Brazil did not withdraw its forces from Asunción until 1878, and Asunción subsequently stagnated, taking decades to recover.

A MODERN LATIN AMERICAN CITY

Asunción is Paraguay's center of government, commerce, industry, transportation, and education and culture. The city's principal industries process the agricultural products of Paraguay's Oriental region, the area east of the Paraguay River. Industries include textiles, food processing (including making vegetable oils), footwear, and tobacco, as well as engineering and a range of consumer goods industries.

The highway network of Paraguay's Oriental region focuses on Asunción, which is linked by ferries across the waterway with the Argentine road and railroad systems. Asunción is Paraguay's most important port, exporting meat, soy, timber, and other agricultural products. The city also has an international airport. In modern times, the population of the metropolitan area has rapidly increased, largely because of migration from rural areas, which have experienced recession, and an economic boom in the city. Most of the growth has been in the neighboring cities in the agglomeration, where land is cheaper, rather than in Asunción itself. The development of Asunción was largely unplanned, and parts of the metropolitan area still lack an adequate modern infrastructure.

Asunción spreads over low hills, surrounding a bay along the Paraguay River. The city has many parks and gardens overlooking the waterway, and the downtown area is characterized by a large number of trees, including purple lapacho trees, which blossom in the spring, and jacarandas. Two main squares—Plaza de los Héroes and Plaza Uruguaya—form the heart of the downtown area, where most streets are relatively narrow. Many street traders sell herbs, decorative art items, food, and a variety of consumer goods, including CDs and DVDs.

Architecturally, the city has single-story colonial era buildings and modern high-rise buildings. Asunción's historic buildings include the Casa de la Independencia (House of Independence) in which the leaders of the Paraguayan nationalist movement met in May 1811 to plot the seizure of the Spanish governor and the declaration of independence. The cathedral and the presidential and legislative palaces date from the nineteenth century, while the domed National Pantheon of Heroes, a striking neoclassical building (built from 1864 through 1936), is the symbol of the city. A memorial to all the Paraguayans who lost their lives in the War of the Triple Alliance and the Chaco War (1932–1935) against Bolivia, it contains the tombs of two Paraguayan unknown soldiers and has a ceremonial guard.

C. CARPENTER

ECONOMY

Paraguay is a landlocked, largely agricultural nation with a relatively small population. The country has great social inequality, extensive poverty, and few natural resources, apart from two major waterways.

Paraguay, located along the Paraguay River, is divided into two by the waterway. To the west, in the so-called Occidental region, are low marshy plains and dry forested scrub, known as the Gran Chaco. The region can support little economic activity and is home to around 2 percent of the national population. To the east of the Paraguay River, extending to the Paraná River along the Argentine and Brazilian borders, is the Oriental region, an area of grassy plains and wooded hills that contains most of Paraguay's agriculture, industry, and resources and 98 percent of the nation's population.

ECONOMIC CHALLENGES

One of Paraguay's main economic challenges is its geographical location. Landlocked, the nation is far from major international trade routes. To export its products and to import raw materials, fuel, and other goods, Paraguay must rely on relatively expensive land routes or transportation along the nation's two principal waterways, the Paraguay River through central Paraguay (flowing past Asunción, the national capital) and the Paraná River in the east, along whose banks is the country's second-largest metropolitan area, Ciudad del Este.

Paraguay's history has played an important role in delaying the country's economic development. While the economy of some other nations in Latin America dramatically grew in the late nineteenth century—as in the case of Argentina and to a lesser extent Uruguay—capitalizing on rich agricultural resources and attracting large-scale migration from Europe and foreign investment, Paraguay remained in deep depression. After being defeated in the War of the Triple Alliance (1865–1870) against Argentina, Brazil, and Uruguay, Paraguay struggled to recover. The war not only devastated the economy but also resulted in the loss of more than one-half of the country's population. Paraguay did not begin to develop significantly again until early in the twentieth century.

In the 1920s and early 1930s, tension increased in the Gran Chaco, most of which was then controlled by Bolivia. The border in the region was poorly delineated and, when international oil corporations prospected in the region (initially confident of discovering commercial reserves of petroleum), the hitherto economically unpromising region became more important. Bolivia, which also wished to gain control of more of the region to secure access to the navigable Paraguay River, attacked Paraguay, sparking the Chaco War (1932–1935). During the war, Paraguay gained the greater part of the Gran Chaco, but the war caused more economic problems, as it was costly both in financial terms and in human lives. The Gran Chaco also proved a disappointment as no hydrocarbons were found in the region.

Facing another period of postwar reconstruction, Paraguay's development was held back by political instability. The military seized power and, after several coups, General Alfredo Stroessner (1912–2006; in office 1954–1989) assumed control. Under Stroessner's military dictatorship, state involvement in the economy greatly increased. Previously, compared with other nations in South America, Paraguay had low levels of public investment, apart from the construction of the transportation network, particularly highways. Stroessner, however, established a number of state corporations to develop the industrial and energy sectors. Established in 1973, the principal corporation, Itaipu Binacional, was a joint Paraguayan-Brazilian enterprise to develop a huge dam and hydroelectricity facility along the Paraná River, along the border between the two nations. At the same time, other Paraguayan state corporations were established to promote iron and steel, cement, and other primary industries. Paraguayan industry was protected from international competition by tariffs. Although Stroessner's regime was one of the most absolute in the continent, it provided Paraguay with the political stability that it had not experienced for decades and, as a result, the government was able to attract greatly increased levels of foreign investment, particularly in agriculture and agribusiness. Consequently, Paraguay achieved high rates of growth through the 1970s.

In 1989, Stroessner was overthrown and, since then, civilian governments have been in power, although the Colorado Party, with which Stroessner ruled, has retained power. The nation's economic policies have, however, undergone dramatic changes.

Standard of Living

In 2006, GDP per capita in Paraguay was $4,800, adjusted for purchasing power parity (PPP), a formula that allows comparison between living standards in different countries. The figure is the lowest in the Southern Cone, the southern region of the continent. In 2005, 32 percent of Paraguayans lived in poverty, one the highest figures in South America.

The level of state intervention has decreased, and foreign exchange controls, which kept the value of the Paraguayan currency (the guaraní) artificially high, have been relaxed. Paraguay now has a market-based economy. Financial reforms have included cutting tariffs (including the establishment of a tax-free commercial zone in Ciudad del Este), introducing tax incentives to encourage foreign investment, and reforming the tax system. Subsequent governments have also attempted a measure of privatization to reduce state spending and have cut the Paraguayan government deficit.

The end of the Stroessner dictatorship also led to changes in the labor market. Under Stroessner, organized labor had no alternative to a single, government-controlled union. As a result, wage costs were low. Since then, other labor unions have formed and, consequently, wages, although still relatively low by regional standards, have risen. The benefits of the dramatic economic growth since the 1970s were unevenly distributed. In 2005, some 32 percent of Paraguayans still lived below the official poverty line. Standards of living rose for people in cities, particularly Asunción and Ciudad del Este, but more than 40 percent of Paraguayans are still poor subsistence farmers, producing their own food and trading any surpluses.

The Paraguayan economy is characterized by a large informal sector, partly as a result of the inefficient collection of taxes and partly in response to resistance to the demands of an oppressive state in the past. Many Paraguayans import consumer goods from neighboring countries and then reexport them to its neighbors, without any transactions being recorded. These activities are particularly widespread at Ciudad del Este on the Brazilian border, which is a center of smuggling, but urban street traders and small-scale unrecorded enterprises are also common in Asunción. The scale of the informal economy not only makes it difficult to gain accurate figures to measure the size of Paraguay's economy and its different sectors but also makes the collection of state revenue difficult. The GDP (gross domestic product, the total value of all the goods and services produced in a country in a fixed term, usually one year) was estimated to be $31.3 billion in 2006, but this figure is almost certainly an underestimate because of the extent of unrecorded economic activities.

Ciudad del Este, which is linked to Brazil by the Friendship Bridge across the Paraná River, is the center of a large tax-free commercial zone. Many Brazilians cross to the city to shop, and its commerce supplies more than one-half of Paraguay's GDP.

Paraguay depends heavily on trade with its neighboring countries, Argentina and Brazil. As a result, when the Argentine and Brazilian economies are prospering, Paraguayan exports to the neighbors increase. When either Argentina or Brazil suffers a downturn, for example the severe Argentine economic crisis of 2001, the problems have a cumulative effect upon the Paraguayan economy. Paraguay, consequently, faces a challenge to diversify its trading partners to make it less reliant on conditions in a few nearby states.

ECONOMY

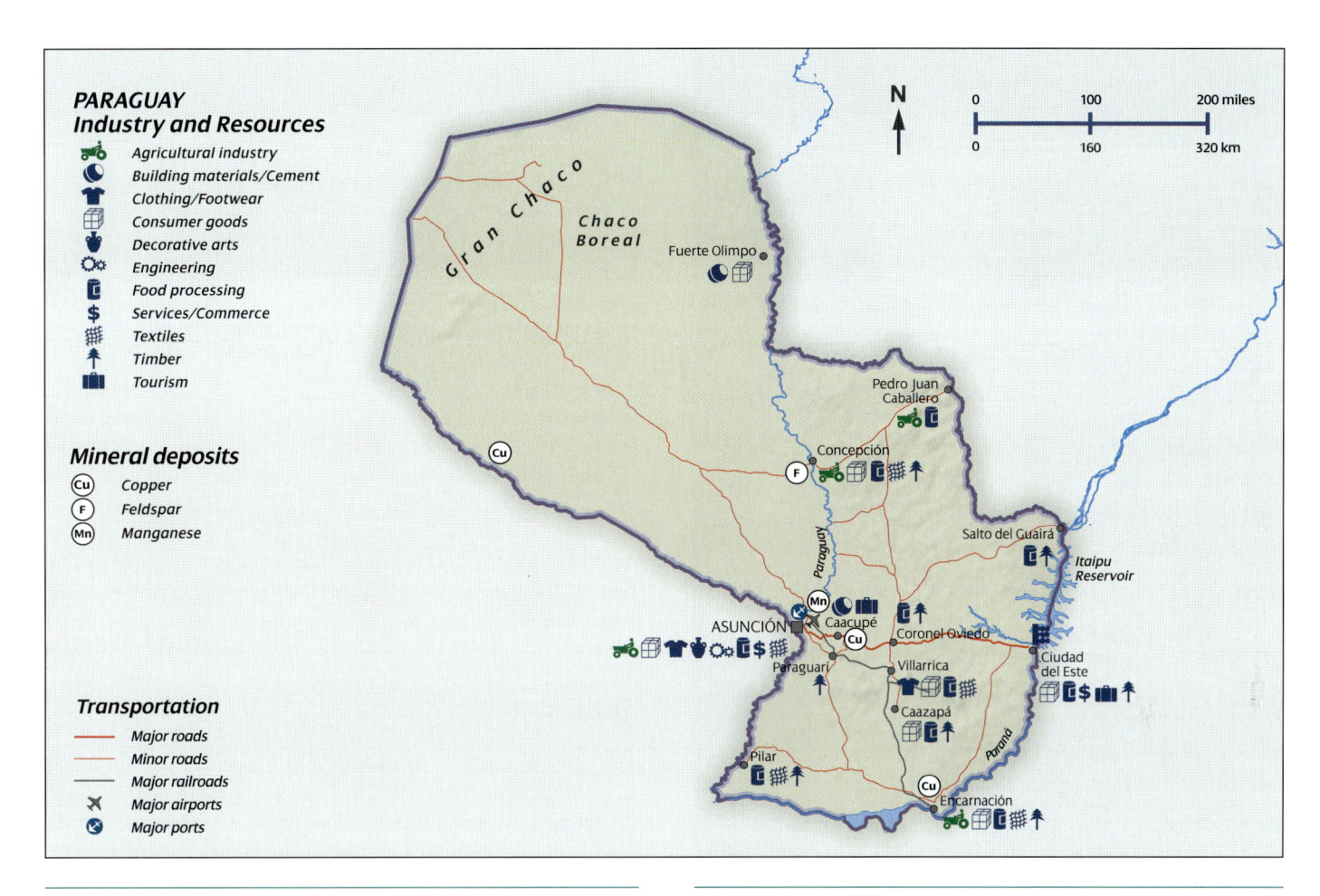

RESOURCES

Paraguay has few mineral resources. Small quantities of manganese, copper ore, and feldspar are mined in the Oriental region, where limestone is also quarried. Despite continued prospecting, neither petroleum nor natural gas has been found in the Gran Chaco. However, the nation has one major natural resource, its waterways, which can be harnessed to produce important hydropower.

The Itaipu Dam on the Paraná River, some 10 miles (16 km) north of Ciudad del Este was jointly developed with Brazil from 1973. The project, which has transformed the Paraguayan economy, supplies one-half of its electricity to Paraguay, which sells its surplus to Brazil. The dam, one of the largest in the world, houses 18 turbines, making it the largest operational hydroelectric power facility in the world, with a capacity of 12,600 megawatts. Completed in 1982, the dam holds back a reservoir that is 106 miles (170 km) long and averages 4.4 miles (7 km) wide. A second major hydropower project, the Yacyretá-Apipé Dam, is downstream along the Paraná River. Jointly owned and run by Paraguay and Argentina, Yacyretá-Apipé has a capacity of around 2,700 megawatts. Because Paraguay has a relatively small population and comparatively little industry, it consumes less than 90 percent of the power produced by the two large facilities, and electricity is therefore Paraguay's most valuable export.

AGRICULTURE

Agriculture employs some 45 percent of the Paraguayan labor force and supplies more than 21.4 percent of the GDP and, until the last quarter of the twentieth century, agriculture and agricultural exports dominated the economy. More than one-fifth of the land can be farmed, but in practice a much smaller percentage is used. Most of the agricultural land in Paraguay is owned by less than 5 percent of landowners. The majority of Paraguayan farms are occupied by subsistence farmers, who rent their land, even though the Instituto de Bienestar Rural (Rural Welfare Institute) has helped large numbers of landless peasants acquire the land they farmed.

The Occidental and Oriental regions have contrasting agricultural economies. The grasslands and marshes of the Occidental region, and the arid Gran Chaco, comprise Paraguay's principal cattle raising region, although cattle are also important in the south of the Oriental region. Paraguay is self-sufficient in beef, surpluses of which are exported, and hides and dairy products are also exported. The Oriental region is more important for growing crops including soybeans, wheat, corn, rice, groundnuts, cassava, sugarcane, cotton, coffee, citrus fruits, tobacco, and vegetables. In modern times, the area under soybeans has greatly increased, and soy is now a major export. Paraguay raises sheep, hogs, and poultry, and is able to supply most of its food needs. One of the nation's most characteristic crops is yerba maté, a

PARAGUAY

Itaipu Dam on the Paraná River houses the world's largest operation hydropower installation. Electricity generated by its 18 turbines is exported to Brazil, earning Paraguay more than $300 million a year.

PARAGUAY'S GDP

Paraguay's gross domestic product (GDP) was $31.3 billion in 2006. The figure is adjusted for purchasing power parity (PPP), an exchange rate at which goods in one country cost the same as goods in another. PPP allows a comparison between the living standards in different nations.

MAIN CONTRIBUTORS TO PARAGUAY'S GDP

Agriculture	21.4 percent
Industry	18.5 percent
Services	60.1 percent

Source: Government of Paraguay

plant that is related to the holly. Maté, an herbal tea, is made from the leaves and stems of the plant. The nation has commercially important forests in the Oriental region, and both timber and tannin are significant exports. Paraguay's waterways supply a variety of fish, but commercial fishing is not highly developed.

INDUSTRY

Industry has traditionally been a small sector of the Paraguayan economy, and, in modern times, industry supplies about 18.5 percent of the nation's GDP. Under the Stroessner dictatorship, the industrial sector grew, with state corporations established to develop a steel industry and cement industries, for example. Other, relatively small-scale industries were protected from cheaper imports by the imposition of tariffs. Since 1989, freer trade policies have included tariff cuts, making imported manufactured items cheaper and discouraging local industry. Although some industries have been established, using cheap hydropower from the Itaipu Dam, the industrial sector remains relatively undeveloped. Most Paraguayan industries are based on processing the nation's agricultural produce, including sugar refining, textiles, wood products, food processing and packing, vegetable oils, and beverages.

SERVICES

The services sector is small but contributes 60.1 percent to the GDP. State employees account for a large share of the sector, including government and administration, education, some sectors of transportation, and two state banks. The retail sector grew in the last quarter of the twentieth century, not only in Asunción but also in Ciudad del Este, the center of one of the world's largest tax-free commercial zones. The city has many stores selling, for example, electrical and electronic items to Brazilians who cross the border to take advantage of prices that are cheaper than in Brazil. Ciudad del Este rapidly grew in the last quarter of the twentieth century, and its tax-free zone generates more than one-half of Paraguay's GDP. Ciudad del Este's commerce attracted large numbers of foreign traders to the city, which now has Arab (mainly Lebanese and Syrian) and, particularly, Taiwanese settlers. Paraguay's tourist sector is underdeveloped, although numbers of foreign visitors are slowly increasing. The main tourist attractions include Lake Itaipu and its shoreline nature preserves and the ruins of Jesuit missions, the reductions, most of which date from the seventeenth century.

TRADE

Legal reexports make an important contribution to the economy. Paraguay imports items, particularly consumer goods, from many countries and reexports them to neighboring Argentina and Brazil, taking advantage of differential tariff rates. In the past, this trade, which is mainly channeled through Asunción and, particularly, Ciudad del Este's tax-free zone, was lucrative, but, because of the establishment of the MERCOSUR free trade area—whose members are Paraguay, Argentina, Brazil, Uruguay,

828

EMPLOYMENT IN PARAGUAY

Sector	Percentage of labor force
Agriculture, forestry, and fishing	45 percent
Industry	about 10 percent
Services	about 45 percent

Source: Government of Paraguay, 2000

In 2005, 9.4 percent of the labor force was unemployed.

and Venezuela—this activity has begun to be less important. In the twenty-first century, growth in the Paraguayan economy has been achieved partly because of membership in MERCOSUR.

In 2006, Paraguay imported goods and services worth an estimated $5.8 billion and had exports valued at $4.8 billion. The nation's trade balance has greatly improved, in part because of reexports. Exports include electricity, consumer goods, soybeans, animal feed, cotton, meat, vegetable oils, wood, and leather. The nation's main imports are road vehicles and transportation equipment, consumer goods, fuel and petroleum products, tobacco, and electrical equipment. Much of the imported tobacco and many of the consumer goods are reexported. Argentina, Brazil, and Uruguay were Paraguay's traditional trading partners and still dominate the country's trade. In 2005, Uruguay (whose share in Paraguay's trade is increasing) received 28 percent of exports from Paraguay, while Brazil took 19 percent, Argentina 6 percent, Russia 6 percent, and China including Hong Kong 4 percent. The principal sources of imports into Paraguay were Brazil (27 percent), China including Hong Kong (21 percent), Argentina (20 percent), the United States (5 percent), and Switzerland (4 percent).

TRANSPORTATION AND COMMUNICATION

Paraguay's highway system covers 18,334 miles (29,500 km), 9,314 miles (14,986 km) of which are paved. Paraguay does not have a railroad system, the nation having only 22 miles (36 km) of track. A line used to operate from Asunción to Encarnación but has largely been abandoned, with only a short section for commuter trains operating at the Asunción end of the track. The country is landlocked, but there are 1,927 miles (3,100 km) of navigable waterways along the Paraná and Paraguay rivers. Asunción, along the Paraguay River (which is navigable for most of its length and is the main transportation artery of the nation), is the main river port. There are 12 airports with paved runways, one of which—Asunción Silvio Pettirossi International Airport—handles international flights.

Paraguay's telephone system does not cover the entire country and is in need of modernization. In 2006, there were some 330,000 main telephone lines, while in 2006 some 3.2 million Paraguayans had mobile cellular phones. In 2006, 260,000 people in Paraguay had Internet access.

C. CARPENTER

Farm workers harvest sugarcane, one of the principal crops of the Paraguayan agricultural sector.

Uruguay

Uruguay is a relatively flat country, largely comprised of grassland. The region was home to Charrúa Amerindians before the arrival of the Spanish in 1516. For several centuries, Uruguay (then called Banda Oriental) was disputed betweenSpain and Portugal. Uruguay gained independence from Spain as part of Argentina in 1816 but in 1821 was annexed by Brazil. Uruguay revolted against Brazil in 1825 and secured recognition of its independence in 1828. From 1865 through 1870, Uruguay joined Argentina and Brazil in waging war against Paraguay. At the beginning of the twentieth century, president José Batlle (1856–1929; in office 1899, 1903–1907, and 1911–1915) reformed the government, laying the foundations for a state welfare system. For much of the twentieth century, Uruguay had a reputation for democracy and stability. However, left-wing Tupamaros guerrillas became active from 1958, when the country experienced economic difficulties, and, in 1973, the army seized power. Abuses of human rights were widespread under the military dictatorship. Constitutional rule was restored in 1985.

GEOGRAPHY

Location	South America, along the South Atlantic Ocean, between Brazil and Argentina
Climate	Warm temperate climate
Area	68,037 sq. miles (176,215 sq. km)
Coastline	410 miles (660 km)
Highest point	Sierra Catedral (also known as Sierra Carapé) 1,685 feet (514 m)
Lowest point	Atlantic Ocean 0 feet (0 m)
Terrain	Low plains and rolling hills
Natural resources	Hydroelectric power potential, fish
Land use	
Arable land	7.8 percent
Permanent crops	0.2 percent
Other	92.0 percent
Major rivers	Río de la Plata, Uruguay, Negro
Major lake	Embalse del Río Negro
Natural hazards	Floods, droughts

METROPOLITAN AREAS, 2004 POPULATION

Urban population	87 percent
Montevideo	1,750,000
Montevideo City	1,270,000
Las Piedras	69,000
Salto	99,000
Paysandú	73,000
Rivera	64,000
Maldonado	55,000
Melo	51,000
Tacuarembó	51,000
Artigas	42,000
Mercedes	42,000

Source: Uruguayan national census, 2004

NEIGHBORS AND LENGTH OF BORDERS

Argentina	360 miles (580 km)
Brazil	664 miles (1,068 km)

POPULATION

Population	3,306,000 (2005 government estimate)
Population density	49 per sq. mile (19 per sq. km)
Population growth	0.5 percent a year
Birthrate	14.4 births per 1,000 of the population
Death rate	9.2 deaths per 1,000 of the population
Population under age 15	23 percent
Population over age 65	13 percent
Sex ratio	104 males for 100 females
Fertility rate	2.0 children per woman

URUGUAY

Infant mortality rate	12.0 deaths per 1,000 live births
Life expectancy at birth	
Total population	75.9 years
Female	79.3 years
Male	72.7 years

ECONOMY

Currency	Uruguayan new peso (UYU)
Exchange rate (2007)	$1 = UYU 24.35
Gross domestic product (2006)	$37.5 billion
GDP per capita (2006)	$10,900
Unemployment rate (2006)	10.8 percent
Population under poverty line (2006)	27.4 percent
Exports	$4.4 billion (2006 CIA estimate)
Imports	$4.9 billion (2006 CIA estimate)

FLAG

Adopted in 1830, the flag of Uruguay comprises nine horizontal bands, blue and white. A yellow sun symbol, the so-called Sun of May, is centered in a square canton (the upper corner nearest the flagpost). The sun symbol has 16 rays, alternating straight and wavy. The Sun of May represents freedom, and the stripes represent the nine original provinces of Uruguay.

GOVERNMENT

Official country name	Oriental Republic of Uruguay
Conventional short form	Uruguay
Nationality	
noun	Uruguayan
adjective	Uruguayan
Official language	Spanish

URUGUAY

Salto, the second-largest city in Uruguay, is at the head of navigation along the Uruguay River. The city is the center of a fruit-growing region and is known for its production of wine.

Capital city	Montevideo
Type of government	Republic; democracy
Voting rights	18 years and over; universal and compulsory
National anthem	"Orientales, la Patria o la tumba!" (Uruguayans, the fatherland or death!)
National day	Independence Day, August 25 (the anniversary of independence from Brazil in 1825)

TRANSPORTATION

Railroads	1,288 miles (2,073 km)
Highways	48,311 miles (77,732 km)
Paved roads	4,812 miles (7,743 km)
Unpaved roads	43,499 miles (69,989 km)
Navigable waterways	994 miles (1,600 km)
Airports	
International airports	2
Paved runways	8

POPULATION PROFILE, 2006 ESTIMATES

Ethnic groups	
European ancestry	88 percent
Mestizo (Amerindian and European)	8 percent
African ancestry	4 percent
Religions	
Roman Catholic	66 percent
(of whom around one-half are practicing)	
Nonreligious	31 percent
Various Protestant Evangelical churches	2 percent
Jewish and others	1 percent
Languages	
Spanish	more than 97 percent
Other European languages	less than 3 percent
Adult literacy	98 percent

CHRONOLOGY

1st millennium CE	The Charrúa Amerindians live in what is today known as Uruguay.
1516	Spanish colonists arrive in the region, but they face fierce resistance from the Charrúa.
16th century	The Spanish initially neglect the region because no valuable minerals are discovered in the area that is now Uruguay. Continuing Amerindian resistance also discourages settlement.
17th century	Spanish settlement in the region increases as Spanish forces overcome the Charrúa. The first permanent Spanish settlement is established in 1624. However, the Portuguese also attempt to settle Uruguay (then called Banda Oriental) from the north.
1776	The Spanish viceroyalty (administrative region) of Río de la Plata, comprising Argentina, Paraguay, and Uruguay, is established.
1806–1811	Banda Oriental is contested by Spanish, Portuguese, and British forces. In 1807, the city of Montevideo, now Uruguay's national capital, is occupied by the British.
1811	José Gervasio Artigas (1764–1850) leads a successful revolt against Spanish rule in Banda Oriental, which achieves independence as part of Argentina.
1821	Brazil annexes Banda Oriental, and Argentina fights a war against Brazil, at the end of which Banda Oriental is lost to the Brazilians.
1825	Uruguay secures its independence; the nation gains international recognition in 1828.
1830	The name Uruguay is adopted for the country.
1839–1854	Uruguay is divided between two political movements, the (conservative) Blancos and (liberal) Colorados. For much of the period, Uruguay is in a state of civil war, the so-called Guerra Grande. Montevideo is under siege from 1843 through 1852.
1865–1870	Uruguay joins Argentina and Brazil at war with Paraguay.
late 19th century	Larger numbers of immigrants come to Uruguay from Italy and Spain.
1903–1907 and 1911–1915	President José Batlle (1856–1929) reforms the government, laying the foundations for a state welfare system.
late 1950s–early 1970s	After a half century of political stability, left-wing Tupamaros guerrillas become active in 1958, as Uruguay experiences economic difficulties. In 1968, a state of emergency is declared and further restrictions to civil liberties are put in place in 1972.
1973	The army seizes power.
1973–1984	Abuses of human rights are widespread under a military dictatorship. Many writers and artists leave the country to escape political repression.
since 1985	Constitutional rule is restored.
early 21st century	Uruguay suffers an economic recession. In 2004, a left-of-center coalition wins power, ending the domination of Uruguayan politics by the Colorados and Blancos.

GOVERNMENT

Uruguay has experienced a greater degree of political stability and civilian rule than most other South American countries. The nation has also had fewer constitutions than most Latin American states.

For most of its history, Uruguay has had an executive presidency. Under the original 1830 constitution, the chief of state was also head of government. However, from 1951 through 1966, the country adopted a new system of so-called collective government, with a collegiate presidency. In 1966, under a new constitution, the executive presidency was restored. A debate concerning the nature of the governmental system followed a period of military rule from 1973 through 1984 and, in 1984, Uruguay readopted the slightly modified 1966 constitution. Since then, Uruguay has again been a functioning democracy.

Under the constitution, an executive president, who is assisted by a vice president, elected on the same ticket, is elected by universal adult suffrage for a five-year term. The president appoints a council of ministers, with 13 members who head different departments. The president also appoints the principal officers of state. In 1996, amendments to the constitution separated municipal and national elections and changed the balloting system for the presidential election.

THE LEGISLATURE

The bicameral Uruguayan legislature, the General Assembly of Uruguay, comprises a 31-member Senate (consisting of 30 senators and the vice president) and the 99-member Chamber of Deputies (lower house). Senators and deputies are elected under a system of proportional representation by universal adult suffrage. The voting age is 18 years, and voting is compulsory. Each department must be represented by at least two deputies in the lower house, regardless of its population.

POLITICAL PARTIES

Uruguay has one of the oldest two-party systems in Latin America. The politics of the nation have traditionally been dominated by the conservatives, or Blancos ("whites"), and the liberals, or Colorados ("reds"). The names of these parties derive from the color of the flags that they adopted in the Uruguayan civil war in the first half of the nineteenth century. The Blancos and Colorados have generally alternated in power, although first one party and then the other has typically held office for long periods. In modern times, these two movements are represented by the (center-right) National Party (the Blancos) and the (centrist) Colorado Party. In the twenty-first century, a left-wing coalition, the Broad Front/Progressive Encounter, emerged as the largest political movement in Uruguay, gaining more seats in the legislature than the Blancos and Colorados combined. The small Independent Party is also represented in the Uruguayan legislature.

LOCAL GOVERNMENT

Uruguay is divided into 19 departments (*departamento*s or provinces), each of which is administered by a governor who is directly elected. The departments are, in turn, divided into municipalities, which have elected councils and mayors (also called *intendente municipal*).

C. CARPENTER

The Uruguayan legislative building in Montevideo is constructed from more than 50 types of marble, each of which represents a different part of the country.

MODERN HISTORY

Early in the nineteenth century, the sparsely populated territory known as Banda Oriental (the "eastern bank") was part of the Spanish viceroyalty (administrative region) of Río de la Plata. The area had been disputed by Spain and Portugal (with its base of power in Brazil to the north), and the path to independence as Uruguay was troubled, including civil war involving its neighbors.

At the beginning of the nineteenth century, Spanish rule in South America began to falter. In 1807, the British unsuccessfully attempted to seize Montevideo, now the national capital of Uruguay, and in the following year, the French invaded Spain, toppling the Bourbon dynasty. As a result of the ousting of the Spanish government, local city authorities in many parts of South America set up local governments, called juntas, which claimed to rule in the name of the deposed king of Spain, Ferdinand VII (1784–1833; reigned 1808 and 1813–1833). The administration of the region had been based in Buenos Aires, across the wide estuary of the Río de la Plata, and had been in the hands of officials from the Spanish mainland. With the removal of direct Spanish rule, Montevideo's *criollos* (creoles, people of unmixed Spanish ancestry born in the New World) saw an opportunity to gain more power for themselves.

In Montevideo, pro-independence sentiment gained strength as the *criollo* population established juntas and promoted local economic interests. Pro-independence elements united around the leadership of José Gervasio Artigas (1764–1850), a *criollo* who had been a captain in the Spanish army.

CONTENDING FORCES

Despite being united by the common aim of autonomy, the revolutionary forces on the two sides of the Río de la Plata did not cooperate effectively with each another. Throughout the struggle against Spanish rule, the strong conflicts of interests between Buenos Aires and the other provinces within the viceroyalty were evident; eventually, these different interests led to the dissolution of the viceroyalty. The situation was further complicated by the intervention of other powers, such as Great Britain and Portugal, that did not hesitate to take advantage of weak Spanish rule as they attempted to expand their own influence in the region.

In February 1811, the so-called Orientales (the *criollos* of Banda Oriental) took up arms to fight for independence from Spain. At first, they were supported by the *criollo* junta in Buenos Aires. Later, not only did they lose this support but they also faced an invasion by the Portuguese army from Brazil. In theory, the Portuguese forces in Brazil were allied with the Spanish authorities in the Río de la Plata viceroyalty, and their intervention had been requested by the Spanish to assist in the fight against pro-autonomy movements in the region. However, the Portuguese were pursuing their own interests. In 1680, the Portuguese had founded Colónia (or Colónia do Sacramento) in Banda Oriental, and they did not finally withdraw from the region until 1777.

THE FEDERAL LEAGUE

Between 1815 and 1820, Artigas established the so-called Federal League (Liga Federal), an initiative aimed at fostering cooperation between some of the Spanish provinces of the former viceroyalty of the Río de la Plata. Membership in the

José Gervasio Artigas began the fight for independence for Uruguay but died in exile in Paraguay after nationhood was achieved.

league entailed giving up neither provincial autonomy nor local interests.

However, despite its initial success, Artigas's initiative ultimately met with failure because of strong opposition from Buenos Aires and because of invasion by the Portuguese from Brazil, both of which were threatened by the league. The league also floundered on internal disagreements when Artigas' leadership was questioned by other politicians from the Argentine provinces, including the governors of Entre Ríos and Santa Fé, who entered into agreements with Buenos Aires. With his plans for independence and broad local autonomy frustrated, Artigas went into exile in Paraguay, where he died many years later. In modern times, Artigas is regarded as the national hero and founding father of Uruguay.

OCCUPATION AND INDEPENDENCE

The Portuguese invasion of Banda Oriental in 1821 ended the region's first attempt to secure independence and, when Brazil became independent in 1822, Banda Oriental remained part of the new Brazilian Empire under a monarchy headed by the Portuguese royal family.

The citizens of Banda Oriental were not content with this situation; after revolts in 1821 and 1823, a new pro-independence movement emerged in 1825, the Cruzada Libertadora (Crusade for Freedom), under the leadership of Juan Antonio Lavalleja (c. 1784–1853), José Fructuoso Rivera (c. 1789–1854), and Manuel Oribe (1792–1857). Independence was declared in August 1825, but between 1825 and 1828, Banda Oriental was once again disputed by two powers, the successor states to the viceroyalty of the Río de la Plata and the Portuguese. The disputing powers were Buenos Aires (which was the leading member of the United Provinces of the Río de la Plata, the loose confederation that eventually became Argentina) and Brazil.

Banda Oriental opted for confederation with the United Provinces, but neither Buenos Aires nor Brazil managed to prevail. Eventually, both sides agreed to Banda Oriental's becoming an independent state. An envoy of the British government mediated between the Brazilians and the authorities in Buenos Aires, and the so-called Preliminary Peace Convention was signed in 1828, committing both Argentines and Brazilians to acknowledge and preserve the independence of Banda Oriental.

In July 1830, the first constitution of the new nation entered into force and, at the same time, the country adopted the name Uruguay. The General Assembly appointed José Fructuoso Rivera (in office 1830–1834, 1838–1839, and 1839–1843), who managed to obtain more support for his nomination as president than Juan Antonio Lavalleja. The country had achieved independence and the establishment of a legitimate government. In practice, however, the establishment of a national identity, the removal of external threats, and the creation of a stable political environment would take some fifty years.

THE URUGUAYAN GREAT WAR

In its early years, Uruguay was destabilized by political rivalry. Presidential authority was systematically challenged by those who, at the time, felt illegitimately excluded from political power. At the same time, at least until the War of the Triple Alliance (1864–1870), in which Argentina, Brazil, and Uruguay joined forces against Paraguay, Uruguayan domestic political conflicts became intertwined with internal disputes in neighboring countries and the aims of contending regional powers.

Rivera was sworn in as president in November 1830. Two years later, the supporters of Lavalleja launched an armed rebellion; Lavelleja's faction was defeated but took up arms again in 1833. Rivera was replaced in office in 1835 by Manuel Oribe (in office 1835–1838 and 1843–1851); however, Rivera would not cooperate with Oribe and fought him until he was overthrown. Rivera replaced Oribe in March 1839, beginning the so-called Uruguayan Great War, which ran from 1839 to 1852.

Defeated by Rivera, Oribe sailed for Buenos Aires where he gained the support of the governor of Buenos Aires, Juan Manuel de Rosas (1793–1877; in office 1829–1832 and 1835–1852). In order to defeat Oribe, Rivera recruited allies in the region, in southern Brazil, and among the Argentine Unitarios, the political enemies of Rosas. In time, Rivera also gained European support and the intervention of the French and, later, the British navies. Oribe, on the other hand, was supported by Rosas and the Argentine Federales faction, which favored a loose Argentine confederation rather than a unitary state.

Uruguayan society polarized during the conflict between Rivera and Oribe into conservative Blancos ("whites"), the supporters of Oribe, and liberal Colorados ("reds"), who favored Rivera. The Colorados generally represented the commercial interests of Montevideo, while the Blancos were supported by the landowners of the interior. In 1841, exiled Unitarios attempted an invasion of northern Argentina from Uruguay and, in 1843, the Argentines responded by invading Uruguay. Argentine forces overran most of Uruguay but failed to take Montevideo, which was then besieged.

The siege of Montevideo began in February 1843 and lasted nine years. Foreigners resident in Montevideo formed armed companies to help the besieged Colorados resist the attack; an Italian company was led by Giuseppe Garibaldi (1807–1882)—later largely responsible for the campaign that united Italy in the 1860s—who was then resident in Montevideo. In 1845, when Argentine ships blocked access to the Paraná River, British and French fleets intervened on the side of the Uruguayans in Montevideo. Rosas reached an agreement with Great Britain in 1849 and with France in the following year, but the siege of Montevideo by Oribe continued.

In 1851, the Argentine political leader Justo José de Urquiza (1801–1870; in office as president of Argentina 1854–1860) united forces against Rosas, forging an alliance of Uruguayan Colorados, exiled Argentine Unitarios, and Brazilians. Urquiza's forces defeated Oribe, lifted the siege, and then entered Argentina to oust Rosas in 1852.

The Great War left a profound legacy; on the one hand, Uruguay was in debt, economic activity (cattle raising and the meat-salting industry) remained depressed, and the population was diminished; on the other hand, the very high social costs of war gave rise to a stronger perception of Uruguayan nationhood.

AFTER THE CIVIL WAR

After the Uruguayan civil war, the nation's political leaders entered an era of cooperation. The war had been caused by disputes between rival political factions gathered under the leadership of military chiefs (*caudillos*). In order to eliminate political instability, the Uruguayan elite advocated a so-called merger policy, to absorb the factions into new political groups founded on principles rather than on personal loyalties. However, the *caudillos* were unwilling to dismantle their power structures and instead began to negotiate among themselves.

In the early twentieth century, Montevideo experienced modernizaton and expansion, including new docks.

In 1863, Colorado leader Venancio Flores (1808–1868; in office 1854–1855 and 1865–1868) revolted against the Blanco president, Bernardo Prudencio Berro (1799–1868; in office 1869–1864). Flores won support from Argentina and Brazil, while the Blancos were favored by Paraguay. As a result, the revolt became subsumed in the wider War of the Triple Alliance, in which Argentina, Brazil, and Uruguay confronted Paraguay. Flores's forces were victorious in the Uruguayan conflict, although their losses were heavy and Flores was eventually assassinated. After the war, negotiation among Uruguayan political leaders gradually became the main key to establishing peace in the country. As a result, Uruguay managed to avoid uprisings and revolts, and Uruguayan politics started to look toward consensus. In 1872, the political parties took a decisive step toward the pacification of the country with the Peace of April, an agreement to share political influence. The government of General Lorenzo Latorre (1844–1916; in office 1876–1879 and 1879–1880) subsequently significantly strengthened state authority and granted increased protection of property rights.

At the same time, economic progress began to transform Uruguay. Cattle raising was improved and new technologies

During his time in office, José Batlle reformed and transformed Uruguay into a stable, democratic welfare state.

were introduced, and large numbers of immigrants came to Uruguay from Spain, Italy, and other European countries. In 1875, the country also launched an ambitious popular education policy under José Pedro Varela (1837–1903; in office 1868, 1875, and 1875–1876), who believed that mass education was essential.

THE COLORADO ERA

Although the Peace of April of 1872 eased tensions in Uruguayan politics, the Blancos were far from satisfied with the status quo. The agreements had relegated them to the status of a minority party. In an attempt to redress this situation, the Blancos (who adopted the name the National Party in the late nineteenth century) carried out a strong recruitment policy in the last 20 years of the century and worked against what they perceived to be electoral fraud. After some years of prosperity, a major economic crisis occurred in 1890, which was related to the fall in prices of the country's main export products (wool, leather, and jerked beef) and to the bankruptcy of important European banks and companies that had interests in the region.

JOSÉ BATLLE Y ORDÓNEZ

José Batlle y Ordónez (1856–1929; in office 1903–1907 and 1911–1915) was elected president of Uruguay in 1903. During his two periods in office, he transformed the government, laying the foundations for a welfare state. The program to consolidate state authority also achieved success during Batlle's first term of office. Until 1903, the country had been effectively ruled by two authorities. The national government had been controlled without interruption by the Colorados since 1865. However, many of the provinces were ruled by the Blancos, and the central government had no effective control over them. In 1904, as a result of military action, the Colorado national government extended its authority to the whole territory of Uruguay.

Apart from expanding its jurisdiction, the state extended its economic and social functions. Some banks and the port of Montevideo were nationalized, while state monopolies were established in insurance and electricity generation and distribution. Under Batlle, the foundations for a generous welfare state also were laid. Labor legislation incorporated significant benefits for workers (for instance, the working day was limited to eight hours in 1915). The social security system included severance pay and old age pensions, while major investment was made in public education.

CONSTITUTIONAL CHANGE

In 1916, Batlle was defeated in the first free and fair election in the country's political history. Uruguay entered the 1920s as a democracy, having completed a strong process of renewal of its institutions. A new constitution in 1917 maintained the presidential system of the 1830 constitution but made important changes. A sophisticated organization of the executive was established (a so-called two-headed executive), in which power was shared and responsibility was split between a president (acting as chief of state) and a national council of administration consisting of nine members. The council was based upon the Swiss system of government, which Batlle greatly admired. At the same time, proportional representation was introduced, thus addressing the demand of the National Party for increased representation.

An economic crisis in 1929 wrecked the highly optimistic atmosphere in which the hundredth anniversary of La Cruzada Libertadora (Uruguay's fight for independence) had been commemorated in 1925. In 1933, when the specter of political instability loomed again because of economic problems, the Colorado Party's Gabriel Terra (1873–1942; in office 1931–1938) decreed the dissolution of the legislature for the "sake of governance." He had the support of a majority of the National Party, and full democratic government was not restored until 1942.

The Colorado Party continued in office until 1958, in part because of division in the National Party and the practice of widespread voter abstention, a method promoted by opposition forces to declare their differences publicly and withdraw legitimacy from elected governments. The opposition considered that they would not be able to win elections and therefore advocated abstention as a political weapon. In 1934, Terra introduced a constitutional reform, which, apart from incorporating some elements characteristic of parliamentary government (government in which the legislature is paramount), gave up the two-headed executive system, focusing government functions on the presidency. The new constitution also granted women the right to vote. The constitution was changed again in 1942 and in 1951, when a plural or collegiate executive, which had been advocated by Batlle, was introduced. Until 1967, Uruguay was governed by a national council, whose president (who held office for one year) was chief of state.

During the same period, the role and the size of the state grew. The 1929 economic crisis had resulted in a major reduction in exports, and Uruguay, like other Latin American countries, was forced to manufacture many products that for years it had been able to purchase abroad. As a result, the development of domestic industry gained momentum. This process was increasingly encouraged by the state, which used public spending to create jobs and regulate the economy.

INSTABILITY AND MILITARY GOVERNMENT

Economic problems developed in the mid-1950s, as production stagnated and inflation increased. At the same time, social problems were on the rise. In 1958, the National Party gained control of the executive after decades in opposition. During eight years in power, the Blancos attempted a liberalization of the economy and modernization of government bureaucracy. However, the economic situation did not improve and social tension grew. Encouraged by the example of the Cuban Revolution in 1959, the left strengthened its efforts to radicalize popular opinion. In the early 1960s, the National Liberation Movement, an urban left-wing guerrilla group known as the Tupamaros, was established in the cities.

In 1967, the Colorado Party regained control of the government, reacting harshly to the growing political mobilization of workers and students, as well as to the actions of the Tupamaros. The Colorados abandoned the collegiate government system and, in 1968, the president, Jorge Pacheco Areco (1920–1998; in office 1967–1972), banned several left-wing groups, including the Socialist Party and their press publications. That same year, a university student was killed by police in a street protest in Montevideo. Uruguay, which a few years earlier had regarded itself as the "Switzerland of South America" because of its stable economy and generous social benefits, gradually slipped into violence and authoritarianism.

In June 1973, the Colorado president Juan María Bordaberry (born 1928; in office 1972–1976) dissolved both houses of the legislature. From that time until late 1984, the country was effectively ruled by the armed forces and a group of civilians who chose to cooperate with the military. Many political prisoners were held and abuses of human rights, including the use of torture, were widespread. However at the same time, economic reforms helped overcome some of the nation's long-standing problems.

CIVILIAN RULE RESTORED

The military regime ended in 1984 when, once again, the Colorado Party won the national elections. The Colorados held the presidency for 15 of the following 20 years under Julio María Sanguinetti (born 1936; in office 1985–1990 and 1995–2000) and Jorge Batlle (born 1927; in office 2000–2005), whose great-uncle was former president José Batlle. The Blancos managed to break this hegemony only between 1990 and 1995, when Luis Alberto Lacalle (born 1931) was president.

The country progressed toward economic liberalism, establishing a customs union with Argentina, Brazil, and Paraguay in 1991, through the MERCOSUR trade organization. However, in 2003, the country was plunged into a deep recession; the unemployment rate reached almost 20 percent and poverty exceeded 30 percent. A year later, for the first time in Uruguayan history, neither the Colorado Party nor the National Party won the election. Uruguayans instead elected a candidate of a center-left alliance, Tabaré Vázquez (born 1940, in office since 2005), of the Frente Amplio (Broad Front).

A. GARCÉ

Julio María Sanguinetti talks with Cuban leader Fidel Castro before the Ibero-American conference in Havana, Cuba, in 1999.

CULTURAL EXPRESSION

Literature

Uruguayan literature has been strongly influenced by European traditions and, unlike the literature of most of its neighbors, shows little indigenous influence. It is famous for its gaucho literature tradition.

Uruguay's literary heritage is largely Spanish, although other European settlers, including Italians, brought their own literatures to the region, and French literature was influential in the nineteenth and twentieth centuries. Among the first important early Uruguayan writers were the poets Bartolomé Hidalgo (1788–1822) and Francisco Acuña de Figueroa (1791–1862), who wrote the words of the Uruguayan national anthem.

GAUCHO LITERATURE

Folk literature, also known as gaucho literature, is one of the oldest literary genres in Uruguay. This literary style imitated the *payadas* (ballads) of the gauchos who traveled around the country singing to the accompaniment of a guitar about love, life, and politics. Some of the most characteristic literature of the nineteenth century comes from the gaucho genre, for example in the classic poem "El gaucho Martín Fierro" (1872; The gaucho Martín Fierro) by José Hernández (1834–1886). Although Hernández was an Argentine journalist and poet, he also lived and worked in Uruguay. Eduardo Acevedo Díaz (1851–1924) was one of the founders of Uruguay's gaucho literature, although he wrote many of his works in exile in Argentina. Acevedo Díaz's first novel, *Brenda*, was published in 1886, and his 1894 novel *Soledad* (1894; Solitude) influenced many gaucho novelists in both Uruguay and Argentina. Other important gaucho writers include Javier de Viana (1868–1926), who wrote about gauchos in the short story "La yunta de Urubolí," and Carlos Reyles (1868–1938), a wealthy horse breeder who provided an insightful portrayal of country people in his novels *El terruño* (1916; The native soil), and the celebrated *El Gaucho Florida* (1932), which deals with the upheavals of ranch life.

MODERNIST LITERATURE

Poetry has always played an important role in Uruguayan literature. The poetry of the leading early twentieth-century poet, Delmira Agustini (1886–1914), whose life was cut short by her murder, is extremely passionate and sensual and stands out among other modernist poetry of the period. Julio Herrera y Reissig (1875–1910) influenced the development of modern Latin American poetry; he and the poets who gathered around him in Montevideo challenged existing poetic conventions and themes, experimenting with language and structure. His best-known work includes *Los maitines de la noche* (1902; The matins of the night) and *Poemas violetas* (1906; Violet poems). Florencio Sánchez (1875–1910) was a respected dramatist who wrote several plays dealing with rural life in and around the Río de la Plata. His work is still performed in Uruguayan theaters.

Possibly one of the most influential pieces of early twentieth-century Uruguayan writing is the essay "Ariel" (1900), written by the writer and critic José Enrique Rodó (1871–1917), who was also editor of *La Revista Nacional de Literatura y Ciencias Sociales*. The essay, which disavows the cultural and spiritual influence of the United States over Latin America, shaped the work of many nationalists and educationalists throughout the region. Other important Uruguayan writers include the short-story writer Horacio Quiroga (1878–1937) and the feminist poet Juana de Ibarbourou (1895–1979), who became known for her poems dealing with naturalist themes and featuring erotic imagery. Ibarbourou influenced many modern Latin American poets.

Novelist and short-story writer Juan Carlos Onetti (1909–1994) is regarded as having written the first modern Latin American novel, *El pozo* (1939), said to have influenced magical realism, a genre popular with modern Latin American writers, in which magic and spiritual elements are used in an otherwise realistic setting. Onetti spent much of his early working life in Argentina. A critic of gaucho literature, which he viewed as old-fashioned, Onetti returned to Uruguay in 1955 and began writing about the fictional town of Santa María. Many of Onetti's books deal with moral degradation and the futility of urban life.

Among current writers, the work of journalist Eduardo Galeano (born 1940) has been translated into more than 20 languages. Mario Benedetti (born 1920), who spent much time in political exile, has received many literary prizes and wrote a study of Uruguayan literature.

J. MONCADA

Art and Architecture

Hispanic art and architecture developed later in Uruguay than in other parts of Spain's colonial empire. Uruguay was not settled by the Spanish until the end of the seventeenth century, but there is limited influence of native peoples on local art.

There are few artifacts from the indigenous peoples of Uruguay. The Charrúa, the most populous pre-Columbian people in the region, made simple clay vessels and petroglyphs (rock paintings and engravings), but, when the Charrúa were wiped out by Spanish colonists, little of their art survived.

The first significant European settlements were built by the Portuguese and Spanish, who disputed the area. The Portuguese founded Colónia del Sacramento, opposite Buenos Aires, at the mouth of the Río de la Plata, in 1680. Typical of Portuguese settlements in Brazil, it had fortress walls of brick and stone, and simple dwellings of adobe (mud brick) and thatch. Farther east, the Spanish built the heavily fortified settlement of Montevideo in 1726. Military engineers who designed such fortifications were also responsible for religious and civic buildings in the region.

ARCHITECTURE

After the final establishment of Uruguayan independence in 1828, the neoclassical style—then fashionable in Europe—was adopted for official buildings, particularly in the new capital, Montevideo, where notable examples include the Plaza Independencia (1837) designed by Italian architect Carlos Zucchi (1789–1849). Greater political stability and economic growth in the closing decades of the nineteenth century stimulated urban expansion, and new housing complexes were laid out, such as the Reus district of Montevideo, with its regular, two-story row houses. The arrival of large numbers of European immigrants and the education of Uruguayan artists and architects abroad furthered the influence of European styles in the country, notably eclecticism (mixing stylistic features), and, in the twentieth century, art nouveau, art deco, and modernism. Influential architects who adopted the modernist idiom included Julio Vilamajó (1894–1948) and Mario Payssé-Reyes (1913–1988), while the engineer Eladio Dieste (1917–2000) designed some of the most unique buildings, including the brick-built church at Atlántida (1958–1960), whose undulating walls make a complex pattern through deceptively simple design.

VISUAL ARTS

The first European art in Uruguay was made by traveling painters such as Emeric Essex Vidal (1791–1861) and Alphonse D'Hastrel (1805–1870), who recorded the country's landscapes and peoples in detailed paintings and drawings. The first important native-born artist, Juan Manuel Blanes (1830–1901), painted historical subjects, portraits, and scenes of everyday life in a romanticized academic style. Alongside the realistic, academic style, the turn of the nineteenth and twentieth centuries also saw the influence of modern European art movements, such as Impressionism, and a desire among artists to explore specifically Uruguayan subject matter. Pedro Figari (1861–1938), for example, was influenced by Post Impressionism and produced paintings with pastel colors and simplified forms that depicted the lives of rural people.

The most influential artist in the development of modern Uruguayan art, however, was Joaquín Torres Garcia (1874–1949). He returned to Montevideo from Europe in 1934, at the age of 60, and through his studio and his manifesto, *La escuela del sur* (1935; The school of the south), promoted a uniquely South American abstract art. In addition to painting and sculpture, in the 1960s tapestry became a medium for exploring experimental techniques and avant-garde imagery, notably in the work of Ernesto Aroztegui (1930–1994).

R. BEAN

Casa Pueblo, at Maldonado, is the unfinished clifftop home and studio of Uruguayan architect Carlos Paéz Vilaró (born 1923), who also designed it. The building, which has no straight lines, shows Arab and Mediterranean influences.

Music and Performing Arts

Uruguay's music and performing arts reflect a diverse range of cultural traditions, drawing on European, particularly Spanish, and African traditions, among others. Compared with many South American nations, the music of Uruguay is little influenced by Amerindian traditions.

Music and dance play an important role in the culture of Uruguay, and the country is home to a wide range of musical styles, from *candombe* (a popular Afro-Uruguayan drum-based genre), *milonga* (a style of music and dance performed in both Uruguay and Argentina), and the tango, to various forms of theater, such as the *murga* (a form of musical theater). The nation also has a tradition of classical music and is home to a distinctive genre of modern music, Uruguayan rock.

CANDOMBE AND INDIGENOUS MUSIC

Uruguayan music and performing arts owe much to the cultures of African slaves who were brought to the Río de la Plata region by Spanish colonists from the mid-seventeenth century onward. Most slaves came from the western central coastal region of Africa, which was home to many different cultures and traditions. *Candombe* arose from groups of slaves meeting to sing, perform, and dance, and describes a percussion-based type of music that developed from this time. Performers gathered to play *tambores* (drums, variously known as *tambor piano*, *tambor chico*, and *tambor repique*) in groups. These gatherings became a matter of concern for the country's European establishment, who viewed them as potential hotbeds for political and social dissent. In the early nineteenth century, such meetings were banned, and, as a result, they were effectively driven underground. In 1846, after Uruguayan president Joaquín Suárez (1781–1868; in office 1843–1852) abolished slavery, the *candombe* came to be a key element of Uruguayan culture, rapidly becoming an important part of the nation's flamboyant carnivals and festivals.

The *milonga*, which is derived from the *candombe*, is believed to come from an Angolan word *mulonga*, meaning "word" or "long story." *Milonga* now refers to music, dance, or the place of a social gathering. Often played to the accompaniment of a folk guitar, the *milonga* style became popular among gauchos in the Río de la Plata region in the second half of the nineteenth century. A fast-paced dance, it is believed to be the precursor of the tango.

During the late nineteenth century, the tango developed in the back streets and brothels of Buenos Aires, the national capital of Argentina. However, both Uruguayans and Argentines claim that the tango originated in their country, and both also claim that their country was the birthplace of the celebrated tango singer Carlos Gardel (1891–1935), who brought the music to world attention. Although traditionally associated with Hispanic music and dance, the tango owes much to African rhythms. The musical traditions behind the tango are mixed, and Uruguayans seem to have made at least some contribution toward the genre. "La cumparsita" (1917), one of most famous tangos, was written by the Uruguayan composer Gerardo Matos Rodríguez (1897–1948). The tango, along with fandangos, boleras, waltzes, and polkas, became popular dances in Montevideo dancerooms. *La gavota* (influenced by the minuet), the *minue montenero* (also called the *national* and influenced by the minuet), and *la media caña* were all popular dances in nineteenth-century Uruguayan society.

THE *MURGA*

Uruguay is known for the *murga*, a type of musical theater performance, particularly popular during carnival season before Lent. A *murga* group consists of up to 17 people, comprising a chorus performing in harmony, and three percussionists, playing such instruments as the *bombo* (a shallow waist drum), *platillos*

A member of the Uruguayan murga *company La Mojigata, an informal theater group, performs on the streets of Montevideo.*

Montevideo's Teatro Solis was built in 1856. The city's principal stage for opera, ballet, and classical music, the theater underwent a multimillion-dollar restoration in 2004.

(cymbals), and a snare drum (*redoblante*). *Murga* music is typically made up of a prominent *saludo* (or opening song) and a *retirada* or *despedida* (finale, or final song). The performers, who are often colorfully made up, usually focus their songs on a social, political, or cultural theme. For example, during the era of political repression of a military dictatorship (1973–1984), some *murga* groups used their lyrics to highlight abuses of human rights. In modern times, some popular bands have adopted *murga* styles in their music. During carnival, temporary theaters, called *tablados*, are set up, where artists perform *murgas* and other types of music.

CLASSICAL MUSIC

As well as more traditional dance and music forms, Uruguay also houses several ballet schools and companies, including the Uruguayan National Ballet School and the SODRE Ballet Company. The nation has a long classical music tradition, influenced by Spanish and Italian music, in particular. Leading figures include celebrated violinist and composer Eduardo Fabini (1882–1950) and classical guitarist and composer Abel Carlevaro (1916–2001), who was taught by the Spanish guitarist Andrés Segovia (1893–1987), who moved to Montevideo during the Spanish Civil War (1936–1939). Héctor Tosar (born 1922) was a prodigy who composed his famous *Toccata* at age 16. He wrote a wide variety of orchestral, choral, and piano music. Composer-conductor José Serebrier (born 1938) has written symphonies, concertos, and chamber music, while the Uruguayan pianist Luis Batlle-Ibáñez (born 1927) gained an international reputation. In modern times, Uruguay has several classical orchestras, including the Symphonic Orchestra, which was founded in 1929.

MODERN MUSIC

The music of a diverse range of American and European artists is popular in Uruguay, as is jazz, independent music, punk, hip-hop, and rock, among other genres. The Uruguayan rock scene began in the 1960s with a local group, Los Shakers, who were influenced by the British band the Beatles. The group and other similar bands, such as Los Mockers and Los Malditos, in turn influenced the development of rock music in Argentina. In the mid-1970s, a genre of music called *canción popular* rose to prominence. Similar to *nueva canción*, a form of protest song that emerged in Chile and Argentina in the 1960s, *canción popular*'s exponents, such as Daniel Viglietti (born 1939), were often politically active and were imprisoned for their views by Uruguay's military dictatorship. In the last decades of the twentieth century, Uruguay was home to several punk, folk-rock, and hip-hop bands, such as El Peyote Asesino, a hip-hop and hard rock band that performed from 1994 through 1999. In 2004, singer-composer Jorge Drexler (born 1962) was the first Uruguayan to win an Academy Award for his song *Al otro lado del Río* from the soundtrack of the movie *The Motorcycle Diaries*.

THEATER

The works of Uruguay's leading dramatist Florencio Sánchez (1875–1910) are still performed in theaters across the country. The Florencia, named for the dramatist, is an annual theater award, the equivalent of the Tony Awards in the United States. In modern times, Montevideo houses a vibrant theatrical community with several independent theater groups. Uruguay's leading modern playwrights include Mauricio Rosencof (born 1933) and Eleuterio Fernández Huidobro (born 1942), who were both imprisoned during the military regime and later wrote about their experiences.

E. M. STONE

Festivals and Ceremonies

Uruguay is a secular country in which public holidays that commemorate important events in the country's history outnumber religious holidays. Many local festivals are also celebrated throughout Uruguay.

Local festivals are among the most enthusiastically celebrated holidays in Uruguay. The festival of the Virgen de la Candelaria, celebrated on February 2, centers on a church at Punta del Este in southern Uruguay. Accessible only at low tide, the site is thought to be the place where Spaniards first stepped ashore and celebrated their safe arrival with a mass. The holiday is marked by parades, colorful costumes, and music.

Las Llamadas is an annual Mardi Gras carnival held in the days before Lent in Montevideo, the Uruguayan national capital. Famous for *murgas* (small informal theatrical productions) and *candombe* music (traditional drumming of the Afro-Uruguayan people), the carnival is the most popular national festival and lasts for two days. A dancing festival to honor Carlos Gardel (1891–1935), a famous singer of tango music, is held annually at Valle Edén, which claims to be his birthplace, although Argentines claim that Gardel was born in Argentina.

NATIONAL HOLIDAYS

The first public holiday of the year in Uruguay is New Year's Day. Desembarco de los Treinta y Tres (the Landing of the 33 Patriots Day) in mid-April commemorates the arrival by ship in 1825 of 33 exiles who began a war that led to Uruguay's independence. Día de los Trabajadores, a national holiday that is equivalent to Labor Day in the United States, is celebrated on May 1.

A holiday in mid-May marks the anniversary of the 1811 Battle of Las Piedras, when a Spanish army was defeated by local people led by José Gervasio Artigas (1764–1850). Artigas is honored as Uruguay's national hero, having twice fought for independence from Spanish rule, but also having resisted Argentine and Brazilian attempts to annex Uruguay. Artigas's birthday, June 19, is a public holiday and, in modern times, is also called Día del Nunca Más ("never again day") to commemorate a period of political violence (beginning in 1958) and the military dictatorship from 1973 through 1984. Those who died or suffered human rights abuses are remembered on this day.

The public holiday on July 18 is called Jura de la Constitución ("swearing in of the constitution"), commemorating the approval by the legislature of the nation's original constitution in 1830. Independence Day, the National Day, occurs on August 25, marking the attainment of independence from Brazil in 1825. Columbus Day, October 12, is traditionally celebrated throughout the Americas as the day that Christopher Columbus (1451–1506) arrived in the New World in 1492. In Uruguay, as in many Latin American nations, the holiday is called Día de la Raza ("day of the race"), commemorating the first contact between Europeans and Amerindians.

RELIGIOUS HOLIDAYS

Only a minority of Uruguayans are practicing Catholics, and nearly one-third of the population are nonrelgous. However, several religious holidays, such as Maundy Thursday and Good Friday, are public holidays. All Souls' Day (November 2), known as Día de los Muertos ("day of the dead"), is also a public holiday, when ancestors are honored. Uruguayans usually spend the day with family and attend local celebrations. Christmas Day is a national holiday, but the secular state calendar names the festival Family Day. Other religious holidays also have secular names; for example, Epiphany, on January 6, is called Children's Day. In the religious calendar, the day commemorates the three kings' visit to the infant Jesus. In modern Uruguay, children traditionally receive presents on that day.

D. TORRA

A carnival band begins the inaugural procession of Montevideo's colorful parade to celebrate Las Llamadas.

Food and Drink

Making use of locally produced meat from the pampas of the interior of the country, Uruguayans are one of the largest consumers of beef in the world. The national cuisine is characterized by many meat-based dishes.

Uruguayans tend to start the day with a light breakfast, featuring bread and jam or *media lunas* (croissants), served with coffee or maté (an herbal tea). Lunch is normally a more substantial meal, and some businesses close for several hours to allow employees time to eat at home with their family. Many people, however, eat sandwiches or a *chivito* (a steak sandwich topped with eggs, cheese, bacon, lettuce, and tomatoes). The most substantial meal of the day is dinner, which Uruguayans eat late in the evening.

ASADO

One of the most typical Uruguayan dishes, the *asado* (barbecued meat), is made from cooking meat in a wood-fired oven called a *parrillero*. Before cooking, the meat is spread with a marinade or *mojo* made of water and salt. The *asado* typically consists of chorizos, *morcilla dulce* (a type of blood sausage sweetened with orange peel), *mondongo* (tripe), and *choto* (intestine wrapped with tripe). It is served with salad and a *chimichurri* sauce (made from oil, oregano, salt, and garlic).

POPULAR DISHES

Other popular meat dishes are *puchero* (beef with vegetables, bacon, beans, and sausages), *churrasco* (grilled steak), and *húngaras* (spicy sausages), which are usually served in a roll. *Cazuela* (stew) is often served, and *mondongo* (a tripe sausage with garlic flavoring) is popular. *Milanesa Uruguaya* consists of a breaded, fried steak, barbecued pork, and grilled chicken in wine.

The heritage of the nation's Spanish and Italian settlers is also reflected in Uruguay's diverse cuisine. Paellas and other seafood dishes, cooked in a Spanish manner, are frequently served in restaurants, while Italian influences are seen in the popularity of both pizza and pasta.

DESSERTS

Uruguayans, like many of their South American neighbors, enjoy desserts, especially *dulce de leche* (a caramel crème). Other popular sweet dishes include *chajá de Paysandú*, a ball-shaped cake filled with apricot jam, coated with cream and rolled in crushed meringue, and *mossini* (cream sponge cake). Lemon pie and *yemas* (crystallized egg yolk) are also favorites.

DRINKS

Coffee houses are an important part of Uruguayan culture. Uruguayans particularly enjoy strong espressos, *café cortados* (coffee with a small amount of milk), and *café con leche* (a half-milk, half-coffee mixture). As in many other South American countries, maté is also commonly drunk and is offered by hosts to their guests. During the military dictatorship (1974–1984), when public meetings were banned, one of the few ways in which Uruguayans could meet and exchange information freely was over a cup of maté. Uruguay also produces good quality wine. *Clericó* (white wine mixed with juice) and *medio y medio* (made from a mixture of white wine and champagne) are popular, and local beers include Prinz and Zillerthal. Local spirits such as *caña* (made from sugarcane), grappa (from grapes), and home-produced whiskey and gin are also available.

J. MONCADA

Uruguayans often go to restaurants to eat asado *(barbecued meat), which is cooked in a traditional manner in a wood-fired oven.*

DAILY LIFE

Religion

Around 66 percent of Uruguayans are Roman Catholics, but only about-half of that figure attend mass. Another 2 percent are members of various Protestant churches, while 1 percent belong to other faiths, including Judaism and Islam. Compared to other Latin American countries, Uruguay has a large number of people who claim to be nonreligious, about 31 percent.

Uruguay is a secular state, and even the names of religious holidays officially have nonreligious names in the state calendar. Christmas Day, for example, is called Family Day holiday.

A SECULAR NATION

Historically, the strong resistance of the country's small indigenous population to conversion to Christianity delayed the colonization of the region by the Spanish, and, although Jesuits established *reducciones* (reductions, or missions) for the indigenous peoples in the seventeenth and eighteenth centuries, they were mostly destroyed after the Jesuits were expelled in 1767. Post-independence Uruguay was influenced by European ideas and adopted many of the anticlerical attitudes popular in France. Subsequently, several laws were introduced endorsing Uruguay's secularization, including a 1907 law that legalized divorce, and a law, two years later, that prohibited religious education in schools. The 1917 constitution confirmed the separation of church and state in Uruguay.

LIBERATION THEOLOGY

In the 1960s, a more radical, liberal movement—that came to be known as liberation theology—began in the Roman Catholic Church in the region. Montevideo-born Juan Luis Segundo (1925–1996), a Jesuit priest, was one of a group of Latin American theologians who, in the 1960s, challenged practicing Catholics about the role of the church in society. Asking practitioners to rethink how their church fit into society, Segundo, along with Peruvian theologian Gustavo Gutiérrez (born 1928), among others, promoted the idea of using faith to help create a more just society in Latin America. Many church officials, teachers, and health care workers, influenced by liberation theology, began working in poor and disenfranchised communities across Uruguay and other countries in Latin America. This new liberalism was also adopted by members of the Protestant community in Uruguay.

PROTESTANT DENOMINATIONS

Uruguay's small Protestant community dates back to the 1830s, when Methodists came from North America. From the 1850s, the Waldensians, a Protestant community that originated in northern Italy and southern France, moved to Uruguay and Argentina, fleeing persecution in Europe. They founded Colonia Valdense along the Río de la Plata, one of the earliest Protestant communities in Latin America. Members of other Protestant groups migrated to Uruguay, including German Lutherans, Jehovah's Witnesses, and Seventh-day Adventists.

In modern times, the Protestant population of Uruguay predominantly comprises Episcopalians, Methodists, Lutherans, and Baptists. Other Christian denominations now include various evangelical churches, Pentecostalists, Mennonites, and Eastern Orthodox churches.

OTHER RELIGIOUS GROUPS

There are more than 70,000 members of the Church of Jesus Christ of Latter-day Saints (Mormons) in Uruguay, which is also home to about 30,000 Jews. Immigration in modern times has also led to the establishment of other faiths in Uruguay. There is a small Muslim population, the majority living near the Brazilian border, and a Baha'i community lives in Montevideo. In the twenty-first century, the Brazilian spiritist community, who were previously restricted in the country, has also grown in numbers. Some Uruguayan sources state that more spiritist centers than new Protestant churches are opening in Uruguay.

E. M. STONE

Family and Society

For most of the twentieth century, Uruguay was a welfare state, with a highly educated liberal society and a per capita income higher than most of its neighbors. A distinctive Uruguayan society and way of life consequently emerged.

Through the twentieth century, the Uruguayan government invested time and money in the well-being of its people, both as individuals and families, creating a liberal and educated environment. Uruguay became known as the "Switzerland of South America." However, economic difficulties in the late twentieth century and the seizure of power by the military (from 1973 through 1984), which interrupted a long period of democratic rule, seriously challenged the accepted Uruguayan way of life.

STRUCTURE OF SOCIETY

Uruguayans are mostly of European origin, some 88 percent being of unmixed European ancestry, largely Spanish and Italian. Another 8 percent are mestizos, people of mixed Amerindian and European ancestry, but Amerindian influences are less significant in Uruguay than in any other nation in South America. Black Uruguayans and a small number of Asians account for the remaining 4 percent. The nation is culturally European, mainly Hispanic, and largely Roman Catholic, although only 66 percent of Uruguayans are recorded as Catholic and only about one-third of the population are practicing.

Compared with other Latin American societies, Uruguay is relatively egalitarian, and the sharp divisions between rich and poor that characterize other South American nations are absent. Nevertheless, sociologists broadly divide Uruguayan society into an upper class (including ranchers, businesspeople, and politicians), a middle class (of professionals, white-collar workers, and small businesspeople), and a lower class (of blue-collar workers, domestics, and peasants).

Uruguayan society was hit hard by an economic recession in 2002, but the nation's welfare system helped cushion some of the worst effects of economic decline, and many Uruguayans suffered far less than citizens in other comparable Latin American nations that experienced downturns in the same period. Nevertheless, unemployment in the country rose from around 8 percent to 17 percent (falling to 10.5 percent in 2006), and family incomes sharply dropped. The middle class, particularly professionals, was most affected, and many people were hit so badly that they came to be termed Uruguay's "new poor." In 2006, according to official figures, an estimated 27.4 percent of the population was poor. As a result of the economic crisis, child poverty increased (by 400 percent since 1985), and some children dropped out of school in order to support their families—a situation that had been rare in Uruguay.

Grandparents play an increasingly important role in child care in Uruguay because in many households both parents work.

Uruguay is a highly urbanized country. Some 87 percent of its population of 3.3 million people live in urban centers, with around 1,750,000 in the metropolitan area of Montevideo, the national capital. However, because of the relatively small distances between Montevideo and most rural areas, the difference between urban and rural life is not as great as in some South American nations. The interior regions of Uruguay are not isolated, nor do they have the relatively low population density associated with rural areas in neighboring countries.

THE FAMILY

Family ties are traditionally strong in Uruguay. Extended family structures are more common in rural areas than in the city, but family gatherings are popular throughout Uruguayan society. The sharing of maté (an herbal green tea) is a popular social custom in family gatherings. Maté is passed around a circle in a hollowed-out gourd with a metal straw. The custom became popular as a way of holding meetings during military rule in the 1970s, when political gatherings were banned.

In modern Uruguayan society, it is no longer common for extended families with grandparents, children, and grandchildren to live in the same household. Nuclear families, comprising father, mother, and immediate children, are the norm, making up more than 60 percent of households in the country. The single-person household is also increasingly common, the result of growing separations of couples and the rising number of people who prefer to live alone. A growing

Marriage is in decline in modern-day Uruguay, and many people are choosing to live together in informal unions or to bring up children in single-parent households.

number of women now head single-parent households, and there is also a tendency for young upper-class Uruguayans to remain single, and, if in a relationship, to be childless.

Attitudes toward the institution of marriage have also changed. Fewer people are choosing to marry and many prefer to cohabit with partners. There are no guarantees that families will last, and divorces, separations, new unions, and blended families are part of the new social fabric. In Uruguay, there are now more divorces than marriages, and no stigma is attached to failed relationships for either men or women. Homosexual unions are still not widely accepted, although, in late 2006, the government passed legislation making such civil partnerships legal.

Family sizes are declining, mainly because women practice birth control as they become more involved in careers. By 2007, the fertility rate was 2.0 children per woman. At the same time, Uruguay's advanced health care system has helped extend the lives of older people, so that, by 2007, life expectancy for women was 79.3 years and for men 72.7 years. The median age is increasing, with 13 percent of the population over age 65. The younger population is mobile, and it is common for young Uruguayans to migrate within the country or to go abroad for employment opportunities.

THE ROLE OF WOMEN

In nineteenth-century Uruguay, society, in part influenced by the traditional Roman Catholic view of families, was traditionally patriarchal, and stereotypes of male superiority were widespread. However, at the end of the nineteenth century and early in the twentieth century, the Uruguayan authorities implemented laws that strengthened women's rights, particularly under José Batlle (1856–1929; in office 1899, 1903–1907 and 1911–1915), a strong supporter of women's equality. By 1885, civil marriages were legalized, and fewer marriages were conducted in church. Divorce on the grounds of cruelty by men was legalized in 1907 and, from 1912, women could file for divorce without giving any cause. Women voted for the first time in 1932. Through the twentieth century, increasing numbers of women opted for careers rather than traditional roles as wives and mothers.

Despite the advances that have been made, full equality for Uruguayan women has not been completely achieved. Women's participation in politics and government decision making is still limited, and wages of women workers are lower than for men, even when they do the same type of work. Violence against women, including domestic violence, is a problem. Single women bringing up children are among the poorest people in Uruguay. Women usually bear the responsibility of looking after children from an increasing number of broken relationships, and a high proportion of Uruguayan men do not contribute to child support. It is also not possible for a woman to obtain an abortion on request in Uruguay, and illegal abortions that may endanger women's lives or future health are widespread.

R. SIMON-KUMAR

Health and Welfare

Uruguay was South America's first welfare state with an innovative system in health care, social security, and public education. However, economic problems brought restrictions and reforms to the system late in the twentieth century.

Uruguay's tradition of social welfare began with the establishment of mutual aid societies in the 1850s. By 1896, the country had implemented a social security pension system for teachers. Under the reformist president José Batlle (1856–1929; in office 1899, 1903–1907, and 1911–1915), the foundations for a state welfare system were laid, beginning in 1912, and the process continued under his successors until 1929. Uruguay, a nation that was known for its stability and the exercise of democracy, was therefore able to establish a welfare program, including subsidized health care and benefits for low-income workers, as well as social security provision for senior citizens and the unemployed.

For most of the twentieth century, Uruguay was ruled by democratically elected governments, which attempted to provide basic social welfare programs for all of its citizens. In 1943, family social security pension allowances were introduced, and the system was consolidated seven years later. However, the pension structure was subject to manipulation since some politicians implemented changes to gain electoral support. The system was also open to abuse, and, in one scandal, more pensions were handed out to alleged garment workers than the actual number of workers in the industry.

By the late 1960s and early 1970s, growing economic problems threatened the continuation of the welfare system unless it underwent radical reform. At the same time, widespread urban violence and unrest spread throughout the country—Uruguay had not experienced political violence for more than a century. Left-wing Tupamaros guerrillas (members of the Movimiento de Liberación Nacional, MLN) became active from 1958, and in 1973 the army seized power. The military regime that ruled Uruguay from 1973 through 1984 made severe cutbacks in health and welfare spending, while military expenditures and government bureaucracy increased. When civilian government was restored in the mid-1980s, funding for social welfare programs increased, but the state welfare system is not as comprehensive as it was before the period of military rule.

THE HEALTH CARE SYSTEM

In modern times, the majority of Uruguay's 3.3 million people live in relative prosperity and have access to adequate medical care (although around 30 percent of the population do not have insurance). The bulk of Uruguay's people are middle class and live in cities, particularly the national capital, Montevideo, whose metropolitan area was home to 1,750,000 people at the 2004 national census. As a result, medical and other facilities are concentrated in the cities, most of which are along or near the coast. There are approximately 60 hospitals and 200 health care centers in Uruguay, with easy access to facilities in most parts of the country. Uruguay currently has nearly 12,400 doctors, 2,880 nurses, and more than 3,900 dentists.

About one-half of the population receives health care through the public sector. The Uruguayan Ministry of Public Health administers health services through the Social Welfare Fund, while the armed forces and police both have their own health care systems. Founded in the late 1960s, the Social Welfare Fund is a self-regulating agency that coordinates social security, among other functions, and additionally acts as a direct provider of health services to children and to pregnant women. Low-cost medical services for Montevideo's needy are available at the city's Hospital de Clinicas, which is a large facility that is also known as a research center.

The rest of Uruguay's population are members of cooperatives, most of which are funded through employee contributions. More than 50 private cooperative agencies exist, and the services available through the contributory private system are widely considered to be better than those provided through the public health sector.

The general standard of health in Uruguay is good, and, in 2007, life expectancy for women was 79.3 years and for men 72.7 years. Communicable diseases are not a major problem, and common childhood conditions, such as measles, have been all but eradicated through modern immunization programs. More than 95 percent of Uruguayans have received all of the standard inoculations. Heart disease and cancer are among the most common causes of death among Uruguayans, as in many industrialized countries.

WELFARE

Most Uruguayans contribute portions of their salaries to pension and social security programs. There is also a noncontributory element to the pension fund, and expenditure on pensions accounts for around 15 percent of Uruguay's GDP (gross domestic product, the total value of all the goods and services produced in a country in a fixed period, usually one year). In 2004, around 90 percent of Uruguayans over age 65 received a pension. The percentage of citizens with a pension is decreasing, however, as larger numbers of older people postpone retirement. Separate army and police pension programs also exist. In 1996, the authorities introduced reforms to the pension system to cover rising costs and increasing numbers of people of pensionable age. As a result, workers now have individual savings plans to pay for their pension. Mothers, who receive low or no wages, receive child care benefits. The unemployed receive payments, and there are sickness benefits for those unable to work for health reasons.

HOUSING

Unlike many other South American countries, Uruguay has few urban slums. Most residents in Montevideo and other Uruguayan cities have access to electricity and running water (around 75 percent of all houses) and are connected to sewers. Most are also in close proximity to medical care facilities. Generally, only the poorest city residents live in tiny shacks on the outskirts of Montevideo. More than 55 percent of Uruguayans own their own home and another 25 percent rent a house or an apartment in the public sector or from a private landlord. Most of the remaining population live in part of a dwelling that is owned by someone else, usually a family member. The public sector is a major provider of housing, and the National Institute of Low-Cost Housing builds homes for low-income workers and for senior citizens.

High-rise apartment buildings line the Rambia, in Montevideo. The district is a typical example of Montevideo's mainly middle-class neighborhoods.

WELFARE IN THE TWENTY-FIRST CENTURY

Although Uruguay has a reputation for providing health and welfare services to all of its citizens, and there is less inequality in the distribution of income than in other Latin American nations, social problems remain. The unemployment rate stood at 10.8 percent in 2006. In that year, according to official figures, some 27.4 percent of the Uruguayan population was poor. The government of Tabaré Vázquez (born 1940; in office since 2005), Uruguay's first socialist president, increased coverage of basic health care to the poor and also implemented a food program. However, attempts to establish a comprehensive national health care insurance program stalled because of funding problems. The International Monetary Fund (IMF) has urged Uruguay's authorities to maintain more restrictive fiscal policies rather than to increase public spending greatly. The Vázquez government has put in place several new health care provisions, and, in early 2006, Uruguay became the first Latin American nation to ban smoking in public places, including offices, universities, and enclosed bars and restaurants.

K. BIAS

Education

Uruguay was a pioneer of universal education in Latin America. Since the mid-nineteenth century, the country has provided mandatory, secular, free education through a public school system.

Uruguay has the highest standard of adult literacy in South America—98 percent in 2006. The country also has the best provision of educational facilities in the continent.

DEVELOPMENT

President Pedro Varela (1837–1903; in office 1868, 1875, and 1875–1876) was a strong advocate of universal education. Although his own terms in office were short, his ideas influenced later Uruguayan governments, which introduced compulsory public schooling in 1877. The 1877 Law of Common Education established a nationwide educational system for primary, secondary (high school), and tertiary education.

In the 1960s, Uruguay's high schools and universities became centers of political activity. Students staged demonstrations and sit-ins to protest government policies and, when a military regime came to power in 1973, the authorities reacted against students and teachers. From 1973 through 1985, the military junta reduced spending on education, student dropout rates rapidly increased, many teachers left the country, and educational standards and achievements declined. Following the return to democracy in Uruguay in 1985, a series of educational reforms, most of which date after 1994, improved the quality of the system, and enrollment of students from poorer households in the later years of secondary education has improved.

SCHOOLS AND UNIVERSITIES

Schooling in Uruguay is compulsory from age 6 through 14, covering primary and basic secondary schooling. There is nearly 100 percent coverage of enrollment at the primary level, and a school meals program delivered through primary schools provides lunches for the poorest children. High school education comprises two three-year cycles: the basic cycle is compulsory and the second cycle prepares students either to enter university or begin vocational training. However, at the second cycle of high school, many students drop out of the educational system. Around 48 percent of students over age 15, mostly from poor households, stop attending high school after the first cycle.

The high school curriculum includes science and math, Spanish, humanities, and the liberal arts. Curriculum reform in 2004 introduced the study of recent history, including the period

The Universidad de la República, which has more than 70,000 students, was founded in 1849 in Montevideo, the national capital. In modern times, the university has also opened campuses in the cities of Rivera and Salto.

of military dictatorship (1973–1985). Improvements have also been made in the provision of facilities, particularly for sciences and computing. However, the number of dropouts from high school after age 15 is still a major concern.

Until 1984, there was only one university in Uruguay, the (state-funded) Universidad de la República, which was founded in 1849. Since then, three private universities began to operate in the Montevideo metropolitan area. Entry to university is open to students who have passed the *bachillareto* qualifying examination or have completed both cycles of high school education. Education is free in the public university, and courses may take up to six years, depending on the subject.

R. SIMON-KUMAR

Montevideo

Montevideo, the national capital of Uruguay, dominates the nation's political, economic, and social life. The city is home to more than 40 percent of Uruguayans.

In 2004, the Montevideo metropolitan area, which includes the neighboring city of Las Piedras, had a population of 1,750,000 and 1,270,000 people lived within the city limits. By contrast, Salto, the second-largest city in Uruguay, was home to only 99,000 people.

CITY DEVELOPMENT

The region that now forms Uruguay was known in Spanish colonial times (from the sixteenth through early nineteenth centuries) as Banda Oriental ("east bank," of the Río de la Plata). Because of the hostility of the local Amerindians, the area was not settled by the Spanish until the seventeenth century, when it was disputed by Spain and Portugal, the colonial power in Brazil to the north. Montevideo was founded in 1726 as a Spanish fort to check expansion into the district by the Portuguese.

Many nineteenth-century hotel, retail, and office buildings are situated in Montevideo's central business district.

Originally little more than a garrison, Montevideo grew during the second half of the eighteenth century, when cattle raising developed in the region inland. By the start of the nineteenth century, Montevideo was a small city of some 6,000 inhabitants and was home to a flourishing merchant community. From 1806 through 1825, British, Spanish, and Portuguese forces—and later Argentine, Brazilian, and local nationalist elements—fought for control of the city. The British occupied Montevideo in 1807. In 1811, José Gervasio Artigas (1764–1850), in modern times regarded as the national hero of Uruguay, led a successful revolt against Spanish rule in Banda Oriental. The region won independence as part of Argentina.

In 1821, Brazilian forces invaded the area, occupying Montevideo. As a result of a revolt in Uruguay in 1825, the area became an independent entity—initially called the State of Montevideo—within the loose confederation that then formed Argentina. The new state secured international recognition in 1828 and changed its name from Montevideo to Uruguay in 1830.

Independent Uruguay suffered a long period of civil war through the 1840s, and Montevideo was besieged by a combined Argentine-Uruguayan force for nine years from 1843, when the governor of Buenos Aires, Juan Manuel de Rosas (1793–1877; in office 1829–1832 and 1835–1852; supreme chief of the Argentine Confederation 1851–1852), attempted to reincorporate Uruguay as a province of Argentina. During the siege, ships were able to maintain supplies to the Uruguayan troops defending the city. At the same time, the French and British, who allied with the defenders of Montevideo, blockaded the Argentine port of Buenos Aires across the Río de la Plata estuary.

Despite the fighting, Montevideo grew, and trade became more important. By 1850, Montevideo had a population of 35,000. In the second half of the nineteenth century, as Uruguay developed economically, the city's population rapidly grew, reaching 105,000 in 1884 and 266,000 in 1900. At the same time, Uruguay's railroad and highway system was extended, with Montevideo as the nation's route hub. The city's growth was rapid through the first half of the twentieth century. By 1928, Montevideo was home to 459,000 people; in 1938, the city's population was 704,000.

In December 1939, during World War II (1939–1945), the German battleship *Admiral Graf Spee* took refuge in the neutral harbor of Montevideo after the Battle of the River Plate against the British navy. British vessels waited outside Uruguayan waters for the German ship to emerge from port. To avoid an inevitable defeat in a one-sided conflict, the captain of the *Graf Spee*, Hans Wilhelm Langsdorff (1894–1939), scuttled his ship off Montevideo. He subsequently killed himself.

The extensive beaches of Montevideo attract many tourists, particularly Uruguayan and Argentine vacationers.

A MODERN CITY

Montevideo lies along the shore of the wide Río de la Plata estuary. The city's economy centers around its port, which handles the greater part of Uruguay's international trade. The port exports meat, wool, and hides and imports fuels, consumer goods, and a wide range of raw materials. Montevideo's industries process the agricultural products of the interior, preparing, packing, and freezing meat, processing wool and dairy products, and making shoes and other leather goods. The city has textile and engineering industries and makes wine, clothes, soap, and cement and building materials, as well as refining oil.

Uruguay is a highly centralized country, and Montevideo is home to ministries, government offices, and other administrative buildings. Until modern times, the city was also the only location of university-level institutions in Uruguay; as a result, it is a major educational center. Montevideo houses the nation's media, cultural, and artistic institutions, including the national history museums and the national library.

Montevideo Carrasco International Airport handles most of the scheduled international flights to and from Uruguay. The city is more European in appearance and character than most national capitals in South America. The mestizo (mixed Amerindian and European) population accounts for only 5 percent of Montevideo's inhabitants, and no Uruguayan Amerindians of unmixed indigenous ancestry are recorded as living in the city. More than 90 percent of the population of Montevideo is of unmixed European ancestry. In 2006, an international human resource center rated Montevideo as the South American city with the highest quality of life.

MONTEVIDEO'S ATTRACTIONS

The city's major tourist attractions are its extensive beaches of white sand. Montevideo attracts large numbers of Argentine visitors for beach vacations. The city's main boulevard, 18 de Julio, stretches from downtown Plaza Independencia, which adjoins Ciudad Vieja, the old quarter. Plaza Independencia is a wide square, which is lined by palm trees and surrounded by most of the city's historic public buildings. In the center of the square, a statue of José Gervasio Artigas surmounts his tomb. The buildings of Ciudad Vieja date mainly from the nineteenth century and the early years of the twentieth century, with some fine examples of the art deco style (a popular elegant style of the 1920s and 1930s). The old quarter also contains a smaller number of Spanish colonial-era buildings dating from the second half of eighteenth century.

C. CARPENTER

ECONOMY

Compared with its South American neighbors, Uruguay is a relatively small country, slightly smaller than the state of Washington. The nation has the region's highest standard of living and lowest levels of poverty and inequality, in part because of political stability through most of its history.

Uruguay, located along the northern shore of the Río de la Plata estuary, is a nation with little topographical variety in its slightly hilly terrain. The country has a temperate climate, and most of the interior is grassland, the Pampas, which is suited for raising cattle. The nation, which has a small population of only around 3.3 million, is dominated by one large metropolitan area, Montevideo, the national capital, which is home to more than one-half of Uruguay's population.

The economy of Uruguay has long been characterized by substantial state involvement. Despite significant structural reforms since the 1990s, including the lowering of tariffs and a reduction in the size of government, the state continues to play a major role in the economy with full or part ownership of firms involved in insurance, utilities, petroleum refining, transportation, and banking. Although privatization is often politically opposed in Uruguay, the economy is based on the principle of free enterprise, and property rights are respected.

ECONOMIC CHALLENGES

The main challenge for the Uruguayan economy has always been the nation's small size. Its modest population means that it cannot rely on domestic consumption to fuel economic growth. Since independence in the early nineteenth century, Uruguay has had to rely on agricultural and primary exports as the principal source of foreign exchange. The source of its wealth in the nineteenth century came from agricultural products such as wool, lamb, beef, hides, and grain, which it traded with Europe, especially Great Britain, for consumer goods. The agricultural sector was so profitable that from 1870 onward, there were sufficient funds to establish a small manufacturing sector.

Uruguay's dependence on foreign markets, and the constraints placed upon it by its limited domestic market, became apparent during the Great Depression (a major worldwide economic downturn; 1929–1933). During this period, most nations adopted trade policies (such as tariffs and import quotas) to protect domestic manufacturers from foreign imports, and world trade rapidly shrank. As a result, Uruguay encountered economic problems. During World War II (1939–1945), export performance (particularly of beef and wheat) improved to meet the war needs of the United States but soon declined once the war was over. Uruguay's exports of wool were particularly damaged by the invention and manufacture of synthetic fibers in the United States from the late 1920s onward. Exports were also hurt by underinvestment in the agricultural sector as profits from the sale of farming products were redirected toward urban consumers (in the form of subsidized food) and the manufacturing sector (for the purchase of foreign-made capital goods, goods used in industry). By the mid-1960s, primary product exports had fallen to just 26 percent of total output from a high of 69 percent in the early 1950s.

During the 1930s, Uruguay implemented a policy called import substitution industrialization (ISI) to encourage the manufacture of goods such as cars and other consumer durables that had previously been made abroad in order to reduce its dependence on foreign imports. However, Uruguay's manufactured goods could not compete with foreign imports in terms of either price or quality, and the small size of its internal market with a low number of domestic consumers made it impossible for the program to solve the country's economic problems.

Uruguay's economic decay was not apparent until the 1970s. In 1973, the military took power, promising to revive Uruguay's economy by increasing foreign investment and reducing inflation. In the same year, however, oil-producing countries quadrupled the price of oil, causing what became known as the first oil crisis. (The second oil crisis occurred in 1981, when prices peaked at three times their 1973 price.) This crisis had a recessionary impact on countries like Uruguay that were highly

---

Standard of Living

In 2006, GDP per capita in Uruguay was $10,900, adjusted for purchasing power parity (PPP), a formula that allows comparison between living standards in different countries. GDP per capita is a notional method of demonstrating how much wealth each person in a particular country has. However, since a country's wealth is never divided equally, other measures are often used. One method is the United Nations' Physical Quality of Life Index (PQLI), a composite indicator that uses the literacy rate, life expectancy, and infant mortality to calculate the quality of live in a given nation. According to this indicator, Uruguay enjoys the highest standard of living of any Latin American country.

dependent on oil imports for their energy needs. The decline of the export sector, coupled with high oil prices, led the military to take two economic decisions, neither of which was successful. The regime borrowed money from foreign banks. In the 1970s, interest payments on loans were low because of the large amount of money in the world economy generated by oil sales. However, global interest rates sharply increased in 1981, raising the value of Uruguay's debt by 400 percent. The military also increased the money supply (printing more money), which spurred inflation up to 63 percent. Spiraling inflation, a growing foreign debt, and poor export performance failed to win the confidence of international investors. The military's economic policies were also undermined by large, well-organized, militant public sector labor unions, which opposed proposed wage freezes and cutbacks in government spending that would have helped stabilize the economy and reduce inflation.

In 1985, the military government relinquished power to a democratically elected administration, and, although the new government failed to reduce the debt or inflation, its respect for democratic norms signified that Uruguay had turned away from authoritarianism as a solution to its economic problems. Since 1992, Uruguay's economic performance has been largely positive. Growth has been high, with the GDP (gross domestic product, the total value of all the goods and services produced in a country in a fixed term, usually one year) growing by 12.4 percent in 2004, and 7 percent in 2005 and 2006.

The growth of the economy has been due in no small part to Uruguay's membership in MERCOSUR (the regional trade pact whose other members are Argentina, Brazil, Paraguay, and Venezuela), which has caused the demand for Uruguayan exports to triple since 1992. However, Uruguay still faces many challenges, both political and economic.

Uruguay is famous in Latin America for its generous welfare state. While providing many citizens with a high standard of living, the welfare system was expensive to run and was the cause of much of the high government spending that fueled inflation and excessive borrowing. During the 1990s, fiscal constraints were placed on Uruguay by the International Monetary Fund (IMF) in return for loans; thus the main political challenge was to reduce social expenditure (money spent on health, education, housing, etc.) to a level the government could afford. This challenge was met, in part, in 1994 when Congress passed a law allowing the partial privatization of some state benefit systems such as pensions. Following a policy of fiscal conservatism (making sure that expenditure never exceeded income), the Uruguayan administration achieved single digit inflation and paid off more than one-half the national debt by 2005. The last $1.06 billion of Uruguay's debt to the IMF was settled in November 2006.

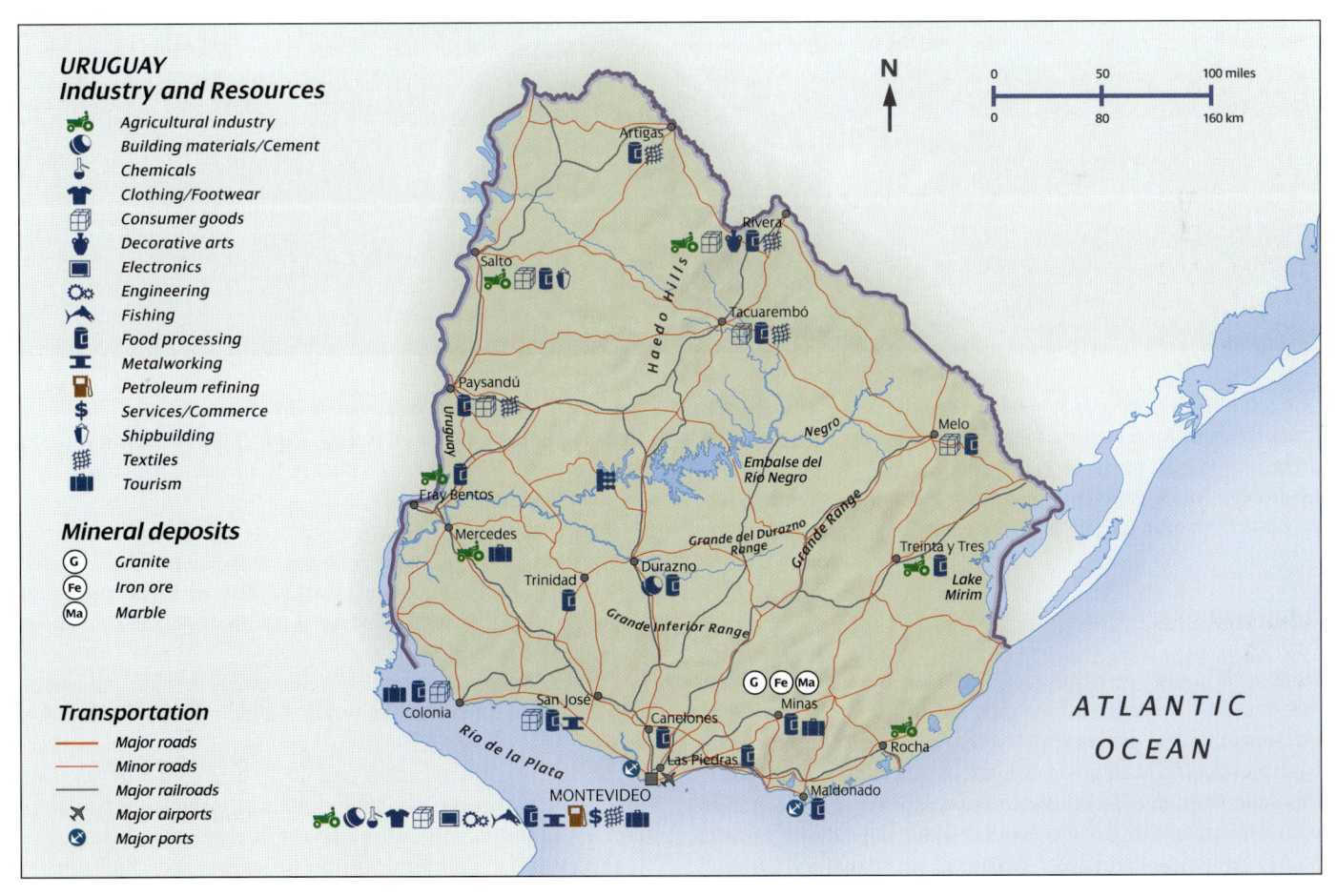

Uruguay's main economic challenge in the twenty-first century is to diversify its exports away from primary products such as beef and wheat. While primary products have undoubtedly created much wealth over the last century, their large share of total exports means that the economy can only grow as long as prices in global commodity markets remain favorable. This dependency has been partially resolved by an increase in manufacturing and services as a share of GDP.

RESOURCES

Uruguay is not rich in natural resources and has no known fossil fuel deposits. However, it does have one of the highest rates of electrification (95 percent) in the region. The country's main source of electricity comes from hydroelectric plants. The largest, the Salto Grande Dam on the Uruguay River, is a joint project with Argentina. The facility produces approximately 1.8 million megawatt-hours of energy, or 40 percent of Uruguay's electricity.

Because the nation has no known hydrocarbon reserves, Uruguay imports all the oil it uses. Much of the oil consumed in the country is refined at La Teja, in Montevideo, the largest refining facility in Uruguay.

The remainder is generated by power stations fueled by imported oil. Since 1998, Uruguay has attempted to break its heavy dependence on oil with imports of gas from Argentina via the Entre Ríos–Paysandú pipeline.

Uruguay has small-scale but flourishing mining industries, extracting nonmetallic minerals including clay, bentonite, broken stone, dolomite, flagstone, granite, gravel, gypsum, limestone, marble, quartz, sand, and talc. These minerals are used for the construction industry, glass and ceramics production, and as inputs for other industrial processes. Local limestone is the essential ingredient for the Uruguayan Portland cement

ECONOMY

Montevideo is the principal port in Uruguay, although river ports, such as Fray Bentos along the Uruguay River, are important for exporting meat.

industry. The mining sector has seen a significant expansion since the 1990s because of a change in the law that allows greater foreign involvement in Uruguay's economy. As a result, limestone production increased by 22 percent in the late 1990s after investment by a Spanish consortium. Early in the twenty-first century, there was also a resurgence in mining precious metals, particularly gold. Before 1997, precious metal mining accounted for only 0.2 percent of GDP; since the 1999 purchase of the San Gregorio gold mine by a Canadian company, the (still relatively small) output of precious metals has been increasing by 4 percent per year. Diamonds and semiprecious stones, such as agate and amethyst, are also mined.

URUGUAY'S GDP

Uruguay's gross domestic product (GDP) was $37.5 billion in 2006. The figure is adjusted for purchasing power parity (PPP), an exchange rate at which goods in one country cost the same as goods in another. PPP allows a comparison between the living standards in different nations.

MAIN CONTRIBUTORS TO URUGUAY'S GDP

Agriculture	9.3 percent
Industry	31.6 percent
Services	59.1 percent

Source: CIA, Factbook

AGRICULTURE

Agricultural products have always been the mainstay of the Uruguayan economy. Although the farming sector only contributes 9.3 percent to total GDP, agriculture is the main source of exports and of the foreign-exchange earnings. Red meat exports (particularly beef but also lamb), especially to the United States, have been the main source of foreign exchange, accounting for 37 percent of total exports. Other important agricultural products are wheat, corn, oats (used for cattle feed), rice, and oilseeds such as sunflower and flax.

Uruguay is split into two major geographical regions: rural and urban. Around Montevideo, the nation's only major urban area, is a district that is devoted to small-scale agriculture, producing vegetables, corn, and fruits for the local domestic market. The far south, near Montevideo, cultivates the Tannat grape, and Uruguay has a growing reputation for its wine. The district surrounding Salto, Uruguay's second-largest city, is also known for its wine.

The southwest of the country produces grains and dairy products and contains extensive pasture land for fattening cattle brought in from northeastern Uruguay. The north and east of the country are home to large estates that raise cattle and sheep. Other farms in the region, particularly along river valleys, produce sugar, rice, and citrus fruits.

Uruguay has a rapidly growing fisheries sector. As a result of government support and subsidies, fish catches increased nearly 600 percent from the early 1970s through 2000. Commercial species caught include Argentine hake, whitemouth croaker, and striped weakfish. The fishing zone from Piriápolis to Punta del Este along the country's southern coast is often considered one of the most productive fishing areas in the world. Catches of dorado salmon are taken from Uruguay's rivers, particularly the Uruguay and Paraná rivers, and from major reservoirs. However, the nation's freshwater fisheries are still relatively undeveloped commercially.

Since the passing of a 1988 law approving the plantation of nonnative tree species in Uruguay, forestry has become a major growth sector. From 1988 through 2002, forestry plantations (particularly stands of eucalyptus and various types of pine) increased around 2,000 percent. Domestic varieties of wood are largely exploited for firewood and fence posts. The nation's forestry industry now receives more than $2 billion in foreign direct investment and is set to become one of Uruguay's leading export sectors. As part of the expansion of the industry, a major pulp mill has been constructed at Fray Bentos. The European Union, which buys 42 percent of Uruguay's forestry exports, is the largest export market for Uruguayan forest products.

Fishers unload their catch at Lake de la Rocha.

EMPLOYMENT IN URUGUAY

Sector	Percentage of labor force
Agriculture, forestry, and fishing	14 percent
Industry	16 percent
Services	70 percent

Source: Government of Uruguay, 2006

In 2006, 10.8 percent of the labor force was unemployed.

INDUSTRY

Industry has never been the main driver of growth in the Uruguayan economy, although, in 2006, industry contributed 31.6 percent of the nation's GDP. After the failure of the import substitution policy, the Uruguayan economy underwent a process of de-industrialization from the mid-1970s onward. Subsequently, manufacturing output shrank annually until 2002. Owing to increased levels of foreign investment and a favorable global economic climate, industry finally began to show signs of recovery from 2003.

The main fields of industrial activity are textiles, tires, beverages, food processing (particularly meat processing, packing, and freezing), shoes, leather apparel, cement and building materials, plastics, wine, and petroleum refining. The production of cellulose from eucalyptus pulp is a growth industry. Most industrial activity is concentrated in and around Montevideo.

SERVICES

Since 2001, services as a share of GDP have declined from a high of 65 percent to 51.9 percent in 2006 because of the expansion of agriculture and industry rather than a reduction in the services sector. The sector is dominated by finance and banking. Uruguay's larger government-owned banks have traditionally held a major share of the banking market. The Central Bank (BCU, Banco Central de Uruguay) formulates monetary policy and regulates capital flows in coordination with the government. Uruguay's financial system comprises the BCU, two public banks, 14 private banks (eight of which are foreign-owned), 23 financial institutions (including offshore banks), and 71 foreign exchange firms. Early in the twenty-first century, Uruguay's offshore banks became an attractive haven for Argentine investors.

A highly educated workforce and relatively low wages have allowed Uruguay to develop a market niche in software and consulting. In partnership with foreign (especially Indian) technology consulting firms, the country has become a major outsourcing hub in Latin America. Uruguay also has an important tourist industry, attracting Argentine visitors to Montevideo and neighboring beach resorts.

TRADE

Argentina and Brazil were Uruguay's traditional trading partners. This trade relationship has been accentuated by the creation of MERCOSUR, and trade with other MERCOSUR member countries has accounted for around 50 percent of Uruguay's total trade since the 1990s. Imports from MERCOSUR countries have remained stable at around 43 percent of total imports from 1992 through 2005.

While membership in the MERCOSUR trade pact has undoubtedly benefited Uruguayan exports (which have more than doubled from 1990 through 2005), the dangers of such close economic integration became obvious in 1999 when Brazil devalued its currency (the real). This made Uruguay's exports to that country much more expensive and consequently less desirable. As a result, Uruguay's foreign trade suffered.

Since 2003, the United States has become one of Uruguay's principal trading partners, receiving 12 percent of Uruguay's total exports in 2006. The export share to Brazil and Argentina stood at 14 percent and 8 percent, respectively. Other major recipients of imports from Uruguay are China including Hong Kong, Germany, Russia, and Mexico. In 2006, Uruguay exported goods and services estimated at $4.4 billion.

In the same year, Uruguay imported goods and services worth $4.9 billion. Uruguay's principal imports are oil and capital goods used in the construction, mining, agricultural, and forestry sectors. The main suppliers of imports to Uruguay are Brazil (which provided 17 percent of imports in 2006), Argentina (20 percent), the United States (9 percent), Paraguay, China including Hong Kong, Venezuela, and Nigeria.

TRANSPORTATION AND COMMUNICATION

Uruguay has a highway system that covers 48,311 miles (77,732 km), 4,812 miles (7,743 km) of which are paved. The limited railroad system of 1,288 miles (2,073 km) includes three main branches extending from Montevideo to various points along the border with Argentina and Brazil, and two other branches eastward to Minas and to the port of La Paloma along the Atlantic coast.

Montevideo is the nation's most important port, and other commercial ports include Juan Lacaze and Colónia, both along the Río de la Plata estuary, and the river port of Fray Bentos. Uruguay has 994 miles (1,600 km) of navigable waterways. There are 64 airports, eight of which have paved runways and two of which handle international flights. The principal airport in terms of both size and passenger numbers is Carrasco International Airport, in Montevideo.

Although modern and efficient, Uruguay's telephone system is concentrated mainly in the Montevideo area. In 2006, there were around 1 million main telephone lines; in 2006, 2.3 million Uruguayans had mobile cellular phones. In 2006, nearly 760,000 people in Uruguay had Internet access.

S. J. LUND-LACK

Further Research

WORLD GEOGRAPHY

Brown, James H., and Mark V. Lomolino. *Biogeography.* Sunderland, MA: Sinauer Associates Publishers, 1998.

Clark, Audrey N. *Longman Dictionary of Geography: Human and Physical.* New York: Longman, 1985.

Lydolph, Paul E. *Weather and Climate.* Lanham, MD: Rowman and Littlefield, 1985.

National Geographic Family Reference Atlas. Washington, DC: National Geographic Society, 2004.

Strahler, Arthur N., and Alan H. Strahler. *Modern Physical Geography.* 3rd ed. Hoboken, NJ: John Wiley and Sons, 1987.

Times Atlas of the World: Comprehensive Edition. New York: Crown Publishers, 1999.

REGIONAL GEOGRAPHY, HISTORY, AND CULTURAL EXPRESSION

Adams, Jerome. *Liberators and Patriots of Latin America: Biographies of 23 Leaders from Dona Marina (1505–1530) to Bishop Romero (1917–1980).* Jefferson, NC: McFarland, 1991.

Bennett, Wendell, and Rene d'Harnoncourt. *Ancient Arts of the Andes.* New York: Textbook, 2003.

Bethell, Leslie. *The Cambridge History of Latin America.* Cambridge, UK: Cambridge University Press, 1985.

Burger, Richard L. *Chavin: And the Origins of the Andean Civilization.* London: Thames & Hudson, 1995.

Clapperton, C. M. *Quaternary Geology and Geomorphology of South America.* New York: Elsevier, 2007.

Drake, Paul W., and Eric Hershberg, eds. *State and Society in Conflict: Comparative Perspectives on the Andean Crises.* Pittsburgh: University of Pittsburgh Press, 2006.

Eisenberg, John, and Kent Redford. *Mammals of the Neotropics,* volume 2. Chicago, IL: University of Chicago Press, 1989.

Greenfield, Gerald. *Latin American Urbanization: Historical Profiles of Major Cities.* Westport, CT: Greenwood Press, 1994.

Harvell, Tony. *Latin American Dramatists since 1945: A Bio-Bibliographical Guide.* Westport CT: Praeger, 2003.

Heenan, Patrick, and Monique Lamontagne, eds. *The South America Handbook.* Oxford, UK: Routledge, 2002.

Hemming, John. *The Conquest of the Incas.* New York: Penguin Books, 1983.

Hennessy, Huw, and Hans-Ulrich Bernard. *Amazon Wildlife Insight Guide.* Washington, DC: APA, 2002.

Lea, David, and Colette Milward. *A Political Chronology of the Americas.* New York: Routledge, 2001.

Lovera, José Rafael. *Food Culture in South America.* Westport, CT: Greenwood Press, 2005.

Kleymeyer, Charles. *Cultural Expression and Grassroots Development: Cases from Latin America and the Caribbean.* Boulder, CO: Lynne Rienner, 1994.

Mayer, Enrique. *The Articulated Peasant: Household Economies in the Andes.* Boulder, CO: Westview Press, 2001.

Peter Standish, ed. *Dictionary of Twentieth Century Culture: Hispanic Culture of South America.* Detroit, MI: Gale Group, 1995.

Parodi, Carlos. *The Politics of South American Boundaries.* Westport, CT: Praeger, 2002.

Radcliffe, Sarah, and Sallie Westwood. *Remaking the Nation: Place, Identity, and Politics in Latin America.* New York: Taylor & Francis, 1996.

Ridgely, Robert, and Guy Tudor. *The Birds of South America.* Austin: University of Texas Press, 1989.

Robinson, John, and Elizabeth Bennett. *Hunting for Sustainability in Tropical Forests.* New York: Columbia University Press, 2000.

Roniger, Luis, and Mario Sznajder. *The Legacy of Human-Rights Violations in the Southern Cone.* New York: Oxford University Press, 1999.

Turner, Frederick. *Catholicism and Political Development in Latin America.* Chapel Hill: University of North Carolina Press, 1971.

Stone-Miller, Rebecca. *Art of the Andes: From Chavín to Inca.* London: Thames & Hudson, 2002.

Veblen, Thomas T., Kenneth R. Young, and Antony R. Orme, eds. *The Physical Geography of South America.* New York: Oxford University Press, 2007.

TRAVEL LITERATURE

Bernhardson, Wayne. *Argentina, Uruguay, and Paraguay.* London: Lonely Planet, 1996.

Box, Ben. *Footprint South American Handbook, 2007.* 83rd ed. Bath, UK: Footprint Travel Guides, 2006.

Fodor's South America. 7th ed. New York: Fodor's Travel Publications, 2006.

Matthiessen, Peter. *The Cloud Forest: A Chronicle of the South American Wilderness.* New York: Penguin Books, 1987.

Palmerlee, Danny. *Argentina.* London: Lonely Planet, 2005.

ARGENTINA

Archetti, Eduardo. *Masculinities: Football, Polo, and the Tango in Argentina.* Oxford, UK: Berg, 1999.

Badsey, Stephen, Rob Havers, and Mark Grove. *The Falklands Conflict Twenty Years On: Lessons for the Future*. New York: Routledge, 2004.

Beccaceci, Marcelo. *Natural Patagonia*. St Paul, MN: Pangaea, 1998.

Brennan, James. *Peronism and Argentina*. Lanham, MD: Rowman and Littlefield, 1998.

Crassweller, Robert. *Peron and the Enigmas of Argentina*. New York: W. W. Norton, 1987.

Crouch, Gregory. *Enduring Patagonia*. New York: Random House, 2002.

Foster, David. *Buenos Aires: Perspectives on the City and Cultural Production*. Gainesville: University Press of Florida, 1998.

Foster, William, Melissa Lockhart, and Darrell Lockhart. *Culture and Customs of Argentina*. Westport, CT: Greenwood Press, 1998.

Gustafson, Lowell. *The Sovereignty Dispute of the Falkland (Malvinas) Islands*. New York: Oxford University Press, 1988.

Kuhnheim, Jill. *Gender, Politics, and Poetry in Twentieth-Century Argentina*. Gainesville: University Press of Florida, 1996.

Lewis, Daniel. *The History of Argentina*. Westport, CT: Greenwood Press, 2001.

Marchak, Patricia, and William Marchak. *God's Assassins: State Terrorism in Argentina in the 1970s*. Montreal, Canada: McGill-Queen's University Press, 1999.

Nouzzeilles, Gabriela, and Graziela Montaldo. *The Argentina Reader: History, Culture, Politics*. Durham, NC: Duke University Press, 2002.

Paolera, Gerardo, and Alan Taylor. *A New Economic History of Argentina*. Cambridge, UK: Cambridge University Press, 2003.

PARAGUAY

Farcau, Bruce. *The Chaco War: Bolivia and Paraguay, 1932–1935*. Westport, CT: Greenwood Press, 1996.

Bulmer-Thomas, Victor. *The Economic History of Latin America since Independence*. Cambridge, UK: Cambridge University Press, 2003.

De Abreu, Capistrano, and Arthur Brakel. *Chapters of Brazil's Colonial History, 1500–1800*. New York: Oxford University Press, 1998.

López-Alves, Fernando. *State Formation and Democracy in Latin America, 1810–1900*. Durham, NC: Duke University Press, 2000.

Miller, Elmer, and Laurie Weinstein. *Peoples of the Gran Chaco*. Westport, CT: Bergin and Garvey, 1999.

URUGUAY

Caudillos, Gaucho, and John Chasteen. *Heroes on Horseback: A Life and Times of the Last Gaucho Caudillos*. Albuquerque, NM: University of New Mexico Press, 1995.

Dominguez, Luis (trans.). *The Conquest of the River Plate (1535–1555)*. Boston, MA: Adamant Media, 2001.

Vanger, Milton. *The Model Country: Jose Batlle y Oroanez of Uruguay, 1907–1915*. Hanover, NH: University Press of New England, 1980.

PERIODICALS AND OTHER MEDIA

Arizona Journal of Hispanic Cultural Studies. Tucson.
www.u.arizona.edu/~compitel/AJHCS_home.htm

The Economist. London.
www.economist.com

Journal of Latin American Geography. Austin, TX.
www.utexas.edu/utpress/journals/jlag.html

"Beyond the Crisis: Economic Globalization and Informal Work in Urban Argentina." *Journal of Latin American Geography* 6, no. 2 (2007): 121–136.

"The Transitional Zone of Western Greater Buenos Aires." *Journal of Latin American Geography* 5, no. 2 (2006): 127–131.

ELECTRONIC RESOURCES

Buenas Aires Herald (newspaper).
www.buenosairesherald.com/

Country Studies: Paraguay. Federal Research Division, Library of Congress.
http://countrystudies.us/paraguay

Country Studies: Uruguay. Federal Research Division, Library of Congress.
http://countrystudies.us/uruguay

Geographia.com.
www.geographia.com/argentina
www.geographia.com/paraguay
www.geographia.com/uruguay
(online coverage of Argentina, Paraguay, and Uruguay).

Montevideo News.
www.montevideonews.com/

Newspapers Online.
www.newspapers.com

Paraguay information.
www.paraguay.com/

The World Factbook. CIA.
www.odci.gov/cia/publications/factbook/index.html
(for facts about Argentina, Paraguay, and Uruguay).

Index

Page numbers in *italic* refer to illustrations.

A

Acevedo Díaz, Eduardo 759
Aconcagua 726, 727, 736, 760
Acuña de Figueroa, Francisco 840
agriculture
   Argentina 797–799, *799*, 801
   Paraguay 825, 827–828, *829*
   Uruguay 728, 858
Alacaluf 745, 759
Alfonsín, Raúl 772, 787
Alvear, Marcelo T. de 769
Amerindians 758, 759, 760, 785, 790
   art 775
   Charrúa 744, 749, 759, 830, 833, 841
   encomienda system 751–752, *753*
   Fuegians 744, 745, 759, 785
   Guaraní (Tupí-Guaraní) 744, *745*, 749, 750, 751, *758*, 759, 785, 804, 813, 814, 819, 820
   Guaycurú 814
   Mapuche (Araucanians) 744, 759, 785
   Quechua 759, 785
   Querandí 744–745, 746
   slavery 744, 751–752
   Tehuelche 785
amethyst 733
Andes 726–727, 728, 732, 734, 735
Antequera y Castro, José de 752
Aramburu, Pedro Eugenio 771
Araucanians *see* Mapuche
architecture
   adobe 788
   Argentina 775–756, *775*, *776*
   Paraguay 814–815, *815*
   Spanish colonial 747, *748*, *749*, 775, 793, 814, *815*
   Uruguay 841, *841*
Areco, Jorge Pacheco 839
Argentina 760–801
   agriculture 728–729, 797–799, *799*
   Altiplano 726
   Amerindians 744–745, *745*, 758–759, 760, 768, 775, 785, 790
   Andes 726–727
   art and architecture 775–776, *775*, *776*
   Buenos Aires junta 756–757, 765, 809
   candombe 777, 778, 842
   civil war 757, 764, 765–767, 790
   concordancia 769
   Cuyo 726, 727–728
   desaparecidos 772, *772*, 786, 792
   Desert Campaign 767, 768
   Dirty War 771–772
   economy 728, 762, 763, 768–769, 772, 787–788, 792, 794, 795–801
   education 789, *789*
   Falklands War 731, 763, 771, 772, 803
   family and society 785–786
   festivals and ceremonies 780, 783, 784
   film 779, 780, 792
   flora and fauna 740–743
   food and drink 728, 782
   gauchos 729, 747, 767, 773, *775*, 779, 786, *798*
   geology 732–734
   Gobierno, Orden, Unidad (GOU) 770
   government 762, 764
   Gran Chaco 724, 726, 727, *727*, 728, 735, 738, 740, 768, 800
   health and welfare provision 787–788
   history 762, 765–772
   hydroelectricity 739, 760, 798, 856
   immigration 758, 768, 785
   independence 756–757, 763, 765
   industry 797, 799–800
   Jesuits 751, 775, 777, 783, 789, 793
   literature 773–774
   Mesopotamia 726, 730
   military regimes 763, 768–770, 771–772, 778, 784, 786, 789
   music and performing arts 777–778, *777*, *778*
   oil and gas reserves 733, 760, 769, *796*, 797, 801
   Pampas 726, 727, 728–729, 735, 736–738, 740, 741–742, 747, 748, 755, 797
   Patagonia 726, 728, 730–731, 735, 739, 740, 743, 758, 768, 785
   Perónistas 770, 771, 772
   population 758–759, 760–762, 785, 786, 796
   religion 726, 762, 770, 783–784, 786, 789
   Roca-Runciman Treaty 769
   Semana Trágica 768–769
   Spanish colonization 746, 747–749
   Spanish language 726, 785
   sports 781, *781*, 786, 792
   tango 777, *777*, 778, 780, 792, 842
   terrorist groups 771
   Tierra del Fuego 726, 730, 731, *731*, 735, 740, 743
   trade 748–749, 765–766, 769, 790, 792, 800–801
   transportation and communication 762, 767, 792, 801
   United Provinces of Río de la Plata 757, 765–767, 790, 836
   viceroyalty of Río de la Plata 726, 750, 754–757, 763, 793, 809
   War of Independence 762
   War of the Triple Alliance 763, 767, 804, 807, 809–810, 815, 833, 837
   wine production 727–728, 782, 798
   yellow belt 742–743
Arigas 830
Arlt, Roberto 774
Artigas, José Gervasio 765, 766, 833, 835–836, *835*, 852
Asunción 724, 726, 730, 732, 739, 746, 765, 790, 804, *806*, 807, 809, 814, 815, 822, 823–824, *823*, *824*, 826
   Spanish colonization 823–824
   War of the Triple Alliance 810, 824
Asunción Arch 732

audiencia 754, 756
Avellaneda, Nicolás 767
Ayolas, Juan de 746

B

Bahía Blanca 729, 761, 801
Banda Oriental 749–750, 756, 757, 765, 766, 830, 833, 835–836
bandeirantes (paulistas) 752–753
bandoneón 778
Bariloche 728
Barrios, Augustín 816
Bastos, Augusto Roa 813, *813*
Batlle, Jorge 839
Batlle y Ordóñez, José 830, 833, 838, *838*, 849
Belgrano, Manuel 757, 762, 765, 780, 794
Bellessi, Diana 774
Benedetti, Mario 840
Beresford, William Carr 755
Bermejo River 728
Blanquet, Ovidio José 778
bola 745
Bolivia
   Chaco War 804, 807, 810, 815, 825
   Gran Chaco 807, 825
   War of the Pacific 810
Borges, Jorge Luis 773, 774, *774*
Bourbon reforms 750, 754
Brazil 724, 726, 749
   annexation of Uruguay 830, 835–836
   Brazilian Empire 836
   Charrúa Amerindians 744
   Gran Chaco 728, 735, 740
   Jesuits 751
   slavery 749, 750, 752–753
   War of the Triple Alliance 763, 767, 804, 807, 809–810, 815, 833, 837
Brazilian Highlands 726, 729
Brazilian Shield 732
Buenos Aires 724, 726, 729, 737, 739, 744, 746, 747, *747*, 748, 750, 756, 760, 764, *769*, 790–792, *792*, *800*, 823
   architecture 775, 776, *776*
   audiencia 754, 756
   conflict with the provinces 757, 764, 765–767
   junta 756–757, 809, 835
   port and trade 748, 750, 765, 790, 792, 801
   Spanish colonization 763
   tango *777*, 778, 780, 792, 842
   United Provinces of Río de la Plata 836
   viceroyalty of Río de la Plata 809
Buschiazzo, Antonio 776, 792

C

Caacupé 817
Caaguazú 804
Cabeza de Vaca, Álvar Núñez 746–747
cabildos 754
Cabot, Sebastian 746, 748
Cabral, Pedro Álvares 746

Cámpora, Héctor J. 771
Campos Cervera, Hérib 813
candombe 777, 778, 842, 844
Carbón, Laguna del 760
Cárcova, Ernesto de la 776
Carrió de la Vandera, Alonso 773
Casaccia, Gabriel 813
Casares, Adolfo Bioy 774
Caselli, Juan José 765
Caseros, Battle of 766
Castillo, Ramón S. 769
Castro, Fidel 771, 839, *839*
Catamarca 727
cattle 728–729, 746, 747, 748–749, 757, 798, *798*, 854
caudillos 766, 837
Cevallos, Pedro de 754
Chacabuco, Battle of 765
Chaco Basin *see* Gran Chaco
Chaco War 804, 807, 810, *810*, 815, 825
Characas 747
Charrúa 744, 749, 759, 830, 833, 841
Chile 726
   independence 765
   Tierra del Fuego 731, *735*, 740, 743
Chono 745, 759
Chubut River 731, 760
Ciudad del Este 730, 817, 825, 828
Cold War 811
Colónia *749*, 750, 835, 841
Columbus, Christopher 780
communidades 784
Comodora Rivadavia 731
compadrazgo 820
comuneros 752
Condor, Operation 811
Contursi, Pascual 778
copper 797, 827
Córdoba 728, 747, 755, 756, 760, 766, 775, 777, 789, 790, 793, *793*, 799–800
Córdoba, Battle of 765
Córdoba Mountains 793
Coronel Oviedo 804
Corrientes 730, 751
Cortázar, Julio 774
Cosquin 780
Creole Grotesque 779
Creoles (*criollos*) 750, 754, 755, 757, 758, 835
Cruzada Libertadora 836
Cuban Revolution 839
Cubas, Raúl 812
Cuchilla de Haedo 730
Cuchilla Grande 730
cuchillas 730
Cueva de las Manos 775
Cuidad del Este 804, 826, *826*
Cuyo 726, 727–728

D

Della Valle, Angel 776
desaparecidos 772, *772*, 786, 792
Desert Campaign 767, 768
Dirty War 771–772

INDEX

Discépolo, Armando 779
Dorrego, Manuel 766
Duarte Frutos, Nicanor *808*, 812
Duhalde, Eduardo 796

E

El Niño phenomenon 735, 736, 739
Embalse del Río Negro 830
encomienda system 751–752, *753*
English language 803
Entre Ríos 730, 836
Espinosa, Fernando 777
estancias 729, 786, 788, *798*
Estigarribia, José F. 811

F

Falkland Islands (Islas Malvinas) 726, 731, 743, 754, 758, 780, 802–803, *803*
   War 731, 763, 771, 772, 803
Fangio, Juan 781, *781*
fascism 769
Ferdinand VII, King of Spain 756, 757, 765, 835
film, Argentina 779, 780, 792
First Coalition 754
fishing 802, *858*
Flores, Venancio 837
Fray Bentos 858, 859
Frondizi, Arturo 771
Fuegians 744, 745, 759, 785

G

Galeano, Eduardo 840
Galtieri, Leopoldi 772
Garay, Juan de 747
Gardel, Carlos 778, 842, 844
Garibaldi, Giuseppe 836
gauchos 729, 747, 757, 767, 773, *775*, 779, 786, *798*, 842
   gaucho literature 773, 840
Ginastera, Alberto 777
González Macchi, Luis 807, 812
Gran Chaco 724, 726, 727, *727*, 728, 732, 735, 738, 740, 800, 807, 825, 827
   Chaco War 804, 807, 810, *810*, 815
   Desert Campaign 768
Great Depression 763, 792, 795, 854
Guaíra waterfall 724
Guaraní 744, *745*, 749, 750, 751, *758*, 759, 785, 804, 806, 807, 809, 814, 819, 820
Guaraní language 744, 759, 806, 809, 813, 820
Guaycurú 814
Guevara, Che 771
Güiraldes, Ricardo 773
Gutiérrez, Eduardo 773, 779
Guzmán, Teodoro H. 777

H

Haush 745, 759
Hernández, José 840
Herrera y Reissig, Julio 840
Hidalgo, Bartolomé 840
Hidalgo de Cisneros, Baltasar 756
horses 746, 747, 775–776, *775*
hydroelectricity
   Argentina 739, 760, 798, 856
   Paraguay 807, 825, 827, *828*
   Uruguay 856

I

Ibarbourou, Juana de 840
Iguazú Falls 730, *733*, 734
Inca Empire 747, 763
Itaipu Dam and Reservoir 724, 804, 807, 825, 827, *828*

J

Jesuits 746, 750, 751–753, 775, 777, 783, 789, 793, 804, 846
   expulsion 753
   Paraguay 751–753, 804, 807, 813, 816, 819, 823
   reducciones 744, 746, 751, 753, *753*, 775, 814, *815*, 819
John Paul II, Pope 812
Juárez Celman, Miguel 768
Jujuy 727, 747, 761, 775
juntas 756–757, 809, 835

K

Kirchner, Cristina Fernández de 772, 786
Kirchner, Néstor 772

L

Lacalle, Luis Alberto 839
Lanusse, Alejandro Agustín 771
La Plata 760, 783, 801
La Rioja 728, 736, 775
La Santísima Trinidad 814, *815*
Latorre, Lorenzo 837
Lavalle, Juan 766
Lavalleja, Juan Antonio 836
librecambistas 765
Lima 748, 750, 754, 809
Liniers, Santiago (Jacques) de 756
literature
   Argentina 773–774
   gaucho traditions 773, 840
   magical realism 840
   Modernismo 773
   Paraguay 813
   poesía gauchesca 773
   Uruguay 840
López, Carlos Antonio 809, 815, 819, 824
López, Francisco Solano 767, 809–810, 815, 819
Lugones, Leopoldo 773
Luján 783, 784

M

Madrid Treaty 750
Magellan, Ferdinand 745, 746
Magellan, Strait of 726, 731, 743
Maipú, Battle of 765
Maldonado 830
Malvinas, Islas *see* Falkland Islands
Mansilla, Lucio V. 773
Mapuche (Araucanians) 744, 759, 785
Maradona, Diego 781
Mar del Plata 729, 760
Martínez, Domingo 746, 747
Massa, Bartolomé 777
maté *see* yerba maté
Mazó, José Ricardo 813
Melo 830
Mendizábal, Rosendo 778
Mendoza 728, 732, 736, 747, 760, 799, *799*
Mendoza, Pedro de 746
Menem, Carlos *764*, 772, 787, 795–796

mesetas centrales 730
mestizos 750, 758, 762, 785, 806, 814–815, 820, *820*
milonga 778, 779, 842
Missiones 730, 751
Mitre, Bartolomé 767, 768
Molloy, Sylvia 774
monopolistas 765
Montevideo 726, 729, 750, 755–756, 765, 830, *834*, 837, 841, *843*, *844*, 848, 850, *850*, 851, 852–853, *852*, *853*, 854, *856*, 857, 859
   British occupation 833, 852
   Guerra Grande 833, 836
   Portuguese invasion 766
   State of Montevideo 852
Montoneros 771
Moreno, Mariano 765
Morínigo, Higinio 811
Mothers of the Plaza de Mayo 772, *772*, 786, 792
murga 842, 844
music and performing arts
   Argentina 777–778, *778*
   candombe 777, 778, 842, 844
   murga 842, 844
   Paraguay 816, *816*
   tango 777, *777*, 778, 780, 792, 842
   Uruguay 842–843, 844

N

Nahuel Huapi, Lake 728, 760
Neuquén 761
Neuquén Jorge Basin 733

O

Ocampo, Silvina 774
Ocampo, Victoria 773
Occidental region 724, *727*, 728, 804, 808, 825, 827
oil and gas reserves
   Argentina 733, 760, 769, *796*, 797, 801
   Chaco War 810, 825
   Falkland Islands 802
   Southern Cone 727, 731, *731*, 733
Ojos del Salado 727
O'Leary, Juan E. 813
Onetti, Juan Carlos 840
Onganía, Juan Carlos 771
Oriental region 724, 726, 730, 804, 808, 825, 827
Ortiz, José Antonio 777
Ortíz, Roberto M. 769
Oviedo, Lino 812

P

Pampas 726, 727, 728–730, *729*, 735, *737*, 740, 741–742, 746, 748, 755, 790, 797
pamperos 728, 737–738
Panama 746
Panama Canal 731
Pantanal 724
Paraguay 804–829
   agriculture 825, 827–828, 829
   Amerindians 744, *745*, 753, 758–759, 804, 806, 807, 809, 813, 819, 820
   art and architecture 814–815, *815*
   Chaco War 804, 807, 810, *810*, 815, 825
   civil war 807, 810, 811

Colorado Party 807, 808, 810, 811, 812, 825
comuneros 752
dictatorships 767 804, 807, 808, 809–810, 811–812, 813, 816, 819, 825
economy 804, 805, 807, 825–829
education 822
encomienda system 751–752, 753
festivals and ceremonies 817
food and drink 818
geology 732–734
government 806, 808
Gran Chaco 724, 726, 727, *727*, 728, 735, 738, 740, 804, 807, 825, 827
health and welfare provision 821
history 807, 809–812
hydroelectricity 807, 825, 827, *828*
independence 757, 765, 804, 807, 809
industry *827*, 828
Jesuits 751–753, 804, 807, 813, 814, *815*, 816, 819, 823
literature 813
mestizos 806, 814–815, 820, *820*
music and performing arts 816, *816*
Nazi war criminals 811
Occidental 724, *727*, 728, 804, 808, 825, 827
Oriental 724, 726, 730, 804, 808, 825, 827
population 726, 758–759, 804–805, 806, 809
reducciones 744, 746, 751, 753, *753*, 814, *815*, 819
religion 726, 806, 817, 819
Roman Catholic Church 809, 812, 817, 819, 820
Spanish colonization 746–747, 807, 814, 823–824
Spanish language 726
sports 817, *817*
trade 826, 828–829
transportation and communication 806, 825, 829
United States involvement 811
viceroyalty of Río de la Plata 804, 807, 809, 823
War of the Triple Alliance 763, 767, 804, 807, 809–810, 815, 824, 833, 837
Paraguay River 724, 726, 727, 728, 730, 740, 801, 804, *806*, 809, 823, 824, *824*, 825
Paraná River 724, 726, 727, 728, 729, 730, *733*, 734, 740, 746, 790, 794, 801, 804, 809, 825, 827
Patagonia 73, 726, 728, 730–731, 740, 743, 758, 785
   climate 739
   Desert Campaign 768
payadores 779
Paysandú 737, 830
Paz, José María 766
Peace of April 837, 838
Pellegrini, Carlos 768
peninsulares 754
Perito Moreno glacier *734*
Perlongher, Néstor 774
Perón, Eva (Evita) 770, 779, 786
Perón, Isabel 771
Perón, Juan 763, 764, 769, 770, *770*, 771, 779, 784, 795

863

Peru, viceroyalty of 748, 750, 752, 754, 775, 790, 793, 809
Philip V, King of Spain 750, 754
Pizarnik, Alejandra 774
population 758–759
  Amerindians *see* Amerindians
  Creoles 750, 754, 755, 757, 758, 835
  mestizos 750, 758, 762, 785, 806, 809, 814–815, 820, *820*
  peninsulares 754
  Portuguese 744, 746, 749–750, *749*, 751, 753
  Banda Oriental 830, 833, 835–836
  invasion of Montevideo 766
Portuñol language 758
Posadas 761
Potosí 747, 748
pucará 775
Pugliese, Osvaldo 778
Puig, Manuel 774

Q
Quechua 759, 785
Querandí 744–745, 746
Quilmes 775
Quiroga, Horacio 773, 840

R
reducciones 744, 746, 751, 753, *753*, 775, 814, *815*, 819
Rega, José López 771
religion
  Argentina 726, 762, 770, 783–784, 786, 789
  Jesuits *see* Jesuits
  Paraguay 806, 817, 819
  Roman Catholic church 748, *748*, 758, 762, 770, 783–784, 786
  Uruguay 844, 846, 847
Resistencia 728, 738, 761
Reyles, Carlos 840
Río Colorado 729
Río de la Plata 724, 746, 748, 760, 790, 830, 859
Río de la Plata, United Provinces of 757, 765–767, 790, 836
Río de la Plata, Viceroyalty of 726, 750, 754–757, 763, 793, 804, 807, 809, 823, 833, 835
Rivadavia, Bernardino 766
Rivera, José Fructuoso 836
Roca, Julio Argentino 767, 768, 789
Roca-Runciman Treaty 769
Rodríguez, Andrés 812
Rodríguez, Gerardo Matos 842
Rodríguez de Francia, José Gaspar 759, 807, 809, 811, 813, 815, 819, 823
Roman Catholic Church 748, *748*, 758, 762, 770, 783–784, 786, 789
  Argentina 726, 762, 770, 783–784, 786, 789
  communidades 784
  liberation theology 846
  Paraguay 806, 812, 817, 819
  Uruguay 846, 847
Romero, Elvio 813
Rosario 729, 760, 790, 794, *794*, 799–800, 801
Rosas, Juan Manuel de 766–767, 773, 794, 836, 852
Rúa, Fernando de la 772, 796

S
Saavedra, Cornelio 765
Saer, Juan José 774
Salazar, Juan de 746
Salsipuedes Creek massacre 744
Salta 727, 736, 747, 760, 775, 782
Salto 830, *832*, 852, 858
Salto dos Sete Quedras waterfall 724
San Carlos de Bariloche 728
Sánchez, Florencio 840
Sanguinetti, Julio María 839, *839*
San Ignacio Guazú 814
San Ignatio Miní 775
San Ildefonso, Treaty of 755
San Juan (Argentina) 728, 736, 761
San Lorenzo, Battle of 757
San Luis 728
San Martin, José de *756*, 757, 765, 780
San Miguel de Tucumán 726, 727, 747, 757, *757*, 760, 765, 775, 782, 798, 800
San Pedro, Cerro 804
San Pedro Caballero 804
Santa Fé (Argentina) 729, 747, *748*, 761
Santiago del Estero 728, 738, 747, 761, 775
Sarmiento 739
Sarmiento, Domingo F. 767, 773, 789
Schmidel, Ulrich 773
Segundo, Juan Luis 846
Semana Trágica 768–769
Seven Years' War 750
sheep 727, 728, 731, 802
Sierra de Aconquija 727
Sierra de Córdoba 728
Sívori, Eduardo 776
slavery 744, 748, 749, 750
  African slaves 750, 759, 842
  Argentina 767
  bandeirantes (*paulistas*) 752–753
  Brazil 749, 750, 752–753
  encomienda system 751–752
Sobremonte, Rafael de 755–756
soccer 781, 817, *817*
Solís, Juan Días de 746
Somoza, Anastasio 812
sondo 737–738
Sosa, Mercedes 778, *778*
Sousa, Martim Afonso de 749
Southern Cone 724, 726
Spanish colonies 744–745, 746–750
  architecture 747, *748*, *749*, 775, *815*
  Argentina 763
  Bourbon reforms 750, 754
  Buenos Aires 763
  Christian missionaries 744, 746, 751–753, 783, 804, 807, 813, 814, *815*, 816, 819
  encomienda system 751–752, 753
  Madrid Treaty 750
  Paraguay 746–747, 807, 814, 823–824
  Spanish colonial system 748, 750
  Tordesillas Treaty 749–750, 753
  trade 748–749, 750, 754
  Uruguay 830, 833, 835
  viceroyalty of Peru 748, 750, 752, 754, 775, 790, 793, 809
  viceroyalty of Río de la Plata 726, 750, 754–757, 763, 793, 804, 807, 809, 823, 833, 835
Spanish language 726, 758, 785, 806, 813
Stanley 731, 802, *803*
Stroessner, Alfredo 804, 807, 808, 811–812, *812*, 813, 816, 819, 822, 825, 826
Suárez, Joaquin 842
Suipacha, Battle of 765

T
Tacuarembó 830
tasajo 748
Tehuelche 785
Tejedor, Carlos 767
Terra, Gabriel 838–839
tierra caliente 735
Tierra del Fuego 726, 730, 731, *731*, 735, 740, 743, 797
  Amerindians 744, 745, 759, 785
tierra fría 735
tierra templada 735
Tilcara 775
Tordesillas Treaty 749–750, 753
trade
  Argentina 748–749, 765–766, 769, 790, 792, 800–801
  MERCOSUR 726, 801, 829, 839, 855
  NAFTA 801
  Paraguay 826, 828–829
  smuggling 748, *749*, 750, 754
  Spanish colonial system 750, 748, 750
  Uruguay 859
Troilo, Anibal 778
Tupamaros guerrillas 830, 833, 839, 849
Tupí-Guaraní *see* Guaraní

U
Uriburu, José Félix 769
Urquiza, Justo José de 767, 836
Uruguay 830–859
  African slaves 759
  agriculture 728, 858
  Amerindians 744, 759, 830, 833, 841
  annexation by Brazil 830, 835–836
  art and architecture 841, *841*
  Banda Oriental 749–750, 765, 766, 830, 833, 835–836
  Blancos 833, 834, 836, 837, 838, 839
  caudillos 837
  Colónia *749*, 750
  Colorados 833, 834, 836, 837, 838–839
  Cruzada Libertadora 836
  economy 831, 837–838, 854–859
  education 838, 851
  family and society 847–848
  Federal League 835–683
  festivals and ceremonies 844
  gauchos 840, 842
  geology 732–734
  government 831–832, 834
  Guerra Grande 833, 836–837, 852
  health and welfare provision 830, 833, 838, 847, 849–850, 855
  history 833, 835–839
  immigration 833, 838, 841
  independence 766, 830, 833, 836
  independence as part of Argentina 830, 833
  industry *855*, 859
  Jesuits 751
  juntas 835
  literature 840
  military dictatorship 830, 833, 839, 849, 854–855
  murga 842, 844
  music and performing arts 842–843
  Orientales 835
  Pampas 728–730, *729*, 735, 736–738, *737*, 740, 741–742, 748, 755
  Peace of April 837, 838
  population 758–759, 830–831, *832*
  Preliminary Peace Convention 836
  religion 726, 844, 846, 847
  resources *855*, 856–857
  slavery 842
  Spanish colonization 830, 833, 835
  Spanish language 726
  trade 859
  transportation and communication 832, 859
  Tupamaros guerrillas 830, 833, 839, 849
  United Provinces of Río de la Plata 757, 836
  urbanization 726, 848
  viceroyalty of Río de la Plata 833, 835
  War of the Triple Alliance 763, 767, 804, 807, 809–810, 815, 833, 837
  wine production 858
Uruguay River 724, 726, 729, 730, 760, 830, 856, 857
Ushuaia 731, *731*, 739

V
Valle Edén 844
Varela, José Pedro 838, 851
Vázquez, Tabaré 839, 850
Vértiz y Salcedo, Juan José 754
Vespucci, Amerigo 746
Viana, Javier de 840
Victoria 737
Vidal, Emeric Essex 776
Vilaró, Carlos Paéz *841*

W
War of the Pacific 810
War of the Triple Alliance 763, 767, 804, 807, 809–810, 815, 824, 833, 837
Wasmosy, Juan Carlos 807
Welsh language 731, 758, 785
wine production
  Argentina 727–728, 782, 798, *799*
  Uruguay 858
World War II
  Uruguay 852, 854

Y
Yacyretá-Apipé Dam 827
Yahgan 745
Yámana 745
yellow belt 742–743
yerba maté 730, 782, *782*, 818, 827–828, 845
Yrigoyen, Hipólito 768–769

Z
zonda 736

Wake Tech. Libraries
9101 Fayetteville Road
Raleigh, North Carolina 27603-5696

DATE DUE

GAYLORD			PRINTED IN U.S.A.

JAN '09

WORLD AND ITS PEOPLES

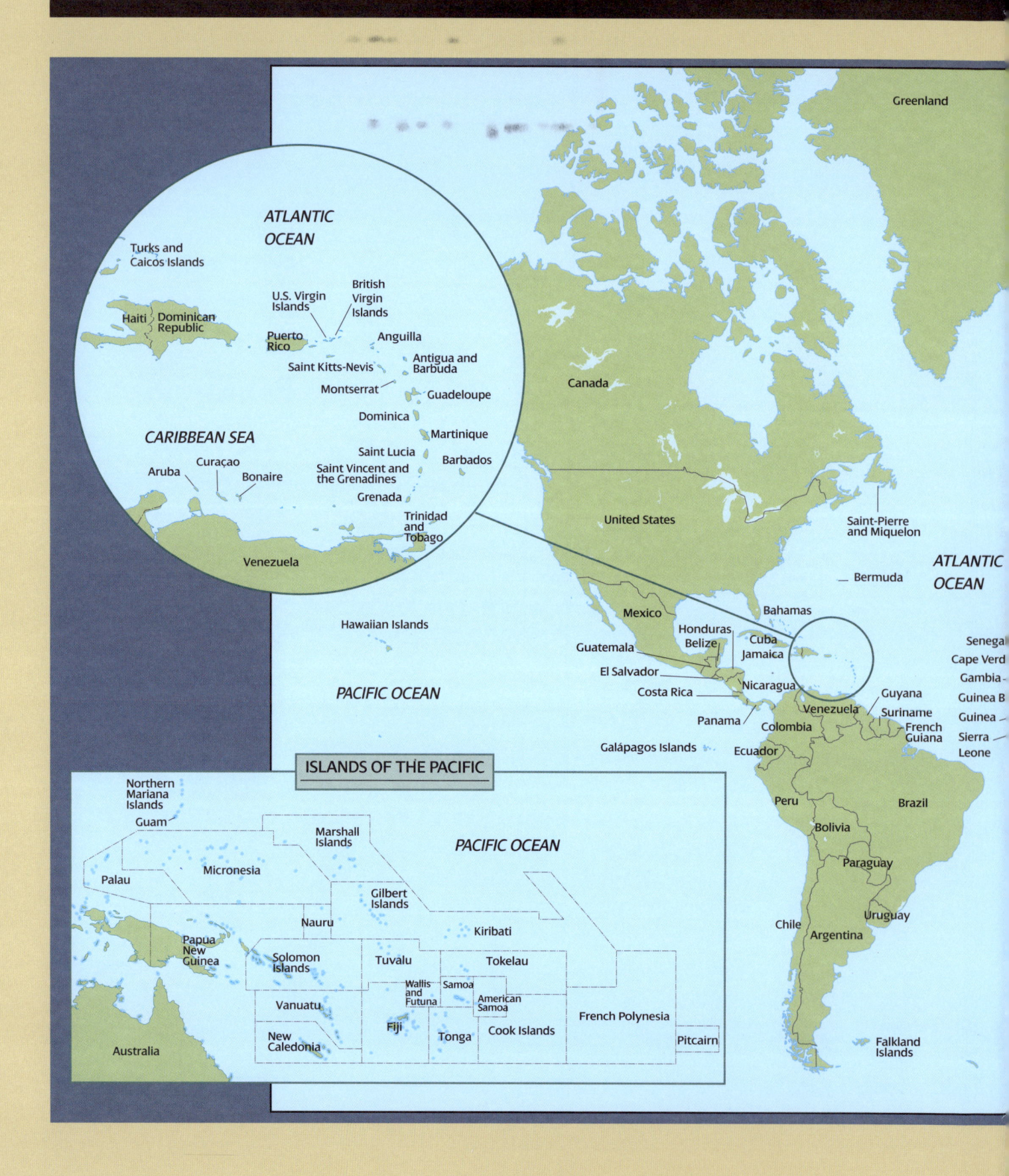